**Praise for *Pretender*:**

"Masterful . . . As usual, Cherryh alternates long stretches of brilliant, often oblique dialogue and complex political maneuvering with shorter interludes of violent, well-executed action. A science fictional equivalent of George R.R. Martin's 'Song of Ice and Fire' sequence, this series represents contemporary SF at its finest." —*Publishers Weekly*

"Cherryh's follow-up to *Destroyer* opens up new aspects of atevi civilization while introducing a younger generation of characters. Superbly realized characters and an intriguing, Asian-based civilization." —*Library Journal*

"Her world building, aliens, and suspense rank among the strongest in the whole SF field. May those strengths be sustained indefinitely, or at least until the end of *Foreigner*." —*Booklist*

## and the "Foreigner" series:

"Cherryh's gift for conjuring believable alien cultures is in full force here, and her characters . . . are brought to life with a sure and convincing hand." —*Publishers Weekly*

"A seriously probing, thoughtful, intelligent piece of work, with more insight in half a dozen pages than most authors manage in half a hundred." —*Kirkus*

"Close-grained and carefully constructed . . . a book that will stick in the mind for a lot longer than the usual adventure rom . . . —*Locus*

"A large ne . . . ne . . . a return to the . . . which she has made su . . . super-latively draw . . .

—*Chicago Sun-Times*

# C. J. CHERRYH
# PRETENDER

**DAW BOOKS, INC.**

DONALD A. WOLLHEIM, FOUNDER

375 Hudson Street, New York, NY 10014

**ELIZABETH R. WOLLHEIM**

**SHEILA E. GILBERT**

**PUBLISHERS**

http://www.dawbooks.com

DAW Books are distributed by the Penguin Group (USA) Inc.
Book designed by Stanley S. Drate/Folio Graphics Co., Inc.

First Paperback Printing, February 2007

1  2  3  4  5  6  7  8  9  10

For Sharon and Steve,
who have walked us off cliffs
and helped us move books.

# 1

The room had suffered, not from the attackers, but from the defenders of the house, who had taken no pains at all about recovering ejected shells—the detritus of combat was scattered about the floor, a few items lying on the rumpled coverlet of the bed, on the table. One, an apparent ricochet, having landed on the floor around the corner, in the large bath. Damage from the attempted intrusion of the enemy, numerous holes pocked the walls and woodwork. At some point during the battle for the house, someone among the room's defenders had shot an exit hole through the door, complementing the several inbound rounds that had taken out the door lock and lodged in an opposing wall ... without, one hoped, catching any of the house's defenders along the way. The door had been kicked open after that, evident by the scuff marks on the paint near the shattered lock, as the invaders rushed the room. But the foremost intruder from the hall had hit a chest-high wire at that point, and Bren was very glad the staff had cleared away the evidence.

He was, considering all the other scars of war, overwhelmingly glad to find his computer where he had left it, hidden behind a stack of spare towels on the bottom shelf of the linen press ... neither defenders nor invaders having had an inclination to open the storage cupboard of spare towels and bedsheets. No stray shot had hit it, nothing had damaged it, and, on his knees, having extricated the precious machine and its accompanying security modem from their hiding spot, Bren sat on the floor in front of the cabinet with both on his lap, too exhausted, mentally and morally, to struggle up again.

"Is something wrong, Bren-ji?" Jago appeared by him, and he tucked the computer case under his arm, clenched the modem in his hand, and made the effort to get up. Jago helped with a hand under his elbow, lifting him to his full height—which, for a tall human, was about equal to her black-clad shoulder. Even Jago appeared the worse for wear at this hour, her Guild leathers and her ebony skin alike streaked with pale dust from the road and the shattering of plaster, her usually immaculate pigtail a little wind-frayed from a wild ride and a wilder night. Bren's own pale hands showed bloody scrapes. He had dirt under his nails, which would have been a scandal to his domestic staff if they had been here and not up on the station. They were all of them, himself and his atevi bodyguard, candidates for a good long soaking bath. He smelled of human sweat, Jago of that slightly petroleum scent, but a bath seemed out of the question at the moment. There seemed too much to do to contemplate such a luxury this afternoon, there was no domestic staff at hand to take care of the cleanup: It was all up to them; and he was sure that once he sank into warm water, he would be completely lost.

"Tired, Jago-ji," he murmured, inserting the modem into a case pocket. "Simply tired." He heaved the precious computer's carrying-strap up to his shoulder, not sure what else to do with the computer, wondering whether he should go on using the same hiding place and being too exhausted to be confident in his logical choices at this point. He hadn't so much as taken his coat off since their arrival in the room, and his clothing bore mud, soot, and the scrapes of hedge branches, not to mention mecheita-spit and bloody rips in cloth he had taken riding through a gap in the estate's wire fence. "But one dares not lie down yet."

"Let us check the bed," Jago said, and left him in order to do that check, electronically, with one of the little handhelds her Guild used.

Checking for bugs. For booby traps. Her partner, Banichi, was over by the windows, likewise engaged, and Tano and Algini, the other pair of his body-guards, were in the bath, also looking for bugs and explosives, one surmised. All of them were gathering up shell casings.

"Is the chair safe?" he asked, meaning the fragile green-and-white-striped and doubtless pricelessly historical item in the corner.

Fragile from the atevi viewpoint: For a human, child-sized on an atevi scale, the chair was more substantial, even well-padded, and he was glad when Jago came back, surveyed it, and pronounced it safe for him to sit in.

Lord Tatiseigi, lord of the estate, had had his domestic and security staff make the first sweep of the premises, and they had cleaned up the bodies, blood, and broken items before they declared the room fit for occupancy. In any event, these rooms had fared better than the suite next door, where Kadagidi clan Assassins had made their actual entry into the house, and possibly left gifts that made one just a little anxious at the moment about standing near the north wall. Bren had less confidence in his host's staff than in his own—Tatiseigi's staff were competent at their work—competent, if woefully underequipped in communications and electronics—but he felt much safer knowing his own staff was giving it their own close inspection, with more skill, recent practice, and far better equipment.

Water started running in the bath, a thunderous flood in that huge, atevi-scale bathtub. It was a seductive sound, and more than a testing of the plumbing, since it went on. Tano and Algini had made an executive decision and started drawing hot water for the household.

And Bren looked at his hands, at the grime, the cuts, the stray mecheita-hair and mecheita-sweat that had gotten all over his sleeves and trousers, reconsidering the bath question and the question of letting the adrenaline run down.

The unpleasant fact was the day was well advanced and they still weren't assured the Kadagidi weren't coming back tonight.

Or, worst of all thoughts, and one that had been at least a passing topic of discussion downstairs, their victory—and the knowledge Tabini was on the premises—might drive the Kadagidi to more desperate measures, even before dark: They might be desperate enough to attempt an air strike, in which case there was no safety and no time to settle in here as if there were. True, the Assassins' Guild had passed a formal resolution condemning attack by air as anathema in clan warfare, and in that resolution declared that the Guild would exercise severe and automatic sanctions against violators. But the Guild as a whole had not turned a hand to prevent the overthrow of Tabini-aiji, had it? It had not bestirred itself to condemn the Kadagidi lord, Murini, for setting himself up as aiji in Tabini's place, had it, then? The Guild had not leaped in to protect Tabini's grandmother and his heir when they, innocent parties in any dispute between the two clans, returned from space. The Guild had not intervened last night to prevent the Kadagidi from attacking them here in a neutral clan's province. So there was a little justifiable suspicion downstairs that the Guild had not supported Tabini-aiji as wholeheartedly as they ought before his downfall, and that their lack of response in preventing a third clan being attacked had allowed some already questionable moves, all on one side of the equation.

Still, a man in the position of Lord Murini of the Kadagidi, who had gotten the Guild to take this dubious position of neutrality, letting him stage a bloody coup in the capital and declare himself ruler of the Western Association—which was to say, the whole continent—still had to worry about one potent force in atevi politics, and that force was public opinion. The various clans only recently united, had a long history of independent thought and independent and regional action. There associations within the Association which were historically much stronger than any modern ties, and Murini was already risking his neck by proclaiming himself aiji before the blood of household staff was dry on the carpet.

More, granted he had gotten the Assassins' Guild to stay out of action, he was beholden to someone for that favor. He dared not go violating publicized Guild resolutions, creating a scandal for Guild leadership, and worse, contravening the Guild's established principles of politics in his new-minted claim to power.

So there were three powers, all teetering out of equilibrium: the people, the Guild, and the man who called himself (with his clan) the new authority. And if any one of the former two tipped away from him, Lord Murini, so-named Murini-aiji, stood to lose all his advantage. It would be calamitous for his authority if the Assassins' Guild decided suddenly to take the side of Tabini-aiji, who was not dead, and who was, in fact, currently lodged four rooms down, his staff going through much the same precautionary cleanup of premises. It was very clear that Tabini would accept Guild neutrality, but hold a grudge for its inaction in preventing his overthrow, and might forgive that grudge if the Guild now budged toward his side.

So the last twenty-odd hours had brought a very delicate time for both claimants to the aijinate: Murini, the upstart would-be aiji, with ancient ambitions of an ethnically different clan, had relied on popular discontent under Tabini-aiji's authority to seize power; Tabini, overthrown, but now with allies—themselves—newly returned from space, now had records and testimony that might change public opinion. In a few days, Murini's unchallenged supremacy had slid a few degrees, and now the whole thing had headed downhill gathering calamity like a snowball provoking avalanche. Step one: the dowager's party, including Tabini's young son, had arrived from deep space and landed onworld, in spite of Murini's plan to keep the shuttle fleet entirely out of action. They had immediately presented themselves on the doorstep of Lord Tatiseigi of the Atageini, the young heir's great-uncle, and by that action, had put Lord Tatiseigi to the choice of sheltering them or turning his young relative away.

Step two: Murini's Kadagidi clan, neighbor to Tatiseigi—who had thought they were going to chastise the elderly and habitually neutral Tatiseigi for receiving Tabini's grandmother and son under their roof—had not only failed in two nights of trying to breach the house and assassinate them all, but last night had found the Atageini's neighbor to the west, Taiben, supporters of the old regime and relatives of Tabini-aiji's clan, coming to the Atageini's defense. It was an unthinkable combination of clans: Taiben and the Atageini had been at loggerheads for hundreds of years, and now they found common cause against the Kadagidi, for the boy's sake.

Then, third step, Tabini-aiji himself, unheard from for the better part of a year, had shown up to defend his grandmother and his heir, risking life and reign on this one dice-throw: rescue Tatiseigi, drive off the Kadagidi, and support a new compact between Taibeni and Atageini lords.

Suddenly the Kadagidi control of their local Padi Valley neighborhood wasn't looking as secure as it had three days ago, and centuries of Atageini neutrality in the region began sliding more and more toward commitment to a cause, namely restoration of Tabini-aiji to rule in Shejidan . . . because that would set a half-Atageini great-nephew up as heir.

So the sun was up. The ancient Atageini house at Tirnamardi still stood, if battered, in the middle of a province now annoyed with the Kadagidi and feeling massively insulted. The historic premises were pocked with bullets, Atageini house stables were burned and its venerable hedges were in tatters, not to mention the damage in the foyer and upstairs, while its lawn held an encampment of neighboring Taibeni and their large and numerous—and now hungry—mounts. The province took these affronts personally and supported their offended lord.

Who overall had fared surprisingly well under such heavy assault, the old premises proving their ancient, blunt-force construction methods had produced very solid walls. The Atageini house stood, and stood well. By the sound of the flood in the bathroom, its plumbing evidently worked and its boilers must be up, producing hot water for the sore and weary household, to judge by comments that wafted out of the bath.

So the aiji-dowager and the aiji had won the first several rounds of the fight, if not the war that was surely preparing. Murini sat in the capital claiming to be the popularly supported aiji while Tabini-aiji sat in a Padi Valley lord's house maintaining that he still was. Meanwhile Lord Tatiseigi, their host, was still muttering about the Guild's general ban on no-holds-barred attacks and its rules about historic properties and premises, as if this was sufficient to preserve the Atageini province and its towns from a repetition of last night. Most of Lord Tatiseigi's security, who were members of that Guild, held far less optimistic opinions on that score; and senior members of Tabini's security and the dowager's were down on the lower floor, laying plans for coping with what they were sure would come with nightfall.

As for one Bren Cameron, paidhi-aiji, interpreter of foreign affairs, Lord of the Heavens and so on and so forth, he sat in the one safe chair in an unsafe world, wondering whether he should open up his computer and look up his notes on the finer print of Guild regulations, searching for loopholes for further attack and simultaneously wondering whether, if he took his boots off to go take advantage of that wonderful hot water in the bathroom, he could possibly get them back on.

He had blisters, he was sure, in places he would rather not describe to his staff. Numerous wood splinters were lodged in his palms. He was amazingly sore.

But he had recovered his computer. And because he had it, he had all his records from space and from the voyage. And because he had those, he possessed detailed evidence which could argue that Tabini-aiji's unpopular actions had produced results well worth the sacrifices. It was a precious record, and there was a backup for what was stored here—but one copy was in orbit over their heads, and another in his brother's hands—he hoped safely back on Mospheira by now. On the mainland, on atevi soil, where it was most needed, this was the only copy he could hope to lay hands on, and he wasn't eager to let the precious computer leave his hands until he had gotten that report to Tabini.

All things considered finally, that was the highest priority, to get a printout or a disk where Tabini could read it and understand what he had. It was the highest priority, even when Tano came out of the bath and reported that the tub was well on its way to being filled, assuming the hot water held out that long.

It was true that in his present state, he was unfit for an audience: even while the world tottered, conventions and custom prevailed, and a man, even the Lord of the Heavens, had to be respectfully presentable to authority . . . especially an authority shaken by events.

"You may have the water first, nandi," Tano began, as Algini also came out of the bath—but at that moment a racket broke out in the hall outside their suite, a stream of angry shouting. He could not make out words. He looked in that direction, down the short entry hall, in some alarm, and Tano went as far as the outer door and listened, while Banichi and Jago waited with Algini, hands on sidearms.

"Cenedi is out in the hall, explaining certain things to the household staff," Tano said wryly, which drew a little amusement out of them all. One was ever so glad to find Cenedi alive today, and clearly indignant: None of them doubted that Lord Tatiseigi's household staff needed certain key points laid out before them and the head of the dowager's bodyguard was the man to do it—not least bringing home the fact that most of Lord Tatiseigi's security equipment belonged in a museum, not active service. Even the paidhi understood certain facts without explanation, notably that there was a very good chance that the intruders who had gotten into the house last night, not to mention spies predating them, might well have installed bugs, and wise servants would not discuss household business in any area until security with proper equipment had cleared it . . .

Proper equipment. That was a sore spot. Security with proper equipment necessarily involved outsiders poking about in Lord Tatiseigi's household security, even bringing in some outsiders, namely Taiben clan, with whom the Atageini maintained a centuries-old feud, while the bodyguard that Tabini had brought in had its own opinions, and certainly Banichi had voiced his.

Outside security having access to house equipment had been one major sticking point of discussions downstairs. In the paidhi's staff's case, certain things they had were unique on the planet, a matter they had not entirely explained to the Atageini; anything that had come in from outside was better than what existed here. The Atageini lord was upset with the implications, his servants were all indignant, and the Guild security employed by the Atageini were in a particularly glum mood, having lost members of their staff due to deficiencies they themselves had doubt-less pointed out to their old-fashioned lord long since. No, no, no, their lord would say: he bought *quality* to defend his house and his province. *Quality* items once purchased ought to be good for decades if not the next generation—Lord Tatiseigi had no un-derstanding at all of how radically the advent of elec-tronics and computers had changed that basic precept of atevi economy. Quality things lasted for generations, did they not? One bought the most ex-pensive and it was clearly going to last for decades.

And, oh, emphatically, one could never trust secu-rity outside one's own man'chi, one's own loyalty. That was a principle to which the Atageini had ad-hered for centuries. It had preserved their power, their autonomy, even within the *aishidi'tat*. It had guaranteed the aiji had a refuge when things came to crisis. Lord Tatiseigi would very tactfully suggest so. Did it not prove his case?

Never mind that a little support from Tatiseigi would have meant joining the detested Taibeni in passing certain bills in the legislature, and made the whole Kadagidi defection more difficult. Things had gotten damned hot downstairs, once history came under discussion, and that had diverted the discus-sion into details unrelated to Lord Tatiseigi's antique defenses.

But Tabini-aiji had, aside from the argument, in-sisted, guest that he was under this roof, and Lord Tatiseigi had quietly and very reluctantly agreed to supplement his own leaky surveillance equipment. Or at least most of it. So the scene downstairs had ended, an hour ago, discussion having gotten around to old pieces of failed legislation, and the Taibeni-Atageini feud, which the aiji outright insisted had to be buried.

The particular source of the near-disaster in the last two days, the item that had cost staff lives, had been Lord Tatiseigi's communications units. It had turned out they might just as well have phoned the neighboring Kadagidi province outright and advised them that the paidhi and his staff had gone out chasing Tabini's eight-year-old heir halfway to Taiben, who were being asked in to aid their old enemies. The Kadagidi could have no doubt now that Taiben had responded, and that they were all, including the heir, the aiji-dowager, and the aiji himself with his Atageini-born consort, reinstalled in Lord Tatiseigi's house, a growing nucleus of the old adminstration reconstituting itself apace, a threat to the Kadagidi's theft of authority.

The latter details had doubtless leaked far and wide among the Padi Valley clans before Tabini's staff had gotten the last die-hard user of the compromised system to shut down transmissions and quit gossiping on the network. The fact of the dowager's and Tabini's presence in Lord Tatiseigi's house was likely on the morning news in Shejidan, for that matter, because reports of the disaster, the attack, the resistence, and the advent of former administration into the Atageini province had all flowed back and forth on that compromised network.

The first result of the gossip had turned up this morning, as ordinary Atageini provincials, shopkeep-

ers, farmers, and town laborers en masse, all linked
into that network, had rolled onto the estate grounds
to join their threatened lord's defense against what
they perceived as an assault against their sovereign
rights. An untidy host of town buses and farm-to-
market trucks had pulled up on the formal cobbled
drive in front of the house, and no few armed farmers had turned up with tractors and small earth-
movers, very truculent and martial arrivals in the
lower hall. Hearing that someone wanted to shut
down their lord's communication system, they had
involved themselves and their outraged civil liberties
in the dispute about the safety of the system, a matter of local pride. They had backed down only because they had finally gotten it through their heads
that the apparent Guildsman in black was not an
Atageini security officer, but Tabini-aiji himself, arguing with their lord, and proposing to improve local
communications, if they could only shut down the
core of it for a certain number of hours.

The whole matter of the civil protest had started
because Taibeni rangers, of that hated neighboring
clan, had set up some sort of competing communications installation in their camp on the manicured
front lawn, a much more state-of-the-art system
about which the Taibeni were as secretive and defensive as the Atageini were about their own network.
Lord Tatiseigi had demanded *that* rival network be
shut down, claiming the Taibeni were spying on his
defenses—the Taibeni being older enemies than the
Kadagidi themselves. That ancient feud had boiled
on under the whole debate, and the presence of the

farmers and heavy equipment operators had provoked a haughty delegation from the Taibeni leadership, arriving to support Tabini-aiji against Tatiseigi's provincials. *That* had been the point at which the paidhi-aiji had decided to retire quietly.

But argumentative as all sides were, and no matter the simmering feuds between Taiben and the Atageini, the presence of those lowland farmers and those high forest rangers alike guaranteed that the Kadagidi would meet more opposition today than had already sent them packing back to their own province last night. The line of buses and trucks out there might give the Kadagidi pause, politically as well as tactically. At least for the daylight hours.

"One has no idea how long it may be, nadiin, before anyone downstairs has time to consider domestic requests," Bren said. "But at the earliest, I should be very obliged if I can persuade our host to let me connect to a printer . . . granted we can disconnect from the network."

The household computers had become an object of extreme contention in the communications issue too. But all he wanted was a computer with available backup, a printer, and a considerable lot of paper to put information out that, in his own opinion, *someone* needed to hear. It was a report, a document which itself might not be prudent to produce in a house likely to be assaulted tonight; but he was down here to make that report, and if it got out, even into the hands of the opposition, it would create gossip and questions—but it was far more useful to get it into Tabini's hands, ammunition against such arguments as proceeded downstairs, if only he could persuade Tabini to hear him on the topic.

"One is reliably informed the aiji has come upstairs, insisting on a bath," Banichi said, pausing in his careful examination of bullet holes in the walls. "We should all be safe for a few hours, Bren-ji, and the aiji has retired, perhaps for the rest of the day. The debate has doubtless exhausted everyone."

Banichi knew his frustration. And knew the importance of what he wanted to print.

"If one might hand the report to his staff . . . if one could gain access to one isolated machine . . ."

"The aiji's staff indicates to us that he will rest after his bath," Jago said, and the subterranean text was that his own staff had tried to get the audience he had asked for—tried, and gotten nothing. The aiji had rebuffed that approach as he had deflected all other attempts. The paidhi's influence had been a major grievance behind the coup. He knew it. He had not gotten his own audience; his staff met opposition: It was a standoff. But even if it made Tabini angrier than he was, he still had to get that document into Tabini's hands and get him to read it.

"Go," Jago said. "Have your own bath, Bren-ji. We have told the aiji's staff the gist of things. More than that, Cenedi will brief them, if they will not hear us."

Cenedi, the dowager's chief of security, was clearly their best hope: whatever Tabini's feelings toward the paidhi-aiji, the aiji-dowager would get through, and Cenedi, in her name, could grab staff by the lapels and talk urgent sense to them . . . all sorts of urgent sense. But one also had to worry whether Tabini, with new staff around him, the others having perished, might not be subject to a new filter of information. They were Taibeni, but not all; and Bren had never known them.

"I shall, then," he said.

"We have sent for clothes," Jago said. "One still hopes."

It was by no means his security's job. But his clothing, adult but child-sized, posed a major problem: It was not as if they could run to a local shop, even for the most basic items, and Tatiseigi's hospitality had provided no domestic services ordinary to such a house. Their host was extremely harried, one had to understand, his housekeeping staff already pressed to the limits, and as exhausted as the security staff . . . but the plain fact was Tatiseigi detested humans as much as he hated Taibeni, with as much history behind the feeling: he hated their look, hated their influence, their technology, and their continued presence on the planet, and having a human house-guest attendant on the general destruction of his lawn, his hedges, and the tranquility of his province had clearly not made him change his mind on the topic.

And if all that were not enough, Tatiseigi personally and as a close relative resented the paidhi's former influence with Tabini-aiji and his current influence with the dowager. Most particularly Tatiseigi resented his relationship with the young lord, the aiji's son—Tatiseigi's own great-grandnephew, who had stood up for the paidhi in no uncertain terms.

Oh, the paidhi was under Lord Tatiseigi's roof on tolerance, no question, no matter that he and his staff—and the aforementioned young lord, with the detested Taibeni—had helped rescue the house from destruction last night. Lord Tatiseigi's view was that the house would never have been attacked and damaged in the first place if not for the paidhi's past influence, his support of this radical new space technology, its economic disruption, and the upheaval it wrought among the provinces. Consequently, the paidhi and his atevi staff could quite nicely go to hell—so long as the aiji-dowager didn't notice his departure. So, no, there were no domestic servants to help them, it was hardly graceful to protest it from his tenuous position, and he had no wish to provoke another argument downstairs.

But the sad truth was, he, born a nice democratic Mospheiran fellow, had grown pitifully dependent on clothes turning up miraculously arranged in his closet, the socially appropriate garments appearing in the hands of servants who would help him dress. Lace would be starched and hand pressed, every detail of his attire and his bodyguards' black leather rendered immaculate without their much thinking about it or questioning what they were to wear on what occasion. Everything would be perfect—if his own staff were here. If he needed delicately hint at something, his staff would talk to house staff, or to any other lord's staff, and miracles would happen, appointments would turn up, protocols would be settled, and he would never hear about the difficulties.

His staff being up on the station, he now had to think about such details, down to finding clean socks. And the paidhi's odd-sized wardrobe, at the moment, consisted of a single change of clean formal clothes packed into a soft traveling bag that had been tossed onto fishy ice, thrown down into dirt, bounced around a bus, tied onto a mecheita, tossed into this room, and shoved against a baseboard during last night's armed assault. What he had worn yesterday was a total loss. The pale trousers were brown with dirt about the seat and knees, black with soot, and stained with blood, not to mention ripped from fence wire and branches. His cold-weather coat, no cleaner than the trousers, was ripped by the selfsame wire the length of the lower arm. His white, lace-cuffed shirt, where the coat had not covered it, was stained with every substance possible to find in the landscape, not to mention human and atevi blood. His boots had a seam parting along the right toe, in addition to the scuffs and mud.

As it was, he decided if Tabini was not going to be available and if no printer was to be had, he should put his computer back into the hiding place that had protected it through the attack—they had no way of knowing at what time another alarm might sound— and see what he could do about the clothing situation on his own. Jago certainly wasn't his valet, and his security staff had enough on their hands.

Hefting the light computer case back up into its

safe place hurt. Getting into his baggage on the floor and searching into the tangled mess of clothing inside discovered splinters in his palms he had not yet found. And the clean shirt he pulled out of the duffle was, as he had foreseen, by no means ready to wear. The lace had gone mostly limp. The body was more than rumpled: it had pressed-in wrinkles. The remaining spare trousers likewise showed fold and crumple marks.

But they were at least clean. He found clean underwear. And socks. He got up and hung the clothes in the closet, which he should have thought to do yesterday, and began, stupidly, to strip off what he was wearing, right there in the bedroom, as he would have done on the ship.

Someone rapped at the outer foyer door. He dived, caught up his pistol from his dirty coat out of the pile of clothing he had just dropped on the floor, and, both sleeves in one hand, held the coat for cover, moving into clear shot of that door as Jago, armed, walked out into the short inner hall to answer it.

Two arrivals. They looked like domestic staff, in Atageini colors, muted green and gold. One was a woman, a rather substantial woman. And with a little bow and the exchange, presumably, of courtesies and names, they excused themselves right past Jago's bemused stare and came in to survey the premises and the situation. Bren stood holding his gun in one hand and anchoring the coat with the other, and the two servants bowed and reported themselves to Banichi as if the lord of the establishment were part of the furniture. Jago had followed them in; she stood behind the pair, hand on her pistol, just stood, wearing no peaceable look. Tano and Algini stood in mirror image, hands likewise positioned.

"We are instructed," the man said with a sideward, embarrassed glance at Bren, "to provide assistance to the paidhi's household."

Staff help. From Lord Tatiseigi. The sky would fall next. Then he decided it might not be a lie. The aiji-dowager or Tabini himself might have requested special dispensation for them—if either had happened to notice the conditions in which the old lord had settled them.

But it would be impolite to seem astonished . . . no matter he suspected their sashay past Jago's forbidding presence might be a reconnaissance for Tatiseigi as much as a desire to report themselves properly to Banichi, as de facto head of staff. House servants might be Guild, just the same as bodyguards in uniform, and if they were reconnoitering, seeing if he had pocketed the bath soap, then he was prepared to be annoyed beyond the slight they paid.

"The premises are presently secure, nadiin," Banichi said curtly. "We need laundry done. Boots seen to." Menial tasks, all. The most menial. Banichi was likewise highly annoyed; if human ears could pick that up with no problem at all, the intruders could certainly figure it out. And as the pair's survey of the room finally included the very obvious human, Bren held his coat in front of him and bowed his head in as pricklishly gracious an acceptance as a man could give while standing naked in view of strangers.

"Clean clothes would be delightful," he said, "nadiin. There has been a problem in that regard."

"Astringents, liniments, and plasters," Jago said from behind their backs. "A medical kit, nadiin, if you please. Ours is for emergencies."

"Soap," from Algini, "nadiin."

"Indeed," the man of the pair said, and looked around the room full circle as if taking inventory of the historic vases and the condition of the furniture—perhaps because of the bullets that had flown last night, but one was still hardly sure. "Is *all* the paidhi's staff lodged in these quarters?"

"Guild security," Jago said frostily from their backs. "We are on duty."

There was additional space and cots in a little closet of a room off the short entry hall. It was an extremely minimal apartment, not designed for a gender-mixed staff ... but where Jago slept wasn't in these strangers' need-to-know.

"Towels, first," Jago reiterated, "nadiin. We shall be very glad of towels."

"Immediately," the man said, with another bow, this last a little more courteous, and aimed toward Bren, as if he had finally gotten his mental bearings or overcome his shock. "My name, nand' paidhi, is Timani."

"Adaro," the woman said, likewise bowing. "One is honored to serve."

Bows on all sides. A little relaxation of manner. "Jago," Jago said. "Banichi. Tano. Algini." It was all staff-to-staff, the sort of thing that might have been done in the backstairs, if this suite had been large enough to have proper servant passages. Introduction of the lord of the household didn't belong at the bottom of that list. The two Atageini servants, after the initial shock, had avoided quite looking at the half-naked human. And still tried not to.

"Honored, nadiin." A bow from staff to staff, and a quick departure.

"Amazing," was Banichi's acid comment. Lord Tatiseigi, actively insulting to a human under his roof, had never evinced the least interest in seeing his human guest properly dressed, fed, or sheltered on their first night. Now he sent his servants, while the house was in crisis, and while the lawn was full of Taibeni rangers? And the servants of this conservative country estate had just conducted their business past the lord's presence, ignoring him entirely, while snippily questioning Jago's presence, a woman on a man's staff?

Bloody hell, Bren thought. He had wanted servants. He was ready to pitch this pair out.

"The aiji may have requested them," Jago said.

Tabini had not seen Lord Tatiseigi's performance on their arrival, and might have no idea they had been only scantly seen to. "Or the aiji-dowager," Bren said, "possibly even without consulting Lord Tatiseigi."

That thought afforded Banichi and Jago a grim amusement. Ilisidi had been romantically and politically involved with Lord Tatiseigi in her reckless youth, perhaps even while married to Tabini's late grandfather, and it was true she had no hesitation in ordering Tatiseigi's staff as if she were still resident here. It was a good guess that Ilisidi was behind it, and if she was, he had hopes of seeing his wardrobe resurrected, if only the precious pair came back with an iron.

Meanwhile, the bath water would not wait forever, which meant the paidhi-aiji should take his pale, skinny human body off to the tub before two servants became fortunate three and then five and seven—granted that they were, in fact, going to be providing clean sheets and towels and pressing his clothes in the bedroom.

And just wait, he thought with grim satisfaction, until they asked more directly where Jago did sleep, and just wait until *that* answer reached the old lord's ears. It was the one particular of their domestic arrangement he had never broadcast for the world's consumption. And if this house had not made arrangements for Jago, then the scandal was theirs to deal with.

He took out his pocket com, the spare ammunition clip, and his pill bottle, taking them with him as things he had no wish to surrender to Atageini servants, and dropped the coat back onto the pile of hopeless clothes on the floor before, gun in hand, he walked into the tiled bathroom. He laid the firearm and the other items safely on a tiled shelf above the slosh-line, but where he could reach the weapon and the clip if an alarm sounded. The tub, which would have qualified as a small pond in any human garden, was nearly full, though water was still cascading in from the fire hose-sized faucet. It was a bath built for socializing. It would have been a bath sufficient for grandest luxury, if its owner had decided to equip it with sufficient towels, scents, and oils, and if he had sent his servants to provide tea and other amenities for relaxation. There was not, in such an upstairs room, a mud drain, as there was in belowstairs baths, for servants, for hunters returning from the field, but there was at least a drain grating around the tub to carry away the water pushed over the edge and he spied, on a tiled shelf, a flower vase devoid of blooms—one of the countless details the Atageini had never properly attended in this room. He took up that antique vase for a pitcher, partially filled it from the tub and poured it over himself as he stood over the drain. He repeated the procedure, sluicing off the worst of the grime, until coming up behind him, Jago took the full vase and poured it over his head.

Both hands free, he raked a twig out of his hair, and laid it on the shelf. A second vaseful followed. He undid his braid, and laid aside the bedraggled, sodden, once-white ribbon. Jago shed her black leathers and boots and tee, and being no cleaner than he was, poured the makeshift pitcher over herself, washing dirt into the drain as the relative chill of the air drove him to the depths of the tub. He submerged, surfaced, embraced by fluid warmth.

"It should be safe for the rest to join us, Jago-ji," he said. "I have no modesty left."

"Oh, they will take their turn," she said. Her black skin showed a few scrapes, a few trails of red film from untreated cuts. Her pigtail, freed of its confines, separated into temporarily curling strands that sent trails of moisture down a broad, strong back, and he watched that beautiful back in absolute satisfaction and enjoyment, rejoicing to see her alive and in one piece. He was, himself, polka-dotted with bruises, with red chafe marks, with scrapes, scratches, and one long raking cut on the leg that was not as painful as the blisters, but it hurt like hell in the water, right along with his splinter-invaded hands.

Still, oh, it was good to duck his head under water, to sink down over his head, and resurface with his nose just above warm, steaming water. He stirred from that bliss, spying bits of straw and twigs that had bobbed to the surface, about to get into the filter. He put them, collected, onto the stone rim, and the next moment his straw bits were awash for a second time as Jago stepped into the bath. She submerged. The water cut itself off, having reached its level, and Jago surfaced, eyes shut, content to sink back against the wall and soak for a moment.

So was he content, blissful, until Tatiseigi's man-servant turned up next to the bath edge with a tall stack of snow-white towels.

"One may put them on the shelf, nadi," Jago said severely, shocking the man, quite surely—one only hoped he was too embarrassed to report the scene to his lord, but one greatly doubted it.

And at this precise moment, Bren said to himself, he didn't give a damn what the servants gossiped.

The gentleman of service went back to the door, delicately took a tray from his female fellow-servant standing oh so modestly and properly outside, then came back and set it down on the bath edge. It held the unguents and oils and linaments Jago had requested. A small box of plasters Timani set above the water-zone, and then stopped dead, staring at Bren's gun on the shelf on eye level with him. Underwater, next to Bren, Jago had braced a foot—to spring, it might be.

But then, without coming near that deadly object, the manservant slipped out.

"One should not have left that there," Bren muttered.

"One should not," Jago agreed: never a syllable of flattery or excuse over a security breach, and likewise she was probably annoyed with herself. Then came the drift of remarks passed outside: Tano, very near the bathroom door, accosted the servants to discuss clothing, clean and otherwise, and the urgent need for shirts and underwear.

"We shall be gossiped about," Bren muttered. "One deeply apologizes, Jago-ji. Not least about leaving the gun there."

"Better to be gossiped about," Jago said, sinking back, "than taken for the furniture, nandi." A wicked smile chased the frown, and a wink. "That is a true domestic. He is not Guild."

That was good to know. Meanwhile Jago was close and soap-scented, and in good humor. For a few moments after, just to spite fate and the local gossip, they indulged in conventions some human, some atevi, some common to both, and several things that downright hurt—but about the pain, he didn't, at the moment, care. Being alive was good. Being with Jago was glorious. He had intended to spend his bathtime extracting splinters, and dismissed the notion for perhaps ten whole minutes—before they got out to give the others the chance at the tub.

Then he found that the hot water had him dripping blood from that gash he hadn't thought amounted to much, not to mention the sensation of air hitting the raw spots.

"I shall ruin the towel," he protested, when she wanted to stop the flow.

"One is very certain, Bren-ji, that the staff has bleach at their disposal." Jago settled him on the dressing bench and set to work with the bottles the servant had brought in on the tray, some preparations that stung, most that he was glad to find didn't. She salved spots he wouldn't have anyone else reach, pulled splinters from his hands, including one quite nasty one on the side of his right hand, and stuck plasters onto several cuts. They were plasters designed for her complexion, not his, true, but they were, except the one on the side of his hand, all in inconspicuous places.

And somewhere in that process the pain greatly eased, pain he'd carried so many hours he hadn't even realized it, until the steady presence of misery changed to the sting of treatments. He returned the favor on her scratches, rubbed liniment left-handed into her shoulders. They had both become far more pleasantly aromatic than the condition in which they had arrived, and were both towel-wrapped, evergreen-smelling and warm by the time Banichi came in. He laid his own gun on the shelf and claimed the bath, sending water over the side. Then Tano and Algini added themselves to the tub, and the slosh-drain became a vital necessity.

Bren retreated from the flood with Jago and took up watch in the bedroom. There was no bathrobe provided by their host. There was no help with his hair from the servants, but Jago put on most of her uniform and he, wrapped in a luxurious huge towel, plaited Jago's damp queue while she sat on the floor in front of him, one of the rare times he could persuade her to take precedence, for duty's sake.

The servants slipped in the front door again. Timani, the man, brought them soap, towels, combs, brushes, and a stack of black uniform shirts, and tried not to notice the impropriety in progress, not looking at Jago nor quite at him.

The two fled back out the door, in haste, and Jago outright laughed at the retreat.

"Hold still," Bren complained, and replaited the last few turns, which, with her movement, had escaped the half-tied ribbon and his unskilled fingers. His own hair was still wet. When braided, it tended to curl right out of its ribbon, unless very expertly handled. Hers was always straight and sleek and perfect.

So was she, once she stood up: straight and sleek and perfect, wearing her last uniform tee and black leather pants.

"I shall track down the servants and see what the laundry staff intends to do about your clothes, nandi."

"And underwear," he said solemnly. "I am down to the very last." He suffered a kiss on the forehead and sat afterward with his eyes closed, listening to Jago put on her coat and leave, listening to the

Atageini house elsewhere recovering from last night's attack, upstairs and down, inside and out. A mecheita in the general direction of the stableyard bawled its complaint at the heavens. Someone had begun hammering with a vengeance in the last few minutes, two someones, or a strong echo, coming from somewhere inside the house—he thought downstairs, and indeed, they had been moving scaffolding in the foyer. Servants shouted instructions and questions at one another in halls that, before the attack, had been orderly and quiet. This room, unprepared and lacking amenities, was probably one they accorded some village lord's third son during the seasonal hunts and otherwise never touched. He had a go at plaiting his own hair, with indifferent results. He could by no means tie the ribbon, but he clipped it into a finish.

And he recalled then he was supposed to be guarding the room, and he had left his gun and pocket com on the shelf in the bathroom. He got up and went after the means for self-defense.

"The door opened," Banichi observed, tilting his head back from his comfortable place in the tub, Tano and Algini having arranged themselves around the other rim.

Atevi hearing. Jago had not been that noisy in her leaving.

"Jago went out to question the staff," he said, "she says about my wardrobe, but likely about other things, too."

"The house is full of strangers coming and going, Bren-ji. Atageini, Taibeni." A high member of the

Atageini house staff having been in Kadagidi employ, it remained a wonder they had not all been murdered in their beds on the first night, if the traitor had once found a way past their personal security. "Your staff earnestly asks you stay away from the doors. If there should be an arrival, even of the servants, immediately duck in here and trust that we shall leave this bath in very rapid fashion."

"I shall sit far to the inside of the room," he promised Banichi. The water around his staff had gone murky. The bathroom smelled of strong evergreen soap. "But the servants have already been here. Shirts have arrived. One assumes there are enough for all of you, nadiin-ji."

"Good," Banichi said, and heaved himself up to his feet, sending tides over the edge. He climbed the ledge, leaving the water to Tano and Algini. "But one does not approve this coming and going of strange servants."

"Jago was here at the time." He was mortally sorry to have disturbed Banichi's bath. "And, Banichi-ji, one is quite sure ill-meaning servants could equally well poison us at dinner or shoot us in the halls—"

"Access," Banichi said, wrapping a towel about his waist. "Everything is a question of access and the propriety of the house. This Timani is vague on the matter of his man'chi, and until someone owns up to him and his partner, we do not allow him—"

The foyer door had opened, not a furtive opening, but a thump. In a single stride Banichi elbowed Bren out of the way, had his gun in hand, and stood to meet an arrival in the bedroom.

"Daja-ma," Banichi said in dismay.

Bren put his head through the door. Only two women alive rated that "my lady" from Banichi. And the visitor was not the dowager. It was Damiri. Tabini-aiji's wife. Mother of the heir. She was resplendent in a silk robe of muted green with the white Atageini lilies. Banichi and he stood there in towels. Her own bodyguard was in attendance, two women in Assassins' black leather, professionally impassive, standing behind her. Dared one suspect amusement in the lady's eyes?

"Daja-ma," Bren said, making his own small bow.

"One trusts the paidhi's welcome now does credit to my uncle's house."

"We have seen two servants," he said. "Are they yours, daja-ma?"

"They are persons we know, at least," Damiri said, "They are not Guild, nand' paidhi, but they are reliable in man'chi to the Atageini house."

"Then the paidhi-aiji accepts them," Bren said, "with all confidence and gratitude, daja-ma."

"Our Ajuri cousins will arrive this evening," Damiri said, "with additional personnel, most domestic—but not all." Ajuri was Damiri's mother's clan, a small fact from the basement of the paidhi's knowledge, one he raked up into memory. He had met Damiri's mother once, at a social occasion: the Ajuri were a small clan to the north of here, a postage stamp of a territory, but a rich one, within Dursai Province, and almost within the Padi Valley. "Local construction companies are assessing the damage to the house and making urgent repairs," Damiri said further. "Certain of my husband's staff have just come in."

Those would be likely more arrivals from Taiben province, Taibeni clan. Ragi, the aiji's own clan, by ethnicity, like most of the central regions. "One is extremely glad to hear," Bren said with a bow of his head. Everything was, on the surface, good news—hasty, too hasty perhaps, the moves of these ordinary citizens arriving as if the skirmish was a single incident, the construction companies coming in as if they were sure the fighting was at least at a long pause, and as if there was no likelihood at all that the Kadagidi would come sweeping in with airplanes and bombs in the next round. He certainly wanted to believe they were safe from further attack. But bombs were not the only danger.

And the arrival of the Ajuri, marginal outsiders to the district, added more than one more clan to what was gathering here; it added intrusion from another association, a situation which, among atevi—given atevi instincts—did not seem to diminish the tension. Modern atevi didn't generally fight wars, knowing they were hard to stop. But this situation was widening.

"We have had at least a preliminary report about your voyage, nandi, the things done, things seen. Clearly our son has grown. And learned new things." There was a mother's regret in that, he sensed it: two years of her son's life had passed in which his mother and father had had no part at all. "You did extremely well for him, nand' Bren. And you risked your life for him, latest. We shall not forget."

He felt heat in his face. "One made every effort, daja-ma." She had graciously not added that his influence over the heir had become a serious liability in this backlash of atevi resentment against human influence in the court. "But he is in all respects your son, and acted as he saw fit." He gave her back a son who'd grown up on *The Three Musketeers* and shared tea and cakes with an enemy alien. A son who longed for dinosaurs and devoured pizza with a circle of human playmates. All these innocent passions had become a liability to the boy and a puzzlement to his parents.

"We have heard things here and there," Damiri said, "that you did at great risk. Things the *aishidi'tat* must know, nandi."

Support. But he needed it not only for his own sake. He needed desperately to make things understood, and he seized on it, perhaps too recklessly. "We hope to give a wider report, daja-ma." With thoughts of the computer lying in its concealment. "We have evidence. We have profound reasons to argue that your husband must be the one in authority."

"Our confidence in you is justified," Damiri said, not a yes and not a no. She added, in a pragmatic vein, "Anything that you may require, nandi, ask of Timani."

Timani. Whom they had deeply and deliberately shocked. God, Bren thought. And *that* act of his might reach the lady's ears, if staff gossip had not embroidered it already.

"Thank you. Our deep gratitude, daja-ma."

She gave a little nod, then turned, gathering her own bodyguard, and left.

This was the house in which she had spent her growing years, in which her Atageini father had died, assassinated. It was the house in which she, a minor child, had come under her great-uncle Tatiseigi's governance—and played childish pranks, so one had heard, faintly. It was a tradition her son had certainly carried on. She was not the lady of the house; she was somewhat greater in power, or had been, until the overthrow.

And every keen golden glance of her eyes had surely noted the deficiencies of her great-uncle's hospitality to a visiting human. He had a feeling that a list was accumulating, between the lady and Timani and Adaro, not least of which must be the lack of separate bedrooms and bath for female staff which the old lord had clearly known was in the party—from that major detail down to the lack of a message tray in the foyer, the sun-fading and mustiness of the bedspread, not to mention the drapes, which had rips in the lining through which the afternoon sun shone in patches, with a few more rents in the rotten, dusty fabric since bullets had come flying past last night. He was sure the suite the aiji occupied and that accorded to the dowager and to the heir were immaculate and *kabiu*—but the paidhi-aiji had been tucked into a room unrefurbished for, oh, two or three decades, if not a century or so.

"I fear I was very indiscreet," he muttered to

Banichi, who, towel and all, had never acted for a moment as if he were caught at a disadvantage.

"One is sure the aiji's consort is very well aware of your personal arrangement."

Could he blush any hotter? "The servants will tell it through the staff, Banichi-ji. It will reflect on Jago and one fears it will reflect on the consort. Clearly, association with me is bad enough without—"

"Do you think you have to cause to be ashamed, paidhi-ji? Do you think you have any reason at all to hide? The discredit is Lord Tatiseigi's, not yours."

He looked up at a man who had cast his lot with him for good or for ill for more than a decade, and whose man'chi would, he was sure, last to the end. Like Jago's. Like Tano's, and Algini's, and so many others . . . it was absolute.

"I shall try to deserve you," he said with a small catch in the throat at that moment, and probably embarrassed Banichi and greatly upset the order of Banichi's universe into the bargain, but he didn't stay to debate his human improprieties, only went to find his change of linen, at least, until Timani and his partner might bring him clothes proper to wear for the remainder of the day. He was still intensely embarrassed at his lapse of judgment, his small fling at an insulting reception. It was going to be an effort to face Timani, let alone the rest of the household staff. They had been sent, Timani had said; the man had made no mention of Damiri. But they were a loan Damiri had specifically engineered, a gift bestowed on him, and he had not done well, not in the least, at a time when his judgment was already questioned in far larger matters, in all the advice he had ever given. He had been in space too long. He had forgotten the ways of the court and the great houses. He had lost touch, was what. And he had to relocate himself in old habits, and mend his rebellious thinking, fast . . . his position advised decorous quiet, and cleverness, and he had been neither quiet nor clever this afternoon.

Banichi meanwhile took black shirts and linen from the closet and went back to the bath. Bren had time to dress, at least far enough to preserve decency under the towel, before the outer door opened, and Timani, indeed, and Adaro with him, arrived bearing his remaining shirt, his coat, his trousers, everything immaculately pressed, besides, in Adaro's hands, a vase of seasonal branches, bare with autumn, whether arranged for them or hastily snatched from some hallway.

"One is ever so grateful, nadiin," he said, newly respectful and grateful for their help. He bowed. They bowed. Adaro unburdened her hands, set the vase on a bare table, and began energetically stripping the bed, while Timani hung his clothes in the closet.

"Additional staff will come and go, by your leave, nandi," Adaro said, "supplying items that may have been mislaid, including fresh linens and towels. We shall introduce them properly to your security, but if you have any question at all, we will stay close by while they are in this room."

"One is extremely appreciative," he said, thinking that he ought to relocate the computer if they were restocking the linen cabinet, and if servants would be going through it; and to Timani, somewhat meekly: "Will you assist me to dress, nadi?"

To dress appropriately for the day, that was, in this tag end of the afternoon—to braid his hair properly, to look civilized, and to begin to act it.

# 2

Left to his own desires for the day he would have gone to bed, burrowed deep, and stayed there for the next week, but he had settled on one urgent objective for the rest of the day, since he had seen Damiri was well-disposed: He wanted above all things to get his report to Tabini, and not to offend Tatiseigi in the process. In order to do that, he was obliged to appear at best advantage, respectful of the house and the persons he dealt with—and he had to manage not to offend the staff in the process.

Adaro had occupied herself discreetly about the bed-making. Timani assisted his dressing, and held the shirt for him, frowning the while—doubtless Timani had never hoped to see a skinny, scratched, and bruised human at such close quarters. Bren was accustomed to a certain curiosity, but given all that had transpired, he was no more comfortable than the servants.

"Forgive me, nandi," Timani said, settling the shirt onto his shoulders, on which black bandage patches were in evidence, not to mention the long gash on his arm, also done up in a series of black bandages. "Would medical attention not be in order?"

"My staff has put me back together well enough," he said, and attempted humor with the earnest fellow. "None of these was the mecheita's fault. Except the fence."

Stiff and proper. "Nevertheless, nandi, if the paidhi or his staff needs any professional assistance—"

"I hope we shall not, nadi. More plasters, perhaps, for them." He attempted his own buttons, with fingers broken-nailed and needing a file, and Timani hastened to take over before his splinter wounds left a blood spot on the linen.

The queue was redone and the white ribbon, pressed, though frayed and warped, went into its proper bow. The boots went on, polished and with the scuffs gone, even the broken seam somehow pulled back into line and repaired. Meanwhile other servants came in with more bed linens and more draperies for the windows, as well as two more massive porcelain vases of a fine pale green. The latter were precious things, older than the Association itself, very likely, and marked a definite turn in the attention given the paidhi in this house.

He sat down under a pretense of reading, quietly took a nail file from his personal kit, and repaired the damage, which tended to snag his trousers, a lord genteely idle and proper while the staff worked.

Then, in a momentary absence of the staff, he sprang up and relocated the computer, in its inconspicuous hard case, to a place with his staff's heavier weaponry in other hard cases and canvas bags, where it looked fairly well at home at a casual glance. A battalion of servants came in with ladders next. The new drapes were hung, meticulously adjusted, tables moved about, vases set just so, as an elderly man, a master of *kabiu,* one had no doubt, arrived, supervised, then left, as satisfied as it was possible to be with an awkward situation. Lord Tatiseigi change his lodgings to something more fit? Admit he had been churlish? A thousand times no.

Patch the situation until Lady Damiri was mollified? Perhaps.

In half an hour, the whole room shifted from sterile and minimal to a heartwarmingly fresh arrangement: *Welcome,* it began to say. *Honored guest of the Ragi court,* it began to say, in the inclusion of small black and red items, the heraldry of Tabini's house, arranged as slight accents within the green and white and gold of the Atageini heraldry. *Welcome to the paidhi-aiji,* the room even began to say, in the white vase now set beside the bed, holding the green and gold and subtler antique white of the Atageini lilies—the arrangement was a little ad hoc, and seasonally questionable, but it spoke volumes about a revised staff attitude.

Meanwhile the nicely pressed coat went on, the lace cuffs and collar were meticulously adjusted, while hammering and sawing reached a frenzy elsewhere in the house.

"One is extremely pleased, nadi," Bren murmured, looking about him, and letting a breath go in a deep sigh, within the comforting, rib-brushing confines of a clean and immaculate coat. "Your efforts are much appreciated."

"With gratitude, nand' paidhi. Will we two suffice for your service? I shall take up residence in the foyer, and Adaro wherever the woman sleeps."

Well, and damn the prickly propriety of this house, which he had previously gone over the line to offend, no question. Now he had to appease their sensibilities, in their best efforts to put a patch on their own lord's discourtesy to a guest. "That does pose an unaccustomed problem, nadi," he said. "We by no means wish the female member of our staff too far separated from her fellows, or from her duty. This is her wish, and mine, and it takes priority above all else."

"Then Adaro and I shall contrive an arrangement in the foyer, nandi, if screens will suffice in this room."

"One has every confidence," he said. "Continue as needed. Thank you."

Damn it, damn it, damn it—he slept ever so much better when Jago was in the bed, but things were as they were, and he was the one responsible for pushing the situation.

And now, if he had Damiri's ear, he had no time to spend on ordering their sleeping arrangements. He had other things to do, urgently, beginning with securing an audience.

At times one so missed Gin's human, shocking style of summons—but *Hey, Jerry!* would be a two century scandal under this roof.

One daren't. But it was perfectly reasonable to ask Timani to walk ten steps to advise Banichi, dressing in the bath, that the lord-of-household needed a Guild messenger in formal uniform to walk thirty paces down the outside hall to advise the aiji's staff to advise the aiji that the paidhi would like to walk that same thirty paces to sit down for a small, hour-long tea and eventually deliver a critical report to the aiji, face to face, oh, sometime reasonably soon.

"Ask Banichi to see me, nadi," was how the routine began, and when Banichi came out of the bath—only his leathers newly polished, doubtless to the detriment of a couple of towels, his queue in good order—in short, ready to face the rest of the day— "An errand, Banichi-ji."

"Nandi?"

"One never once thought to advance the matter with the consort, Banichi-ji—and doubtless the aiji is due his rest— One ever so greatly regrets the haste, and understands the delicacy of asking so urgently—but under all circumstances, certainly the aiji will wish to hear my report as soon as possible."

It was ordinarily a tranquil, gracious routine of inquiry, staff approaching staff, arranging things in back corridors that doubtless existed for the suites in this grand hall, but not for this modest room. The attempt at formal inquiry and request of an audience lost a little more graciousness with the house ringing with hammers and voices of staff hurrying about in a mad rush. Shouts at that moment echoed in the hall outside.

"Yes," Banichi said, with the same economy of motion, and completely understanding him.

Shortcuts. No laborious use of seals and exchange of message-cylinders, which he still lacked, a circumstance which could render a gentleman near incommunicado. He instead hoped to gain the aiji's summons to him, approaching Tabini via the security network, a disgraceful shortcut, for what had become an ungracious, breakneck situation under Lord Tatiseigi's oh-so-proper roof. But one did as one could. Banichi immediately slipped away and out to the hall, sans written message, and was gone long enough for Bren to wonder where Jago was at the moment, and to look cautiously out the window to investigate one source of the hammering.

The repair of the stableyard's eastern gate seemed to be the focus of a great deal of activity. Never mind the stable behind it had burned down. They needed fences to give the Atageini mecheiti a sense of territory, to keep them from challenging the Taibeni mecheiti—if one of the big bulls took it into his thick skull to start a fight, it could be very nasty indeed. At the moment, presumably, the hedges kept them apart, but those barriers only lasted until a mecheita decided to walk on through.

Jago came back.

He looked at her, lifted a brow in mild question regarding her business.

"One delayed, consulting with Cenedi," Jago said.

"How is the dowager?"

"Quite well, nandi, though Cenedi himself is suffering somewhat."

"Wounded?" He had not heard that.

"Minor, but an impairment in hand-to-hand. We

discussed alternatives. Places of refuge to which we might retreat, if things grow chancy. One has a rather better notion of alignments in the region—some business the dowager gathered from her grandson."

A very useful conference between those two, then. A notion how the political map lay, and what doors might welcome them, and what ones would not, as a next step after Atageini territory. But this was not a staff that liked the word *retreat*.

"One rather hopes the Kadagidi would have reconsidered their reception here," he said, "and at least delay for consultations."

Consultations with their lord Murini, who was still sitting in Shejidan, at their last report, while his clan went at it hammer and tongs with the previously neutral Atageini . . . and now had outsiders coming in. Provoking a region-wide war ought to require at least some consultation with the self-proclaimed aiji.

"Couriers may have gone to the capital," Jago said. "Unfortunately, though the Kadagidi had an agent here, Lord Tatiseigi does not seem to have had particular success at installing his own among the Kadagidi."

Of course not, Bren thought. Tatiseigi had spent all his best men infiltrating the paidhi's household—and very good men, too, not to mention a better cook than he could otherwise have found. *He* was the great threat Tatiseigi had been keeping an eye on, not the neighboring clan who had been plotting against the stability of the *aishidi'tat* for as long as that entity had existed.

"One wishes we knew what would be the wise

thing, Jago-ji. Staying here much longer seems rash. The servants, however—Damiri-daja has affirmed she sent them."

"So Cenedi said."

"Damiri says Ajuri clan is coming in—for a familial visit in crisis, one supposes. And all the farmers and townsfolk out there arriving and picnicking, as if it were a local harvest fair—one worries about this situation, Jago-ji. One is very concerned for their safety."

"Well we should," Jago said. "But, understand, it makes a statement—one does wish you would stay farther from the window, Bren-ji."

He moved. Instantly.

"The servants intend to install privacy screens," he offered. "Perhaps we should add them to the windows."

A rich, soft chuckle. "Privacy screens indeed. After what the gentleman saw in the bath, nandi?"

"I greatly regret the embarrassment, Jago-ji," he said. "I profoundly apologize."

"For what possible offense, Bren-ji? And privation will not last. Likely we shall indeed be leaving soon."

"Where?"

"One can only guess," Jago said. "As for the harvest fair out on the lawn, clearly the lord has encouraged it. He has met with these locals. He has praised them. He has sent out word."

"Is that from Cenedi?"

"It might be." The Guild kept its secrets. "Clearly Lord Tatiseigi wishes to rally the clans and meet his neighbors in force if they come in. Tabini-aiji has choices to make."

"God." The last in Mosphei', but Jago understood him. Tatiseigi, whose equipment had nearly gotten them all killed, proposed to raise local war against the clan whose lord claimed Tabini's office, pushing the aiji to move now or move on. "I have to talk to Tabini while we still have some means to print a file. I just sent Banichi to reach him."

"Banichi was going downstairs."

"Downstairs?" To find Tabini's senior staff, was it?

Then Tabini was in conference, or his staff was, with Tatiseigi or his household. Perhaps Tabini was trying to talk Tatiseigi out of provoking a second round with the Kadagidi while things were still within the realm of negotiation and finesse.

The faint thrum of an engine, meanwhile, had barely intruded into his awareness. He had thought at first it was another bus coming up the front drive.

Then it seemed more like something else. And Jago had heard it, clearly. She seized his arm.

"An airplane, nandi."

Air attack. She wanted to pull him to cover. His heart doubled its beats. "My computer. Above all else, my computer." He broke away and rushed to get it, Jago right on his heels, and when he had it she seized up a heavy bag from the same stack: armament. Tano and Algini dived in, arming themselves likewise.

The plane buzzed over the roof to a rattle of small arms fire.

No bombs dropped. The plane flew away and sounded as if it reached a limit and perhaps turned to come back somewhere over the east meadow.

"That plane came from the west," he said; the west was not from the Kadigidi side of things. And since the engine sound was still far away, he darted back out of the bath to risk a quick look from the window, Jago and Tano and Algini in anxious attendance.

It was a very small plane, a three-seater at most. It looked to be landing on the broad meadow of the eastern mecheita pasture. Its fuselage was yellow striped with blue.

"Dur!" he exclaimed, seeing those colors, remembering a young and determined pilot who had scared the hell out of a scheduled airliner. "Jago-ji, come with me! Tano! Algini! Call security! Stop them from shooting at that plane!"

He was still encumbered with his computer. He ran back and shoved it into the pile of baggage, not even knowing whether the landing had succeeded against the small arms fire that renewed itself. He headed straight for his foyer and the door of the suite, ahead of Jago, for once. She overtook him, seized his arm with one hand, and opened that door to the outer hall, by no means stopping him, but not letting him dash recklessly ahead of her.

"Tano is calling Banichi," she said, as they walked doubletime down the upstairs hall toward the stairs. They were alone in the upper hallway—servants might have ducked for cover or run to windows within unoccupied rooms, but there was no sign of anyone as they reached the stairs and hurried down.

There was a broad landing in front of the foyer, the juncture of the main floor and the stairs that led outside, a region now the domain of workmen setting up scaffolding and repairing the outer doors. As they arrived the door to the adjacent drawing room opened, and Tabini-aiji himself strode out through the collection of Guild security that ordinarily guarded the doors of any conference in progress—the aiji was in Assassins' black, still, with an identifying red scarf around his arm, much as he had appeared when he had turned up last night, if less dusty.

Elderly Lord Tatiseigi, in muted pastel green with abundant lace, accompanied him out, looking entirely vexed with the proceedings. Banichi exited the room with them, pocket com in hand.

"They must not shoot!" Bren said at once. "The colors of the plane are yellow and blue! They are Dur!"

"In my winter pasturage!" Tatiseigi cried.

"See to its protection," Tabini said to staff. "Quickly!"

Bren himself veered for the foyer and ran down the steps under the scaffolding to the massive front doors, while workmen who had stopped their cleanup and repair stared at the sudden commotion. With Jago and now Banichi in close company, and right behind Tabini's own head of security, he exited the house onto the wide front steps, above a clutter of buses and farm trucks that now jammed the hedge-rimmed drive. Ordinary townsmen had taken cover from the overflight behind the flimsy cover of vehicles, armed and waiting with their pistols and hunting rifles.

"This may be an ally that has landed!" Bren shouted at the nearest. "Pass the word, nadiin! The colors are the island of Dur!"

And to Banichi and Jago: "Make sure no one fires, nadiin-ji."

"Go," Banichi said to Jago, and Jago dived among the cars and beyond, leaving them behind. By the way heads came up over fenders and truck beds in her wake, she was passing the word as she went, not relying on word of mouth.

Bren's desire was to take off and run flat out toward the plane in the meadow before some accident intervened but a lord ought not to breach dignity; a lord, in view of strangers, was held to, at most, a brisk walk, and necessarily Banichi stayed close by him, armed and formidable, and making their way just behind Tabini's man. Armed gawkers jumped back out of the path of black-uniformed Guild, and a handful of mounted Taibeni rangers that had ridden through the hedges to get over to this path fell in behind him, mecheiti snorting and fussing at being reined in, another reason to want to hurry the pace.

Down the side of the house, along what had been the stable path so long as the house had had a stable, past the ongoing fence repair, and around to the east meadow, where Bren caught a good view of a handful of rifle-bearing house security behind a low stone wall, holding a vantage on the sloping meadow beyond. Engine noise had sunk in volume. The small plane was taxiing in the middle of Tatiseigi's pasture.

He still was constrained not to run. He walked, walked with that mandated dignity that lent calm to a volatile situation. That, as much as the radioed orders, made it less and less likely that some agitated townsman behind him would take a shot at the pilot as he climbed out. He walked, with Banichi, beyond the gateless stone wall and the spectators, walked over the cultivated pasture, a beloved patch of fine graze that had already suffered trampling, vehicular traffic, and fire last night. On the lowest flat, the plane came rolling to a stop.

Jago caught up with them as they came within hailing distance of the plane, and only at that point did cold second thoughts rush in. What if he were in fact mistaken about the color pattern? What if loyal Dur had turned against Tabini along with so many others? A thousand doubts—a human could be mistaken in his assumptions, here in the heart of atevi feuds and upheaval.

But the door of the little plane banged open and the young pilot climbed up onto the wing, a silhouette against the bright fuselage, carrying his coat on his arm. He jumped down with that boundless enthusiasm that was the very signature of the young man Bren remembered.

He wanted to run up and hug the boy for very joy. But Jago had gone forward to meet the lad, and the young pilot came walking back toward them, putting on his formal coat in the process—a rich azure blue, it was.

And once he had his arms in the sleeves, the young gentleman, dignity to the winds, set out toward them at a moderate jog, letting Jago follow at a more deliberate pace.

"Bren-nandi!"

It was Rejiri of Dur, no doubt in the world, and when they met, Rejiri seized Bren by the arms just to look at him—a young man now, no boy, and he had grown half a foot; but his eyes were as bright, as blithe as ever. "Back from space, nandi! What an excellent, auspicious day!"

"Nandi-ji," Bren saluted the young man, carried back to far happier times. Rejiri had stayed steadfast. The planet still turned on its axis.

"Dur is coming in," Rejiri said breathlessly. "My father has sent a hundred thirty-two of the clan here, with our bodyguards, arriving by train this evening, to support the aiji!"

God, another clan to support the aiji, this one from the coast—as if Tabini had joined in with Tatiseigi's crazed notion of going to war against the Kadagidi. The wiser course for the aiji was certainly to fade back into the hills and conduct a far more reasoned assault on the Kadagidi, with organization and pressure levied against the capital. Such wild enthusiam beamed out at him; and the boy from Dur, now a towering, broad-shouldered young man—Rejiri could not take the train with the ordinary folk of his clan, oh, no. He had had to make a dangerous, officially forbidden flight and execute a landing in the middle of Tatiseigi's winter pasture, all to convey the news of Dur's intentions—and have himself right into the thick of things long before clan authority arrived.

Not a hair of the youth was changed.

"You are our good luck, Rejiri-ji," Bren declared. "You are ever so welcome."

"Not just Dur, but our neighbors the Tagi and the Mairi are coming, too!" Rejiri said. And before Bren could muster any rational objection that the aiji himself might be taking off elsewhere, to a safer vantage— "And Banichi and Jago! Good to see you in good health, nadiin-ji! You look not a bit changed. Did you rescue the stranded humans? Did you see wonders out there?"

"We did both, nandi," Banichi said. "But nand' Bren will tell you that, in much greater detail."

By now the row of onlookers back at the ruined fence had doubled in size, spectators gathered there, while on every floor of the house, multiple heads had appeared in every window facing the meadow.

"You will indeed tell us the whole adventure," Rejiri said—words, with Rejiri, always flowed like quicksilver, affording no time for organization, no opportunity, sometimes, for basic common sense. "We look forward to hearing it, every bit. And might there be tea, nand' Bren? Intercede for me with Lord Tatiseigi. Might I prevail upon your good offices to do so? One does apologize profoundly for the tracks in his meadow. It has rained here, has it not? I felt the tires resist as I came in. And is there a chance one may see the aiji? He is here, is he not? It is true, surely?"

All this in his first few steps toward the house.

"The aiji is indeed here, nandi-ji. In very fact, I was preparing to seek an audience with him and with Lord Tatiseigi when we heard your plane pass over . . ."

"Oh, excellent! It was good weather for flying, an entirely auspicious day, as I told my father when I set out. Clear skies made me just a little worried, in case, of course, these wretches should send up planes of their own, which one doubted they would dare, even so, over Atageini air space—but the heir to Dur has a perfect right to fly where he likes over the northern associations, does he not, nandi? Certainly he has!"

"Is the north that fragmented, that one speaks only of the local associations?"

"Oh, you have scarcely heard the list of outrages, nand' Bren! The so-named aiji has made flight regulations, laws, rules, and taxes, all of which Dur refuses to countenance. We despise his laws and his tax collectors!"

"And does your father stand in good health?"

"Oh, extremely, extremely. Do you know, I have two new sisters!"

"Twins, Rejiri-ji?"

"No, no, a new marriage. The girls were born in successive years. Beautiful little sprites. My mother swears she is quite jealous, except I am indisputably the eldest, and papa is indisputably connected to her, and has treaty ties to her house which he will never break. My mother is Drisi-Edi, you know. And the

Edi may well send forces here, too. I would be surprised if not. Have you seen Lord Geigi? Did he come down with you?"

Atevi marriage went by contracts, for thus and such number of years. The Edi were one of the coastal peoples, allied to Lord Geigi's people. And, my God, Bren thought, mentally reeling from the zigzag course of information: Geigi's province? His people were leaving their sanctuary to throw in their lot with Tatiseigi and Dur?

"Lord Geigi remains on the station," he managed to say. "He remains in excellent health, and maintains close control over matters on the station. Jase-paidhi is back, safe and sound, and he will assist Lord Geigi. Mercheson-paidhi, too, is safe on Mospheira, in close harmony with the Presidenta as well as with the ship-aijiin aloft."

"We have had news of the mainland from the radio, nand' paidhi! From your university."

Was *that* how rumor was reaching epidemic proportions? Radio, from across the strait?

"What did they say?"

"Oh, that the shuttle is preparing a return, that the legislature is passing a resolution of support for Tabini-aiji and for the station-aijiin, that the Presidenta has urged citizens along the coast to keep a sharp watch and report any untoward intrusion."

Aimed at the shuttle, it might be. One could only dread what might happen to the two others, here on the mainland.

"And do they know where Tabini-aiji is, Jiri-ji?"

"One remains unsure. It was never mentioned. But

we heard. A car came to us, from Meiri. They had heard, because a Meiri woman has a son with the chief accountant of Ceiga . . ."

Which was an Atageini town. Which meant rumors had been flying at record speed, a veritable network sending out word, possibly starting with Tatiseigi's leaky communications system.

Rejiri went into detail as they passed through the ranks of wondering spectators, no few of whom were house security, and nonstop as they walked up and around the side of the house, Rejiri asking a barrage of questions all the way—had the voyage been successful? What strange sights had he seen?

Then onto the drive, where town buses and farm trucks vied for parking space.

"Taiben has come in," Bren thought to inform him.

"Taiben! Then *they* are the mecheita-camp!"

"Indeed."

"Now that is a wonder," Rejiri pronounced this partnership of Atageini and Taibeni, and, casting his gaze up to the top of the steps that confronted them, he climbed energetically, security trailing them, house security standing at the top of the steps to confront and challenge them.

"The young lord of Dur," Banichi said as they approached that cautious line, "come to confer with Lord Tatiseigi." Oh, that *Lord Tatiseigi* was politic. Opposition immediately gave way.

"Our lord will see the visitor in the sitting room, nadi," the seniormost of Tatiseigi's security informed them, and doors immediately opened and staff folded in with them, past the scaffolding and repair work inside . . . up those steps, then, and onto the level of the sitting room. To judge by the collection of various bodyguards standing about that door, Tabini, Tatiseigi, and the dowager had gone back into conference in that room; and if one could judge by the Taibeni present, Keimi of Taiben was inside, and likely a couple of Atageini mayors, granted a couple of clerkish types in the mix.

And now another pair of participants arrived, racing down the stairs from the rooms above: Cajeiri, eight years old, as tall as a grown human, and accompanied by one Jegari, his young Taibeni guard.

"Did he fly the plane, nandi?" echoed and re-echoed in the stairwell, and Bren paused to introduce the aiji's son to the son of the lord of Dur.

"Nandi," Rejiri said, with a grand and sweeping bow to the boy, and Cajeiri likewise bowed, clearly entranced by the daring landing, the young pilot, and the brightly painted plane out on the meadow—doubtless estimating that if other young lords could do such a reckless thing, *he* could do it: One had only to know him to imagine the gears turning in his young head.

But by then the drawing room door had opened, and security inside had taken a look, exchanged words with security outside, and questions from the assembled lords were bound to come out to them if they did not now go inside quickly.

"Nandiin," Bren said, and ushered Cajeiri and Rejiri both into the room.

Tabini-aiji sat at the center of the arc of chairs inside, with Damiri and the dowager on either hand, with Lord Tatiseigi. The young lord of Dur, facing the aiji that the news services under Murini's control had claimed for months was dead and lost, bowed profoundly, as Cajeiri piped up with, "This is Rejiri, the lord of Dur's son, nandiin! He landed just outside!"

"Aijin-ma," Rejiri said in modest grace. "Nand' dowager."

Welcome was a little less certain on Lord Tatiseigi's face—his age-seamed lips disapproved any commotion in his meadows, any further destruction of his lawn. Others present, Keimi of Taiben, and, yes, two Atageini mayors, to judge by their pale green and gold lapel rosettes, remained impassive, offering that inscrutable face one presented to strangers.

"Nand' Rejiri," Bren said, "reports himself in advance of his father's associates, arriving by train this evening from the coast."

"He landed right at the bottom of the hill," Cajeiri said, unchecked, and improving the account, "right on the grass. We saw him, and he flew the plane himself!"

"Did he?" Tabini-aiji surely recalled a general chaos in air traffic control, in the very heart of the association, in which this particular plane had been involved, when the young pilot had made his first visit to the capital. But he rose from his chair and welcomed the young lord with extreme warmth. "Loyal, and arrived to join us, and the lord of Dur with him. Who could doubt Dur's man'chi?"

"Is he prepared to fight?" Tatiseigi asked dourly, still seated in the privilege of age, though most had risen and now settled back again. "With that great noisemaker? Nevertheless we welcome the young lord from Dur. Well, well, welcome, Dur. We shall offer every hospitality. We shall have a go at those miscreants across our border, teach them to observe our hedges ..."

"And how are things on the north coast, young sir?" Ilisidi asked sweetly from her seat, neatly cutting Tatiseigi off.

Another bow, deep and gracious, in that direction. "Free, aiji-ma, free and unshaken—only awaiting the real aiji's summons."

Summons, had it been? Bren, having found a vacant chair at the end of the arc, darted a sharp look at Tabini, who said nothing to deny such a summons had gone out.

A summons. Aircraft. People arriving by train. The Ajuri coming in this evening—relatives, and intimately concerned with their daughter Damiri. And now there was talk of Edi coming in. All this motion and commotion suggested that he had been wrong in his estimations. The thought that the aiji and his men could somehow melt back into the woods seemed less and less practical. Clearly the paidhi had not quite gotten the picture until now: He was not sure that Lord Tatiseigi entirely had it yet, but that word *summons* rang like a bell. Tabini was not here simply to meet the dowager and reclaim his son.

They sat here in the open now. And Atageini had become involved to the hilt. Taibeni had come in. The Ajuri were coming to their defense, and Dur, and others from the coast, if there was a bus left at the railhead to get them here this evening. Or worse, they might have to fight their way in past Kadagidi agents, if the attack renewed itself at dusk.

"There might be trouble at the train station, nandiin," Bren said quietly, aware it was by no means the paidhi's job to give the aiji defensive advice, but he lacked information: He wanted someone to think of these things, and let him know what in all hell the aiji was planning. "We removed a bus and left it in Taiben. One is by no means sure there are enough buses left at the station to serve."

"An excellent point," Keimi said: The bus in question was still capable of being moved, if Taiben could send it back.

"My father and his guard are armed," Rejiri said, with a gesture toward the outside. "And there are plenty of buses and trucks here to bring them, nandiin."

There were certainly plenty of Atageini vehicles which Tatiseigi might not particularly want shot full of holes but neither did they want their allies shot full of holes getting here; it was easier to move a few of them by the shorter, open country road.

"We can send buses," Tabini said decisively, without so much as a glance at Tatiseigi, who sat glumly chewing his lip and perhaps recalculating the shooting match he was planning with his neighbors. "But the Kadagidi may have moved on the station."

"One could take the plane up," Cajeiri suggested, "and see what the Kadagidi are doing."

Leave it to Cajeiri to think how to get that plane involved in the commotion.

"A dangerous venture," Damiri said.

"But perhaps a useful one," Rejiri said. "Aijiin-ma, one would gladly undertake it, observing all possible discretion, but the plane needs fuel."

"What sort of fuel does it use?" Tabini asked.

It used what the trucks and buses used, it turned out.

"There must be a fuel station in the nearest town," Rejiri said.

"The estate has its own tank," Tatiseigi volunteered glumly, wonder of wonders. "And if we refuel this machine, you will keep an eye to the east, young sir, and advise us by radio what you see from up there, before nightfall." A vague wave of the elderly hand, outer space and the air corridors being likely the same thing in Tatiseigi's concept. "There may be a use for this thing."

"By all means, nandi!" Rejiri said. All this meeting and conversation had left the new arrival standing practically in the doorway, assaulted with observations and questions with no time at all taken for tea or consultation—an outrageous haste by atevi standards. One could all but hear Ilisidi say, the thousandth reminder to Cajeiri, that gentlemen did their conversing seated. But Rejiri was difficult to keep still and no one had insisted on tea.

And with very little more than that exchange of words, the young lord of Dur declared he would go fuel his plane immediately—if the lords would be so gracious as to give him leave to do that.

"My staff will assist, young Dur," Tatiseigi declared, with a wave of his hand, and that unseemly haste was that. Off went the young lord of Dur with several of Lord Tatiseigi's servants trailing him from the doorway, bound outside to provide the fuel, one supposed.

"Certainly a very forceful young gentleman," Lord Tatiseigi said, as if a hurricane had just blown through the hall; and: "*Tea,* nadiin!" No *nadiin-ji* for his servants, not from this stiffly formal lord, an elderly gentleman who looked quite harried, quite disturbed, and, like all of them, very short of sleep. Tatiseigi might not be up with the times in technology, but very few had ever outfigured him in politics, and perhaps he, too, was rearranging his concept of Tabini's intentions—all the while muttering: "Looking over neighbors' borders. Buzzing over roofs. Not even time to sit down in decency to consult. Can a rifle shot possibly do damage to such a machine?"

"It can," Tabini said. "And the young man very well knows it, one is quite sure. No, no tea for us, nandi. We are inundated with tea. Lunch, however, would be welcome."

"Indeed," Tatiseigi said, clearly rattled, unaccustomed to being ordered in his own hall.

And somewhere in the swirl of servants and security in the general area, Cajeiri had left his chair, and was nowhere in the room. Bren became aware of it, leaped up and went to the door, where Banichi and Jago waited with the rest of the bodyguards. "Cajeiri," he said abruptly. "Banichi-ji." That was all.

"Yes," Banichi said crisply, and immediately left, doubtless having known the boy had left, and needing only an instruction.

No possible doubt where the boy had gone. To

watch fuel being pumped into the plane. To watch buses rallied for a run to the train station, and—thank God he was with his young bodyguard—to be underfoot in all possible operations.

"Tell Cenedi," Ilisidi said from her chair, cane poised before her, "that my great-grandson should not go within stone's throw of that plane."

"Cenedi-ji." Bren was the one nearest the door. Cenedi, salt-and-pepper haired as his lady, was also among the bodyguards outside.

"One hears," Cenedi said without his saying a thing, and left on the same mission as Banichi, to be absolutely sure where Cajeiri was when buses left or when planes took off.

Bren turned back to the room, somewhat easier about the boy, and realizing only then that he and the dowager had both just leaped into order-giving regarding the aiji's own son, in the aiji's and the consort's presence and in front of witnesses.

Habit. Two years of habit. He was mortified.

Tabini wore the faintest of considering looks, and Damiri offered no expression at all. Bren gave a little bow, knowing that what he and the dowager knew about the boy's habits and inclinations his own father and mother could only guess at this point, and the middle of Tatiseigi's drawing room was no place to discuss the heir's failings. They should have done what they had done; he only wished he could have been subtler.

Meanwhile at Rejiri's urging, buses and trucks would be loading up with armed guards, themselves likely refueling and moving around out there, one could only assume. He took his seat again with the conviction that Banichi and Cenedi would keep the boy out from under the wheels. The plane would go up, and at least one bus or truck would go off into Taiben, to approach the train station, to come back this evening loaded with forces from Dur . . . God knew how or when Ajuri planned to arrive, but things were definitely cooking here.

They only had to hope, in the process, that their unasked air support wandering the skies near Kadagidi territory didn't provoke an answering escalation from the other side—take a look to the eastern border, indeed. A damned dangerous look, and, considering what he suspected Tabini was setting up here, and what the Kadagidi might be preparing to counter him, he worried about it going wrong.

But he wanted that information, too. He had spent two years and more in a transparent universe where people couldn't sneak about behind bushes or hide behind hills. He longed to go outside and ask for current information from Tatiseigi's Guild staff, who might more likely know what movements were happening on the other side—but in the same way farmers weren't supposed to get involved in lords' disputes, lords weren't supposed to meddle in security.

He'd formed some disgraceful habits in the long voyage, he decided, impulses that had flung him out of his seat and after the boy, and habits proper gentlemen might consider far more pernicious than ordering the aiji's heir about. He'd gotten the very dangerous habit of involving himself in his own security's affairs, and the very fact that he wanted to be out there right now, giving advice and getting it, where the paidhi flatly didn't belong— that was a habit he had to break, a shocking breach, for outsiders, doubtless an embarrassment to his own staff.

No matter that Lord Tatiseigi, the least qualified person to be giving orders in that department, was laying down his own set of priorities left and right, including repairs to the foyer, repair and rewiring of outmoded devices in his hedges, and rebuilding the mecheita pen, which would divert hands from more useful occupations.

But Tabini, meanwhile, was up to something entirely deliberate, something that had clearly had time to draw people clear from the coast, and had not yet heard his report. From his vantage at the end of the arc of chairs, he cast Tabini a desperate look and failed to make eye contact—possibly Tabini was ignoring him after that last embarrassment, was reminding him to observe protocols. Clearly the aiji had things better in hand and much farther advanced than he had known.

"Aiji-ma, aijiin-ma," he asked, clearing his throat, desperate for one critical piece of knowledge, "may one ask—shall we indeed stay here tonight?"

"It seems so," Tabini said placidly. "Does the Lord of the Heavens have grounds to recommend otherwise?"

Not the warm and familiar 'paidhi-ji,' translator for human affairs, but his other office, his capacity as atevi lord, and in that address, he found his window of opportunity. "One has a host of recommendations, aiji-ma." He got up, remote from the aiji as he was, bowed, received the little move of the hand that meant he could approach, and he did so—bowed in front of the chair, then, undiscouraged, dropped to his knee at Tabini's very chairside for a quick, private piece of communication, with only Damiri adjacent. "We met other foreigners out there, aiji-ma, foreigners to humans, too, and, all credit to the dowager and to your son, aiji-ma, these new foreigners are expecting—our whole agreement with them rests on it—to find you in power and able to answer them. We have assured them you *sent* our mission out to them, to unwind all the mistaken communications between them and humans. We have assured them you are in charge, and will take charge, a situation for which they have reasonably high hopes."

"We have heard something of the sort." It could only have come from the dowager. "You have been quite busy in remote space, paidhi-aiji."

"But there is a grave complication, aiji-ma. These foreigners themselves claim powerful and dangerous enemies, still another batch of foreigners, aggressive and with a bad history, on the far side of their territory. In short, aiji-ma, these foreigners are involved in a situation we do not understand, nothing that threatens us yet, but there are details—everything—in my computer, aiji-ma, including linguistic records and transcripts of negotiations in which the dowager and your son were deeply involved. They will tell you events; but I have a long, long account to give, information which the legislature and the Guild must understand, information absolutely critical to our safety. If one could engage the media, we have a reason it is absolutely essential for you to be safe—"

"We have already heard something of the details," Tabini said, "which are neither here nor there at the moment. There are more urgent things."

"We might publish the news, aiji-ma, attack the Kadagidi with information, unseat Murini from the capital. If we were to go back to the hills, we could—"

"*Back,* nandi? *Who* said where we have been?"

It was information the paidhi had not been told, precisely the sort of information the paidhi-aiji could never afford to let pass his lips anywhere he could be overheard. The tightly contained ship-world he had lived in had given him very bad habits, and his staff, even Banichi and Jago, could fall into extreme and deadly disfavor if Tabini suspected they had told him classified matters they had learned from *his* staff.

"Aiji-ma, your whereabouts was my own guess, unfounded, probably entirely inaccurate. One can only apologize, and urge—"

"A *guess,* indeed."

"One unfounded on any particular information."

"A very clever guess, paidhi."

"Only a surmise, aiji-ma, knowing that this entire unfortunate business has centered around me and foreign influence . . ."

"Around you!" Tabini outright laughed at the temerity of his notion. "Around *you,* paidhi-aiji!"

"Indeed," Ilisidi said, leaning forward on her stick, as she sat on Tabini's other side. "Around the paidhi, around this galloping modernity which you promoted far and wide, grandson, from shuttles we needed, to television, which we might—gods less fortunate!—have escaped. *Kabiu* violated. This modern device become the center of attention. You never would listen to advice."

"Oh, indeed," Tabini said, and his position had by now become very uncomfortable to hold, kneeling for conversation with one of the powers of the earth and having another primal force suddenly going at her grandson on the other side, in what could well become a lengthy debate. Bren cast about for a graceful way to get up and back to his chair and found none, none at all.

"So you went up into the high hills, did you," Ilisidi said, "and settled your presence on the innocent Astronomer, who was bound himself sooner or later to be a target? Our esteemed human had no trouble reasoning out this brilliant move. How long before the Kadagidi approach the same conclusion and do harm to the distinguished man and his students?"

"Aijiin-ma." Peacekeeper being the paidhi's job, it seemed time to perform it, urgently so, at the risk of extreme disfavor. "It was by no means an apparent guess, if that was where the aiji indeed resided."

"The hill provinces sheltered us," Tabini said, "but no longer. They will be here, mani-ma, presently, in force."

My God, Bren thought. The hillmen, a hundred little clans at tenuous peace with each other, and for centuries ignoring the rest of the world—what in all reason could move *them* to come down to the Padi

Valley? They'd detested flatland politics. They'd desperately wanted the University that Tabini had finally built up there, and then argued with its modern advice and advisements once they had it.

Not to mention the Observatory, the precious Observatory, adjunct to the University—all the students there. They were set at risk. The University library and all its generations of work, the center for the space program, the shuttle work, the translations of human-given books, the technical translations, many of which were only available by computer reader manuals . . .

Perhaps the look was transparent. "At the University," Damiri said, looking directly at him, "there was, this year, a general suspension of classes, nand' paidhi, by order of the pretender. There was a particular attack on the library."

The bottom dropped out of his stomach.

"The night previous, warned by computer messages, the students dispersed in all directions," Tabini-aiji said with evident satisfaction, "and took the new books with them. Some have gone back to their homes, some sheltered in the hills, and no few of them have set up on the coast, taking resources with them, spreading word wherever they go, and establishing their own communications network. They have the portable machines. And we are informed they will be here."

"Do you say," Uncle Tatiseigi asked querulously from across the room, and, with debate opening up to yet another quarter, it seemed time for the paidhi-aiji to get up and get out of the way. "Do you say not only the hill clans, but next, those ragtag radical students? Those upstarts that deny their clan?"

"Indeed," Tabini said, and shot out a hand and seized Bren's arm as Bren attempted to rise from his awkward position and remove himself from the verbal line of fire.

"Aiji-ma."

"There will be ample time for us to hear your records, paidhi-ji. But for now the books are all in hiding. The shuttles are under Kadagidi guard, and the pilots have all fled to the outer regions and taken their flight manuals with them. The Kadagidi have the University computers, but their mathematicians are so unwilling to accept the computers' calculations that, the last we heard, they are paralyzed in debate and argument, refusing to let their own people use the machines. The traditional mathematicians cannot justify what the computers tell them. Their political supporters support the Kadagidi mathematicians, because the computers are, of course, a human idea." Grim amusement danced in Tabini's eyes. "And you know best of all, do you not, paidhi-ji, what that means?"

Intellectual turmoil. The new mathematics. University teachers had so carefully skirted any confrontation of belief against demonstrable mathematical proof, had constructed examples to avoid direct offense, and now that confrontation, blindly pushed forward by the conservatives, had run straight into the University computer department. "Yes, aiji-ma," he said, envisioning that moment, the traditionalists afraid to destroy the computers, afraid to let information out. The books, the translations would go if the Kadagidi became too frustrated—or too frightened—by their impasse. Everything he had built, everything the University had built, was on the brink not just of hostile rule, but destruction. A return to the precomputer world. A denial of everything the University taught.

"Leave matters to these fools, paidhi-aiji, and let them ban the new books, and deny the evidence and hide what will not fit their numbers, and we will be two hundred years climbing back out of the pit. They say your advice was wrong. Is that not so?"

He was inches from Tabini's face. Tabini's grip cut off the blood to his lower arm, the arm an ateva had once broken with his bare hands. It was irrelevant, that old pain. The atevi world swayed, tottered, threatened to crash.

"I might have done things better, aiji-ma. Even if what I said was my best advice."

"Tell me, paidhi-ji. If one opens a door and discloses a room afire, is the fire one's fault?"

"If it spread the fire, aiji-ma. If the paidhi has to be at fault, one is ready to be at fault."

"This fire, this fire, paidhi-aiji, has been eating at the timbers under our feet for a very long time. It would have dropped us all into the flames sooner or later. You knew the hazards. You warned us. And we likewise are not fools. You showed us numbers that the counters could not refute, nor take into their systems, did you not? Have you fed us poison?"

"No, aiji-ma." But he had dismissed the danger of disturbed philosophers and outright fortune-tellers

as secondary to greater dangers ever since the ship
had arrived in the heavens, the ship that had
brought them Jase, with all the attendant troubles.
Humans on Mospheira had begun to politic with the
ship-folk and some of them had decided to determine the future of the atevi whose planet this
was . . . which was wrong, by his lights, morally
wrong. He had fought that fight, for atevi ownership
of their own world. He had gained atevi their place
in the heavens.

But he was not, in the long run, atevi. He could not
feel what atevi felt. His 'place in the heavens' had
meant earth-to-orbit flight, and computers, which had
meant human mathematics. Human ways of viewing
the universe had come flooding into an atevi culture
that rested so heavily on its mathematics, its percep-
tions of balance and harmony, its linguistic accommo-
dations, its courtesies and orders of power and
precedence. He had loosed the genie, he had known
what he was doing, he had foreseen the danger . . . that
he might compromise what was atevi, even while trying to save them. Atevi could fix the problem—the
mathematics embedded even in the atevi language
was able to accommodate a mutable universe . . . of
course they could. Was there not the dowager? Was
there not the Astronomer, and the mathematicians of
the University? Didn't they adjust their thinking and
come back with uniquely atevi insights?

He had thought they could ride the whirlwind, and,
being no mathematician, he had left the details to the
scholars to hammer out.

And had not the aiji-dowager herself warned him

that the whirlwind could not be dismissed? Wrong. Very dangerously wrong. And Tabini had reinforced those rural fears, by more and more gifts of dazzling technology to even out the economy in the remoter regions, the aiji trying to balance economic advantage, and risking the whole structure. He had had his misgivings all along. He had progressively stifled them, in worse and worse revelations from the heavens. He had never argued with Tabini's economic policy, his awarding of new construction to depressed regions. It ought to have lifted the whole country up.

He saw, as in a lightning flash, a landscape in convulsion.

And Tabini-aiji, son of a bloody, dangerous man, grandson of a conniving Easterner, had listened to him, attempting to be a different, modern kind of atevi ruler.

"Well, well," Tabini said, "so we are where we are, paidhi. Our enemies have steadfastly refused to advance their philosophy or their mathematics in the last three hundred years. They may be factually wrong. But, gods less fortunate, they are persistent."

"Television, an advancement," Lord Tatiseigi scoffed. "And these computers are questionable and impudent."

"You would never take the Talidi part, greatuncle." This bit of politics from Damiri. "They decry computers. One is gratified to know Atageini clan has the sense to own them."

"A damned nuisance," Tatiseigi muttered. "They were supposed to report from the valley. And did they?"

"The Kadagidi destroyed the sensor," Tabini said darkly, "and it reported that, nandi."

"And what good is it after?" Tatiseigi retorted. "A telephone could have told us how many, and what direction."

"Your telephones are compromised, nandi."

"Not Atageini doing! We accepted this Murini under our roof in the interests of peace, when the whole region was in upheaval. What alternative did we have but further conflict?"

"Did we not say," Ilisidi interjected, "no mercy for Talidi leadership back when we had the chance? And did I not warn you, Tati-ji, that sheltering their ally was no solution?"

"What were we to do? Slaughter a guest? If *you* had moved in, he would have moved out sooner."

"We had our own beast to hunt," Ilisidi said, leaning on her cane, "and a great deal on our hands, nandi. We have our own province. And where were *you* when matters turned difficult, Tati-ji?"

Bren found his hand gone numb.

"Dare you," Tatiseigi cried, "and under our roof, and us sheltering Ragi guests, to our personal danger, accuse us?"

"Nandiin," Bren said, "nandiin, one asks, one most earnestly asks—" Tabini was looking him past him when he spoke, but immediately those uncanny pale eyes snapped back to his, at close range. "One most earnestly asks," he resumed, suddenly short of breath, and felt Tabini's grip ease, as if Tabini had remembered whose arm he was holding. "Moderation in these events," Bren finished.

"Moderation," Tabini said. "Moderation, indeed." Tabini let him go, and rested the same hand gently on his shoulder. "Baji-naji. The world is in upheaval. So do you have advice to give us, paidhi-aiji?"

His moment. His opportunity. Or the aiji was mocking him. "I have my report to give, aiji-ma."

"The report," Tabini said, as if such things were very far from his mind at the moment. "There will be many reports, paidhi-aiji, piles of reports. We have already heard where you have been, and what you have done, and promised in our name."

"You say you hear," Ilisidi muttered.

"We have never failed to hear your opinions, grandmother."

"Heard us, and disregarded us," Ilisidi said. No one daunted her in argument. "After which you hurled us off to space and went your own way!"

"We put you in charge of educating our heir, establishing atevi authority in the heavens—and making agreements in our name and in the name of the *aishidi'tat*. This was not an inconsiderable job for an Easterner and an outlander, grandmother! Wherein was this any disrespect of your views?"

"Well, well, outlander is it, blood of mine? And we have accomplished both tasks quite well, have we not? Now need we straighten out this current mess for you? Dare these fools in the south say it was the paidhi's choice? It was yours! It was nothing but yours!"

It was decidedly time to move aside. But the aiji still rested a hand on his shoulder.

"Mani-ma," Tabini said. "In all due respect—"

"Oh, pish! Are we fools? This movement has been brewing and bubbling for far more than the mere decade of the paidhi's close involvement. Toss a treasure into a crowd and all dignity and common sense vanish in the scramble, and everyone emerges bloody. Toss human treasure into the same situation and watch sensible folk start scrambling for this and that piece of value, for factories to spoil their skies and new goods to corrupt their common sense! You loosed the prospect of wealth, new importance for whole provinces, new fortunes, entire new houses elevated or created by this rush to space, with all the upheaval in rights of precedence and legislative power— Gods less fortunate, grandson, what did you expect in this condition but a riot?"

"And confusion," Tabini said. "Never forget confusion and folly, which always attend change, do they not? Change what exists, and toss what-will-be into the air, and, yes, certain fools lose all certainty about the rules."

"Have we not said so?" Tatiseigi said from across the room. "Human influence comes in, human goods, human wealth, and now we have a confusion in man'chi and a galloping calamity of unrest in the rural provinces. Did we not warn at the outset this would be the result, aiji-ma? We warned you not to promote this human!"

"In the calamities you name," Tabini said sharply, "is the fault in the paidhi-aiji, that greed and ambition break out among us? *Power* is the question. Power has always been the issue, and whether there will *be* an *aishidi'tat* in future, or whether this moment will give a toehold to the lurkers-in-wait who want power and who will carve the *aishidi'tat* into regions and interests, even if all they gain is the chance to battle each other for scraps of interest to themselves. Ambition of that sort has existed from the foundation of the world. Outright folly and selfish greed! And blame the paidhi-aiji that folly found an opportunity? Never lay that failing at the paidhi's feet. Was it my folly not to have broken the houses of the conspirators? The paidhi may have counseled moderation but the power to act was constantly in my hands."

"Oh, let us not forget the Kadagidi," Ilisidi said. "Let us not overlook their flaws. Think of that, Tati-ji. You relied on their promises. *You* listened. The Atageini took them for houseguests and even married into the clan."

"I listened to them?" Tatiseigi cried. "Three hundred years sitting on our boundary, the upstarts, and sending their feuds across our border, politicking with the Ragi, with the Kaoni, with the Edi, and with us—*yes,* we have connections with the Kadagidi. One cannot live as neighbors for three hundred years without some connections, however unfortunate, and indeed we took our turn believing in the *aishidi'tat,* in ignoring the numbers, in attempting to mend old feuds and patch up old differences with our neighbors, precisely the Kadagidi, as we were advised to do, as we were even threatened with high displeasure if we failed to do! Yes, thanks to the *aishidi'tat* we have cross-connections, lately forged, against our better judgment and by the blandishments of young fools hot to marry—but the *aishidi'tat* was created precisely to knit associations together and overcome these old feuds, was it not? It was to give us all advantage! And where is the usefulness of the *aishidi'-tat* now in protecting us, when we fritter away our resources, fling our wealth off into the ether, and create this house in the heavens where we mix what experience has shown us should never be mixed, not just Atageini with Kadagidi, gods more fortunate! But humans with atevi, which has always brought war! Have we forgotten that?"

The grip had closed on Bren's shoulder. He was sure he would have bruises, so tight had it become. And never mind the chief offender in politicking with the Kadagidi through the most recent years had been Tatiseigi himself . . . attempting to straighten out these tangled old and new connections, that might be the truth, but at the same time forming a close association entirely troublesome, even threatening to the *aishidi'tat*. The whole Padi Valley sat as the geographical heart of the country, and, partly due to Tatiseigi, it was always in a flutter.

And never doubt this old curmudgeon would have made a move to take the aijinate for himself years ago if he remotely had the backing. That a descendant of his was Tabini's heir was the *only* reason they were safe under this roof.

Tabini said not a thing to that argument.

But Damiri, Atageini herself, had no such reserve. "And have Atageini never contributed materially to the Kadagidi's indiscretions? Have you not looked for your own advantage in their upheavals, encouraged their conniving with the south? Where were you when a simple refusal to shelter their dissident members would have put them within reach of the Guild and saved us all this trouble?"

"Oh, now, indeed, niece!" Tatiseigi said.

"Indeed?" Ilisidi said ominously. "Indeed you have done so repeatedly, nor can deny it, Tati-ji. And did I not tell you where this double-dealing would lead? We told you to dispose of Murini. Now we have arrived at the destination of this policy of yours. We are clearly there, at this moment."

"Bren-ji," Tabini said quietly, easing his grip and massaging the shoulder he had abused, "at this threshold of a memorable family fight, do us a great favor and go outside. Be sure our son stays safe. Go. And we shall see you this evening, if these households survive."

"Aiji-ma." He got up, still feeling the impression of fingers and a tingling in his arm. He bowed, and bowed generally, then specifically and very politely bowed to their host. "With your permission, nandi," he said to Tatiseigi, and immediately headed for the door.

In one part, oh, he wanted to know exactly what Tabini meant to say regarding the family business between the Ragi clan and the Atageini that had been simmering all his career. But in another, more sensible part he was absolutely sure that it would by no means improve a human's welcome with Uncle Tatiseigi if he stayed to witness the family laundry laid out in order.

All was still decorously quiet as he shut the door,

nodded a quiet courtesy to Tabini's chief of security, then picked up Jago.

"We are to find the heir," he said quietly, "on the aiji's request. One assumes Banichi and Cenedi are already on the track." It was still all too quiet behind that door, but then, atevi fights were sometimes exceedingly quiet, phrased in extravagant politeness, interspersed by long silences, and occasionally with whole pots of tea, simply because the recourse to misstatement could be deadly. In very fact, the aiji under anyone's roof was the one who gave the orders, with quiet, polite acknowledgment of his host, it was true; but Tabini would give the orders.

And the warlike half of those gathered on the lawn and up and down the drive, the really experienced fighters, as opposed to the farmers and shopkeepers, were all the aiji's forces. Lord Tatiseigi had no means to object to the aiji's presence or his decisions, and no profit in doing so. Tatiseigi had always skirted the edges of conflicts, never directly stood for or against anything, and now, in the heir, he had a route to power, if only he stayed quiet, and if only the aiji won the day. So he was quite, quite confident Tabini would have his way, whatever that way was.

It was, however, very likely that the paidhi was going to be a central subject of debate inside that room. Words might be passed that Tabini had no wish for him to hear.

At very worst—

"The young gentleman has his young escort with him, nandi," Jago said as they moved. "He ran down to the steps and out the door."

"To find the house fuel tank," he murmured as they negotiated the steps off the main floor and into the foyer, under the scaffolding.

"The fuel tank?" Jago asked.

That did sound entirely ominous, in mental review. It might become even more ominous, if youthful security grew distracted in a press of the curious and enthusiastic around the young stranger. There was a remote possibility of Kadagidi infiltrators on the estate, more apt to conceal their movements within a crowd. In that thought he hastened his steps, under the scaffolding around the damaged frieze of the entryway, across a scatter of carpentry shavings at the door, and emerged into the afternoon sun, on steps high above what had been a stately hedge, elegant lawn, and cobbled drive.

The jam on the cobbled drive now stretched out of sight among the hedges and over the hill. Mecheiti grazed the lawn, among tents, and the hedges were in tatters. The nearest vehicles had become gathering points for a motley collection of townsmen armed with hunting rifles, some ladies and gentlemen, doubtless town officials, wearing brocade coats by no means suited to rough living. The latter were local ladies and gentleman who had not, thus far, found lodging in the lordly house, to which they would ordinarily be entitled. They might be late arrivals out of Heitisi, the neighboring aggregate of towns in this area of the Padi Valley. But as he passed the corner of the house, he saw they were not at all the whole of the crowd. There was a sizeable gathering as well beyond the eastern hedge, near the charcoaled uprights that had been the stable.

"The fuel tank," Jago said, "is there."

The boy was not immediately visible, but he caught sight of Banichi and Cenedi. Dignity be damned, Bren thought, and began to run.

# 3

The fuel pump, thank God, did not sit close enough to the stables to have been involved in the conflagration. The station was an inconspicuous little concrete pad, bearing tire marks, with a small pump at the side, the sort of thing one might have tripped over in the dark. But it must be working. A small group had already left the area, bearing fuel cans down the hill toward the plane in the meadow, and entraining a straggle of spectators from up on the hill.

The straggle included the young gentleman and his companion, to be sure, in plain view, at the head of the advance, and available to any sniper, right behind Rejiri and the strong men bearing gas cans, Banichi and Cenedi in close attendance.

Bren took out down the hill in the wake of the crowd, Jago beside him, both walking faster and faster, until they reached Banichi and Cenedi—who, absent a clear threat, had not been able to stop the young rascals. It took a lord who outranked him, and he could, a little out of breath, and with his security, just overtake Cajeiri as they reached the bottom of the hill.

"Nandi." A little nod as they arrived at their destination "I am obeying my father."

"One is absolutely certain the young gentleman is exercising prudence." One could make clever, light remarks. One could attempt to make his presence out here other than what it was, a retrieval mission. Neither would fool Cajeiri, who had just marched ahead of his great-grandmother's security. "But this is not the closed environment of the ship. There might be rifles, the other side of the meadow. We have no idea who may be in the neighborhood. I do not personally know all these people. A Kadagidi agent could be walking right beside us, in all this crowd. Banichi will not be pleased with this. Nor will Cenedi."

"A professional would not risk his life to assassinate us, would he?"

Oh, the arrogance of having overheard too much. And not nearly enough.

"There are circumstances, young sir," Banichi said quietly, in his deep voice. "Once you have lived long enough, you may hear of them. This is not wise."

A little upward glance. The lad had had Banichi for a teacher, in the corridors of the ship. If Cajeiri had a personal deity, it was likely Banichi, who had taught him to build remote controls, and once converted Cajeiri's best toy car to a weapon. And that particular tone in Banichi's voice, coupled with arriving authority, finally brought a little worry to that young face.

The can-bearers and Rejiri had reached the plane, meanwhile, and Rejiri began to unfasten the fuel cap.

"Stop here, young sir," Bren said, as Cajeiri kept walking.

The boy hesitated half a step. "I want to watch. I have walked all this way perfectly safely. Assassins would have shot us by now, would they not? And the airplane would be cover if there were trouble."

"Indeed," Bren said, "with all that fuel about. And all this crowd around us will take their limit from you, young lord. The obligation of a person of conse-quence is to set limits and not bring all this crowd to the side of the plane to hamper the pilot."

A half glance toward the goal. And not quite a glance—one could all but hear Ilisidi's reminder to observe stiff-backed dignity. Prudence might not have figured anywhere in Cajeiri's intentions, and he had defied two missions sent to stop him, but he had come to a stop now, and the onlookers, adult and many of them also persons of consèquence, had accordingly stopped, providing a modicum of cover and a certain weight of inertia in the crowd. Cajeiri took in a deep breath, drew himself up perhaps a hand taller—or he was standing on a small hummock—and scowled at this development, this check on his freedom.

The vantage he had, however, preserved a view of the fueling, and of where the fuel went in. They sub-sequently had a good view of Rejiri prepping his ma-chine. Then Rejiri got in, started the engine, and with a very satisfactory roar, maneuvered the plane on the meadow.

"Aircraft must face the wind during takeoff," Bren explained during this move, "and it needs a long run to get into the air, another excellent reason to keep the crowd out of the way. That propeller could dice a person into small bits."

Cajeiri looked at him, and then at the plane, suitably impressed.

"Note the moveable panels on the wings, young sir," Jago said. "Those will shape the wing for maximum lift on the wind. Lift will carry it off the ground and keep it aloft."

"One thought the propeller carried it off the ground, nadi."

"Speed from the propeller and lift from the wings and body are the means, young sir. A small, light plane can actually have its engine fail in the sky and still land safely . . . given a smooth landing area, and the lift it still enjoys from wings and body. As it descends through the air, it gathers speed and lift much as if the engine were running. Like Toby's boat, which will not steer at all until it moves fast enough, do you recall? The plane has a rudder, on its tail, which also directs it. See?"

The plane was gathering speed now.

"Oh!" Cajeiri exclaimed, and then did not bounce in place. He folded his hands behind him, fingers tightly locked, the perfect young gentleman. And he added, glumly, "One wished to see inside," as the crowd at large applauded the takeoff. The locals clearly found an aircraft at close hand quite as much a novelty as Cajeiri did. The plane soared, roared deafeningly over the crowd, and banked steeply toward the west, as cries went up from the hill.

"Is it all right?" Cajeiri asked in sudden alarm.

"A turn," Bren said, and true enough, Rejiri leveled off and gathered altitude, headed toward the railway, the noise of the plane fading, as the rear of the crowd began to turn back toward the hill.

"Now we should go," Bren said. "Back to safety, young sir. Back to the house."

They walked. Cajeiri and his young guard walked with them. "I want to fly a plane," Cajeiri said.

Was one in the least surprised?

"I want to fly the shuttle," Cajeiri added.

One could still be surprised.

"You should talk to the shuttle pilots regarding that matter, young sir," Jago said, a definite rescue from the topic, perhaps a new and dangerous ambition, granted they lived through this day.

They walked up the hill, passing many slower walkers in the crowd, then a handful of other persons filling fuel cans at the pump . . . whether or not authorized was itself a question, but the fuel pump had been unlocked, its existence made known, and others took advantage.

Some other arrival was in progress in the meanwhile, a large bus that, ignoring the jam on the driveway, which might stretch for a kilometer and more, had gotten around the long hedge. Now it came rolling across the open lawn between the jammed drive and the Taibeni camp, bouncing and bumping in its haste. Perhaps its driver had been alarmed by the aircraft passing over their heads, and had made an emergency move to try to gain the house, but its course across the lawn had come very close to the Taibeni camp. Mecheiti bellowed protests to the heavens and vexed Taibeni came out to the edge of their camp, bearing weapons.

"Get to the house, Bren-ji," Banichi said, and only then did the full range of possibilities occur to him. Rifles were out. Guns were drawn, all facing that bus across the hedge.

This is insane, Bren thought, hurrying Cajeiri and his escort up the house steps. Surely no Kadagidi invader would dare.

But he climbed, and cast a look back only when he had reached the top of the steps. The errant bus had stopped, just on the other side of the hedge.

It had stopped, under a hundred guns, and a lordly passenger was debarking in considerable indignation.

"Uncle will not be pleased with them for parking on the lawn," Cajeiri said, "whoever did that."

To say the least, uncle would not be pleased.

But more than the untoward incursion of the bus, he had the sudden image of all those vehicles on the driveway, constrained by the hedges on either side, attempting to move under hostile fire. Or trying to evade some vehicle carrying explosives across that same lawn.

Folly, his own sense said. He was sure Banichi and Jago saw the same.

But this bus at least had brought only another set of passengers, servants, bodyguards, and baggage.

"Come inside," Bren said, laying a hand on the young gentleman's shoulder. "Here is far too exposed. We are sure they are safe, but this is long enough for—"

"Those are Ajuri colors!" Cajeiri said suddenly, and neither pointed, that dreadful human gesture, nor raised his voice too high as he indicated the bus, the self-important arrival that had come in on the lawn. "That will be my great-grandfather and my uncle on my mother's side that just ran over uncle's grass."

Ajuri clan. Well, Damiri had indicated they would be here by evening. And the sun had entered the last third of the sky. Ajuri had pushed it, and come a little early, perhaps in fear of traveling close to dark.

"Then I suppose we shall wait for them," Bren said, from their vantage on the steps. They did seem safe. The plane and its noise had vanished, the outraged Taibeni had quieted the mecheiti, rifles and guns were put away, and the bus had by now disgorged a collection of staff and, behind the first lord, an elderly man who was very likely the aiji of Ajuri clan, Damiri's grandfather. The first to alight, the younger gentleman of note, might well be Damiri's uncle, second highest lord. There were a couple of other aristocrats, and a collection of still younger individuals, including young ladies. The middle tier of aristocrats were all carrying hunting rifles, some of them flashing gold baroque ornament on the stocks, and with ammunition cases in evidence, quite the martial addition; but more to be feared, black-uniformed Guild security moved around them, watchful and bearing automatic weapons, and not at all favoring the armed Taibeni in their lords' vicinity. In the background, a few harried domestic staff began to hand suitcases out of stowage, a pile which grew and grew. The Ajuri, a burgeoning small platoon of them, had every intent, it was clear, of claiming lodgings in the house . . . suitcases and staff and all.

Indeed, it might be a reasonable expectation, under ordinary circumstances. They had certain rights of approach, being Damiri's relations, with Tabini in residence.

But Tatiseigi, the boy was right, would have different thoughts. They were already limited in space. Tirnamardi's upstairs had suffered in the attack. The staff and the boilers were already taxed to the limit.

Perhaps they should at least wait and try to slow the advance, and put the overhasty Ajuri in a calmer frame of mind. Their position on the steps was sheltered by the house, by the presence of Banichi and Jago, and the new arrivals pushed their way through the shattered hedge with some dispatch, weaving through the barrier of parked trucks, baggage and staff following, in evident intent to reach the house quickly. The elderly gentleman had taken command and walked ahead of the rest, in no mood to wait.

Damiri's grandfather. Bren searched his memory for the name. Damiri's uncle, a handsome fellow, was named Kadiyi, Bren recalled, out of the depths of his memory: He walked second. The old lord, the one who looked to have swallowed vinegar, was Benati, Bejadi, or some such.

Cajeiri descended to the midsteps landing, a little to the fore, and bowed properly as the old lord came up the steps, but the old man paid his young kinsman not a scrap of notice—climbed, in fact, right past him. The second lord did the same, to Cajeiri's indignation, and up the steps they came, head-on toward Bren.

"You!" the old man said. In Ragi, that address was inestimably rude. "Foreigner! Out of our way, damn your impudence!"

"Honored sir," Bren said. Clearly he had made a mistake in delaying to welcome the arrivals—there was no way in all the world the old man mistook him for anyone else on the planet, and clearly the old man meant exactly what he said. And finding it prudent and politic to let the insult slide off for the moment, and let Tabini-aiji and Tatiseigi deal with this brusque advance, Bren gave a slight bow and moved aside, cueing Banichi and Jago to let the affront pass, outraged as they might be.

Not so Cajeiri, who now boiled up the steps with Jegari in close attendance, right on the old lord's heels. Cajeiri brushed past the second lord, past the old man, right to the top of the steps and the landing, to plant himself and his young Taibeni bodyguard between Ajuri clan and Tatiseigi's front door.

"Outrageous! Outrageous action, sirs!" Did one hear the aiji-dowager's tones ringing in that young voice? Bren was appalled, and hastened upward to try to patch up matters, hopeless as it seemed.

The lords of the Ajuri had stopped in anger and startlement, and perhaps, in that half-heartbeat, both of them had figured out that the child on the steps, Taibeni guard and all, was not a local Atageini—a surmise a young boy's presence near the paidhi-aiji might instantly have suggested to the quick-witted. But Cajeiri was not through.

"Shall the paidhi-aiji have an apology, nandiin?" Direct quote from his great-grandmother, a question directed at the young gentleman, not once, but several times, at key intervals in their voyage. Bren stood stock still, but gathered the presence to bow profoundly as the Ajuri swung a collectively outraged look in his direction. "He had better have it!" Cajeiri said. "Now!"

"Nandiin," Bren said in a low voice, and with a deep bow.

"Is this Damiri's son?" the old man snapped. "Is this rude young person my great-grandson?"

"I am my father's son, and the aiji-dowager's great-grandson," Cajeiri said, head high, eye to eye with his uncle and great-grandfather, whom he omitted from the genealogy. "And my mother is inside, and my father, and my great-uncle, and my great-grandmother the aiji-dowager. All of *them* esteem the paidhi very highly."

"Well, we see all around us the result of *that* policy," the old lord said, and shoved past, brushing past the boy and his guard, this time with no excuse of ignorance.

"Jegari!" Cajeiri snapped, and, oh, my God, Bren thought, and moved to prevent a weapon being drawn, but not faster than Banichi and Jago, not faster than the Ajuri bodyguard—while young Jegari, do him credit, had only put his body between Cajeiri and the indignity of being shoved aside by his own great-grandfather.

Atageini Guildsmen, cooler heads and uninvolved, had by that time frozen, standing stock still in confrontation, blocking their doorway to access as the Ajuri lords reached the upper landing. The intrusion ran right into the roadblock.

"You will not lay hands on my lord, sir," Jegari pursued the Ajuri from behind, in a voice very quiet, and full of dignity, despite the fact it was a young, high voice, and he was not Guild, nor remotely a match for those tall, black-clad individuals in the old man's company who were.

"Truce," Banichi said, shoving between, confronting the five Ajuri Guildsmen face to face, and a head taller than four of them. "Truce. Let all pass. This is best settled inside."

"Open the doors!" the Ajuri lord demanded, which did nothing to convince the Atageini guards, who continued to stand in his path.

Diplomacy seemed the civilized recourse, and being the only diplomat on scene, Bren moved very quietly up a step or two, bowed, said, "May one suggest," as the Ajuri lords simultaneously turned a burning look his way. "This is a sorry misunderstanding," Bren said, ever so quietly, and, not giving way in the least, "and one regrets having been a provocation to it. You have grown considerably, young sir, and you have borrowed your clothes from staff, so clearly your own kin failed to know you. Your great-grandfather has had a very tiring, very dangerous trip." A deep, collected bow to the old lord, with absolutely no hint of his own outrage and the host of other feelings he had no business to let well up into his job—tiring trip, hell! He'd lay his own and Cajeiri's against it, hour for hour, and throw in the last two years as well. "Some very reasonable people consider the paidhi-aiji at fault for his advice to your father. That is solely for your father to judge. But your estimable great-grandfather and your uncle have surely come here at great trouble to support your mother, nonetheless, young sir, and in supporting her, they have come to support you, as well. Do consider that, and let them pass."

The old man had gone quite impassive, somewhat recovering his breath and his dignity, and one would have to have known both gentlemen, the older and the younger, to know what emotions were actually going on behind those faces. There was a lengthy pause, all the Ajuri staff and luggage-bearing servants gone almost as expressionless. A far-traveling human could quite lose that knack of impassivity, in close shipboard society—but it was vital he recover that skill in himself, and he had to encourage the boy, whose face was still like a thundercloud . . . the boy who, one had to reckon, in two years of shipboard life, only his great-grandmother had ever sharply reined in.

"True," the old lord said darkly, as if it were a bad taste in his mouth to agree with the paidhi in anything at all. "Altogether true." The younger, the boy's great-uncle, still glowered.

"Great-grandfather." A little scowling bow, but thank God the dowager's training had sunk in more than skin deep. She had seen to it the boy had the social reflexes to take an adult hint and make that gesture, without which, at this moment, things could only have gotten worse.

"Grand-nephew." A bow, finally, from the second lord.

"Great-uncle." A second proper bow, finally a blink in that confrontational stare. "But we say again, you must respect the paidhi-aiji, great-uncle."

"Nand' paidhi." It was not a happy face the second Ajuri lord turned in his direction: The expression was still completely impassive, and Bren returned the infinitesimally slight bow with measured depth, his own expression under rigid control now, not ceding anything but an agreement to civilized restraint on both sides.

The Guild, meanwhile, on all sides involved, had at no moment relaxed, and did not ease their stance in the least until Cajeiri directed his great-grandfather to the doors and the Atageini guards deemed the situation settled enough to let the lot of them into their lord's house.

In they went, past workmen noisily sawing away at a piece of timber and shedding sawdust onto their heads. That stopped. There was embarrassed silence in the scaffolded heights, and the Ajuri marched on through, with Cajeiri behind them.

Bren followed, Banichi and Jago on either side of him, still alert, past the damaged lily frieze, the rest of the group having ascended the slight rise onto the main floor, where hammering likewise gave way to silence.

The boy had called on his bodyguard to deal with his uncle. That single sharp word still had Bren's nerves rattled. "Perhaps one should advise Ismini and Cenedi," he said to Banichi and Jago under his

breath as they hastened up the steps, and Jago immediately took the steps two at a time, skirting around
the group in an effort to reach the aiji's and the aiji-
dowager's bodyguards—before the collective situation reached the drawing room.

Bren climbed the steps behind the cascading
calamity.

"Well managed, nandi," Banichi muttered, treading beside him.

"One can only regret to have placed my staff in an
awkward position," he murmured, echoes of footfalls
hiding their voices.

"Your staff has absolutely no regret in that regard," Banichi said.

Banichi's and Jago's steadfastness was the only
warmth in a world gone suddenly much colder. And
it posed a weight of responsibility. He wondered if he
had the personal fortitude to approach the drawing
room door at the moment, following the Ajuri entry
into that conference. Or if it was wise at all to do so,
risking more confrontation.

But Jago was beside that door, waiting for him
among the bodyguards posted outside—now number-
ing Ajuri among them, the lords having gone inside—
and Jago caught his eye with a look that said she had
delivered her message and was going to keep her station out here.

More to the point, Ilisidi's chief of security, Cenedi,
and Ismini, head of the aiji's guard, had just disappeared into that room, to have a quiet word with their
lady and lord doubtless, and to advise them of the
confrontation outside. Cajeiri went in on their heels.

And if the dustup between the great-grandfather and Cajeiri continued in there, and involved Ilisidi—well, that would frost the cake, as his mother used to say, and threaten agreements that had been made with dynastic purpose. The whole trembling association was at risk of fracture, the consort's relatives on one side and Tabini and the heir and the aiji-dowager on the other.

Not to mention Uncle Tatiseigi, whose lawn was being parked upon, now, by a heavy bus of a clan nominally his ally by marriage, but clearly a clan with notions of special privilege, notions derived from Damiri's parentage and *their* rival connections to the aijinate.

He had no choice, he decided. He left Banichi and Jago, passed the doors. The Ajuri lord, Benedi—that was the name, thank God he finally recalled it—who at the moment was being received by his granddaughter Damiri—cast a look over his shoulder and let a scowl escape his impassive mask. Damiri's face still preserved a grimly held smile, for him and for her father's surviving brother.

Bren, for his part, avoided all eyes and gave a private nod of gratitude to the Atageini servant who quietly slid a chair into position near him, at the very bottom of the social order. He sat down there in silence, sat through the slight exchange of formal courtesies between the Ajuri, Tabini, and Ilisidi, and finally listened through the Ajuri's extravagant praise of Tatiseigi, who perhaps had not looked outside since dawn. The family was making some effort to keep the peace, at least.

But the conversation immediately took a sharper edge as Ilisidi, hard upon Tatiseigi's pleasant greeting, quoted a very obscure machimi writer about, "late to the contest, ah, late and bringing flowers to his kin." Bren studied his hands, racking his brain in vain to remember the rest of the line, which came from some rarely performed machimi they had had on tape on the voyage. An Eastern playwright, from Ilisidi's end of the civilized world. He was sure the next line was something less than complimentary, something about sailing this way and that and arriving to his lord's aid long after his lord's enemies had slaughtered the household. One only hoped the Ajuri were not conversant with obscure Malguri poets.

And, God, need they have Ilisidi start a war, as if they lacked all other impetus? Ilisidi had Cenedi at the back of her chair, Guild threat lurking in very senior form, and Ilisidi's expression was sweet, familial malevolence, as if she truly hoped the Ajuri lord did understand her. Cenedi had been leaning near Ilisidi a moment ago, and he was now convinced Ilisidi had gotten the story of events on the step outside, particularly including the brusque treatment of her cherished great-grandson. Cajeiri meanwhile had settled, politically savvy for his years, right between his parents, and sat there like a young basilisk, regarding his maternal relatives with still smoldering ire and looking very satisfied with his great-grandmother. Cajeiri knew the quote, damned right he did, part of two years under Ilisidi's tutelage.

Bren kept from meeting any eye, not encouraging the dowager to find another, plainer quote from her considerable repertoire. And Tatiseigi immediately rose to the social challenge, quoting from a better known and safer author, something about "their tents arrayed across the plain," and "drinking rivers dry," with a mournful reference to his ravaged house grounds, one was sure, and then to the enemy "lurking in the east," "to come down with the gathering night." That at least added up to a welcome, Bren was sure, parsing through the references, although the part about the enemy in the east raised a little uneasiness among the Ajuri.

"You expect yet another assault, nand' Tatiseigi?"

"We have taken precautions," Tabini said in his deep, attention-getting voice. "We have set out alarms and given orders to the foremost of this unlikely assemblage of buses—the vehicles are refueling."

"Refueling," the Ajuri lord echoed him uneasily, settling on a fragile chair, his son next to him. He accepted a cup of tea, and a plate of cakes appeared on the table between the two Ajuri, like the smaller stack that arrived, with a portable table, at Bren's elbow. Bren found no appetite for the teacakes, and they went untouched, but the Ajuri lords washed down several apiece. The Ajuri were some distance from home, and if they had come all the way by bus, avoiding the trains, they had certainly been traveling since dawn. They might expect this snack as a prelude to supper . . . to which they expected to be invited, one was sure. "To what purpose, may we ask, aiji-ma?"

At last, that *aiji-ma,* that personal acknowledgment of the head of association. No one twitched. But if human nerves reverberated to it, Bren was sure atevi ones did. Ajuri had not wriggled sideways, not for a moment, and committed.

Good, he said to himself, and in Tabini's answer, that they had to be ready for anything, talk came down to specifics: The current state of the roads, Murini's likely response to the increasing gathering of support here, the placement of patrols on the estate and out across the border between Atageini clan and the Kadagidi, and all manner of things the paidhi could be very certain were also the topic of conversation outside the door among the various guards, who would have far better specifics on Tabini's intentions.

But what a listener could gather just inside this room drew a vivid enough picture: That Tabini was determined to make a stand here, to have the buses for heavy assault vehicles if need be, or mobile fortification to prevent an incursion into the grounds.

It might be the most convenient place to rally supporters—but this house, with wide-open rolling meadows and fields around it, was hardly a protected position. And with Tabini-aiji's supporters swarming over this and the adjacent province to reach Tirnamardi, they were concentrating themselves into an increasingly attractive target in the process.

A human would do things atevi wouldn't, he reminded himself. But, God, it felt chancy, relying oh so much on atevi notions of *kabiu* and acceptable behavior, in apparent confidence that Murini absolutely would not use aircraft and bomb this building . . . simply because it was not *kabiu*.

For a listening human, straight from space, and having the concept of defense in three dimensions fresh in mind, this gathering added up to a very queasy situation, one in which he kept reminding himself, no, no, no, human nerves did not resonate at all reliably. No, atevi truly would not expect certain things to happen, for a complex of reasons, some of which were simply because, instinctually, atevi would not, could not, sanely speaking, go against the bounds of *kabiu* and would not breach the bonds of *aishi,* that indefinable instinct of group, of obligation, of . . .

There was just no human word for it, beyond a comparison to mother-love and so-named human decency. A sane ateva just didn't *do* certain things, didn't attack the head of his own association, for starters, while *aishi* held. He didn't attack the remoter associations of his association for the same reason—and it was beyond *didn't:* It was all the way over to *being in his right mind, couldn't think of it.* Unless . . .

Unless the ateva in question was that odd psychological construct, an individual *to* whom man'chi flowed, who didn't particularly think he owed man'chi upward to anyone else. That psychological construct added up, in atevi terms, to being born an aiji. A born leader. Or at least an ateva who by birth or experience was immune to constraints that applied to others. In human terms, a psychopathic personality.

Among atevi such a person, at the top of the pyramid of responsibilities, made society work. He actually prevented wars by his very existence, in the best application of man'chi. He stopped wars cold, by preemptive action, and his assurance of having followers enough to carry out his objectives.

Tabini was certainly one such personality, trained from infancy to expect man'chi to flow upward from others, taught to drink it down like wine, in judicious sips, not wholesale gluttony. So, one day, everyone expected Cajeiri to be that sort of leader.

But dared one remember such a personality was also capable of going way out on an ethical cliffedge? A strong enough aiji was capable of taking himself and his followers over that aforementioned edge of behavior the followers would by no means risk on their own, and the only possible brake on the situation was when enough followers simultaneously came to their senses and decided the person they'd followed was not a good leader. *That* was ideally how the system worked. A bad leader lost followers, someone turned on him, someone stuck a knife in his ribs, and another leader rose up from among the group. Atevi instincts somehow triggered that change of opinion at the right moment. Logically, things began to balance again, and sane people en masse adjusted the situation until the group found itself a new leader.

But in the meantime people died. Sometimes a lot of people. And sometimes things ordinarily unthinkable did happen.

It was no comfort at all to be human and thinking quite readily of the physical possibilities of a massed target out in that driveway, an attraction for bombs, planes, poison gas grenades, or anything else a murderous and over-vaunting intention could come up with.

But one thing he knew: Setting forward the possibility of someone doing such things, in this conservative company, could only convince Tatiseigi and these suspicious Ajuri aristocrats that humans were depraved beyond belief and just naturally bent toward bad behavior. He was not the individual who could lead them over such a brink.

Give Tabini the benefit of his advice—hell, yes. Tabini had frequently asked him such dark questions, in private . . . and might now, if they ever could achieve ten minutes' guaranteed privacy in this place.

What would a human do? Tabini had asked him in the old days, before the voyage. What things would you warn against, if it were your own people, paidhi-ji?

It always gave the paidhi-aiji a queasy feeling, answering that question honestly, worrying that he might be giving Tabini ideas—the same way he'd worried when he counseled Tabini to mercy and moderation in the face of treason. Maybe he'd generated ideas he never should have let loose among atevi. Or maybe too much mercy was the key damage he'd done, urging Tabini not to slaughter his defeated enemies. They were sitting here under assault, because certain people had remained alive. They'll concentrate your opposition, he'd argued; you can keep an eye on them. Leave them alive.

So here he sat under siege by those same enemies, wishing Tabini would ask him for advice one more time, and fearing he would give the wrong advice one more time if Tabini did that.

And meanwhile, roiling about in the basement of his mind, was that other application of *kabiu,* that word which ordinarily applied to the room arrangement and those flowers in a green vase over on the table: *Kabiu,* that meant *fit* or *decorous* or *appropriate,* if one was setting a table. *Kabiu* could also apply to battlefields.

To honor. To proper behavior.

*Kabiu,* on this occasion, he divined as the reason otherwise sensible people, even the Ajuri, had to set themselves in a target zone, making their statement for this aiji over the other, declaring for civilized behavior, and most of all—maintaining the degree of civilization that underlay atevi culture even in conflict. Man'chi was driving it, an instinct as fatal and as basic an attraction as gravity.

And if, in a great ebbing tide, man'chi left a leader like Murini of the Kadagidi, he was done. He would have no prospect for long life, considering his numerous enemies, and he would find himself instead of well-received under many roofs, suddenly with nowhere in the world to go.

And what answer would Murini the man deliver to this passive attack on his rule? Fatalistic acceptance? Tame surrender?

One didn't think so. No. He had been a man of subterfuge and connivance, but that didn't mean he'd go out quietly, nor would those more violent sorts who had supported his claims.

Would the Kadagidi clan, seeing the tide starting to turn against Murini, itself make some redemptive gesture, and fall away from their own lord, who was absent in Shejidan, to keep armed struggle away from their territory?

Murini, as aiji of the whole country, had to leave his own clan and go to Shejidan to rule, expecting the Kadagidi, ironically left leaderless, to stay steadfast in man'chi while the man who should be attending their interests was off claiming the whole continent—was that not the way Tabini-aiji and his predecessors had dealt with Taiben, leaving the clan loyalty behind and hoping for man'chi to survive?

The whole arrangement among the Kadagidi was still new enough that Murini had likely retained control of the Kadagidi in his own hands and not fully allotted clan authority to a strong subordinate. Such adjustments, such as Tabini had with Keimi of the Taibeni, took time, and one could imagine such relationships were sometimes troublesome, and fraught with second thoughts. It took time for reward to repay sacrifice of a clan's own interests. But it all seemed queasy logic for him to follow, answers wired to buttons that didn't truly exist in the paidhi's instincts. He constantly made appeal to analogs and like-this and like-that-but-not, and, in the outcome, found himself utterly at sea, still trying to find the reason all these people were all sitting here waiting for dark and likely attack.

All right. All right. For a moment accept that all these well-dressed people weren't crazy, accept that the Kadagidi wouldn't bomb the grounds or attack a dozen clans at once for very practical reasons, like public opinion, or for moral reasons like *kabiu,* a virtue Bren didn't for a moment believe Murini possessed . . . he'd shown damned little sense of it before now.

For a moment assume that the Kadagidi would be sane, middle-tier atevi and that they would make a rational atevi response. What *would be* a sane and *kabiu* response from their side of this contest?

Scaled response. Targeted and scaled response rather than a general assault with massive loss of life and subsequent bloodfeuds. That was how the Assassins' Guild was supposed to function, and that was what was anomalous in this whole upheaveal. The silence, the non-involvement of the Assassins' Guild, the leadership of which was presently sitting in Shejidan deadlocked and refusing to take either aiji's side, when it should have stepped in immediately to protect Tabini's household and to prevent the coup in the first place. Now it categorically refused to budge. It had lawyerlike procedures, like a court. It had to hear evidence, receive petitions. An assassination to be obtained involved a Filing of Intent and might see counterfilings on the other side: There were Guild members just like Cenedi, or Banichi and Jago, or a hundred others under this roof and out on the drive—members whose man'chi was to a particular lord, a particular house, above all else. So Guild members would be on both sides of a Filing—but likewise they took a dim view of wildcat operations, movements without Filing and particularly movements that destabilized, rather than stabilized, the government of a region.

Could the Kadagidi, without Filing, move an Assassin into a neutral clan's territory, and take Tabini out personally? Wipe out the ruling family, down to the youngest? They had tried—at Taiben, when they had hit the lodge and attacked the residency in She-jidan—and the Guild had taken no official action. It had been proven that Tabini had survived the move, and had gathered force, when he had gone out toward the coast, toward Yolanda Mercheson—and the Guild had done nothing to support him.

That had to be troubling Banichi and every other Guild member on the continent. What in *hell* was going on at Guild Headquarters? Ordinarily, lords didn't undertake wildcat operations against one another, precisely because the Guild and the aiji in Shejidan would alike take a dim, lethal view of that behavior. But had it become clear to the Kadagidi that the Guild was not going to act, that there was no argument or Filing that was going to protect Tabini at all?

That would encourage actions far more profitable to the Kadagidi than a frontal assault on a neighbor's land.

That indicated one action that began to make sense in this situation, one delicate, surgical action that would fragment this gathering and bring down the hopes of restoring the Ragi clan to power. And all the fire and fury might be intended only to mask the process of getting an Assassin into position.

And these various people who had assembled to protect Tabini by their presence and position had incidentally brought an impressive attendance of Guild Assassins as their own bodyguards. The Guild might be neutral, deadlocked, and stuck in Shejidan, but local man'chi was healthy and thriving, and, at the moment, armed to the teeth and sitting on Tatiseigi's lawn, and probably on the Kadagidi's front porch, at the same time, if they could get a view of what was happening beyond the hills. Both sides were furnished with Guild enough to spend some time infiltrating and manuevering at this stage—but in the nature of things, Tabini, for his part, had, at every reception, to bet his life that none of these arrivals of other villages, towns, clans, masked some Assassin whose man'chi was secretly to the Kadagidi.

That was surely what the conference *outside* the door was dealing with, among other things Bren wished he had a clear picture of. They were screening every Guild member who came through the door, and seeking information on every Guild member who might be on the grounds: "Do you know that man, nadi? Did he come with the lord's wife's clan?"

He had been in space too long, Bren said to himself. As long as he'd been in atevi society, he had encountered such blind spots in his vision, dark spots, situations where he just didn't automatically draw the obvious conclusion without asking Banichi or Jago—and even then their plain answer didn't always evoke all it should. But he had known that very certainly staff was vetting everyone who got past that door: they always did. The Guild in some respects was a sort of exclusive lodge, and the senior members, the really dangerous ones, knew each other by sight, in and out of uniform.

That was why Tabini's loss of the staff who had protected him so long was such a heavy blow—not alone the emotional loss at their murder, but the practical consequences of new staff not knowing things that had gone to the grave with the previous holders of their offices. The well-oiled machine that had operated so smoothly to protect and inform Tabini was suddenly gone—replaced by new people who had attached themselves to him during his exile; and one only hoped the current chief of Tabini's personal bodyguard, Ismini, knew his men as well, and that information flowed through that staff with something like the old efficiency. Banichi and Jago had had ties in the aiji's old household, but they were at least two years out of the loop, and perhaps underinformed and unconnected for much longer than that: they couldn't reconstitute it. Ismini—Bren had no idea where he had come from, or who these men were who surrounded Tabini these days.

The whole situation conjured all the machimi he had ever seen, disasters which involved breakdowns of Guild actions, the sort of thing that laid bodies in heaps on the stage, when what should have been a neat, *kabiu* action, or a sure deflection of an attempted assassination—turned out a real damn mess thanks to new men filling positions they ill understood or outright pursuing divided loyalties, their ties to other agencies imperfectly severed.

The whole train of thought upset his stomach, as if the encounter on the steps wasn't enough. But the dust around the Ajuri arrival settled in a round of courtesies and sips of tea, never mind the rural Ajuri were themselves a wild card—bringing in a collection of somewhat lower-level Guild that weren't necessar-

ily as well known to the aiji's men, or to other staffs.
They got in. It would have been a major incident, if
Ismini and his men had not let Ajuri in to protect
their lord—but bet that they were asking questions
out there, and sending runners out to ask among
those who might have connections to the Ajuri.

Meanwhile, in the general easing of courtly tensions, at least, Tatiseigi began, inanely enough, to propose a formal supper—trying to put a patch on the
fact that, no, the house didn't have any suitable room
for the Ajuri, who were going to have to lodge downstairs in what Tatiseigi extravagantly called the Pearl
Room, which one understood would be cleared of
records and desks and provided with beds. The Ajuri
were not happy. And Tabini meanwhile took the
chance to request a special buffet for the staffs, allowing the individual bodyguards the chance to eat
on duty and discuss, discussion which would never do
at table, oh, no, never, ever discuss business at a
proper table, even when the lawn was full of im-
promptu militia . . . but most of all, find out what the
Ajuri had brought in, and try to resurrect some of the
knowledge which had died with Tabini's original
head of staff, investigating, too, the connections the
Atageini might know about—since the marriage that
had produced Lady Damiri herself, under this roof.

Meanwhile Tatiseigi rattled on, went on to propose
the menu, God help them, in meticulous detail, and
to recommend a special game delicacy of the region,
with a glowing description of the pepper sauce.

Bren laced his hands together across his middle
and tried to look appreciative and relaxed instead of

grim, desperate, and increasingly anxious about the proceedings—an attack of human nerves, he said to himself, and meanwhile he knew Tatiseigi himself was no doddering fool, and that this performance was purposeful. The dinner in question was going to be one of those formal affairs where meaning ran under every syllable, and where, granted no one was poisoned at the table, atevi felt one another's intentions out. But he himself wasn't up to it. He *didn't* want to attend a formal supper with the Ajuri. He didn't want to sit there eating custard and sauce and wondering what was going on in the woodwork, while staffs were just as energetically trying to parse loyalties and connections running back decades if not centuries.

Most of all he wanted, dammit, just five short minutes, in all this expenditure of valuable time, one short chance to talk to Tabini privately for a single interview outside this carefully monitored gathering. He wanted to turn in the report he had risked his life developing, and he thought he deserved that chance . . . never mind Ilisidi's staff had doubtless done their briefing, not an unfavorable one, he was sure, and never mind his own report, coming from a human mind when all was said and done, had probably become superfluous in the press of time and threat, at least in Tabini's estimation. Tabini probably thought it a headache he didn't need at this point, raising questions he wasn't ready to deal with—but it *wasn't,* dammit, superfluous. He wasn't sure by any means that Ilisidi would have covered all the essentials the way he would have wanted: He wanted the t's crossed and the i's dotted with Tabini, he had spent two years picking his words carefully, choosing very precise ways he wanted to set out certain facts of the outside universe to Tabini, and dammit, he was going to have that report riding his mind and weighing down his conscience until he could offload it and say he had done his best.

No matter what then blew up and no matter what blame public opinion laid on his shoulders . . . which was the other looming threat, that when the dust did settle, he might not be able to get to Tabini at all. He'd had a taste of unbuffered atevi opinion on the steps. He began to ask himself if Tabini's distance from him didn't already have something to do with Tabini's desire to separate himself from human influence, or Tabini's outright dissatisfaction with him, turning away from the advice he had once relied on. In that estimation, he was lost. He didn't know what his status was with Tabini, and he couldn't gain a clear signal one way or the other.

A servant loomed, with a tray. He waved off another offering of cakes, allowing his tea to cool, and wondered meanwhile if anyone had yet taken potshots at Rejiri's plane or ambushed a trainload of inbound west coast supporters. He tried once, furtively, to catch Ilisidi's eye: no good. She was not open to inquiry.

And after that he tried to think of an excuse, any excuse, to take his superfluous presence outside, where he might be able to get information.

The dowager was, at the moment, arguing her grandson's determination not to change his dress for the occasion.

The door opened. Three more individuals arrived, two young ladies and an elderly woman, all of whom suddenly nudged hard at memory: Damiri's sister Meisi, Bren realized in a little flood of embarrassment. Damiri's aunt, whose name momentarily defied memory, and a young cousin, now teenaged, nicknamed Deiaja—all Ajuri clan, the female contingent only now arriving from the buses, one supposed, to take their places in the general madness. They seemed quite surprised to see him in the gathering; and the dowager; and next descended on Cajeiri, who scowled at them and refused to be fussed over. Deiaja had outright shot up a foot since he had last seen the child: Small wonder he hadn't known her when she appeared. And there she was, all cordial bows, with her hair in braids and Ajuri clan ribbon— preparing to be a target right along with all the other fools who had come here. He was completely appalled. Ajuri clan was here, with its younger generation as well as its lord exposed to risk, right along with the Ragi.

Was it a statement, a commitment to a stand, equal risk with the Ragi, the Atageini, and the Taibeni?

But this particular young cousin, this pretty teenager Deiaja, he recalled, was half Kadagidi herself, was that not so?

Ajuri clan had linked to both eastern clans of the Padi Valley, the Atageini and the Kadagidi; and the long-nosed aunt—Geidaro was her name; it came to him in a flash—the aunt was the link in that situation. She had been married to a Kadagidi, a cousin of Murini's, for at least a decade of her life, the contract now allowed to lapse, since, oh, about the time Cajeiri was born . . .

And were those events connected—an Ajuri-connected heir born to the Ragi aiji, and Geidaro severs ties with her Kadagidi husband, retaining the daughter in Ajuri possession, however, not to give up the Kadagidi tie, not quite?

Meanwhile Cajeiri rose and bowed to the girl, who had at least six years on him, but not a smidge of height. The courtesy won a pretty smile from Deiaja, even a little simper. Bren rose, guided by habit, despite the urge to flinch from all Ajuri at the moment, and bowed in his turn, quite gravely.

"Nand' paidhi." A pretty bow from the Ajuri girl.

"One is honored." She was a tiny miss, for an atevi, and had Damiri's willowy look in miniature. She smiled as blithely as if they had met at a summer fair, went her way to bow to her aunt's Atageini great-uncle, and Bren took his seat again, wishing he were not professionally suspicious and asking himself whether this obliging child had had a vote in coming here, or where, precisely, this child's Kadagidi father was at this exact moment.

Over the eastern border, over in Kadagidi territory? Absolutely.

And did that father know he had a daughter newly arrived over here, in the target zone?

Less likely, unless the Ajuri had simply phoned the Kadagidi and said, "Oh, by the way, we shall visit Tatiseigi this week. We shall greatly appreciate quiet while we do so."

It did limit Kadagidi options in dealing with this

uprising . . . as uprising it was, even while it got a number of people past the doors.

And on that thought, darker human worries leaped up, despite all thoughts of *kabiu*, thoughts that kept him mute and obscure in the general exchange of greetings and courtesies. Dammit, the outright artillery or bomb attack on this peaceful gathering that *kabiu* called unthinkable *was* in fact perfectly conceivable to atevi, or what in all sanity was the point of them all coming here and laying their bodies on the line to prevent it?

And *was* there anything the Ajuri could possibly gain in the scheme of things, except by coming in to take Tabini's side, when Tabini's heir was half Ajuri? Did they fear that young Cajeiri would be killed, and that the clan would be sucked into a bloody feud willy-nilly on Tabini's side of the balance?

They were clearly moving closer to power. The old lord, frail as he was, was no candidate—but Damiri's uncle, Kadiyi, had a strong a presence, and if anything happened to Cajeiri's other guardians, he certainly could assert himself as a relative.

Bren remained worried and silent, listening to the polite social chatter as the aunt settled down next to Ilisidi and chattered on, and (a flurry of servants with chairs and teapots) as Meisi settled in beside Damiri and Deiaja plumped down beside her. "Did you have a safe trip?" Oh, yes, no difficulties, but going by road was such an uncomfortable way to travel . . . discussion of absent relatives, another cousin in childbed and oh, so much regretting not being here—

For God's sake, Bren thought, as if the whole undertaking were a family picnic.

Then, then his ears pricked up at a few chattered bits from the half-Kadagidi girl: Uncle *Murini* was still in the capital. Indeed, said Ilisidi, brows lifting. And oh, yes, in the last few hours, the aunt said, he had called the tashrid to assemble and come into session.

The tashrid, the aristocratic half of the legislature, the half that approved successions and heard challenges and Filings.

It was the body that initiated a declaration of war or called for a Guild action.

"Has he the numbers?" Tabini asked, meaning, knowledgeable ears understood, the quorum and the favorable numbers of date and attendance to conduct any legitimate legislative action.

"Indeed, no, aiji-ma. The lords, being no fools," Damiri's uncle said, "are many of them finding travel difficult, mysterious breakdowns, disruptions in the rails between their homes and Shejidan."

"Not to mention," Aunt Geidaro said with a wicked smile, "an outbreak of sore throat circulating in the capital itself, a remarkably contagious affliction. It travels by telephone."

Tabini looked amused. Others laughed. Bren, seeing that look of Geidaro's, felt a band loose from about his heart at this strangely conspiratorial tone from a woman who had personal ties to the Kadagidi.

God, were they winning? Were there disaffections? Was resistence against Murini rising up in the capital itself, among the lawmakers?

And in this thawing of manner did he detect a certain glee in the Ajuri attitude toward the situation, and possibly—possibly, to judge by the aunt, even a little rift within the Kadagidi themselves, a resentment rising toward their power-grabbing lord? Was *that* what the Ajuri were here in such numbers to signal—full participation, and maybe some special connections for this little clan to contribute or to claim, by being here in such numbers?

At least the legislature itself seemed to be having second thoughts, taking a cautious, though stingingly public step away from Murini, a small step starting with, doubtless, a brave few. It was a step which—if their unity held, if their numbers were sufficient, if fear that Tabini might come home and demand an accounting had begun to trouble their thoughts—might infect still others with this sore throat.

But such a movement in the capital might throw fear into Murini and start other forces maneuvering, might it not—perhaps recklessly and desperately so in the rebel south coast and the loyal west coast, where armed force might come into play?

And just when had this disaffection begun to whisper through quiet meetings, with nudges and glances and backroom whispers?

Perhaps it had come the moment it became clear the dowager and the heir were back on the mainland and were receiving support from two and three clans.

Perhaps it had begun when it became clear a growing number of dissidents from Murini's rule were all gathering here, defying calamity, daring Murini to do anything and suggesting by their growing presence that he couldn't. Maybe the Ajuri represented a power struggle within the Kadagidi clan themselves, increasingly alienated from Murini, the more he tried to be a national leader and compromise their particular interests—that had happened in the past. What was the proverb? *Kaid' airuni manomini ad' heiji. It is hard to see the provinces from the capital.*

"If one might suggest," Bren said, ever so cautiously, "if there is any phone link possible to the Guild, nandiin, perhaps the aiji might at this moment seize the initiative to inform them—"

"The aiji needs no lesson!" the lord of the Ajuri snapped, cutting him off.

"Grandfather," Damiri said, a gentle intervention for which Bren was personally grateful, and in the same breath the ferule of Ilisidi's formidable cane came down hard on the tiles.

"My grandson is no fool, to ignore advice," Ilisidi said.

Then Tabini, in that distinctive voice that could knife through a parliamentary brawl, said, "The paidhi-aiji has a sensible point. Hear him."

A hint? A momentary caution, when favor and disfavor were on a knife's edge?

The aiji needed desperately to keep the peace and not create difficulty with these clans.

"With most profound regard for the lord's wise caution," Bren said, trying not to hyperventilate, "and the aiji being most sensible of the true situation—the paidhi-aiji should go to Shejidan, to present the facts he has brought back from the heavens, namely that, without the mission the aiji ordered, the business

with the human settlement would have brought foreign enemies to the world—a threat which—"

Tabini himself lifted a hand, stopping him right
there. Bren braked, brimming over with facts and figures Tabini apparently had no interest in hearing or
allowing to be heard, not here, not now, or not in
front of these witnesses.

"Aiji-ma," he said, and subsided into silence.

"We understand your position, nandi," Tabini said
with finality. "Go speak with the staff."

And do what? Bren asked himself. He had wanted
out of the gathering. But he was dismayed to be so
unexpectedly dismissed.

And say what to the staff, and learn what? He murmured a courtesy, nonetheless, and rose and bowed
to one and all, finding he was truly, absolutely exhausted, frustrated with a situation out of control,
and personally out of resources, now that Tabini
tossed him out of the gathering, and presumably out
of the state dinner as well.

Was it now secrecy from the Ajuri the aiji wanted
around that report of his? Why? Did Tabini suspect
that Kadagidi connection?

He reached the door, heard a rapid footstep, and
found the heir at his elbow, outward bound along
with him.

"And where is our great-grandson going?" That
from the Ajuri lord.

"He is leaving in good company," Ilisidi said
sharply, and with a blow of the cane's ferule against
the tiles. "We were all awake all night. Doubtless we
shall get little rest tonight. We are weary, out of pa-

tience, and *hungry*. Sandwiches, Tati-ji. At least give us sandwiches, or hasten this dinner! No more sugar!"

"Indeed," Tatiseigi said, ordered about in his own hall, and the dinner discussion proceeded as Bren quietly let himself and Cajeiri out of the room, in among the waiting bodyguards.

"My apologies, nand' Bren," Cajeiri said stiffly. "My mother does not agree." And rapidly, in Mosphei', a language an heir of the *aishidi'tat* probably shouldn't have picked up quite so fluently, but had: "My father's *mad*."

That, Bren himself had picked up, quite clearly.

"I hope not at me," he said in Mosphei'.

"At Ajuri clan," Cajeiri said pertly, and, as they gathered up Banichi and Jago, along with young Jegari: "My mother is mad, too. They're pushing, is that the word, nandi?"

All these years, and an eight-year-old could read better what was going on in that room. He had suffered his moment of desolation, of being the outsider, at a time when he held some of the pieces that might make a difference—but he had lost all sense of the undercurrents in that room, and Tabini was right: He was being of no help and he had better get out of there.

"One is hardly surprised," Banichi muttered in Ragi, at his elbow—Banichi and Jago alike understanding more Mosphei' than they ever admitted. "But pushing whom, young sir?"

At that moment Cenedi caught up to them.

"More buses are coming," Cenedi said in a low

voice. "We have forerunners already at the eastern fence, nandi. We do not know the clan, but we suspect they are from the north."

More buses. More lives at risk.

"We have had a report," Banichi said, "that the Kadagidi themselves are bringing clans up from the south to join them at Parai."

The Kadagidi stronghold. "Coming up by train?" Bren asked, envisioning rival clans having it out at the train station, if Dur came in at the same time.

"Sources say so," Cenedi answered. Sources. Spies, that meant, perhaps observers inside the other household, or maybe spies at the train station—certainly observers at the estate fence. God knew how word of further movements was getting back and forth to Cenedi, but Tabini's people had surely brought in far better equipment than Uncle Tatiseigi's antique establishment owned, and reports were now moving in some security, not only on the estate and within the province, but very probably through channels involving Taiben in the west and north and maybe up into the eastern hills—so he surmised, at least, by the degree of information that Cenedi had gathered. Tabini had been here long enough to have spread out a network, given the usual efficiency that surrounded the aiji, and if that had started into operation, reports of hostile movements might become more specific.

"The aiji said in there that the hill clans are coming," Bren said, information which did not seem to surprise anyone.

"Tirnamardi cannot hold any more guests," Jago

said. "Or feed them all. They have sent for more supplies from Marim, which also have to be safeguarded, and which cannot be quiet."

Marim was an Atageini town some forty klicks east.

"Meanwhile," Banichi said wryly, "there is a quarrel between Lord Tatiseigi's domestic staff and certain of the aiji's security as to whether there should be a formal dinner with others still arriving—the kitchen is in utter chaos, and many of the Atageini have come in without supplies, expecting to be fed."

The kitchen was overwhelmed. So was he. Fatigue might play a part in it. The calculation that everything he could possibly learn now was secondhand and late had its part in it, definitely. He felt every one of his blisters and bruises, and wished he could do something, but clearly staff was well ahead of him and its emergencies were mostly of a practical nature. What would come next—whether the Kadagidi attacked again or waited—wasn't even anyone's immediate concern.

But one worry came crystal clear, and he had within reach three staffers he absolutely trusted. "Do we, nadiin-ji, rely completely on the aiji's bodyguard? Do we know these new men, and does information flow?"

"Information does not flow to us so readily as before, nandi," Cenedi said. "We know them. They were lesser men in the aiji's service before the calamity. But their man'chi is firm."

"Capable men?"

He saw his staff's faces, not quite impassive, admitting a slight worry on their part—a great deal of worry, one could suspect, if they were not in front of a not quite discreet eight-year-old who was waiting, all ears. The paidhi had expected a simple confirmation; if he were not so harried and dim-brained, he would not have solicited a detailed answer, and if staff were not so harried, maybe they would not have given it in front of the boy who been part of the furniture for two years.

Not to mention his teenage bodyguard, who had not been.

A rare lapse. Or not a lapse at all. The thought sped through Bren's brain and Banichi's large hand simultaneously landed on Jegari's slight shoulder, drawing Cajeiri's bodyguard into their circle. "Understand," Banichi said, "we do not judge these men, your seniors by ever so much, to be in any particular unreliable, but they do not tell us as much as we would wish. When one accedes to a post unexpectedly, without briefings, and without equipment, it may make even an experienced Guildsman very nervous, little inclined to take advice, cautious of releasing information."

"One makes every attempt to learn," Jegari said, quiet under that grip.

"There is no blame for them," Banichi said, "only a situation. Listen, young sir. Even Guild, and they are Guild, can err by taking on too much responsibility and by refusing to consult. They will not abdicate their decisions and zig and zag with every breeze. That is a virtue; but when more experienced hands offer help and information, they insist on deciding, feeling the weight of their enormous responsibility, one can only surmise. They bring an improvement in communications. What the aiji's guard knows, they have begun to share, this last hour, but they still keep too many secrets, and we have no idea how many more they keep. We would not like to see such errors in our own staff. Information should flow to us. It is necessary, nadiin, that information reach us."

"Yes," Jegari said breathlessly.

"We will stay close," Cajeiri declared, at the likely limit of his understanding. "And if we had guns we could fight."

"Your guard will have a weapon, young sir," Banichi said. "As should be. And you will keep your head down."

"Yes," Cajeiri said, no lordly tone, just the quiet *yes* of a subordinate taking an order.

"Good," Bren said.

"But we could tell my father's men to rely on Cenedi!"

"They will defend your father and your mother," Cenedi said sternly, "but they may not even extend that defense to your own valuable person, young sir. They take no chances on anyone they do not know, and you have surrounded yourself with your own security—including us."

Paranoia meant trusting no one but themselves, and atevi paranoia meant knowing, though Cenedi did not say so, that a live aiji could produce another son; but a dead one's policies would fall, taking institutions down in the process. One did understand.

"Dangerous," Bren said. Trust the staff. Always trust the staff, or things fell apart. "They suspect us?"

"They will speak frankly to a few on Tatiseigi's staff, nandi," Jago said. "And of all the ones we would rely on—Tatiseigi's staff is certainly not foremost in our choice. One wonders if there is some suspicion of all of us who have been on the ship."

Young ears were still absorbing the situation, young eyes very attentive. A sudden glance caught the wheels turning in Cajeiri's eyes—turning in silence, which was decidedly the most dangerous situation of all.

"Young gentleman," Bren said, "rely on Cenedi, who has surely spoken to your great-grandmother."

"I could talk to my *mother*," Cajeiri said, jaw jutting. "*She* would talk sense."

And the aiji-consort was Ajuri, not Ragi, and possibly expendable, if push came to shove, if there was purely Ragi aristocracy trying to preserve Tabini at all costs—and maybe not as happy with the Ajuri connection Damiri represented. If Tabini heard that set of priorities, a human guess said Tabini would skin his security alive.

The boy's idea about talking to Lady Damiri wasn't entirely foolish.

"Discreetly, young sir," Bren said, one precarious step into defying the aiji's orders and footing it around a cadre of persons who had established their own channels to the aiji's authority, channels purposely excluding him ... and possibly inclined to wish the aiji didn't have a wife or an heir of Ajuri-Atageini blood.

But in that case, expending one human was negligible.

"Speak with extreme discretion," he said, "counting that your father's guard are not incompetent men—only very tired, and among strangers, and extremely concerned for your father's safety for a very long time. They may care very little about us."

"Well, *we* can speak to them and inform them," Cajeiri said, and started off in that direction, but Bren gently snagged the boy's arm and gained his momentarily startled attention.

"Young sir, no. Report what you have heard to your *great-grandmother.* That is your best avenue. You know your great-grandmother will find your father's ear, and advise him far more cleverly than any of us."

A series of thoughts floated through those young eyes, from astonishment to gratifyingly deeper and more shadowy things. It was not a shallow boy he dealt with: He staked his life on that.

"I shall," Cajeiri said in great solemnity, recovered his arm, and straightened his coat. He stood straight and still, a credit to his great-grandmother.

"Be ever so careful who hears you," Bren said. Standing on eye level with a precocious eight-year-old, it was frighteningly easy to make the mental slip into thinking Cajeiri older and wiser than he was; and maybe, he thought, his own size made Cajeiri more apt to confide in him. "But never assume, young sir, that your father has ever shown his true thoughts to us, not when he is in conference and not when so many important maneuvers are going on. He may have had good reason to wish me to leave the room, so he can talk with Ajuri without my hearing their opinion of me, which may be very harsh."

"Why?" That eternal question, but indignant, and backed this time by comprehension of the situation.

"Because people blame me, young sir, for advising your father to build a space program, and to send atevi into space at all. It is less going to space that is the question, but the modernization—does one know that word?"

"One knows it very well, nandi. My great-grandmother detests it."

"Well, people think the paidhi's job was to prevent modernization happening too fast for people's good, and they blame me for a great many things that resulted from it."

"Mani-ma says if you had not translated the space books we would have the ship-aijiin in charge and the aiji could throw rocks at them for all the good it could do."

He was astonished. And gratified. It terrified him that he had fallen into a discussion of politics with an eight-year-old. But Cajeiri had just spent two years discussing politics with Ilisidi, and that *why* of his was an extremely loaded question.

The paidhi inclined his head in respect. "It may be true, young sir. I think it is. But many good and honest people only see the disturbance and the change in their neighborhoods. One would not say your father's guards are bad men—unless they oppose you, young gentleman. In that case, one opposes them. And I may be completely wrong. They may be thoroughly honest men and in favor of you as your father's son. But if you can catch your great-grandmother's ear—in particular hers—be guided by her, not by me."

For a moment those young eyes bored straight into him, his father's very look—then a darted look aside at Cenedi, and back to him, dead-on. "Mani-ma says you are smarter than any other human, nandi, and I should pay close attention to you, except a few things. That one should understand why you say things."

"One is flattered beyond all measure, young lord, by your great-grandmother's good opinion. One hopes never to fail it. Particularly in this. Be ever so careful, young sir. Rely on Cenedi. Rely on him, and on your great-grandmother."

It was a worried look. And a boy had confronted the edge of a political breach he was born to span.

"A Ragi father, a Malguri great-grandmother, an Atageini mother, young sir, along with an Ajuri great-grandfather and Kadagidi relatives with ties to the south coast—these are considerable advantages, once you reach your majority. Your heredity spans the whole continent, have you considered that? It *is* a great advantage for you someday, but it requires a certain patience at the moment. It requires living to be a man, and aiji in your father's place. Cenedi is the one who will protect you."

"Do I have to rely on the Ajuri? And my great-uncle?"

"One must not offend these relatives. Leave that to your great-grandmother."

Golden eyes flickered—a swing between suspicion

of humor and grim determination. From inside the door, a moment ago, the sharp crack of Ilisidi's cane, a family fight in full spate.

"Cenedi-ji," the boy said then, ever so quietly, and with a shift of his eyes past Bren's shoulder, "is this good advice?"

"It is extremely good advice," Cenedi said.

"Then I shall talk to my great-grandmother," Cajeiri said. "Tell her so, Cenedi-ji."

"Not in there, young sir," Cenedi said, "but one will pass this word."

"We should all go upstairs," Jago said in a low voice, as a clot of other security passed them in the hall, not within earshot, one thought, but there were electronics, despite the hammering that echoed throughout, from two independent sources. "There are situations in progress, and one does not count this hallway secure."

Never disregard staff's warning. "Yes," Bren said. He longed for the peace and quiet of his own quarters, removed from this gathering horde of strange guards and potentially deadly tension in the household. "Young sir, you may come up with us."

"What shall we do up there?" The eight-year-old was immediately back in the ascendant, and strode along with them as they turned toward the stairs and climbed up to the next, the residential floor, catching a step as he tried to match Banichi. But no one answered the heir's question in the echoing stairway, not past Ilisidi's quarters and not past Cajeiri's, where, presumably, Jegari's sister Antaro was still watching the premises.

Banichi knocked at their own door, tested the handle, received some sort of signal, or gave one, via the pocket com, and opened the unlocked latch.

Algini sat at a small table near the window. He had a curious black box deployed and plugged into house circuits. He had not locked the door or secured the entry corridor against adventurous house staff on their proper and innocent business, but Algini was very much on alert, had a com-plug in one ear, and a pistol laid beside him on the little table.

Astonishing, Bren said to himself. An operations center had materialized out of their luggage.

Banichi was not astonished. "Any news?" Banichi asked matter-of-factly, and Algini shrugged.

"Too much radio traffic for our safety," Algini said. "The house itself no longer chatters freely, and we have our new guarded communications, besides the aiji's staff and their network, but these newly arrived staffs are a liability. Every bus out there has a common-channel radio, and the citizens are by no means cautious in calling their relatives in the far reaches of the province."

"The Kadagidi know by now there is a large component of common citizenry to this gathering," Jago said, with a glance at Bren and at Cajeiri. "This is to our good, nandiin. They cannot press ahead with an attack and claim ignorance of the situation."

"They will not attack, Jago-ji?" Cajeiri asked.

"One did not say so, young sir. But the Kadagidi will have to be much more cautious, not to proceed without finesse."

"Finesse," Cajeiri echoed.

"Indeed," Jago said.

Assassins, Bren thought. The only way to get in a deft strike, and such a strike would aim at the house and the high-value targets.

Meanwhile Cajeiri had restrained himself from a look out the windows and instead sidled close to Algini's black box device—had gained the sense not to reach out an inquisitive hand, but pointed at it. "Is it a com?"

"One might say so, young sir." Algini flipped a switch and took out the earplug, with a look toward Bren. "Nandi."

Offering his full attention, that was to say, and implying a question regarding their return to the room.

"It seems safer up here," Bren said. "The aiji is having a family discussion downstairs. The plane is off and about to reconnoiter and Ajuri clan has come in, with its junior and senior members."

A wry turn of Algini's mouth. That situation needed little amplification.

"So what is funny?" Cajeiri asked.

"Very little, young sir."

"The other installations?" Jago asked.

"Done," Algini answered her. "Tano has been busy. One would recommend the young gentleman and his staff relocate to these premises or to the dowager's for safety tonight."

"My great-grandmother," Cajeiri said with no hesitation. "We have to—" Talk to her was the probable next statement, but Jago cut that off with a sharp move and a finger uplifted to the ceiling, their code for possible listeners.

"Probably wise," Bren said.

"So Jegari will bring Antaro here until then, shall he not, nand' Bren?"

Pert. Entirely too pert, Ilisidi would say, but the boy was thinking, clearly.

"Excellent," Bren said, and Jegari made a dart for the door.

"Halt!" From all his bodyguard at once. Jegari skidded to a stop and faced them, shock writ across his young face.

"*Now* the door is disarmed," Algini said. "Make deliberate speed, young man, and inform your sister. And when you come back, knock. Always knock for admittance where Guild is involved and pray do not dart at doors. This is not Taiben Lodge."

"Nadi." A very chastened bow, and Jegari made a quieter departure from the premises.

"One assumes that vital instruction need not be repeated for others," Bren said in a low voice, "young sir."

"By no means, nand' paidhi." Oh, so quietly. Cajeiri's eyes were wide and alert. Two reprimands in a handful of minutes, after his very adult response downstairs, and he was clearly off his balance.

"Come," Jago said, "and one will instruct the young gentleman in other needful precautions."

"Yes," the lad said respectfully, and just then a distant hum obtruded, even to human ears. "The plane!" Cajeiri cried, and made one abortive move toward the window.

"Boy!" Banichi, in that tone, but Cajeiri had already frozen in midstep.

"I would not have touched—" Cajeiri began, and then the aircraft roared across the roof from east to west, distracting him.

"Keep your mind on business, young sir. Consider your staff, and restrain *them* from such moves. This is no game. This is never a game."

"Yes, Banichi-nadi." Meekly. Very softly. The plane buzzed in the distance, meanwhile, coming about for a landing, and Cajeiri did not even look toward that window to see.

"Excellent that you stopped," Bren said, deciding such contrition deserved a little praise, ever so little, since a small dose was often overdose with this lad— but Banichi's tone of voice would have chilled the dead. "House defenses are up, young gentleman, but more, defenses are up which you never saw used on the ship, things which might take a hand or a foot off. Jago will explain them for you and your staff, if you will attend her. In the meanwhile, one assumes the young gentleman from Dur is landing safely, if prematurely, and might have news for us. Tano-ji," Tano had just come into the room, from the bath. "Will you inquire? And ask nand' Rejiri to accept our hospitality in these premises immediately, if he cannot penetrate the family discussion below."

"Nandi," Tano said, and went off on his own errand, with—one hoped the boy noted the fact—a signaled coordination with his partner, who threw switches on a pocket remote.

"How shall I warn my bodyguard, nandi? Might I please go down the hall to advise them?"

Clearly thinking farther than himself and farther than the moment, now, twice in one half hour. And oh, so polite.

"Jago herself will go and advise them. It is an excellent idea, young sir, but security should handle security."

The boy was getting the picture, and had a good head on his shoulders, which might ensure it lastingly stayed on his shoulders. He stayed still, touching nothing, going nowhere, watching while Banichi did a walkaround tour of the windows and their precautions.

Meanwhile, switches had to be flicked off and reset again as Jago went out, then came back with Jegari, Antaro, and the all young company's meager luggage—Jago settled that burden into the front cubby of a room—bringing with them, one noted, a bowl of seasonal fruit tucked into Antaro's open carry-bag, a welcome little amenity which the forest bred youngsters did not leave behind in their transfer of residence.

The incoming luggage—saddlebags, in the case of the Taibeni youngsters—settled with their bags, the fruit bowl went onto the hall table, and the young trio followed Jago's quick and thorough lecture, this time with embellishments from Cajeiri, who was a very quick study, in the dire things he had heard from Banichi.

There was, however, no Rejiri. The young man had not even entered the house to report, but had quickly gone off in a bus, so Tano said on his return from scouting. The contingent from Dur was about to reach the train station, the train coming in full bore, and they needed transport and guidance immediately—if not outright defense.

"The folk from the coast are coming in with Dur," Tano reported, "by the same train, and with that group, notably, nandi, Adaran and Desigien."

The fishing village where they had made their landing on the continent and the railhead village from which they had continued their journey, villages which had already risked a great deal in the dowager's support.

"One should remember them," Cajeiri said solemnly, with no one prompting.

"Indeed," Bren said.

Two more contingents added to the vulnerable lot already sitting here, a target for Kadagidi mayhem as the sun declined in the sky. Brave folk, as they had already proved. He was far from easy in his mind. Finesse, Jago had said. But there might be gunfire at the train station in very short order, and there might be ambush on the way—God knew where it would end up. Rejiri had apparently scouted things out, including, perhaps, the position of forces trying to control access to the Atageini train station, and then opted to ground the plane and go back by bus—a good move, Bren thought. If he had appeared over Kadagidi forces, they might have claimed illicit attack, and that could escalate what was already in progress.

So while Jago instructed three eager youngsters in the meticulous details of avoiding disaster—and specifically cautioned them against trying to bypass Algini's black box device, which involved skills the Guild did not divulge to novice security and an inquisitive princeling—Bren found no further use for himself at all, except to get out his computer and attempt to condense a report, paring thousands of pages down to essentials, in the hopes that if they did have a quiet night, and if Cajeiri did get his great-grandmother's ear, Tabini might have time to look at it this evening.

No phone connnections to Mosphiera, not from this house. He had his modem, but without the landlines, it was no use to him; he mortally regretted that the communication network had never gotten beyond Mogari-nai's solitary dish. He wondered how good the informal network was, the illicit radio traffic across the straits, whether that had maintained any mainland contacts, and consequently whether President Shawn Tyers knew what kind of a mess he was in, and that Tabini had knowingly put himself in a target zone? Yolanda Mercheson, his liaison with the spacefarers, was sitting over there on the island, in a hotel beside the landed shuttle, perhaps having been clever enough during his absence to have tried to create such links, but she had not made contact with him if they existed. At the moment, she was still waiting to relay information to the station, and he couldn't tell her what was going on, either—though the increasingly massive traffic jam out there might by now be seen in orbit, who knew? The station had been on the verge of deploying observation satellites with very good optics, but that project, once certain hidebound humans and atevi had gotten wind of it, had bogged it down in security concerns on both mainland and island. Had it ever

happened? One assumed if it had gotten into operation the captains up there would have given him
suitable equipment, knowing the situation on the
mainland. One assumed—

Well, what the station knew or could see or gather
from clandestine networks or doggedly determined
spies in rowboats was not his problem, at the moment. Tabini was. Tabini's gathering force was.

Tabini's highly protective guard was.

"What has the dowager's staff been able to tell
Tabini's guard?" he asked Tano, as the one of his staff
who at least looked unoccupied. "What success have
you had passing information to them?"

But Tano answered: "Algini would know better,
nandi," and quietly replaced Algini in control of the
black box, freeing Algini to come and confer with
Bren.

"What information has Cenedi relayed to Tabini's
staff on our mission?" he asked, for starters. "And
what are they saying?"

Algini hunkered down by his chair and, staring
into space in the manner of a man recalling minute
detail, spilled the essentials, an amazing flow, almost
a chant.

And all coherently organized, more the marvel,
carrying the agreements, the persons present at the
negotiations, the representations made on both sides,
exactly as he would have outlined it—though not the
reassuring content he would have wished. The aiji's
guard had given no reaction to news that there were
more foreigners out in space, and as to what the
dowager had said to Tabini himself, only Tabini's staff

had witnessed that—and Tabini's security staff was not talking to them.

After all these years, he was still amazed at the detail, the precise picture of who had been standing where and overheard what. He began, in some despair, to fold his computer away. The essentials had come out. Tabini had not wanted his report.

His movement interrupted the flow. Algini, rare gesture, touched his hand, preventing him. "Our accounts are necessarily missing some detail, nandi."

"Clearly it misses very little," he said, and decided to consult Algini, who rarely talked but who seemed communicative at the moment. "The aiji has men about him who seem commendably protective of him, Gini-ji. But Cenedi is not pleased. What would his former guard have said?"

"We are meeting obstacles in communication," Algini said bluntly. "One cannot speak for the dead. But these men are different."

"Their man'chi?"

"One detects very faint ties to the hills, and perhaps to the south."

"To the south." Alarming. "And the aiji has accepted that knowingly?"

"Certain of us question, Bren-nandi, how much the aiji knows of those ties."

Twice alarming. "Who truly knows these men, Gini-ji?"

A very slight hesitation, half a breath, if that. Algini's gold eyes flicked into rare direct contact at so blunt a question. "Various of us have formed independent impressions of the situation. Certainly the aiji and the consort have slept safely under their guard."

"So their objective, whatever it may be, is consonant with the aiji recovering Shejidan."

"One believes they do oppose Murini, and the aiji has continually been the strongest opposition available. Your return and the dowager's have created somewhat of a stir: Your renewed influence challenges them."

Clearer and clearer. "There is no likelihood this opinion of me will improve."

"The paidhi and the dowager represent an arrangement of new numbers," Algini said, "bringing in Lord Geigi and the establishment in space, as well as other coastal folk, who are now arriving here in considerable number to add their voice to the discussion."

The coast and the hills had never been united before the *aishidi'tat.* There was still conflict of interest. The middle south and Lord Geigi, up on the station, had never been allies in policy except, again, as the *aisihdi'tat* united them.

"It would seem then," he paraphrased the subtext, "that the elements of the *aishidi'tat* who are against the Kadagidi, but who have not been favorable to me or the dowager, have been the primary refuge of the aiji in this time of need, and they are greatly dismayed to see us returning easily and moving back into our former position, snatching away the influence they feel they have justly earned."

Algini's gaze flickered just slightly. "That would be one theory, nandi, and generously phrased."

"Would they ultimately mean the aiji ill?"

"The elements we suspect have never favored the *aishidi'tat's* establishment, and may use it now only as a convenience. To see all central organization fall apart would well suit some of the hill lords, and some of the south."

"Disaster, in dealing with the ship-humans."

"Your staff thinks so. The dowager thinks so. But the aiji's staff is limiting what information reaches him."

"Painting a picture in which their advice is wise and politically safer."

"Exactly so, nandi. And the Ajuri themselves are seeking a position of more importance through their connections. They may be northerners, but they represent a certain discontent up to the north, a minority—they have been a minor force throughout, but the news that the aiji is here, again, under Lord Tatiseigi's roof—and that you and the dowager are back—has galvanized them and filled their eyes with great expectations. They are a hinge-point, on which other borderline elements may base their reactions."

"They thoroughly detest me."

"The heir, their grandson, is a critical matter. They wish to see him with their own eyes, to establish his man'chi, where it lies and may lie in future. He departed as a child. He returns having been under your influence and the dowager's for two formative years. He speaks fluent Mosphei'. This fact will shock them immeasureably."

"His fondness for pizza and ice cream will not help us either," Bren said wryly; so great was his confidence in his staff that he had not questioned Algini discussing these things aloud with him, in this lowest of voices, but now his heart gave a thump and he remembered where they were. "Dare we say these things, Gini-ji?"

"One knows now exactly who is doing the monitoring and why," Algini said. "We have established ourselves. We have installations in several rooms. We are secure."

The black box. The monitoring. And "installations." God knew how installations had gotten into other rooms.

"Downstairs, too?"

Algini's face became incredibly hard to read, and Bren broke off, assuming his staff's secrets were not for him to penetrate.

"So must we approach the Ajuri in a conciliatory way?" he asked, and seemed to have startled Algini for once in their association. It was as if he had hit a nerve.

"One should not, by no means," Algini said, "but rather trust that they will swing to the prevailing wind. They are not a ruling clan. They have not the heredity. Yet."

"They need Cajeiri."

"They need his good will," Algini said, "if they have any hope of prominence. They are ours because it is not in their interest the heir should perish."

Cajeiri being their only claim to power and prominence.

Politics made strange bedfellows indeed. And Tatiseigi let the Ajuri under his roof and into his hospitality when other, higher ranking claimants to that hospitality were likely to sleep on bare ground or in their buses tonight. The Ajuri lord had certainly been caught off guard, meeting him and Cajeiri on the steps, as if they were there solely to confront him and prevent him reaching that goal. The old man had not recognized the heir, in his borrowed coat, but he had certainly recognized and affronted the paidhi—only to be set straight by an eight-year-old. Ajuri had been thoroughly discommoded, and hit Tatiseigi's hall not in smooth advance, but in a fit of embarrassed outrage.

A delicious moment, if he had had the hand in planning it that the Ajuri must have thought he had . . . no wonder the old lord had been put out with him, and now thought him more cunning than he was.

"Interesting," he said. The member of his staff that had been sitting here at a table all afternoon proved to be a fount of information on everything in the house, while Banichi and Jago had been busy keeping him safe and Tano had been back and forth in the room, running clandestine errands, one had a slight suspicion, on the backstairs servants' routes and wherever else he could reach within the secret ways of the building. Unlike Banichi and Jago, who had gone to deep space with him, Tano and Algini had spent the last two years at the station, hearing all the reports of disaster from the world below their feet, developing their own picture of politics as all order fell apart. Trust Algini to have a very good grasp of where lines of power ran.

"Interesting indeed, the position the Ajuri now find themselves in," Algini said, "and their staff is making very cautious approaches to Tatiseigi's and to the dowager's staff."

"To the dowager's?"

"She is respected," Algini said, which was no secret from anyone, "and feared. You are the unadded sum in many equations, nandi. We have received approaches from out on the lawn. So has Lord Keimi of the Taibeni, at no few points. Now that you and the dowager are back in the numbers, there is some feeling of familiarity in the structure of the world, as certain people see it. This restores a sort of balance of tensions which some find comfortable."

"One can see that," he murmured. Certain ones might oppose him, but he was a known quantity. "The heir, however, is a new quantity."

"Indeed," Algini said, "and he is young, nandi. Youth is always a cipher, when it comes to what his influence may become. You are the fixed point. No one believes you will break man'chi."

"I?"

"You will not leave the aiji," Algini said.

"Or the heir," he said. "Or the dowager."

Algini nodded. "A point of certainty. You are stability in these matters. More than the dowager herself, you represent a simple, sure number in all calculations. This reassures even your enemies, nandi."

He was startled into a grim, soft laugh. "One is glad to perform a service."

"A vital service, at a time when the aiji has issued a call."

His heart sped. "Has he, Gini-ji?"

"As of this morning," Algini said. "But certain people were already coming."

"The Kadagidi have issued a call, on their side."

"Momentum. Momentum and the will of the people. One wonders where the summons will bring a muster."

"Well," Bren said, "I shall not leave him, and he will not leave the people out there, and you for some reason a human can never understand will not leave me, so here we sit, one supposes, until the sun goes down, deeply appreciative of your analysis, Gini-ji, ever so appreciative."

"Salads," Algini said.

He had to laugh. He had to laugh aloud, touched to the heart. "Extraordinary salads, Gini-ji."

Algini was a grim fellow. But he smiled, all the same. "Aiji-ma," he said, not nandi. Not nand' paidhi, not even Bren-ji. And one could hardly believe one had just heard that word. He supposed he stared at Algini for a second.

"Nand' Bren." Cajeiri bumped the other side of his chair. "Antaro says she and Jegari can go downstairs and get us food for tonight, if we are not going to great-uncle's dinner. They will *ask*," he added, as if to dispel any notion of theft.

"One might accompany the youngsters," Algini said wryly, "and lay hands on a bottle of brandy."

As if he and Cajeiri had not eaten their fill of tea-cakes. But in all the arrangements for getting staff fed, staff had had much more opportunity to drop below-stairs and take advantage of the offerings. If there was a buffet laid out, the two Taibeni youngsters, otherwise without useful employment, might carry a basket up here in reasonable safety. "Go with them, Gini-ji. But *not*," he added, and got only that far before Cajeiri dropped crosslegged onto the floor at his side.

"Not me," Cajeiri said glumly. "Never me."

# 4

The sun sank. It grew dark out, or dark in that last stage of twilight. A human eye might take it for full night. Not an atevi eye.

And the hammering went on downstairs, incessant, which argued either workmen driven by Lord Tatiseigi's fraying temper (unimproved by the family discussion, one might guess) or workmen on a project on which security depended. Presumably dinner was in the offing down there.

Jegari and Antaro, with Algini, missing for the better part of an hour, attended Adaro and Timani up from downstairs, a party loaded with paper-wrapped packets and baskets redolent of savory meats—and clinking with bottles far in excess of the promised brandy.

"Ah," Banichi said, diverted from his small wiring project. Bren would have sworn he could have no appetite of his own after all that sugar and tea, but his appetite perked up at that wonderful smell.

"The lords have gone to supper, nand' Bren," Algini reported. "And it seems at least that all parties have gone to the dining hall. The argument beforehand was loud, but they are all at the same table."

Encouraging, at least. And the kitchens, whether with Adaro's and Timani's urging, or because they had cooked up a precautionary surplus of food, had provided them a very handsome supper, which one had to trust.

Adaro and Timani began to search for a serving surface, the apartment not being provided with a dining table. The computer table was obliged to serve that purpose, and several chairs besides, holding the various dishes. The informal arrangement left only the bed and the floor for sitting, but there were glasses and utensils enough, and bottles of ice water as well as wine and the fine brandy.

The servants served while the household sat crosslegged on the floor, Cajeiri as well, lord and bodyguard and servants all safely below the level of the windows as night came down, as they appreciated the first morsels of a grand dinner which Algini had assured them had come from the same dishes which served the whole household—and Banichi and Jago instructed the sober Taibeni young folk in the subtle arts of assassination the while, while pointing out some of the features of the black box, and some delicacies of the art of poison. It was to be noted that Algini had a com-plug in his ear since he had come back; affairs in the kitchens were not all he had been arranging.

"Poisoning rarely happens in a well-managed kitchen," Jago said cheerfully, "and this kitchen, whatever the failings of the electronics in the house, does not allow people to wander through at liberty. The cook manages the pantry under lock and key, and only allows observation, not touching. If one wishes food, one obtains it from the table outside."

"Could *you* not break in, Banichi-ji?" Cajeiri asked, appealing to the greatest authority in his young experience.

"Probably," Banichi said in some amusement, which gave Bren a certain niggling doubt about the bite currently in his mouth, but, hell, he said to himself, in a household which had just purged itself of all the Kadagidi spies it *knew* about, likely if there was one topflight man in all Tatiseigi's household, it was the cook, seeing that Tatiseigi was still alive despite his long-standing feuds and the onetime presence of Murini under this roof. The cook of a stately home was up on food safety—in all its senses. Witness Bindanda, his own cook and staffer back on station—who was incidentally connected with Tatiseigi's household. There was a man who managed his kitchen with great skill.

A little polite laughter, and the servants offered the next course.

Downstairs, the hammering stopped. Abruptly.

Everyone in their little circle stopped eating and cast bemused looks into the ether, and then toward each other.

Someone of note from the camp might have walked in past the workmen. Possibly Rejiri had just arrived with a sizeable delegation.

Or not.

"Did we hear a vehicle engine?" His staff's ears were far keener than his.

"Yes," Banichi said. "Not the first such, but a moment ago, yes."

"Guild," Algini said. *He* still had the com device in his ear, and suddenly had an intent, distant look. "A Guild delegation has arrived."

News of it had just reached Algini's downstairs contact.

"It has come, then," Banichi said solemnly.

Bren swallowed the last of the bite he had in his mouth and looked at Banichi, who was looking at Jago as if *they* both understood something and then at Tano. As if everyone in the universe would understand, if they had any wit at all.

"From Shejidan?" he was obliged to ask the stupid but necessary question.

"They are expected," Algini said, dinner forgotten as he followed the information flowing into his ear from presumably secure systems. Or Tatiseigi's compromised ones.

But withholding the knowledge of Guild official presence would not be in their interest. The Kadagidi would hardly attack with Guild officials in the house. All sense of that seemed off.

"Perhaps the Guildmaster received my letter," Bren said quietly, hopefully, while Cajeiri positively had his lip bitten in his teeth, restraining questions. His eyes were taking in everything.

"Perhaps he has," Banichi said.

Bren moved his napkin from his lap. "I should go downstairs."

Cajeiri moved to rise as he did, oversetting a water glass, which Jago's lightning reflexes rescued as the boy scrambled for his feet. His bodyguard jumped up with him.

"At this moment," Bren said, "my company is not the most auspicious for your own introduction to the Guild, young sir. First impressions are difficult to overcome."

The jaw halfway set. But there was a sensible worry on that brow, too. "So the Guild is the paidhi's enemy, like my great-grandfather?"

"Now, you must not speak ill of your Ajuri relations or the Guild either, young sir."

"You rescued the kyo! You saved all the humans! You brought us home!"

"That we did, young sir, but we have to have their confidence to tell them those things."

"Then they are fools!" Cajeiri said. "And if they can speak to my father, so can I."

Dared one say the paidhi felt control of the situation slipping though his fingers? It was not only history and diction the boy had learned from his great-grandmother.

"Patience, patience," he said. "Reconnoiter. Has Banichi taught you that word?"

"Cenedi did. We are quite cognizant of the word."

"One very much advises meekness and modesty in front of the Guild," Bren said, hoping to nip that pert attitude in the bud. "Leave policy to your father and do not limit his resources by presenting him with a difficult situation."

A deep sigh. "I am not aiji *yet*." Clearly another Ilisidi quote. "But one will not permit them to lie.

Timani and Adaro are my mother's servants. And they can tell *her* things."

That *can tell* was a drop of caution in a burgeoning sea of regal indignation: Cajeiri had not blurted everything out, not about the problem with Tabini's guards; he had not taken his usual tack and made things irrevocable—a breathtaking prudence, when one considered what damning things the boy could blurt out.

"One doubts they will have time to do so, young sir, nor may they wish to be put in that position. But you are not aiji. Nor will you ever be, nor perhaps will your father by morning, if this encounter with the Guild goes wrong. Caution and prudence, one begs you. Information is life, here." Timani, whose ears were doubtless burning, was utterly deadpan through this—he had brought a change of coats, a considerable finery that had likely been cloth on a bolt as late as this afternoon, and stood with it in his hands, distressed. "Thank you, nadi," Bren said, and put one arm in, then the other, while Cajeiri stood silent and brimming over with things bubbling up inside him.

The coat was deepest purple shading to red in a serpentine, shining brocade, a finer coat than the lace on his shirt could possibly do justice, and he could only wonder how the servants had put this together in a handful of hours, or whether Tatiseigi might recognize the fabric as not a very petty theft.

"Extraordinary," he murmured, by way of appreciation as Timani brushed down the sleeves.

"It fits, nandi?"

"Very well, nadi." With a little adjustment of the cuffs, while the maidservant, Adaro, adjusted his queue past the collar. "Excellent." He was shaken by the boy's little outburst, knowing what a desperate pass they had come to down there, and how he was going to have to defy Tabini's dismissal, at least to appear in the vicinity. But he felt, at least, the equal of any lord down there, as flashy, in this mode, as Tabini was deliberately martial. The aiji was completely out of the fashion wars that meant psychological advantage, and remarkable in the statement he did make—but for his part, no ateva wanted to give way in argument to a peer who looked like a rag-bin. It was core of the court mentality. It was like a suit of armor, this purple-red coat.

He drew in a deep breath. "And the young gentleman?" he asked Timani.

"Mani-ma has my best clothes in her closet, nand' paidhi," Cajeiri said, unasked. One saw the boy was upset, that rash behavior was very near the surface and wanted calming.

"Then we had better find them, had we not, and get you down to your great-grandmother?"

Pointed remark. Cajeiri's pupils widened, a little jolt of comprehension that this was a very adult game from which he was *not* excluded.

"Nandi." From Algini, a sober look.

"Is there a difficulty?" he asked.

"One has heard a name," Algini said, with reference to that com device in his ear. "Gegini."

Jago shot Banichi a look, a decided look.

"Who is he?" Bren asked, and Banichi, with a

glance at Algini and back, grimaced. "One can hardly name names," Banichi said, "but if the Guild has moved from neutrality, clearly this visitation is not one according to your wishes, Bren-ji, or in response to your letter."

That was three times around the same corner and no direct information. "Are you saying this arrival could be a Kadagidi expedition, brazening it into the house? A lie, nadiin-ji?"

"Oh, they would be official, at highest level, under Guild seal," Banichi said.

"The question is, always," Algini said, "what is the state of affairs within the Guild, and does Gegini have a right to that seal?"

"Would this be notice of a Filing, do you think?"

"Or outright illegal conduct," Algini said. "Such action is a possibility, Bren-ji. This is not a man the Guildmaster we know would send. We are by no means sure the Guildmaster we know is alive. This man is acting and speaking as if he *were* Guildmaster."

Looks passed among his security. Timani and Adaro had left or, one thought, that name Algini had named and the details Algini referred to might never have come out; the name itself, Gegini, meant nothing to his ears, except it was a name not that uncommon in the Padi Valley.

A new power within the Assassins' Guild, someone his staff knew, and did not favor? Someone Tano and Algini had been tracking in their absence from the world?

The Guild, in new hands?

He had been accustomed to thinking of that Guild

above all others as unassailable in its integrity and unmatched in its outright power. It operated inside every great house on the continent, though its individual members had man'chi to the houses and their lords.

But with power over half the civilized world at issue, clearly anything could change if the side favoring Murini had quietly slipped poison into a teacup. His staff, hedging the secrecy of their own Guild, was giving him strong hints about an entity his space-based staff particularly knew from the inside, in all its hidden parts . . . a name, moreover, that meant something to Banichi and Jago.

"Maybe you should not go down there at all, young gentleman," Bren said directly to Cajeiri, and saw the boy go from wide-eyed absorption of the situation, and a little confusion, to jut-lipped disapproval of the order in a heartbeat. "In the sense that you should preserve a politic distance from me and my doings, young sir, perhaps you should not be here, either."

"Then I should be sitting with mani-ma downstairs," Cajeiri said, "and *she* will not tolerate bad behavior. My bodyguard can escort me down by myself. And no one will stop *me* at the door."

All eyes turned to the paidhi for the ultimate decision in this political arena. And the best advice seemed to come from the eight-year-old.

At least moving Cajeiri downstairs while his staff moved his baggage back to Ilisidi's suite would put him under Cenedi's protection, not to mention Ilisidi's, leaving no trace of the boy's evening sojourn here. Ilisidi in particular was, it always had to be reckoned, an easterner, from that most tenuously attached half of the *aishidi'tat,* and the eastern half of the continent was a force that had to be reckoned with cautiously—very cautiously. In any general upheaval, Ilisidi stood a real chance of being among the few left standing, if her staff could move quickly enough.

"Never mind your coat, young sir. Take mine. Go."

"But—"

"I shall manage, young sir." He shed it, and with his own hands held it out for the boy.

The purple coat was a fair fit, even if Cajeiri was growing broader in the shoulders. Bren took Cajeiri's plain day-wear in its place, a fine coat, nonetheless, a pale green brocade that just happened to be in the Atageini shade, while the purple and red was very well in color key with the Ragi colors: It was dark, it was dramatic, and if the seams held up, it lent a handsome boy an extremely princely look in a time of crisis and threat.

He straightened Cajeiri's collar himself, the servant's role, and looked the boy squarely in the eyes as he did so. "Be canny. Judge the room ever so carefully before you walk in. If Cenedi or Nawari is not at the door, or if things look wrong, come back up the stairs immediately. If things go very wrong down there, and you have to get away, figure to get outside and get back to the window here or upstairs to our door—do not use the servant passages if that has to be the choice: They will surely guard them first. But do not forget the knock. Do not for a moment forget the knock. Do you understand me clearly, young sir?"

"One understands, nand' paidhi." Cajeiri was entirely sober and attentive, young eyes wide and, for the first time, truly frightened.

"If you have to run outdoors," Jago said, "remember there will be other Guild with night-scopes. They can see you in the dark."

"If you must escape, Bren-ji," Banichi said, "escape outside. Never mind the baggage. We will stay by you and the young gentleman."

If things went wrong down there, getting the heir away became a goal worth any risk, any sacrifice, not just for the continuity of Ragi rule on the continent, but for the stability of government that had to deal with the kyo when they arrived—*everything* hung on either Tabini or his son surviving. "You have no other job, if things go badly, young sir, except to use your head and to get yourself to safety. That is how you help your staff, by helping them help you. Go. Quickly now."

The boy cast a look at his own young staff and headed for the door.

And stopped, with a scared look back.

"Defenses are down now," Tano said. "Go."

A quick study. Bren never doubted that. It was why he placed his hopes in the boy.

And if the boy came running hellbent back up here, with Cenedi not where he was supposed to be— all of them might have to take the window route.

"The Guild will have made more than one approach to the house," Banichi said. "There will be the delegation, and observers that we will not see, Jago is quite right. They will likely have been here before the delegation. And possibly within the house."

"As simply so as contacting an amenable Guild agent on a given staff," Jago added, leading one to wonder, not for the first time during the years he had dealt with these particular Guild members, if there were agents who worked directly for the Guild planted in key houses throughout the *aishidi'tat*.

He didn't ask. He had become privy to enough Guild secrets as it was, information that didn't make him confident of their situation at the moment. If, as Banichi hinted, the Guild had just become a player in this game, if the old Guildmaster had gone down, and if rules were all suspended, then what the Guild *could* do was extensive, and extreme, and bloody.

And not on their side. Not even neutral any longer. They could be walking down there to hear a Filing against Tabini. And if that was the case, they had to listen and let these people walk out safely.

Deep breath. He straightened his own queue, which had gotten crushed under his collar. He was, he decided, as dressed as he could get. "Time for us to go," he said, and cast a look at Jago, at Banichi, then at Tano and Algini. "The boy," he said, "nadiin, should anything happen that seems to require it, any one of you take him somewhere, and the rest of us do not ask to know where that would be. We will find one another."

"Yes," Tano said, agreeing to back up Algini, that partnership working together, and that was that, as Bren headed out the door with Banichi and Jago.

Out into an otherwise quiet hallway. The boy had gone downstairs, and at least there was no uproar from below. Bren walked calmly, quietly toward the stairs, with Banichi and Jago, one on each side of him—walked toward what he had asked for, in one sense, with his letter to the Guild—but he very much doubted now that it was what had brought this mission to Tirnamardi.

He took his cue from Banichi and Jago and kept his brain entirely in present tense, in the moment, his eyes scanning recesses and alert to any move. He had one fleeting inner imagination of the Guild officers, inbound, diverting attention with a small dispute at the front door while a different, more stealthy approach came up through the scattered camps—everyone out there, however nervous, would tend to assume that a stranger walking through their camp was just some stranger from an allied village or that an inbound bus weaving its way across the lawn was part of the Dur contingent, never mind that it unloaded heavy weapons among its baggage.

Was he scared at that moment? Oh, not half.

Down the steps next to the foyer, where the workmen who had been hammering away at the doors stood idle amid lumber and their scaffolding, looking confused and doubtful as to whether they ought to take up their work again.

"Have you seen strangers from the Guild, nadiin?" Banichi asked them.

Several hands pointed silently and solemnly toward the drawing room. Bodyguards were no longer in evidence at the door. They had all drawn into the

room, it seemed, indicating a prudent move to protect the lords who held their man'chi not from some
external threat, this time, but from the high officers
of the Guild itself, and some shift in policy that immediately concerned them.

"Come in with me," Bren said, "nadiin-ji."

He started to touch the door, hesitated, just that
heartbeat of doubt, but Banichi and Jago, who were
wired and doubtless reading those devices and signals they had not used in two years, simultaneously
put out hands and opened both the double doors.

It was a dramatic, two-door entrance, to be sure.
Every eye turned. The weapon hand of every bodyguard in the room moved.

And stayed and relaxed, as they recognized him.

Cajeiri had gotten a seat next to his mother. New
arrivals stood in the middle of the half arc of chairs,
men and women in Guild black and silver, a grim, tall
old man who did not look at him, and his two bodyguards, whose gold eyes locked on the intrusion for
one paralytic moment. Smooth as a well-oiled machine and deadly: The older Guild, rarely seen, was
like that.

"Nandi," Bren said, as the old man slowly swung a
look toward him and as one of the old man's guard
looked, machinelike, toward the assembled lords.
That was the address appropriate for a newly arrived
Guild official, and Bren gave a careful, measured
bow to the old man.

"Paidhi-aiji," Tabini said. "Come sit."

That shocked him. Scared him, in fact. Tabini made
a point, made a defiant statement in that invitation,

in fact, in a morass of political quicksand, and with his guard behind him and these Guild strangers in front. Bren felt his heart skip, covered his shock as smoothly as he could, and went to sit where Tabini pointed, as servants managed to insert a chair between Tabini and the dowager.

Don't do this, he would have fervently advised Tabini. Don't make statements that you might have to deny before sunrise. But one did not hesitate at the aiji's order, not when it was so deliberately, so knowingly given.

Cajeiri, he noted, kept a stone face to the whole proceedings. The boy's chair was on his mother's left, between her and the Ajuri, and Cajeiri's two young guards stood behind his chair as if they were Guild— if there was anyone in the room whose position was less enviable than the paidhi-aiji's, it had to be those two brave youngsters, facing senior Guild who would take a dim view of anyone intruding on Guild prerogatives.

Bren sat. He did not turn his head to see, but a faint sound declared Banichi and Jago were taking their positions behind his chair.

A minor disruption. "We have begun inquiry into the Ragi clan request," the old Guildsman resumed his statement. "We have come here to gather evidence."

"One comes damned late, nandi." From Tabini. And in no conciliatory tone. "Honest members of your own guild are dead in this delay."

"We are here at the *right* time," the old man said in a soft voice, and his golden eyes shifted subtly until they stared straight at Bren, cold and terrible. That gaze went on to Ilisidi, and last of all to Tatiseigi, on Ilisidi's far side. "You have called Council, nandi," the old man said at last, directly to Tatiseigi. "You claim a complaint against a neighboring clan. You have appealed to the Guild. We are here."

"I have a justified complaint!" Tatiseigi said, rising with more alacrity than the old gentleman usually managed. "Damage to these premises, a national treasure. Kadagidi have attacked non-Guild on our land, when we have done them no injury at all! You have seen the ruin of our foyer!"

"The Kadagidi likewise have a complaint against the Atageini," the Guildsman said, "in your fomenting rebellion and dissent against the aiji who now sits in Shejidan."

"They *dare* say so!" Tatiseigi fairly frothed at the mouth. "There was absolutely no cause for this assault, less for the damage to a historic house! We were at no time involved in any political cause, nor has our clan!"

"You host the former aiji. This is provocative."

"Think twice," Tabini said ominously. "Murini does not exist. And *we* visit this house in the name of the *aishidi'tat,* which is not dissolved, and which does not release the Guild from its contract. Show me any signing to the contrary."

The Guildsman's mouth opened, his brows contracted, and then, perhaps, perhaps—what he would have said failed to find exit. "We do not carry such papers about. And the Ragi lord's claim to Sheijidan has been judged by the citizenry of Shejidan, judged and dismissed."

"We have no need for debate," Tabini said. "But while this house keeps records, we will state our position. Kadagidi have attacked my underage son, tried to visit murder on this house, of another clan, and *we* intervened while the Guild sat paralyzed and debating in Shejidan over decrees from a Kadagidi who has no authority, no man'chi, and lacks the mandate."

"He has the mandate," the answer snapped back.

"He has called the legislature. Have they assembled?"

The Ajuri's information. Tabini committed them all on a dice roll.

And Guild silence met that question, for at least three heartbeats.

"Equal evidence exists on either side," the Guildsman said, lines deepening around his mouth. "No one will move from current positions tonight. No attack, no retreat. We are here officially to make Guild judgment, in response to a request from the Atageini lord, and we demand lodgings." This, swinging his gaze from Tabini to Tatiseigi. "This is a demand, nand' Tatiseigi."

"You are our guests," Tatiseigi said, not happily, and waved a hand at the desperate servant staff, namely the major domo standing by the inner door. "The green suite," he said.

The old major domo came close and bent down to his lord's ear to whisper a protest, but he managed perhaps two words before Tatiseigi cut him off with, "The Ajuri will still take the east." In a furious not-quite-whisper, and with a wave of his hand at a sec-

ond, anguished protest. "Move my grandson somewhere, beneficent gods! He is a minor child!"

It was an ungraceful moment; it embarrassed the
old lord, who was not coping well with the situation.
The displacement was a family embarrassment, the
Ajuri were already unhappy, but perhaps not so unhappy as Ilisidi, and the Guild was not a comfortable
neighbor to anyone.

"They may have my room, great-uncle," Cajeiri
said in his high, distinctive voice, "since I am moving
in with Great-Grandmother."

"He is perfectly welcome," Ilisidi said frostily,
"since this visitor is so arrogant as to make demands
the aiji of Shejidan himself would scruple to make on
a historic and damaged house. He has interrupted
our supper with his demands, he has tracked sawdust
on the floor, he has been inconvenient, inconsiderate
and *late!* He brings no documentation, he begins his
investigations in the dark of night, and he disrespects
his host . . ."

That alone, echoing in the lofty ceiling, accompanied by the sharp crack of Ilisidi's cane for emphasis,
created a stir in the room, and at that very moment,
piling confusion dangerously atop disorganization,
an entirely new party arrived through the double
doors, escorted in by a handful of Taibeni rangers and
a cluster of young men in an unlikely mix of worn
hunting gear and lordly dress and casuals.

The center of the arriving commotion, hurried
along by this unlikely guard, was a frail and elderly
gentleman, his queue half undone and his white hair
wisping about his beaming face.

Grigiji, Astronomer Emeritus, blithely ignored the glowering Guild, ignored Tabini-aiji as if he had seen him not half an hour ago, and his face lit in thorough, undisguised, childlike delight as his eyes discovered Bren and the dowager.

"Ah, dowager-ji! One was absolutely sure you would be here! We saw the ship from the little telescope. My students informed me, we informed the aiji, of course—" A little bow toward Tabini. "And we came here as fast as we could. How was the voyage? Have you brought data for us?"

Bren rose desperately in a hall not his own, and gave a little bow, trying to manage the situation with this good old man before Guild indignation unraveled everything. "The dowager has brought back the most astounding things, nand' Astronomer." No lie at all, but with that lure, he had gained the Astronomer Emeritus' absolute attention, and was aware simultaneously the hostile Guild was hearing all of it—not with the same delight that shone in the old court Astronomer's face, and possibly to very different political effect. He aggressively expanded on his statement. "We have documents. The mission was an unqualified success. The danger to the *aishidi'tat* is much abated—but grown complex."

"Indeed," Ilisidi said.

The Guild, meanwhile, stood clearly upstaged in its own moment.

"A chair for the Astronomer," Tatiseigi said meaningfully, but in vain, as Grigiji moved to pay a bow to Ilisidi, to exchange a few pleasantries, and only then meandered on to Tabini and Damiri, all as if he were at some social gathering—and knowing Grigiji, one could think perhaps that great and childlike mind had quite missed the significance of the Guild presence: They weren't people he knew, and Bren held his breath for fear the old man would wander on and introduce himself to them. The Guild for its part was thoroughly insulted, no doubt of it, and they glowered at the major domo who had let the Astronomer in, and who attempted, in the small lull, to inform the Guildsmen where they might lodge.

The Guild senior muttered something ungracious. Then in a voice that suddenly carried over all the chaos: "We are here to observe, and what we observe we will take into account, nandiin. Where we wish information, we will ask it. We may and we may not proceed to formal hearing on your question."

With which the Guildsmen turned and walked out, a black clot of ill will, in a silence still quivering with those deep tones.

The doors shut, hard, with no one to manage them.

"Well," said Grigiji, "well." With those perpetually astonished eyes. He was out of breath, windblown, so frail-looking his physical body seemed faded. The life that was in him burned through, all the same, like a star through the fear the Guild had brought in, while his students dispersed about the peripheries of the hall as his bodyguard. These youths, of various social classes, in various shades of dust and informality of dress, mingled with frowning Guildsmen all about the hall. Grigiji's bodyguard: His students, a motley group of gangling collegiates, but far more martial were his second escort of graceful, silent Taibeni, with their personal armament of hunting rifles and knives. "Those gentlemen seem rather out of countenance, do they not?"

"One doubts," Tabini said dryly, "that they depart more disturbed than they arrived."

"Ha," Ilisidi said, leaning on her cane. "Very welcome termination of that sorry display. Bravely done, Gri-ji."

"Very dangerously done," Lord Tatiseigi muttered. "And under my roof!"

"Pish! Wisely handled, Tati-ji, wisely and deftly managed. Nand' Bren, *very* deftly done."

"Nand' dowager." Bren managed a bow and sank back into his chair, wishing he were back upstairs, and far from confident he had been at all wise to drop that information into the pool.

"But where are these records you name?" the Astronomer asked. "Might we see them?"

"In due time, nand' Astronomer," Tabini said, getting to his feet. "A staff meeting may be in order at this point, to bring everyone up to the moment. Will any of your young gentlemen choose to attend, nand' Astronomer?"

Staff meeting. Almost universally Guild staff, that was the irony—a meeting regarding the deadly presence that had entered their midst, with events and perhaps other Assassins subtly percolating through the countryside, all aiming here, at Tabini. And new information in the mix: the non-appearance of legislators summoned to the capital, the claim of these three Guild officers to an authority the validity of which no outsider to their Guild had the means to determine. The whole business had the ominous tension of a landslide just on the verge, and at least the Astronomer's students, not being as unworldly as the Astronomer, all looked worried at their inclusion in that suggestion.

"Aiji-ma," the senior of that lot said, bowing his head, while Kadiyi of Ajuri clan moved close for a word with his niece, Damiri casting up a worried, frowning glance at that whispering.

Bren sucked in a deep breath and cast a look to his own right, where Banichi loomed; not a word had he had from Banichi or Jago, although he was sure they had observations.

The Atageini and the aiji's guard had fortified a line out there with buses and trucks and farmers with hunting rifles but clearly that wasn't how the greatest threat had come to them. It had come up as three men at their door, answering a letter, and demanding to spend the night under their roof, right in the heart of their defenses.

And they still weren't that sure of the men around Tabini.

"Are we to have supper at all?" the older Ajuri lord asked petulantly, amid all this. "Are we finally to be served the rest of our supper at some time this evening, respecting the noble efforts of your poor cook, nandi?"

The very thought of food turned Bren's stomach.

But on the other hand having dinner was a practical notion. It fortified them against the night. It flew the banner of the completely ordinary in the face of that arrogant intrusion. It gave staffs time to confer without lordly interference. Tatiseigi, appearing quite glad to have the distraction from present dangers, gathered himself up and said yes, they should resume their dinner, and in short order, too—the new arrivals were to have a cold supper sent to their quarters.

By Tatiseigi's tone, one had the feeling the supper offering might not be much beyond bread and cold sausages—a gesture of hospitality only, since even the paidhi could guess that the Guild on a mission would be very little likely to trust the house cuisine. One decidedly didn't want them near the kitchens, the other alternative, letting them observe down there.

No. Not at all a good idea, Bren thought. One wanted those three shut in their quarters, not stirring out, and one very much doubted they remotely had that intention . . . except to the degree they had agents slipping about in the bushes, while their officers diverted attention to themselves.

It seemed, in that light, a good moment for the paidhi, excluded from the dinner invitation, to retreat and consult. Bren got up quietly and slipped to the doorward side of the room, Banichi and Jago with him. They opened the door. He turned, bowed—no one showed interest—and left, entrusting Cajeiri to his great-grandmother and Tabini to his own devices.

"Come," Jago said quietly once that door was shut and they stood outside, amid a very small scattering of other Guild. "We should go back upstairs, nandi, where we have some control over the perimeter."

The operationally dual we, with the -ta, the numerical compensator, as if *she* were going with him, but as if Banichi were not.

Staff meeting, Tabini had said, but Bren had a terrible suspicion, given the businesslike frown on Jago's face, that what happened next could be far more active than a debate. People could die, right in the meeting, by way of a vote. And he had no doubt at all there were Guild out on the grounds, if not already inside the house. They might have begun to lose this battle without most of the house knowing they were in it.

But what could he say, out here in front of witnesses? "Yes," he said, and to Banichi, with a lingering look, "Take utmost care, Banichi-ji."

"Always," Banichi said smoothly, and Jago brushed a gesture against Bren's shoulder—move now, that meant. Go.

No arguments. No choice at all.

# 5

It was quick passage up the stairs, back to Bren's own rooms, where Jago's patterned knock drew a sound of soft footsteps from inside. Tano answered the door and let them in. Algini waited, gun drawn, at the end of the foyer. That gun slipped quickly back into its holster.

But a rapid set of hand-signals passed between Jago, Tano, and Algini, while Bren stood in the foyer thinking quite desperately what he could possibly do to help them.

He found no practical use for himself in what was going on apace—he did catch the signal that meant going downstairs, which might be Jago reporting Banichi's going down into the workings of Lord Tatiseigi's house, down to the guard stations and other establishments. But there was another sign that meant hostile movement, and they signed understanding, agreement.

Then Jago did a curious thing. She went into the room, retrieved his computer from its hiding place, and set it on the table.

Maybe there was a use for him. Bren went to oversee this handling of an instrument so precious to their affairs. She meaningfully drew back a chair in front of the machine and signalled Tano and Algini to come over.

Bren sat down and silently brought up the typing function, keying over to Ragi as Jago drew up a second chair beside him.

She drew the machine over into range and typed, for the two looking over her shoulder, perhaps most of all for his benefit: *Gegini has arrived with two of his lieutenants, claiming to speak for the Guild regarding a letter from this household. There will be others outside who have not made themselves evident.*

Algini and Tano, reading over her shoulder, assumed a grim look—Bren flung a glance in their direction, then looked again at the screen, where Jago had typed quickly:

*The old Guildmaster should have sent. Clearly he has not. Either he is dead or this is an unauthorized mission, attempting to claim authority over us. Gegini is a Padi Valley man, Madi clan. He is here acting as if he were Guildmaster.*

That was a small clan, attached—Bren raked his years-ago memory—to the Ragi on one hand, to the Taibeni and to the Kadagidi by blood and marriage. This Gegini, a name he had never heard, was a man with ties in all directions; a dangerous man, if disposed to be—and acting as if he were Guildmaster? To his experience, that entity never admitted his identity, never advertised his office—he permitted no likeness, gave no interviews, wore no identifying badge, and carried no special credentials. So rumor said of an individual only other Guild could identify, by signs outsiders didn't know.

*Atageini Guild reports numerous things. The vote for the Guild to act to overthrow an aiji requires a two-thirds majority, and it was reported to the Guild that the coup against Tabini-aiji was an accomplished fact, and that he was dead. When it was reported within a few hours that he was alive, the Guild should have moved in his support. It did not act. When it was proposed the Guild should throw Murini out of Shejidan, there was a vote on the question, which legally should not have happened, since it falsely supposed that the two-thirds majority rule was needed to overthrow Murini under those circumstances. It was a clever move, calling the vote that way, and calling on short notice. We and the dowager's staff and Lord Geigi's were absent in space. Others who would have voted for intervention were at Malguri and on the coast. Atageini Guild were not notified at all, except to send proxies, who were not properly instructed as to the question. The aiji's staff, half of whom were dead and should not have been counted, were counted, along with the living members of that staff, as wilfully absent. Several other large contingents were called back by attacks aimed at their interests.*

"*God,*" Bren said finally—sure that his staff had known this much from Lord Geigi's staff before they ever left the station—everything but the bits that involved Tabini: Those had likely dropped into the pot here, only filling out the scandal. The Guild never talked about its private business, he wasn't entirely sure any lord downstairs had heard the half of it, and he was sure he was reading this now only because his staff was dangerously willing to breach Guild silence. Maybe it was because he was human, maybe it was *because* he didn't twitch to the same instincts or have a wide and entangled man'chi.

Maybe it was because there was nowhere he could even accidentally pass such deadly secrets . . . secrets deadly to public confidence in the Guild itself, if this shameful business leaked.

God, did they possibly want *his* advice what to do, the head of their own Guild having proved unable to stop this?

It went on.

*The meeting hour was moved up and proxies did not arrive until the vote was over. Two of Lord Geigi's house were killed on the way, and no one has heard from the Guildmaster since the hour of the vote. The rumor in this house is that he is dead. This has been the state of affairs since the day after the attack on the aiji's household.*

No wonder his staff had gone about with very grim faces.

Jago typed: *Now Gegini has made his first public move, coming here as if he were Guildmaster. We believe he is no more than Murini's agent, and that any vote in the Guild that he has had a hand in is no legitimate vote. His presence here is ostensibly in response to the gathering and to the letters. By coming here and taking a hand as judge, he is effectively calling himself Guildmaster, and since no one knows the face or the age of the Guildmaster, no one but Guild can contradict him. We, along with the Atageini, suspect the old Guildmaster has died or is under duress.*

A thought leaped to mind. Bren reached for the computer and slid it back. He typed: *Have the Atageini Guild told their lord these things? And are not the Ajuri in effect a part of the Kadagidi Association? Are they possibly here as Gegini's allies?*

Jago slid the machine back to her section of table. *As for the Atageini staff, they have said little to their lord.*

With good reason. Tatiseigi, honest old man, would have exploded and thrown Gegini off his doorstep when he showed up, putting the fat well and truly into the fire.

*The Ajuri position is ambiguous and cannot be comfortable at this moment, if indeed the Ajuri Guildsmen have informed their lord. It was clear that Tabini-aiji places some confidence in the information the Ajuri brought him, and it did not seem to be information known to Gegini. That may have embarrassed him.*

Tabini's citing Kadiyi's information about the legislature in rebellion. In retrospect, throwing that information onto the table assumed the character of a major risk—though it did appear to have scored, when Tabini had used it . . . as if perhaps Gegini's information was not as thorough or as free-flowing as he might have thought.

He snagged the computer back again. *Tabini used Kadiyi's information, seeming to rely on it. It appeared to hit unexpectedly. Is it possible the Ajuri in coming here and delivering this news are representing a hith-*

erto silent segment of the Kadagidi Association itself, and signaling possible opposition to Murini within his own clan?

Back to Jago, rapidly. *We have attempted to find such indications in these events, but the Ajuri Guildsmen are close-mouthed and large-eyed.*

A proverb meaning they said nothing useful and were nosy in the extreme, poking into household business.

*But we are speculating in all this,* Jago wrote.

In writing his letter of appeal to the Guild, he had thought he knew who he was writing to. He had assumed a true impartiality on the part of the Guild and Banichi and Jago had never warned him otherwise. He slid the machine back: *Did you know these things when you aided my sending the letter?*

She typed, *It was useful, though risky. For the record, it signaled a willingness of your faction to talk with Guild leadership. This was a valuable move.*

*Valuable.* He was utterly aghast, for half a breath, that his staff had let him make a critical and dangerous move, and not informed him that he might be writing to a dead man, and asking Tatiseigi to send a provocative letter under his seal.

Then he recalled Guild strictures, Guild secrecy, which it was worth their lives and his to breach. The wonder was that they were telling him the truth now. Something major had shifted, notably when Gegini had shown up on the doorstep, notably when that letter had stirred a response out of their enemy.

*Banichi has gone to talk to house security,* Jago typed, *and to any domestic staff who has gone down to the basement, of which there may be no few—a flood of persons wanting to exchange information between staffs, one suspects. We let the letter go out because it is a step that should have been taken, legally. Gegini attempts to use it as a key to Tatiseigi's door, and a way onto his grounds. If Murini was ambitious—so is Gegini. No one ever proclaims himself as Guildmaster in public . . . the Guildmaster only comes and goes, and we know, but not even the aiji knows for certain. That power exists in secret. It supports the aiji. It is not only the hasdrawad and the tashrid that vote on the succession, Bren-nandi.*

Dammit. Dammit to bloody hell. He had the notion that the word *Gegini* had informed Tano and Algini instantly of everything they had to fear.

Hell—maybe more than Jago herself or Banichi knew, when they had come down here. Tano and Algini had spent the last two years up on the station where they could monitor what was happening on the mainland, if not communicate back and forth with any freedom. They had *known* what was going on before they even boarded the shuttle to come with him . . . they had known at least whatever Geigi's staff could get from their estate down on the coast . . .

No, but the dish had gone down with the coup. Mogari-nai had stopped transmitting, and all the orbiting station had had to go on was Yolanda Mercheson's translation of the illicit radio traffic back and forth across the straits. There was no way Guild business could get through that filter, no way Yolanda, of all people, was going to get that kind of confidence.

So Tano and Algini—and all Geigi's staff, for that

matter—hadn't known; had likely known enough that they'd burned to get down here and find out, and any opposition to Murini had taken to the hills along with Tabini.

Like that staff his own didn't trust.

God, there were a thousand questions he wanted to ask his staff in a give and take fashion, not this pecking at keys—but with Gegini's crew ensconced in the building, and likely more conversant in Mosphei' than he would wish, there seemed no—

"Jago-ji," he said, and launched into kyo, a language it was absolutely certain only those of them who had been in far space understood—and Tano and Algini were not themselves in that company. "Say."

Her eyes sparkled. Kyo took a moment or two of mental adjustment. A deep breath, a refocus. Then: "They come to make war inside the house. Remove Tabini, the dowager, the heir and you, all at one time. No Tabini, no opposition. All this gathering dissolves. This man rules. Even Murini will not be safe in his bed."

Their collective command of kyo was not that deep: they had had only weeks to gather vocabulary. But it served. And in a handful of words, he had the finishing touches on the whole disturbing picture.

Jago then went back to typing, specifically for Tano and Algini. *We must prepare for assault inside the house. The question is whether we shall take this opportunity to remove Gegini. He knows he is taking that chance, which is a point in favor of his survival: There is even the chance he is buttering both sides of*

*his bread and hoping to test his power if he should
shift to Tabini-aiji and let Murini fall. He will be reading the tides of public opinion. What the aiji said about
the legislative disaffection has given Gegini pause.
This may cause him to attempt to contact and check
his associates on the grounds. We must not misjudge
such movements.*

Bren shot her a look. Jago, offering mitigating
opinions on this villain? He doubted it . . . though
hers was a profession which routinely thought the
unthinkable, did the undefendable, simply because it
was, in the service of some house or other, reasonably
practical. The Jago who shared his bed and the Jago
who defended him could not be divorced from one
another, but he had the most queasy thought that he
had let himself slip into a reality of his own devising
in that regard, that he *did* not understand what was
going on within his own staff. Would they support this
man, if he turned coat yet again?

"I am doubtful," he said in kyo, and Jago looked at
him—looked at him with what an outsider might
judge as no expression at all, but which he saw very
keenly: it was Jago completely on guard, Jago following the essentially ruthless line of thought that her
Guild required. It was Jago as scary as hell in that
moment, and he thought it was probably time for a
wise lord to shut up, go read a book, and let his staff
operate in their own way, bloodshed and all—it was
beyond talk. They were in operational mode now,
where the paidhi had absolutely no useful function
except to stay alive.

Misjudge Gegini's movements. That had a lot of

meanings, too, not just that Jago thought they might have been wanting in charity toward the man. It might mean Jago was worried she *didn't* know what the man was up to—a usurper in her own Guild, someone senior and clever enough to have taken out the Guildmaster.

Now, indeed, if Murini, under the threat of their return, was weakening, who knew what Gegini was up to in coming here, or even if—God help him, the brain had to spin in circles, dealing with the Guild—Gegini might be unwilling to support an ephemeral candidate. Who knew whose hand was steering this thing, or whether there was another lord waiting in the wings, ready to doublecross everyone? Clearly his own staff had a lot to think through.

Algini threw off a flurry of handsigns. Jago signed back.

It was not right. It just was not right. His staff was attempting to maneuver in an increasingly cramped set of alternatives, and assets—assets which were unusable, except with the risk of an ungodly amount of bloodshed.

Risk. Hell.

He snatched the computer. *If I went out on the steps tonight, if I went among the crowd and told them what we have to tell them, we could stir popular opinion, and maybe tilt the balance, if one is in question.*

A quick, signed negative. Emphatic.

He typed: *If I have any use in the world, Jago-ji, if I came back to any advantage, it rests within that computer. Tabini-aiji finds it inconvenient to hear my report. I do not understand why he refuses me. But perhaps the details may still help his case and explain things to the crowd out there. If they collectively petitioned the Guild—*

Second sign. Negative. Jago drew the computer back forcefully and typed: *If the aiji hears you first, he cannot then swear that he does not know the content of the report nor had a hand in it. You will clearly bring this document to the tashrid yourself, with the full case to lay out for them in your own name, on the aiji's behalf.*

*Legislative* rules. A petitioner—Tabini—could not influence evidence to be presented before the legislature, not without greatly diminishing its value.

My God, he thought. He knew the rule. But himself, not Tabini, to stand and present the case for Tabini's argument against Murini? The master manipulator, Tabini, intended to bring his controversial human adviser right to the center of the debate, and let him give his report there, where they probably had enough Filings against him to paper these walls?

Jago had drawn that conclusion, at least, and if she was right, then Tabini had made up his mind to that course the moment he had gotten the staff reports from the dowager. The stunning announcement, maximum controversy—the appearance of himself—in the capital, in the Bujavid, which at present was under Murini's control . . .

How in hell were they going to pull that off?

"How, precisely," he began aloud, all he needed to say, and Jago typed:

*This will have to be finessed.*

Finessed. That lethal word. His fingers began to go

numb, that sign of blood rushing to brain and body core. Oxygen seemed short even so, and he rubbed his fingertips together to remind himself of his physical body, so deep his dive into intellect and hypothesis. He recalled his own apartment in the Bujavid with such vividness he could see the pattern in the porcelains, the details of his own bedroom, the central hall, the foyer with its little filigree basket beside the entry . . .

If there were messages waiting for him in that bowl, what would they say?

Traitor?

Foreigner, go home?

Your fault, paidhi, all the loss of lives?

The destruction of our traditions, our values, our way of life?

The outer halls, then, the residencies, marble halls with priceless antique carpets and room for the old families, the old houses, in all those suites of rooms— into whose midst Tabini-aiji had installed him—*him,* asking more and more from him. Tabini had lifted his human adviser out of his old modest apartment with the garden door, down across from the aiji's cook, the aiji's secretaries . . . the rank paidhiin had always held in the aiji's court.

Years ago, the aiji had elevated not only him, but the chain of contact he represented, to a dizzying preeminence in the court, a preeminence that had gotten higher and higher, until it greatly offended essential supporters—

Until it at last fractured the *aishidi'tat* and he had now to preside over what might become a catastrophe, one to equal the War of the Landing?

What was he supposed to do now? Stay alive long enough to bring his case before a legislature the majority of whom, even if denying support to Murini, sincerely wished him and his influence in the aiji's family to fall, so that they could start warring among themselves?

"Does Banichi think this, too?" he asked in kyo, which drew a blank look from Tano and Algini, but not from Jago.

"Yes," she said firmly, with that fire in her eye that said somehow, perhaps in code passed hand in hand, she and Banichi had already agreed on measures.

Something was moving then, and maybe moving fast, and it was high time he took himself out of his staff's way. He got up, left the computer to Jago, if she might need it.

But he saw now a flurry of handsigns between Jago and Tano and Algini, most of which he couldn't read—they involved the windows and the baggage, he thought, but he couldn't be sure.

What shall I do? he asked himself. If we start a fight—God, what am I supposed to do? All those people on the lawn, all Tabini's man'chi . . . if they lose a fight here . . . if somehow something happens to Tabini—

"Yes," Algini said aloud, in answer to Jago's sign, and went to the console, flipped a switch, went to the window, opened it onto the dark, and threw a leg over the sill.

There's no foothold, Bren thought in alarm, wondering what possible good it could do for Algini to hang out the window—but he didn't hang: he vanished straight down into the dark with a mechanical whirr, leaving only a silver hook embedded in Tatiseigi's woodwork and a taut metal line cutting a nasty gouge in the painted wood.

Jago walked over and matter-of-factly picked the hook loose and tossed it out, returning it, presumably, to Algini, who was now, equally presumably, safe on the ground below.

What in hell are we about to do? Bren asked himself, concluded that Algini was in considerable personal danger loose on the grounds, and hoped that he was only on his way to Banichi for personal discussion.

He concluded that, and wished he knew for sure. Tano looked worried about his partner, as if he wished he were out there, and would give anything to follow him. But Tano dutifully sat down at the little black box's console and adjusted a com-plug in his ear, keeping up with things on a communications network which no one now dared use—presumably.

Bren cast Jago a look, wanting explanation, and Jago just folded the computer up, slipped it into its case, and handed the case over to him—more than handed it over: slipped the strap onto his shoulder. Keep up with it, that was to tell him, without saying anything that listeners might pick up. She was through typing and through discussing.

Damn, he thought. He went and sat down out of the way with the computer on his lap, and Jago paced the floor, not consciously so, perhaps, but she kept moving between Tano's console and the vicinity of the bath.

Something was damned sure happening, and he feared it wasn't just a meeting with Banichi and Cenedi.

If our staff gives these high-ranking Guildsmen the slip, he thought, it's going to be a professional embarrassment to some very dangerous people. A career embarrassment.

It's going to be war, out there.

He got up, still with the computer strap on his shoulder, and stayed out of Jago's path, not even making eye contact with her while she was thinking and watching over Tano's shoulder. He went to the cabinet where he had stowed his pistol, his ammunition, and his pills. A breeze blew in from the open, unbarriered window as he stuffed his pockets. His warmer coat, to his regret, was with the servants. The heavy pistol made the dress coat hang oddly, and he told himself that one of these days he was going to have to have to get a holster for the thing before he shot himself in some embarrassing and fatal spot.

On his next trip to the Island he would do that. Better than having it customed over here ... not that personal apparel wasn't always handmade on this side of the water. It was the patterns, the proportions. He'd get a half dozen warm coats when he got back to the Island. Some gloves. That was one of the hardest things, getting human-proportioned gloves ...

Gloves, for God's sake. His mind, if he let it work, wandered helplessly in the dark outside the house, wondering what Algini was doing and where he was—he was their demolitions expert, if one had to assign Algini a speciality: Tano for electronics, Algini for blowing things up, and while he worried, Tano was sitting over there listening to something he wished he could hear. From time to time Tano and Jago traded handsigns, both of them privy to that information flow, as he wasn't.

He slipped back to his chair and sat down, arranging his coat as he did so, putting the computer down beside his chair, the gun in his pocket and that pocket arranged for a quick reach. He sat and waited. And watched that dark window.

Tano signed to Jago, who came and took his place at the console while Tano went and delved into their baggage, and pulled out a particularly nasty automatic with several clips of ammunition in a shoulder loop.

Bren watched that, too, still not moving or offering comment, as Tano simply walked down their little entry hall and left them.

It was just him and Jago now. Just him and Jago, and Jago now had all her attention focused on that little console. Once she interrupted her attention to make a sign he knew: Banichi. Just that, for his benefit.

Was Banichi in trouble? Was that why Tano had armed himself and left? No. If it were Banichi in trouble, Jago was his partner. Was it Algini who had run into a problem? Whatever was going on, he knew his security would be far more efficient if both teams were whole—and Jago couldn't leave *him*, dammit to hell.

He couldn't stand the waiting. He got up from his chair, taking his computer with him, and stood near Jago, who gave him another sign, one he raked his brain to remember. It was, perhaps, the sign for *all our people lying still.* Or the one for *stealth.*

An explosion rocked the floor underfoot, a shock into his very bones, that made him stagger and grab for the gun in his pocket.

"Quickly," Jago said, and left the chair, grabbed the computer from him, grabbed a rifle and an ammunition belt from the baggage in the corner, and motioned him toward the outer door.

He went. He seized the computer from her as they hit the hall, headed for the stairs.

Down, then, down the public stairway as fast as he could manage it, which was far less fast than Jago could have done it, but he was only a little to the rear as they hit the main floor and met a gaggle of alarmed staff, all asking what it had been and whether a boiler had blown up.

Jago grabbed his arm and hauled him away from Tatiseigi's people, ignoring their questions, pulling him toward the lower stairs. They went down again, down to a pale stucco hall, plainly lit, punctuated by a long series of doors, some open—servants' territory, the underbelly of the stately home. He thought they would go to one of those rooms and find Banichi, but Jago jogged right past all such choices, down the whole length of the hall. "Outside," she said, not even out of breath, as they reached a short stairway. It led up again, to an exterior security door, the sort that was usually alarmed.

It was ajar at the moment, with a rock holding it open. A sliver of night showed at its edge before Jago elbowed that door open, and they exited into the dark, the two of them, emerging right by the end of the hedge and the newly restored stable fence.

Jago turned right, along the side of the house by the hedge-rimmed path, and onto the floodlit drive, where the buses had cleared back a little and rendered themselves a wall of defense.

Beyond that next hedge, across the drive, was the Taibeni camp and their mecheiti—that was where he thought they were going, but Jago drew him left, along the row of buses, passing one after the other.

Off to the distant left, an engine coughed to life, down toward the meadow. The plane, he thought. Rejiri.

His breath came hard now, and the light and shadow jolted and jagged in his blurring vision. They ran along the drive, weaving through the crowd that had gathered, and dodging more questions: "What happened at the house? Was it the Kadagidi?"

It had not been the Kadagidi attacking, he was sure of that. It was most likely the Guild they were fighting, and God and Jago only knew what they were running from or to. Blood had been spilled, possibly to get them out of the house—and to get Tabini out, he hoped above all else, all their lives depending on that one life. He was sure whatever was going on, staff was communicating, Jago doing exactly what she and Banichi had agreed had to be done . . .

She dived among the trees, then drew him past the tail ends of two buses and a truck, and into full shadow and brush, then past a thorn thicket. He hoped to stop just there and catch his breath.

No such luck. Jago kept going at a steady jog, seizing him by the arm as the going got rough. She kept him moving and directed him deep among the trees of the little decorative copse.

"I can follow you," he gasped, out of breath. "Go, Jago-ji."

No question, no protest from her. She trusted him to run, and kept going.

Meanwhile the plane buzzed over their heads, headed south.

*South.* Toward the heart of the country.

That would be Tabini, he hoped, Tabini, and maybe it was the prevailing wind that indicated south rather than east. Maybe the plane would turn, veering off to the mountains, to safety. Rejiri would do anything in his power to keep the symbol of their resistance safe, but that plane only held three people at most, and that meant if Damiri was in that third seat, no body-guard was going with them—safest, maybe.

Or a decoy? Was Tabini somewhere out in these woods, running the way they were running?

His legs ached. His side ached, breath a knife in his ribs, and still Jago kept jogging on in near silence, repositioning both of them to some refuge, it might be—someplace to wait for the rest of the team. He could hardly hear past his own breathing, and beyond them rose a tumult of shouted questions in the drive-way, compounded with the bawling of mecheiti across the hedges. He was all but blind in the dark. Atevi hearing and atevi eyesight guided them, and he kept in Jago's tracks, trusting her utterly.

After that one explosion there had not been one intimation of hostile action in return. What proceeded, proceeded stealthily beneath the confusion of the general assemblage, stealthy as his and Jago's exit from the building, their dive aside into this grove of ancient trees.

She stopped near the edge of the copse, the farther meadow and part of the line of buses visible through the trees, and there she stood listening. Bren found himself a tree to lean against, fought to quiet his breathing, and not to cough or move at all, rustling about the leaf litter. The least sound might mask any untoward approach she was listening for. There might be any number of Guild Assassins loose out here. And here he stood in a pale, easily-seen court coat, trying to blend in with the trees. The shirt he wore underneath the coat was no better. He wished he'd at least stolen the bedspread. A curtain. Anything to wrap in, to mask the pallor of his skin and his dress.

A soft chirr sounded, off in the brush. Jago answered it. A moment later, a shadow slipped like a soft breeze through the woods and joined them. Tano, then another shadow: Algini, Bren was sure—he was vastly relieved to find them safe, but he was greatly concerned when another moment failed to produce Banichi. He dared not say a thing or ask a question, least of all to Jago.

Suddenly he felt a heavy leather jacket whipped between him and the tree, enveloping his shoulders in its protective darkness. A push at his arm, a signal to move, and he hitched the strap of the computer high on his shoulder, hooked his free arm into the black coat, and struggled not to lose it in the brush as he ducked and followed Jago, Tano, and Algini behind him. The coat was warm, hot, even, in the general chill of night air. It weighed like lead, which it all but was—body armor against a stray shot, and his having it around his shoulders meant one of his team was working without protection at the moment.

Their course through the edge of the trees veered more and more toward the right, until they paralleled the end of the cobbled drive, where it became the unpaved road from the west gate.

Questions welled up, all but choking him, life and death questions about Tabini's welfare, about Banichi, about Ilisidi and Cajeiri, and others' whereabouts, after that groundshaking explosion—and he dared not distract his bodyguard with chatter. Were there other Assassins actively on their trail? Was Banichi coming? He hoped Tabini had been in that plane, that it had eventually banked toward the east, toward the long meadows near the mountains, where a plane could land.

Or maybe Rejiri would fly his passenger all the way west to Dur, which had hiding places aplenty, not to mention boats—or with that plane, he could even fly Tabini to Mospheira, where a shuttle crew was prepping for a return flight to the station: He had never proposed that course of action to Tabini—he had never had the chance to pose it as a choice. But Tabini surely knew that he would be safe to go to Mospheira, that he would have a welcome there from President Tyers, and he had surely gathered from the dowager that the shuttle was waiting there on an airstrip. If Tabini got up to the station, he had Lord Geigi and all the atevi aloft to rally around him, and the radio to make contact with his supporters on the ground, with Mospheiran help. If Tabini got up there and took power, there was no way in all the world for his enemies to reach him, ever, and he would be there to meet any trouble that came . . .

But it seemed to him now that the noise of that plane had tailed off into the distance, still on a south-ward course.

South, toward Shejidan.

Chilling. Blood-chilling.

And he knew Tabini's disposition, that running from a fight was the last thing Tabini would ordinarily choose. Tabini had run from Taiben coastward only when he'd been hit by surprise and had no choice. He'd had his chance then to cross the straits to Mospheira and gain help from the heavens.

Clear enough that he wouldn't do it this time, either.

# 6

They waited in the woods, in a small parcel of dark—himself, Jago, Tano, and Algini, who breathed or moved gently, nothing more. They stayed isolated from the larger, noisier dark out on the road, where voices disputed in high passion, vehicle doors slammed, and mecheiti groaned and protested. The noise of the plane had long vanished, and still the commotion out on the driveway persisted.

A shiver started up again. Bren pressed his hands against his legs, trying to still the tremors—he was cold by now, at least his legs were, while his upper body sweltered under the borrowed bulletproof jacket. He didn't ask where Banichi was, or where Tabini was. He was resolved not to interfere with his bodyguard, no matter what.

But he saw Jago check her watch. That was the most hopeful thing. He saw the shadows that were Algini and Tano do the same, all of them privy to some forthcoming event that the paidhi didn't know, and desperately wished he did.

A soft movement stirred the brush, not the gusting wind, he thought, and he eased his hand past the jacket, into his own coat pocket, where he had the gun and the clip. Clearly his bodyguard had heard that noise, their hearing being far more acute than his.

Bus engines had started up and another near them now coughed to life, momentarily deafening the night. More voices rose from that direction, some sort of excitement or confusion. He couldn't make out the shouted words above the engine noise. He wondered if people were having second thoughts about their gesture of support, if they were going to desert Lord Tatiseigi, or if Tatiseigi himself had had second thoughts about holding out here at Tirnamardi.

No. Hell would freeze over before Tatiseigi abandoned the historic premises to Kadagidi looters.

More and more vehicle engines started, until the racket on the drive drowned their hearing and the lights blinded them to the deeper dark.

A whistle sounded near them then, low and perfectly audible above the noise. Bren's heart leaped up. Jago whistled back, and a shadow joined them.

Banichi was back—Banichi and several other accompanying shadows whose identity Bren didn't guess and didn't venture to ask. Shadow-signals passed, in too dim a light for human eyes, but enough, clearly, for his bodyguard to communicate, possibly even to recognize faces.

And Banichi was safe and had brought reinforcements with him. Thank God.

Might one be Tabini, and the airplane a diversion? None were tall enough.

"Come," Jago said, and a grip on his arm rescued him immediately as he foolishly caught his foot in a root and nearly fell flat on his face. Jago settled the jacket back onto his shoulder. He forged ahead, trying to keep an atevi pace, blind in the dark. Jago, who could see, cued him with pressure on his arm where to dodge an obstacle, steered him through a gap in the hedge where headlamps blazed and trucks and buses loomed up like strange lumpish beasts. Fumes from their engines stung the ordinarily pristine air, hazing the light like fog.

Banichi took the lead of their group, and slipped through the gap between two buses. Headlamps threw him into distinction for a moment. Those few newcomers with him—illumined for the instant in the lights—proved to be Taibeni, and one other who looked like one of Tatiseigi's security staff. Bren sucked in his breath and kept with Jago, moving quickly in the lights and feeling like a pale-skinned prime target as she directed him on Banichi's track, around into the second lane of vehicles.

Banichi had stopped by a bus door, holding the mounting rail and, the moment Jago brought him up, Banichi seized Bren's arm and propelled him up the three towering, atevi-sized steps onto the deck.

Bren stumbled onto the last step, used a push of his hand on the flooring and a snatch at the passenger rail to haul himself aboard. Another hand seized his shoulder and hauled him into the aisle as the rest of his team clambered up after him, their strength and weight rocking the bus, which, unlike others, sat dark and quiet, its aisle and its occupants all in shadow.

"Nand' Bren!" a young voice exclaimed—a voice he knew as well as he knew the dowager's. Cajeiri was aboard. And the bus seats—headlamps of other vehicles provided a glow through the windows, enough, at least, for outlines and shadows—filled with passengers, might contain the Taibeni youngsters, at least, if not the dowager herself—he expected her, and Cenedi, and the men he knew.

"Here," that high young voice said, and a hand reached across the back of an empty seat, patting it—a whole vacant bench seat in an otherwise crowded bus. Doubtless the young folk had preserved it for him. He set a knee in the seat and strained his eyes forward, searching among those standing in the aisle, concerned to make sure all his own bodyguard had made it aboard—whatever this hurry meant, wherever they were about to go.

To the mountains, maybe. To safety—masked by all this to-do, this shifting of pieces on the board.

A shadow loomed above him. A heavy hand rested on his shoulder. He sensed rather than saw Banichi's presence shutting out the light from that direction.

"Are you all right?" he asked Banichi as he heard the bus door shut. "Where are we going, Banichi-ji?"

"To Shejidan," Banichi said.

"The Guild officers," he began.

"They and theirs are no longer a concern," Banichi reported.

Not a concern. Just that. There had surely been fa-

talities in that explosion—fatalities that encompassed the self-proclaimed highest leadership of
Banichi's own Guild—not men they supported, but
not easy men to take down, all the same.

And the Assassins who might have come onto the
grounds with that pair? Disposed of, just like that?

One noted that they still weren't turning lights on
inside this particular bus. A handful of other vehicles
were lit up inside, interior lights recklessly blazing
out into the night, while ordinary folk, townsmen and
others, got to their seats in what one could only take
as a general departure of the massed vehicles.

"Sit down, Bren-ji," Banichi advised him. "We shall
be moving in a moment."

Shejidan, Banichi had said. All of them, evidently,
were headed straight into confrontation.

Banichi left him. He subsided into the seat next to
the window. He had not seen Tano and Algini board,
but he was convinced by now that his entire contingent had made it onto the bus, though there were
only shadows and occasional profiles to tell him so . . .
seated as he was, and with the backs of heads to look
past, he saw one profile that looked very much like
Tano talking to one he was sure was Jago.

The red and blue taillights of the bus in front of
theirs flared to life, and white light stabbed rear to
front of their bus, the headlamps of the bus behind. It
was indeed Tano, without his jacket. Algini was with
him. Thank God.

In that moment a human-sized form slipped
around the end of the seat and scrambled in beside
him, breathless and excited, a young hand catching at

his arm. "Nand' Bren! Did you hear how someone blew up the Guild officers?"

"One understands that to be the case, young sir." He schooled his voice to evenness and dignity, appalled, even so, by the enthusiasm in that young voice. "Is your great-grandmother aboard?"

"Up there," Cajeiri said, pointing, one thought, to the bus ahead of them "Papa said we should not all be together in the same vehicle, in case of bombs."

"A very good idea, one is sure." But not a good idea in public relations, dammit, to put the heir so publicly into the paidhi's care. A shiver ran through him. Bren worked his fingers, trying to drive out the night chill that had his hands like ice, trying at the same time to render his breaths even and composed and, thinking that the boy knew far more than he did: "Do you know if we are going to the train station, or just where, young sir?"

"We think we shall go all the way to Shejidan."

"Do roads even go there?"

"Except a very short bit in the south, which Cenedi thinks we can cross with no trouble. Uncle Tatiseigi has a whole book of maps!"

Thinks we can cross, echoed in Bren's head, as he numbly braced his computer next to him in the seat, an armrest on the left, against the wall. A *book* of maps, probably the very finest, most expensive, fifty years ago.

No trouble, is it? He was more than dubious about the information. Shejidan? Not likely, he said to himself.

Cajeiri got up on his knees on the seat and turned

around to exclaim to his young bodyguard, "Have you the packets with our breakfast, Gari-ji? The paidhi will be very hungry."

The paidhi's stomach was upset. Breakfast was very far from his mind, but a packet came forward, and Cajeiri handed him a fruit bar, taking another for himself.

And no sooner had the boy gotten up on his knees again to lean on the seat back than the bus ahead of them started to move, slowly lumbering forward.

That seemed to indicate that other buses in line ahead of it were moving, but how they advanced any distance at all in that direction, considering the complete fender-to-fender jam-up in the hedged driveway, Bren was far from sure. Cajeiri twisted back forward and plumped down in his appropriated seat.

The bus ahead of them turned where Bren was sure there was no turn, right into the hedge, as happened, a parting insult to the manicured planting that had separated the drive from the Taibeni camp.

Their own turn followed, broken hedge branches scraping the sides and bottom of their bus as they ground, lurched, and bumped their way over the roots.

Then it was soft lawn. The Taibeni must be on the move, camp struck, mecheiti all moved out. Their bus gathered speed, following a line of taillights that snaked ahead in the dark, a line of about two dozen or so buses and trucks.

"Where is your father at the moment, young sir?" Bren asked Cajeiri. It was one of those things which ordinarily they might not be supposed to know, but if the boy did know, the knowledge was on this bus already.

"He flew!" Cajeiri said, and did one imagine within that awe a profound indignation that he had been left behind? "Cenedi made up nine gasoline bombs out of wine bottles!—and papa went with nand' Rejiri, and they are going to drop them on the Kadagidi if they come at us while we move."

My God, he thought, bombs from airplanes were illegal as hell—and he could no longer restrain himself, no matter the bus was bouncing over the turf in a general advance back toward the hedge and the road. He got to his feet, holding to the seat in front of him, eased his way past Cajeiri, and holding to other seat backs as the bus bucked and jolted over the turf, he searched faces and forms in the dim, diffused light of headlamps behind and taillights ahead. They were passing the estate boundary, crossing past the open gate, and turning off south, he was sure it was south. Toward the train station.

"Jago-ji." He identified her standing in the aisle with Banichi, and she obligingly moved a few steps back to him, bracing herself against the seat on the other side of the aisle.

"Is the aiji indeed flying with Rejiri, Jago-ji?" he asked. "Are they planning to bomb the Kadagidi?"

"Only if they need to, nandi. Only if we come under attack. Such an action is hardly *kabiu*."

To say the least. "Do they hope that they can actually land in the capital?"

"By no means, at this moment, nandi. But the

young man seems quite skilled at finding landing places in open territory."

The young man in question had a notorious history of seat-of-the-pants flying. One could only envision some pasturage, some meadow which would set Tabini and the boy alone, with nine—fortunate nine!—damned wine bottles full of petrol, somewhere far removed from help, after making enough noise to alert enemies from half a dozen townships.

"What are we doing, meanwhile?" he asked. "What do we hope to do?"

"We shall go to the capital ourselves," Jago said. "The paidhi must go. They are calling the legislature, Bren-ji."

The legislature, in whom there had been, within the day, an outbreak of acute sore throat. A body which had defied a summons from Murini. But Tabini believed it would answer *him* and come in.

"*How* has he called them, Jago-ji? Are we public, on the air?" To do anything involving general broadcast would set the whole country in an upheaval—and he had no idea how they would do that.

"We have our means," Jago said, that *we* almost certainly encompassed immediate company, her partner, her hijacked Guild, and electronics to which outsiders had no access. They were matters into which prudent outsiders were not supposed to inquire, and into which he had by no means meant to trespass, God help them all. It meant they were not broadcasting for general hearing, and it meant there was far less chance Mospheira knew what was happening right now. It was, as far as a roaring great column of buses could be, a clandestine advance.

"But the Guild officers," he began, still aching for information, any small bit she could give him. "Have *they* gotten out a message?"

"These persons were so imprudent as to lodge in an upstairs room in an ancient and hostile building. These historic houses are barrel vault upon barrel vault and massively built—precision in such matters is quite possible."

"Were we in an upstairs room, nadi?"

A tone of amused shock. "But, Bren-ji, *we* never allowed enemies to occupy the room beneath us!"

Tatiseigi would have an apoplexy about his missing floor, was all he could think for the moment. The enormity of what his staff had done, in terms of assassinating Guild representatives—perhaps Guild leadership—he could hardly grasp. But no message to Shejidan had gone, it seemed; clandestine hardly described them, and certain forces were likely scrambling to meet their challenge.

And the Guild officers were dead. If the two had imagined that they had actually installed any proper precautions in the room below them, if they had had confidence in the man'chi of someone within the house, in the Atageini staff or otherwise to aid and abet their movements—

Clearly someone had prevented those particular precautions from moving into position in the room below. His staff seemed extraordinarily well-briefed on what had happened, even smug, if he could read Jago's tone.

And he knew their ways. He knew that Banichi had no inclination to be the second man into an action he could much better direct, or to take a purely defensive position when someone aimed at their lives. Neither was Cenedi so inclined, nor was the dowager he served—Tatiseigi might have hesitated, even Tabini might have paused to consider. But the only likely argument between Cenedi and Banichi after two years of running operations together would have been which of them moved first.

The Guild officers, the biggest threat to come at them directly from Murini's side, hadn't even made it to supper.

And what did Banichi do next? Now what did one possibly do, when one had blown up one's own officers, and was running buses full of farmers into the capital?

At the moment he felt inclined to sink down into the nearest seat and let his stomach settle, but his own seat was a few rows back, and the nearest was occupied, like most of the seats, by an ordinary provincial, a man in a rough canvas jacket, with a hunting rifle in callused hands. The type was everywhere. In all those buses. Tabini was in the airplane, and Banichi and Cenedi were calling the shots, never mind Tabini's personal bodyguard.

He was suddenly overwhelmed by the scale of it. By the force of what they had launched.

"You should sit down, Bren-ji," Jago said.

"This is a war we bring, Jago-ji." Atevi society had known no open warfare since the War of the Landing—skirmishes, yes; civil unrest, yes; sniping be-

tween bodyguards of lords in conflict, constantly—
but not a conflict that swept up every clan on the continent, flagrantly involving bystanders. Not involving
middle-aged men with hunting rifles.

And assassinating Guild officers, the Guild being
supposedly the keepers of the law and the peace, the
impartial, every-sided court of appeal . . . impartiality
and fairness had clearly gone by the board; so had
legally mandated support for the sitting aiji. But his
staff had delivered an answer for it.

"Bren-ji?"

"Do we hope simply to drive all the way into Shejidan, Jago-ji?"

"Perhaps." Far too lightly.

"Or are we going to the train station?"

"We refuel there, nandi, at the station pump."

"And the Guild? Are they moving against us?"

"We have moved to convince certain forces within
the Guild, persons of certain man'chi, nandi—that
Gegini was no fit leader."

Not from the grave, he wasn't, that was quite clear.

Cenedi and Banichi. Extravagant action, high and
wide action, of a sort subordinates didn't undertake
on their own.

It was not just to protect him, he thought. It was
much beyond that. Banichi and Jago had been
Tabini's staffers before they were his. In the nature of
things, there always was one higher man'chi that
overrode what they owed to him.

So had Tabini appropriated them? Given them
such an order? Or had the dowager herself?

And coordinated it, dammit all. The echoes of that

explosion had hardly died before Tabini was airborne, headed into trouble ahead of them, precipitating this flood of buses and trucks.

Follow, Tabini was saying to all who had ever followed him—irresistible as the mecheiti leader, dashing hellbent for whatever destination, in the echoes of that explosion. Atevi of the Ragi man'chi were feeling more than an emotional tug at their hearts. Their whole being plunged toward that leader, pell mell, an attraction not in his wiring. *He* might be immune for the hour, capable of a second, critical thought—deciding things on love, that slower, more anguished emotion. But his staff wasn't wired that way. It was the aiji who'd called, and they'd moved. Ruthlessly, comprehensively, without consulting him . . . dammit.

"The aiji ordered you," he said to Jago. "Did he? He didn't rely on his own security."

Jago's hand closed on his wrist. "We may die in this effort, Bren-ji. And our Guild resists emotional decisions. But this time, yes, we are obliged to go."

"The paidhi is likewise obliged," he said, closing his hand atop hers, a contact atevi ordinarily did not invite or accept. "We humans have our own feelings. We understand." He did. Tabini had called in a debt, drafted his staff, the dowager's, his own. They could get killed. But if it was the time to do it, if his staff was going, then he damned sure was. "Are the Atageini going into this on the same grounds? Are they solidly with us?"

"They must," Jago said, and it made sense. Tatiseigi's historic premises now had suffered at least two rooms in utter wreckage, the upstairs premises and the room immediately below, not to mention the lily foyer, the stables, and the driveway hedge. Ridiculous items on the surface—but a matter of Atageini sovereignty.

Add to the stack of circumstances, the self-claimed Guildmaster was dead within an hour of his arrival under Tatiseigi's roof—it could be argued it had been about an hour short of their own intention to assassinate Tabini—a first strike against Ragi power, but the Atageini had been the site of the response, and they had had to make a fast decision.

As Murini had been prepared to make. His own shaken wits informed him that if Guild had come in to assassinate Tabini, it was not going to be the final blow, and it was not going to stop any time soon. There was much, much more intended.

Tatiseigi had had no choice but become involved—the epicenter of the event, exposed to any outrage, beginning with that Guild intrusion, and expanding to every alliance the old man had. The old man had seen it come over the horizon when the dowager had showed up at his gates. Murini had sent in the Kadagidi, Tabini had moved in immediately after with his counterrevolution, the Guild had come in next to take Tabini out in a finessed strike, one that would leave the dowager alive, for her unique value to national stability, and no one had ever seemed to care about Tatiseigi in the process—but only one outcome of this whole affair possibly led to Tatiseigi's grand-nephew being in supreme power over the *aishidi'tat,* and he wasn't letting events pass him by this time.

An entire lifetime of evading conflict until the dust was already settling, a lifetime of being moderately obstructionist to Tabini's modernization policy, and suddenly Tatiseigi was taking his whole province to war behind Tabini-aiji to put him back in power.

He found his way back to his seat, Cajeiri meanwhile kneeling and talking volubly to his two young escorts, who held the seat behind. Cajeiri turned around as Bren eased past that obstruction and sat down in his own place next to the window.

"The other buses are supposed to keep this bus on the inside," Cajeiri informed him. "So snipers will have no targets. But we should keep our heads down if shooting starts, nand' paidhi, Nawari said so, because it will be very heavy guns and they could blow this bus to bits."

Cheerful lad. "Whose bus is this, does one have any notion?"

"It belongs to Dur," Cajeiri said, which was Rejiri's clan. "The lord of Dur and his bodyguard and the fishers' association, too, nandi! They came in from the train station while the young lord took the plane! —I know where Dur is," he added, apropos of nothing about the bus itself. Ilisidi had kept him at his lessons during their flight, and he did know his provinces. "Dur helped mani-ma in previous times."

"That they did, young sir," Bren murmured. He had an inner vision of a nightbound coast with fire and smoke on every hand, and an improbable ferryboat plowing in toward the beach at the most critical of moments. "And so they help her again, for which we all shall remember them with great favor."

If any of them lived long enough to remember this current madness. But it was what a proper nobleman said, regarding a favor. Favors lived long past the favor-doers. Favors bound the generations together. It was one of those givens, that a house never forgot an obligation. And his house must not—if he could have any progeny. The thought had dawned on him long before this, that this boy came as close as he himself could ask, the child of his teaching, the boy he was going to send into years beyond his reach.

Remember them. Remember the favors, boy. Keep the old alliances.

"And if bullets do start flying, young sir, I shall rely on you to hit the floor with me. You *and* your body-guard. And no guns, if you please. This is a situation where experience counts. One is obliged to be an extremely accurate shot, firing out these windows. There are too many allies wandering around out there."

"One hears, nandi." Cajeiri slumped down a little in his seat, arms folded, perhaps remembering his own baptism in fire, not long removed, when he had, though justifiably, killed a man. Tabini's son was not, of course, if one should ask him, afraid. Tabini's son, the dowager's great-grandson, was given no opportunity to be afraid.

Or at least he had never had permission to show it. Delight in gore was, perhaps, his one means of defying the things that scared him very badly.

"Good lad," Bren said, resisting any human notion he might have of patting the boy on the shoulder. The days when he could do that were passing, hurtling away by the second, as fast as the boy's childhood. "Brave lad."

He ought in fact to tell Cajeiri to move away from him and not come near him again on this entire journey. The windows were no protection from snipers, and he was in all respects conspicuous, one pale target shining in any scope. It would be the ultimate tragedy if someone aiming at him accidentally killed the heir.

Some vehicle passed them in the dark, two gold headlamps and an entirely improbable sight coming up from behind—an open convertible, with driver, guard, and two conspicuous occupants, the passenger seats facing backward as well as forward. He leaned forward, not quite believing his eyes, and finding they had not deceived him. It was indeed Lord Tatiseigi and Ilisidi in that open car, passing them at a rate that had to tax that antique vehicle. One had thought Lord Tatiseigi had only owned one automobile, and that surely gone with the stables. Clearly not.

Cajeiri had to see what he was looking at so concentratedly, and leaned hard against him, peering out the window.

"Great-grandmother and great-uncle!" Cajeiri exclaimed in distress. "With Cenedi, one thinks, nandi, in that old car!"

"Indeed it is," he said, and had a very uncomfortable feeling about what he saw, so uncomfortable a feeling that he excused himself out of his seat and went up the aisle to point out the sight to Jago and Tano. "The aiji-dowager and Lord Tatiseigi just passed us in an open car!"

Tano bent for a look out the windows. So did Jago.

"This is very reckless," Bren protested, compelled by atevi idiom to a towering understatement. "This is extremely reckless of them, nadiin-ji. What can they be thinking?"

Jago cast him a shadowy look which, in the near dark, he could not read; but she went farther forward to inform Banichi of the situation.

Ilisidi, deciding to make the grand gesture, Bren thought to himself. Tatiseigi, who had been late to every battlefield, whose house had been assaulted, was making his own grand, potentially fatal gesture, right along with the aiji-dowager, who had mixed herself in every conflict of the last half century and more. Now she had shamed the old reprobate into joining her, one romantic fling at destiny . . .

God, no. They couldn't.

He staggered his way, burdened with the armored jacket, down the aisle, intent on having his own word with Banichi.

"Banichi-ji, they are trying to kill themselves. They are trying to compel the rebels, are they not, by force of example and man'chi and the dowager's allies? We cannot allow this!"

"One hardly knows how to stop them at this point," Banichi muttered, bending low to have a look at what now was out of sight.

"We can at least keep up with them, nadiin," Bren said.

"Yes," Banichi said, and moved forward in the bus, up to talk to the driver, and presumably to the old lord of Dur, who, conspicuous in his court dress, in a seat next the driver, and accompanied by several dark-clad bodyguards, was surely due the courtesy of an address. Bren moved up into the general neighborhood, and heard Banichi pointing out the situation to the lord of Dur. The lord—Rejiri's father—got up from his seat, leaned on the rail, gazing out the front windows at a fading column of lamplit dust, and waved commands at the driver, who with powerful moves of the wheel, swung the bus out of the column in relatively hot pursuit.

"Keep up with them!" the lord of Dur urged his driver. "Go. Go!"

"Your lordship," Bren said diffidently, edging into the lord's presence. "One is grateful, for the sake of the young gentleman and the dowager. I am Bren, the paidhi-aiji, an old associate of your son . . ."

"As who could ever mistake the paidhi-aiji!" Dur cried, and gave a little nod by way of a bow. His personal name was Adigan, Bren recalled that detail the moment the man spoke, immensely relieved to have old resources coming back to him at need. "The distinguished associate of my foolhardy son! Indeed, we are honored, nand' paidhi, extremely honored to provide yourself and the aiji's heir our stolen transport. In the haste of boarding and departure, there was little leisure, nor any desire to distract your lordship from needful orders . . . but one is extremely glad to find you well."

"The honor is very much mine, nand' Adigan. One

offers most profound gratitude for your gracious welcome, above all for the steadfastness of your house and that excellent young man, your son—" The courtesies flowed desperately on, needful as a steady heartbeat, while the bus engine roared and the driveshaft and the oil pan somehow survived the impact of rocks flung up from underneath as the bus lurched.

Then brush scraped under them, the bus running outside the column onto rougher ground. They chased those dust-veiled taillights, bouncing and bumping so that Bren had to hook both arms around an upright rail. "To you and yours we are profoundly indebted, Lord Adigan. Your son—"

"The boy and that machine, baji-naji, the delight of his days!" The bus jolted. Adigan caught himself by the overhead rail, at the same time making a grab to steady Bren, no slower than his bodyguard. "Faster, Madi-ji! Will an Atageini driver lose us?"

Faster it was. The bus passed others, roaring off into the dark wherever there was an appearance of flat ground, finding its way over open meadow, hitting brush, then falling back into the column where it must, not giving up on the car, in no degree, only seeking a chance to get by. Another bus had swerved aside from the general column, veering into their path, and the driver honked vigorously, while Lord Adigan swore and waved as if the other driver could see his indignation.

"Now! Now!" he cried, and the bus veered far out and around.

They passed the second bus. And hit a depression

at the bottom of the hill, a streambed. The bounce of stout shock absorbers nearly threw them all in a heap as they went over the bank. Water splashed up into the headlamps, splattered the windshield. Then they met the far bank, lurched up and over, and climbed, wheels laboring, then clawed their way up at an angle, until one and then the other wheel rolled over the crest. Banichi steadied both of them, and the Dur bodyguard had likewise stood up, prudently holding on, trying to urge their lord to safety.

"The fool!" Adigan cried, ignoring the guards, waving at the other bus, now behind them.

"Best sit down, Bren-ji," Banichi said quietly—in point of fact, Bren had little to see at all past that wall of atevi, but a fleeting glimpse of that pair of taillights, like a ruddy will of the wisp, flitting ahead of them. Questions came from the rear of the bus, what was going on, were they under attack, had the brakes failed? One was a high young voice, demanding information.

Adigan turned and shouted to his household and his provincials:

"We are following a car in which the aiji-dowager has taken passage with the Atageini! That fool driver will never leave Dur in the dust!"

One certainly understood where Rejiri derived his notions. A cheer went up from the folk of Dur, a general approbation of their lord's defiance, and in that commotion Bren began to find his way back to his seat.

"The paidhi-aiji is with us," Dur shouted out, "and the young heir of Tabini-aiji!"

"Hai!" the cheer went up, to a man.

Well, it was something, being cheered by an allied clan that still owned itself allied, after all the troubles. It set a warmth into one's bones.

"Thank you, Dur!" Cajeiri waved his arms above adult heads, in mid-aisle, silhouetted in the glare of headlamps behind them. He had a sure grasp of politics, even at his age.

"Hai for Dur!" his young escort yelled out, everyone congratulating everyone else, while Adigan's bus driver fought manfully not to be wrecked or overset, and Bren clawed his way past and into his seat. Cajeiri hung onto the seat back rail to cheer with his young bodyguard, and the bus bounced and lurched. Their objective, meanwhile, was nimbly eluding them, and they had not even made the train station, let alone Shejidan.

But they were still in pursuit.

If our transmission holds up, Bren said to himself, bracing himself at an angle between the wall and the seat ahead of him. They were going to die in a bus wreck, never mind enemy fire, and it was his fault for suggesting they give chase . . .

But they could not let Ilisidi go commit suicide alone, could they? He knew the dowager's ways, her absolutely outrageous ways, and in his mind, she was likely challenging the Kadagidi in that open car for a reason—her popularity—her absolute idolized status in the east. Let the aiji-dowager die in an outrageously heroic action against Murini and the whole east would blow up, that was what she was about. He could think of half a dozen eastern lords who would break from any western hold over them if Murini was remotely shown to have targeted her. He could think of a dozen more lords in the midcontinent that would become untrustworthy if the far east ever broke away from the *aishidi'tat*—

The whole *aishidi'tat* would break apart, was what—shatter into a hundred rival states. Kill Ilisidi, and it guaranteed Murini would not be in charge when the kyo finally showed up in orbit, even if not a single member of Tabini's household survived.

And if it did happen, if they failed in this mad venture, someone else would make a power grab, to be sure, name himself or herself aiji and cut Murini's throat in the process—give it two weeks, at maximum.

Meanwhile Mospheira would lose no time stabilizing the situation by appointing Yolanda Mercheson *his* replacement. *There* was an idea worth staying alive to prevent.

And they had visitors coming in from space who expected to deal with a stable, reasonable authority down here.

God, if only Ilisidi had consulted him. He would have flung himself bodily in the way of her getting in that car. He would have argued with her that they— he, the dowager, and the heir—should run for it if Tabini had the notion of going back for a frontal assault on Shejidan. Run for the hills, hell. They should just go back to the coast, go to Mospheira, get back into space and use technological means, like a meaningful near-earth-orbit satellite system and broadcasts and even weapons they controlled, to become an unassailable nuisance to any usurper—

But he hadn't had a chance to pose that argument to her. Security staffs had separated their assets, and right now there was no way in hell this overloaded bus was going to overtake that touring car on rough ground—not until their refueling, presumably at the train station.

Then he had to dive off this bus, try to get hold of the dowager and talk sense into her in precisely those terms—appealing to technology which she and her household could understand, alone of atevi within his reach.

If he could reason with her at all at this point. If she hadn't taken some damned public stand from which she couldn't back down . . .

He would send Banichi to talk to Cenedi. *That* was the one agency that could persuade the dowager—get Cenedi to take his side. With reason. With logic. And a concrete plan.

First thing in the plan, they had to overtake that car.

The estate road joined the general provincial road at the southern estate gateway. The bus rolled through broad open gates, still not foremost among the buses that had set out—notably not the foremost, Bren thought, seeing how the lights went on up the curve their column made, and he would bet the dowager's car was up in the lead by now. He heard the tinny radio advisements that someone near him, perhaps Dur's security, picked up from other members of the column—it was, thank God, a verbal code that he could not penetrate; but then, blood-chilling, he heard a voice speaking clear Ragi:

*"The aiji-dowager has returned in triumph over foreign connivance and calls on every village to rise and take back Shejidan from the usurper! The aiji-dowager is at this moment on the move, with all the true numbers of the heavens in her hands! Rise up, arm, and join her! This is the fortunate moment!"*

My God, my God, he thought, feeling that chill run down his back. *She's challenging Murini head-on, no question. She's using Tatiseigi's communications system. If that doesn't bring airplanes down on us with bombs, nothing will. Does she want that?*

*If Tabini starts dropping those illegal gas-bombs himself, all restraint goes on their side and ours . . . but he's* the liberal: *he can conceivably do things like that, can't he? Murini, with his conservative claims—he can't. He daren't. And it's exactly the sort of thing the dowager wouldn't stick at, not in this situation, even if all hell breaks loose.*

*No phones at the station that will let me get through to Mospheira, no radio that won't be monitored. Shawn can't order an intervention without going to the legislature and the legislature won't move in time. No way I can stop this, not once that call to the tashrid has gone public, and Mospheiran military intervention wouldn't help Tabini's cause, anyway.*

*We're in it. We're in it for sure.*

He had his pistol in his pocket. Tano had told him he should take better care of it. Clean it more often. Truth was, he hated carrying it, hated thinking he had it, hated ever needing it, treasure it as he did because of the source from which it came. Now he thought he should follow Tano's advice and clean the thing before he had to fire it, if he didn't set it off by accident in all this bouncing about.

He didn't have a cleaning kit. Needed a brush. He didn't want to be handling it with the boy next to him.

He didn't want it to fail him, either. He got up again, made his way as far as Algini's seat, which he and Tano shared by turns, the bus having many more people than seats. "Gini-ji." He passed Algini the weapon, holding on with his elbow around a pole. "This needs cleaning, if you would do me the kindness, Gini-ji."

Algini took it, ejected the clip and the shell in chamber, not even thinking of the motion, one was sure. Natural as breathing. An occupation for his hands. And Bren took a less painful grip on the seat back railing, held on as the bus lurched and bounced.

"Is there a chance we may overtake the dowager at the refueling stop, Gini-ji? Is there a chance Banichi can reach Cenedi?"

"We shall see what we do there. We may lose certain vehicles, as this assemblage drinks the fuel up, nandi. It will be a difficult matter to get so many vehicles to the capital, all with fuel. And some will not withstand the trip, mechanically."

Clearly they could go stringing dead vehicles and stranded people from here to Shejidan, and it was no good fate awaiting those thus stranded, if their advance failed or stalled. "One has had an unpleasant thought. What if they figure out our path, and start blowing the fueling stations in front of us, Gini-ji?"

"This is our gravest concern, nandi," Algini said, and blew through the open barrel before he added. "Certain fast-moving private cars are going ahead of the column. We hope to take fuel stations in advance. We hope, too, that certain local folk in favor of us will think of our needs and guard their own premises from destruction, such as they can."

"Against Guild?" Ordinary folk contesting the Assassins' Guild seemed the weakest link in their whole plan, even ahead of the vulnerability of the fuel supply, and the sheer mass of all these hungry vehicles. It seemed uncharacteristically fragile, this threat they mounted, even with the support of lords and professional Guild: Most of their supporters were farmers and shopkeepers, completely untrained except in hunting. "They can stall us out, Gini-ji, can they not? They can strand us in the middle of the countryside."

Algini rarely met a direct question, or returned a direct gaze from anyone. In the dark, fitfully lit by bouncing headlamps from other vehicles, he not only gazed back, but did so with uncommon earnestness. "That they can do, Bren-ji."

"What, then, shall we do? Are we to fight, wherever we run out and stop? Or have we a plan to get to cover?"

"The vehicles of high priority will refuel more often than absolute need, and if we are stopped— indeed we may have to fight, nandi, but one trusts a number of measures are being taken in advance of us."

Algini lapsed into the passive voice precisely where the critical *who* would logically be other Guild, as clearly as if he had shouted it. Guild or operatives of the aiji, which would still be Guild—were implied to be taking those measures, out in front of the column.

That answered his query as to whether the aiji and his supporters had taken leave of their senses.

"We killed the Guild officers, Gini-ji." Implying that the rest of the Guild might not be favorable to such action, and fishing for information.

"We did," Algini said, clearly unwilling to disburse too much information to anyone. And then he added: "But do not by any means take Gegini-nadi as the Guild, Bren-ji. He elected himself."

Not Gegini-nandi, then, no title so high accorded to the Guildmaster who had walked into Tatiseigi's sitting room and started laying down the law. The late Gegini-nadi, then, and his associates were no longer an issue in this action, or not an active one. Algini hinted there was no majority behind him, and did not think that the Guild as a whole would be too disturbed.

And Algini, their demolitions man, Bren suddenly suspected, had been intimately involved in taking them out.

Never the most forward of his staff, Algini. Always quiet, always ready to slip into the background. In *Algini's* Guild, the thought suddenly struck him, one never sought publicity, one never discussed Guild affairs, one never gave up one's secrets, not even to one's closest non-Guild associates.

Perhaps, dared one think, not even to other Guildsmen?

And that dark thought having struck him, he looked down at Algini's light-limned features, so tranquil a face, and he wondered what Algini actually *was* within this most secretive of all Guilds.

Granted Banichi and Jago had come from Tabini's staff—exactly what agency had lent him Tano and Algini? And why, after all these years, did he know so little of Algini's opinions?

Curious thought to have occured to him, bouncing along in the dark, face to face with Algini over a piece of enigma Algini politely—and correctly—declined to discuss. It was an embarrassing position, having asked questions, having gotten another, deeper enigma back.

And why? Why did Algini tell him as much as he had, after years of no information? It seemed maybe a direct hint to a very dim-brained human, a human with non-atevi wiring, that there was something else going on—the sort of hint Algini had never been the one to give, because the dim-brained human had always been Jago's and Banichi's responsibility.

But one knew that the connections that wove the great houses into associations were not all lines of marriage. The passing of staff from one house to another, even the less social act of spying on one's neighbors, was an important surety between houses. Verification meant honesty, behavior-as-advertised, creating trust between houses whose relationships spanned not just individual promises, but generations. Banichi and Jago had continually reported to

Tabini, he was very sure, so long as they were neighbors within the Bu-javid. His cook Bindanda he knew reported constantly to Tatiseigi and his housekeeper likewise, making sure the paidhi pulled no humanish chicanery.

While Tatiseigi—being a key lord of the Padi Valley—

Had Tatiseigi's checking up on the paidhi's household also been Tatiseigi's way of checking up on Tabini's behavior—a Ragi lord with an unprecedented lot of power, and married to an Atageini woman?

Perhaps his welcome in Tatiseigi's house would have been better this time had he brought Bindanda with him. He had never been asked about Bindanda's absence. It was hardly the sort of thing the old man could have asked him . . . Welcome, nandi, and where is my chief spy? If his brain had had atevi wiring, he might have had the basic cleverness to drop the information unasked, gracefully, without quite making it a challenge . . .

But nothing answered the essential question of *why* his staff on such short notice had felt entitled to blow the hell out of the Atageini premises and take out the self-proclaimed Guild officers on their own. The aiji's staff should have been the ones to move—and he had the most uneasy feeling that Ismini hadn't been involved; that Ismini hadn't been consulted in the operation at all.

*Do not take Gegini-nadi as the Guild, Bren-ji.*

In a tone downright proprietary and prideful, as if Algini had a personal ax to grind in the removal of their visitor, as if he had conceived a personal offense in the shift of his Guild onto Murini's side.

The old Guildmaster might be alive or dead at the moment. One had no idea what was going on in the Guildhouse, and one never knew.

But, in the way of atevi politics, not all the old Guildmaster's personal operatives would be dead—the same as when a lord went down by assassination, there was always the chance of one or two still in the field whose man'chi might lead them to act.

And one doubted any such operatives would feel any man'chi at all toward someone Algini called self-appointed, a usurper of the Guild's highest authority—possibly even the murderer of the Guildmaster, if the man had met his end.

And if such agents were still in the field, still where the old Guildmaster had placed them, where were they?

Had, for instance, Guild operatives been inserted in *his* house, a means of the Guild checking up on Tabini as well as the human official who was that close to Tabini's ear? It certainly made sense that if he had an assortment of agents on his staff from the Ragi, from the Atageini, and a dozen other lords all watching him, the Guild *not* sending someone of their own would be odd, would it not? They would move through channels that already had access. They would maneuver to get someone ideally not on domestic staff, who would not accompany the paidhi everywhere, at every moment, but into his security, which was only four people, two of whom he knew very closely . . . two of whom found it so, so difficult to call him by anything but his proper titles, until very, very lately . . .

God, what a string of chilly perhapses!

"Here, nandi." Algini handed him back the pistol, cleaned and reloaded. "You should get a holster for it."

"I shall," he said, feeling the air he breathed had gone a little rare. He tucked the heavy object into his coat pocket. "As soon as I find the opportunity, Gini-ji. Your advice and Tano's, both, and one does take it to heart. But one still hopes we shall get through this without my ever needing it."

"Stay behind us," Tano said, out of the dark above his head. "And stay down. You shine in the dark, Bren-ji, and we are not facing farmer-folk, not in this action."

"Yes," he said, the way one took an order. He had been glad of the darker coat: Guild opposition would not hesitate to target any lord on their side, with the human one a priority, no question. But Tano's jacket crushed him with its weight. He found the occasion to shed the jacket, and hung it on the seat back, the night air welcome relief. "With gratitude, Tano-nadi. I shall stay out of view, one promises, most earnestly. Take it. Take it."

"Do," Algini said, just that, and quietly, efficiently, Tano shrugged it on, a more potent defense to him and his than the jacket itself posed.

With that thought, he took himself, his fair skin, his light coat, his newly-cleaned pistol, and his surmises back to his own seat, where Cajeiri was kneeling backward, talking with Jegari and Antaro.

"Is there news?" Cajeiri asked.

News.

There was plenty of guesswork, was what there was in the paidhi's mind at the moment, a good many scary surmises, none of them fit for youngsters' gossip.

"We shall stay close behind your great-grandmother's car, is all." The bus gave a violent lurch, scraped through brush, and then seemed to have gone onto a road. Bren caught a look outside the window, and suddenly they were blazing along a dedicated roadway, throwing gravel from the tires. "One understands we are going to the rail station," he said to the young people. "That being the nearest fuel stop on our way. If your great-grandmother fails to stop there, one hopes we will have enough fuel to follow them to the next such place."

"We shall find them. We shall persuade mani-ma to get onto the bus," Cajeiri said. "And Lord Tatiseigi and Cenedi, too, and Nawari and all of them. The car can go on and be a decoy." The boy had learned that tactic on the ship, under circumstances in which no boy his age ought to have to learn his lessons. "But she will be very stubborn about it, nandi. You can persuade her."

"She is likely to be that, young sir," he said, as the bus swerved around a turn, top-heavy and slewing alarmingly. "And one greatly doubts she will listen to the paidhi, either. But I shall ask Banichi to talk to Cenedi."

"And I shall!"

"You," he said, "will stay on the bus, young sir!"

Arms folded. Cajeiri sulked, an eight-year-old again.

Up hills and down, and onto the flat again, as fast as they could go. They were not quite foremost in the column now, but they were close, only a handful of trucks and cars still kicking up a cloud of headlamp-lit dust in the sandy spots ahead of them. Tatiseigi's car was in the lead of the whole column, one was quite sure, and it was beyond any doubt a far more modern car than the one in which Tatiseigi had first met them, a light and maneverable vehicle with good suspension.

One could hardly say the same for the bus they were riding. It slewed and rocked alarmingly, the driver taking wild turns to avoid major obstacles, and as they pitched wildly along the side of a drainage ditch, Bren braced a foot against the seat in front, of him against the chance they were going over at any moment.

Cajeiri imitated his stance, excited out of his mood, taking delight in the swerves. "The driver is going very fast, nandi!"

"Indeed," Bren said, all the while hoping that if they did overset, it would not be on some steep hill-side or into large rocks.

Up and over the hills, it was, and through woods that might mask Kadagidi ambush, branches raking the top of the bus. By now Bren had gathered half a dozen bruises on the side facing the window, and Cajeiri, laughing, caught him when his foot slipped and he all but dashed his face against the seat in front of him.

"One is grateful, young sir." He righted himself and took a grip on the seat back with his hand. They had swerved onto a stretch of gravel, actually keeping on the road all the way through the woods, the tail of the bus tending to slew somewhat on the turns. Then, with a last such skid, they definitely left the trees, and turned what Bren calculated was due west, and not that far from the rail station.

People standing in the aisle had crowded forward, blocking his view. There seemed some discussion in progress between Dur and the driver—he had no idea what the subject was, but the bus was already going at a reckless pace, and now the driver added speed.

Then a set of red gleams lit the crowd in silhouette: taillights from the several vehicles in front. Braking.

Jago worked her way up against his seat. "We are coming to the station now," she said. "There will be a delay here, and we will try to find the car. We will force our way in as far as possible, but there is no surety the car will stop. It has a fair-sized tank, and utmost priority at the pump, if it does. We do not wish to discuss matters with the others on the radio. Banichi is going out when we get to the pump."

He didn't like the notion of Banichi leaving them. He didn't like the odds the car might have kept going, with some destination of its own in mind, and, as Jago said, no recourse to radio possible.

Damn.

But Jago had immediately gone forward again, and

the bus, moving more sanely behind the other vehicles, hit a much smoother track, still rolling through an enveloping cloud of dust that lights coming up behind them rendered entirely opaque. There was sand under the wheels now—there had been a lot of that around the train station, a typically soft surface for a fairly major road. If the driver could see anything at the moment but the taillights of the vehicle immediately in front, he would be surprised.

"Great-grandmother has a better driver," Cajeiri commented glumly, which was not precisely fair to the driver they had, but it added up to the truth.

Buildings appeared through the haze. More red lights ahead of them. Red light and the hazy headlamps of vehicles behind them lit the interior of the bus as they slowed to an absolute stop near those ghostly buildings, and then their forward door opened. Several people got out of their bus, some likely to go investigate the fuel supply or consult the drivers in front of them, or argue their precedence in getting to what would surely be one fuel pump.

And Banichi, trying to locate the car among these buses.

"Are we looking for mani-ma?" Cajeiri asked, as his young bodyguard leaned over the seat to hear.

"One hopes so, young gentleman. We have reached the train station and no one has shot at us. This is good."

"Guild would have been ahead of us, nandi," Cajeiri said with a wave of his hand, "and taken care of any problems. Cenedi would see to that, too."

"He would certainly do that," Bren agreed. "But

we do not take for granted we are safe here, young sir."

Damned sure he didn't. Cenedi might be out there somewhere. Banichi was. But his view of seats in that car indicated Cenedi was the only one of her staff with her. He hoped Nawari at least was somewhere close in the uncertainty of this blinding dust and dark, and that she was not totally reliant on the competency of Tatiseigi's long-suffering staff.

And, in the matter of unreliable staff, God knew where Ismini was at the moment. Certainly there was no room in the plane for more than three, if that, with the fuel bombs: Tabini, Rejiri, and someone. If the aiji's bodyguard was cut loose to operate, they would not be happy about it, *they* were ignobly set on a bus somewhere in this mess, and whether they were reliable in man'chi or whether they were in fact gone soft—that lot, with or without Ismini, would be up ahead of the column, no question, demanding precedence for themselves, maybe in a position to move near the dowager, who knew? The whole train of thought made him extremely uneasy.

Their personnel—he thought it might be Banichi with them—reboarded the bus. The door shut, and the bus rolled slowly into a turn that led it on an extreme tilt along the margin of the road, passing other vehicles. Cajeiri gave a bounce in his seat.

Had it been Banichi? Or was he still out there?

"So have they found her? Are we going to the head of the line?"

As the universe ought to be ordered, in Cajeiri's

intentions, indeed. And it had not been Banichi boarding. They were moving up to fuel. They negotiated their way past ten to fifteen vehicles, including three cars, and made it to the single pump, where they stopped. The door opened. Several of their people got off to attend the mechanics of it. But there was no car.

Cajeiri immediately got up and began to force his way through the aisle. Bren flung himself out of his seat and caught the princely arm, only marginally ahead of Jegari and Antaro.

"The young gentleman should by no means get off the bus," Bren said.

"We were not getting off," Cajeiri said, indignantly freeing himself, and simultaneously managing a look out the other window. "We are looking for great-grandmother out the front window. It is our right! And Jegari will go."

"Jegari will not go," Bren said, laying a hand on the boy's shoulder. "By no means. Banichi will be out there talking to Cenedi, if the dowager is here, and that is quite sufficient. A young man could as easily be left behind by accident, and this is no safe place to be walking about, young sir, not for you nor for your staff."

The fuel cap was off, a great deal of clatter at the rear. He heard the nozzle go in, he thought, hoped they were fueling apace by now. Adult privilege, he worked his own way forward to see what there was to see up by the door.

There Tano found him, in the press in the aisle. "The dowager has fueled and gone ahead," was

Tano's unwelcome news. "It would be foolish not to top off fuel now that we are stopped, nandi. We do not know what the way ahead may present us. But we do have this station secure, and a team has gone up the line by rail to control the switching point up by Coagi. No train coming from Shejidan will get past that barrier."

That was good news. The rail would be physically shunted over to divert any train coming toward them out of the south, not only from the direction of Shejidan, but, the way the rail lines branched, out of the extreme south, where Murini's strongest support lay. And any such hostile train, once stopped, would be boarded and dealt with, no question.

"More," Tano said, "we have been given maps of where more widely scattered fuel can be had, and they are passing these to the column. Certain of the rearmost of this column will fan out from here and use farm tanks and rejoin our route later. More are coming in to join us."

"Do you know whether the Kadagidi are coming, Tano-ji?" Bren asked. "Will they attack Tirnamardi, or come after us?"

"They will not attack an empty house," Tano answered him, confirming his own opinion. "But they have not been as forward to attack us as one might expect, nandi. And we have passed word of our movement to Guild in the capital."

How? And meaning what? Bren asked himself, his heart skipping a beat. "To Guild officials?" he asked. "We blew up their leader, did we not? Forgive me, Tano-ji." The last, because Guild affairs had fairly well spilled out of him, asking what he should by no means ask.

"We have advised certain Guild members, nandi. Forgive me." The radio was active again, a faint tinny voice to the rear. Tano ducked away through the press in the aisle, having given his question a broader answer, one was sure, than most lords would get regarding a dispute within the Guild, and it came from a source that recent suspicion informed him might itself be somewhat—almost—nearly—official.

Cajeiri, appearing at his elbow, where he should not be, had just asked him a question. He was not sure what it had been, something about Murini. "One has no idea, young sir."

"But," Cajeiri said, and pursued the question.

"One has no idea," he repeated, tracking the noise of the radio, but unable to hear the transmission. Tano was back there, near it.

Meanwhile he worked his way back to his seat, entraining Cajeiri behind him, and burdened with the thought that if Algini and Tano were more than Guild members, this ungainly bus might itself be a higher-level target than he had imagined, a traveling Guild office—

They hadn't contacted Guild *offices* in Shejidan, Tano had said, but certain Guild *members*.

So communications were functioning, maybe including Tatiseigi's leaky communications system, which Ilisidi was using with abandon, alerting the whole reception area. They were not isolated. They had control of the railroad switching point at Coagi. They had maps, had support in the countryside, and the means to route their hindmost vehicles to alternative fueling sites: farm tanks, village stations, all sorts of hitherto unimagined sources.

He sat down in his own seat, dazed by the number of vectors this business was taking, trying to think of anything he could personally do. Cajeiri plumped down beside him.

"We must have a very large fuel tank, nand' Bren."

"That we do, young sir."

"How much fuel does this pump have in it?"

"One has no idea, young sir. The tank itself is underground. A very large tank, one hopes."

"Like the one at Uncle Tatiseigi's house."

"Yes." His mind was skittering off ahead of the moment, toward the rolling countryside around Shejidan, the scores of towns and villages in the most populated area of the country. Roads were not the rule on the mainland. Vehicular traffic did not go town to town; it went, generally, to rail stations, taking merchandise to market, people to passenger stations, and that webwork of small lanes knit the villages together in the process. One wanted to visit a neighboring town? One hitched a ride with a commercial truck or the local village bus on its way to the train station, as they had done. People didn't ordinarily even think in terms of *driving* to the capital: Rail carried absolutely everything, goods and people alike.

But the web of roads grew and linked villages, lumpy, bumpy, and gravel in most instances, tire tracks through meadow in others, even in areas where buses ran once a week.

The sheer novelty of vehicles massing and converging along that network of roads, natural as it might be to human culture, might well be utterly off the map of Murini's expectations, and carry them farther than any assault by rail—if they just took to rail from here, Murini might have cut them off by tearing up track. If they had trusted only to rail, Murini might have picked up the telephone to learn just where they were, and where to stop them. But there were hundreds of village overland routes, through meadows, through woods, and along village centers—across small bridges they could only hope held up, once they reached the stream-crossed meadows near the capital. And their mass could spread out and reform, down this web, taking fuel at farms, gathering strength, Tano had said, and regrouping. Meanwhile their forces were penetrating the rail system, taking switch-points, guaranteeing Murini couldn't use that system.

Sheer audacity might carry them through the night, might get them a fair distance before Murini figured out what was happening and decided how to stop this assault.

And more villages *might* come in along the way. If there was any district in the *aishidi'tat* that had little reason to support Murini, it was that stretch of Ragi ethnicity that bordered Murini's Padi Valley, from Taiben to the Shejidan countryside. The feud between Tatiseigi of the Atageini and Taiben was only a fractional part of that old rivalry. The Ragi atevi of Shejidan could not be content with some Kadagidi upstart from the Padi Valley suddenly claiming to rule the *aishidi'tat,* with his accent, his traditions, his history of skipping from side to side of previous coup attempts, as Murini had notoriously done. There was no reason in the world that Shejidan district should rise up to defend any Padi-born ruler.

Rush to arms en masse to overthrow authority? That was not the atevi style. But lend a slight helping hand to tip the balance in favor of a Ragi prince while professional Guild sorted out their internal struggle?

That would start a chain reaction of minor disobedience that might become an avalanche. It *had* started, when a few brave members of the tashrid had decided to get contagiously ill at Murini's summons. Had they known where Tabini was when they did it? Had they signaled their support through the Ajuri lord?

Now, when it looked as if the whole Padi Valley except the Kadagidi was coming in to support the father of a prince of mingled Valley and Ragi heritage, it remained to be seen whether the tashrid would still sit at home with sore throat or answer *Tabini's* summons to assemble a quorum. Now that the dowager was back from space, Tabini *could* provide the *aishidi'tat* his evidence—never mind the economic mess the paidhi had counseled Tabini-aiji into, the advice that had started this mess. Now it was apparent that an upstart Padi Valley lord, in a bloody overthrow of the existing order, had taken his primary support from the detested south—*that* would never sit well with the Sheijidan Ragi or the Taibeni, under the most favorable of circumstances, once it became clear to them. Murini's seizure of power might have gotten their acquiescence early on, when it had seemed part of a general tilt of the whole Association away from Tabini's policies and toward a restoration of things-as-they-had-been, but once the Padi Valley peeled away from the Kadagidi, led by the Atageini, and once the Taibeni Ragi joined them, and once the mixed-blood prince came home from space, along with Ilisidi, she of the eastern connections, then, God, yes, the whole picture had changed. The north had repudiated Murini. The islands had repudiated him, in the person of Dur. The coast, under Geigi, had never supported Murini at all. The east had never been anyone's but Ilisidi's.

Now the very center of the Association, the Padi Valley and Ragi highlands districts, had turned soft—turned soft, hell, they were in full career toward Sheijidan to make their opinions heard: *there* would be the dicey part. Loss of the center and the east of the *aishidi'tat* left Murini clinging only to the south and his own Padi Valley clan, which was now itself isolated in its violation of neighboring Atageini territory—

Murini was in deep trouble. That exhilarating chain of assessments dimmed all the world around him, leaving vague just what anyone was going to do to reunite the individual pieces of this avalanche into a stable structure. The avalanche was pouring down toward the capital. Murini would have increasing trouble mustering any support whatever, and the self-appointed Guild head who had entered Tatiseigi's estate to bring their agents in position for a surgical strike had done so perhaps foreseeing that the gathering *would* move on the capital and that only taking out Tabini could stop it without shattering the *aishidi'tat* beyond repair.

Now that man was dead, along with, one hoped, every agent he had brought with him.

Nasty thought—that there might be other agents scattered through the buses, maybe on this bus, still intent on stopping them.

Presumably, however, the lord of Dur knew his own and Banichi and Jago could vouch for any others. That might not be the case on more motley vehicles, those that had piled on people from various villages.

The thought drove him up from his seat again, pressing past a bemused Cajeiri, to find Tano, where he had gone.

"One had a thought, Tano-ji, that perhaps on some of the trucks, some of the Guild operatives might still pose a threat."

"There are cautions out, nandi," Tano informed him. "One has advised other buses to take careful account of passengers and quietly report any suspicions at the next fueling stop. Rely on us."

"You heard the radio operating," he said. "You know the dowager is using it."

"One has heard," Tano said.

The bus engine coughed to life. They started to roll. Those of their people who had been outside scrambled aboard as the bus moved, and the doors shut. One hoped Banichi had made it. One saw a tall man talking to the driver, and to Lord Adigan, silhouetted against the light outside.

He went back to his seat as the bus rocked onto level road, eased past, and dropped into it.

"How far can we go on a single tank, nand' paidhi?" Cajeiri asked him.

"One assumes a very large tank, could now that it is full, take even this vehicle most of the way to Sheji-dan."

"See?" Cajeiri bounced to his knees, his whole human-adult-sized body impelled to impose itself over the seat back, to win a bet, one supposed, with his bodyguard. "We can get most of the way there on one tank."

"The lord did not say 'all the way,'" Jegari retorted; the debate continued and the paidhi, who had other concerns on his mind, thought about going back and taking Tano's seat by Algini, where there was quiet.

"How much of the way?" Cajeiri asked him, quite familiarly and quite rudely abrupt, as happened.

"What would your great-grandmother say, young sir?"

"Nandi," came the amendment.

"Indeed, young sir. But I have no precise answer for your question. Excuse me."

He gathered himself up and slipped back into the aisle, an escape from innocence and good humor. It was Banichi's and Jago's company he wanted at the moment, and information, information of any sort, as much as he could get.

He found them together, up by the large front windows. The view was of dust-veiled taillights, not so many of them as before, and the bus shot along a gravel road, throwing rocks and receiving them in equal number. The windshield had taken several hits, and had lost chips.

He came armed with the youngsters' question. "Can we make it to Shejidan, Banichi-ji, on what fuel we have?"

"Possibly so, Bren-ji. We only topped off, is that not the expression?"

"How is the dowager faring? Did you hear?"

"There was no opportunity to overtake her, Bren-ji," Jago said. "So we hear, Tatiseigi has taken the loan of that automobile from the mayor of Diegi, who has habitually driven to and from the trains in a notoriously reckless rush. Murini, with the fuel shortage, has forbidden the driving of such private cars. The mayor is delighted to lend it in this cause, and accompanies them, personally."

One seat given up to another non-Guild. So *only* Cenedi was with them, give or take the man riding with the driver.

And a fuel shortage at the pumps, which meant chancier supply for their convoy. *Nothing* had been working right, in this anti-technology reversal of policies . . . in the flight, as they had begun to hear, of certain notoriously human-influenced, technologically-skilled occupation classes into obscurity and inaction.

So town lords, on their way to the capital to answer calls to the legislature, had evidently been compelled

to take the usual truck or bus to the stations. And
Lord Tatiseigi's coming to meet them in his elegant
automobile that night had itself been a political gesture, it now seemed, a gallant statement, if they had
been aware how to read it. The old lord had had a
touch of the rebel about him from the start, downright daring in his reception of the dowager and the
heir, and in the style of it. One might somewhat have
misjudged him . . . failed to realize how deeply Murini
had offended the old man.

Or how strongly the old man was inclined to commit to the dowager. *There* was a thought.

Subcurrents. Implication and insinuation and hint.
He was back on the continent, for sure. He clung to
the upright bar against the chance of a hole 'in the
road and asked himself how far he had gotten out of
touch with the pulse of the mainland—of the whole
planet—during his absence. So much hardship, so
many lives impacted—

A rock hit the windshield. His imagination made it
a bullet for a split second, and he flung himself back,
bumped into Banichi, who steadied him on his feet.

"We are not yet under attack," Banichi assured
him, releasing him. "But we shall be. Best rest while
you can."

"Next to the young gentleman?" Bren asked, resolved on remaining where he was, and drew a quiet
laugh from his bodyguard.

"Indeed," Jago agreed, and for several moments
the cloud of dust sparked with taillights was all their
reality, the bus going blindly behind the others.

"Someone has gone off in the ditch," he realized,

as they passed a bus pitched over beside the road, nose canted down in the drainage ditch. Their bus whipped past and kept going.

"The hindmost will help pull them out," Jago surmised, which was the only reasonable help: They could not stop the whole column behind them to render aid, and it had not been the dowager's car in the ditch, which alone would have gotten their attention. Their bus bucketed along, itself swerving violently as the road turned for no apparent reason—one such turn had betrayed the vehicle now well behind them.

The progress became a hypnotic blur of headlamp-lit dust and sways and bumps, the driver working the wheel furiously at times to keep them on track, the engine groaning intermittently to get them up over a hill. Then they would careen downward, keeping their spacing from other lights, the whole rushing along at all the speed they dared.

No telling what Tatiseigi's driver had achieved, or how far in the lead they were. They passed a small truck that had pulled over. The passengers were gathered out in front of it with the hood thrown up, attempting to find some problem in the steaming engine. And it was gone in the night. Machines that had never driven farther than the local market were pressed to do the extraordinary, and they passed a large market truck, this one with a flat tire. The passengers held out hands, appealing for a ride, but their bus was already more crowded than afforded good standing room.

"We cannot take them on," the lord of Dur said, in

Bren's hearing. "We are charged to overtake the dowager. We have the heir and the paidhi aboard. Someone will take them."

The scene whipped past them, and was gone.

# 7

Another low range of hills, another diversion to the east, as the driver spun the wheel wildly. One of Dur's men held a flashlight to a map and shouted instructions into the man's ear the while. Intersections with other country lanes went past, and Bren found a small place to sit on the interior steps by the door, down next to Banichi's feet, seeking to relieve his knees.

"No, the paidhi is quite well, young sir," he heard Jago say. "He is trying to sleep at the moment."

Not precisely true. He heard his young companions had come looking for him, or Cajeiri had, personally, and he did not lift his head from his knees, while the rumble of bus tires over gravel made a steady, numbing din at this range. The door had three slit windows, and he could make out brush.

Perhaps he did sleep, in that position. He woke with a squeal of brakes and a rattle of gunfire, that sound he had heard all too often.

"Banichi-ji," he exclaimed, and started to get up, but Banichi's large hand on his head shoved him right back down. A little rattle became a barrage, and he sat, crushed by his bodyguard. Banichi and Jago were keeping low, everyone ducked down. Something cracked through the windshield, but the bus kept going, and then someone toward the righthand rear of their bus must have had a window slid back, because someone inside their bus let off a full clip. The bus never slowed. He heard Dur exhorting his bodyguard to shield their driver.

Damn, he said to himself, crouching there, thinking of that vulnerable, open car ahead of them.

"Cajeiri!" he heard Banichi say, then; and Jago's weight left him. With the worst of thoughts, Bren heaved himself up and scrambled through a press of atevi who tried to give him space.

Cajeiri was on his knees in the seat, he and his young guards, struggling to lift the window they themselves had dropped. Banichi leaned across and did it one-handed.

"What are you doing?" Banichi challenged them.

"There was a flash in the woods, nadi!" This from Antaro, defending her young lord. "We were shooting at that!"

"We?" They were all exposed to the night, but the spot which had roused their alarm was long past in the dark: The bus had sped off at the column's speed. "Your task," Banichi said in that dreadful voice he could use, "your *task,* young woman, is to protect your lord, which may require your flinging him to the floor, not abetting his youthful misjudgement."

"Yes," Jegari said.

There was a draft still coming in, a hole in that window, difficult to see in the dark. A bullet had gone through, and missed. Bren spotted it. He was sure Banichi already had.

And Ilisidi and Tatiseigi in that open car, Bren thought with a chill.

Whoever had shot at the column had fired blindly—which argued non-Guild forces, maybe Kadagidi coming cross-country, having learned they were no longer at Tirnamardi. In the latter case, the attackers surely had no way of knowing they had had the heir in their sights—

Or they *were* Guild, Bren said to himself, and had tried an impossible shot.

Which the fool youngsters had tried to return, and never mind Antaro had used the indefinite, child's *we,* the child's language which she had doubtless left behind entirely seven years ago, Banichi and Jago and everyone else in hearing had to be sure who had drawn a gun and not ducked his vulnerable head—damn, one could be sure of it.

"Keep your heads down, and rest," Bren suggested, employing the fortunate three-mode. "We shall all have to sleep an hour or so, no matter they shoot at us. I shall sit with you."

Which probably did not please his staff, but his backside was numb from the chill of the deck, and he slid past Cajeiri and took his former place, by the window. He took out his handkerchief—a gentleman had a handkerchief—and stuffed that white object in the bullet hole, high up. Well enough, he thought. A sniper might take that pallor for a target . . . above their heads.

"Nandi," Jago said, she and Banichi taking their

leave, moving back to their former position, they and Tano and Algini, who had held the curious back. The aisle in their vicinity cleared, people getting back to their seats.

It was the moment in which an adult might have a word with a foolish young lad, and his desperately inexperienced staff. One prudently declined, letting them think about it, think about the dangers out there.

Young nerves had clearly had enough for the moment. Cajeiri had turned about in his seat, trying to find a comfortable place. He tried turning his head away, pretending to go back to sleep, but in lengthy silence, the bus bumping and thumping at its high speed, he ended up turning over, and finally sliding against Bren's shoulder, exhausted.

Fair enough. Bren provided a shoulder; the weight was warm and provided a brace against which Bren himself could lean, the bus wall being cold and all too vulnerable. Bren found himself able to shut his eyes, even to drift a bit, in an interval of relatively smooth road and dark.

The bus jolted. Brakes wheezed. Refueling stop, Bren decided, at once aware that there was light outside the window. He began to think about getting up and finding out where they were.

Suddenly the bus roared off in a scattering of gravel, making no stop at all.

Cajeiri lifted his weight from Bren's shoulder, braced himself with a hand on the seat in front. "What was that, nandi?" he asked. "What are we doing?"

"One has no idea," Bren said, and hauled himself to his feet and past the boy, in search of information, in what was near dawn. Details hung in a dim gray light, where before had been dark and silhouettes, and faces were weary and watchful, facing the windows.

Tano was the one of his staff closest by, he and Algini having traded off their seats to Banichi and Jago. He took a grip on Tano's seat rail.

"What happened, nadiin-ji?" Bren asked.

"An isolated station, nandi. The pumps are booby-trapped. A team is working to clear it, for the hindmost. Our driver believes we can make it—if not, still to another pump, with a small detour."

Communications must still be working. They had hardly slowed down to find this out. "Is there word of the dowager?" he asked them, "Or the aiji?"

"There is not, Bren-ji. But we have not passed the car, either, baji-naji."

"What shall we do, then? Drive straight into the city?"

"Perhaps," Tano said. "Perhaps, Bren-ji."

Perhaps, if the fuel held out in sufficiency to keep the column together. If, baji-naji, the buses held together mechanically and they didn't run head-on into ambush. Worse, they were going into a narrowing cone on the map, making it clearer and clearer to anyone that the city was their destination, and offering ample time for their enemy to put up a meaningful roadblock and a determined resistence.

He worked forward in the crowded aisle to have a look ahead for himself, and had an uncommonly clear view of the column in front, no longer a dust-obscured scatter of taillights, but a gray string of five small trucks and one bus stretching ahead of them down a hill, on a well-traveled market road. No car. No hint of a car ahead ... whatever that meant. One hoped it meant that the dowager had gone off the route and tried some clever maneuver. It was no good asking. Whatever they got by radio—and it was even possible that his staff could reach Cenedi at short range—there was no news for him, or his staff would have waked him to inform him. Banichi and Jago were in a seat forward, themselves catching a few moments of sleep. He decided against interrupting that rest.

He went back to his seat, answered Cajeiri's sleepy questions—the boy had finally, absolutely run out of energy—and when Cajeiri dropped off again, he watched out the window, watched grain fields pass, finally making a pillow of his hand against the outer wall and catching a few hazy moments of sleep.

Then the tires hit pavement. He jerked his head up, saw buildings, realized they were passing right through a town—a town he knew, by that remarkable red building on the hill, the old fortress. It was Adigian, firmly in Ragi territory.

And it was sunrise, and people were out on the roadside waving at them, cheering them on, some of them with weapons evident.

Cajeiri's head popped up. "There are people, nandi!"

"Adigian. A Ragi town. Wave at them, young gentleman."

Cajeiri did that, but soon they ran out of people, and only saw three trucks waiting in a side street, trucks crammed with passengers, a sight that whisked by them.

More would join them, had his bodyguard not said so?

His nerves were rattled. As the last of the little town whisked past the windows he found another priority. The bus had what genteel folk called an accommodation in the rear, which he visited, and returned to his seat. The bus meanwhile kept up its steady pace, never slowing once, not as they left the brief patch of pavement and struck out on the usual dirt surface.

If there was fuel in Adigian, they had declined it, because the driver judged they had enough. Most everyone had waked, but now heads went down again. And amazing himself, he dropped his head over against the seat edge on folded hands and caught a little more half-sleep, his mind painting pictures of the space station over their heads, the white corridors of the remote station where they had fought to rescue the colonists . . . so, so much detail the world didn't know. He remembered a boy playing at race cars in the ship corridors, Banichi on his knees helping repair a wreck . . . all these things. A curious dinner, with floating globes of drink, and fear of poison . . .

Odd-smelling, dark halls, then, the interior of a kyo ship. The wide, strange countenance of their own kyo guest, his broad hand descending on a pile of tea-cakes . . .

His head spun. There were so many changes, so much water under the bridge.

Adigian. Home territory, if he had a home anywhere besides that mountain over on Mospheira. The Ragi heart of the *aishidi'tat*.

For the first time since returning from space, even in his sojourn in Tirnamardi, he began to have a real sense of location, as if a missing true north had settled back into his bones and reached conscious level. He knew where he was with his eyes shut. Shejidan was *there,* just there, ahead of them, a little off dead-ahead, as the road wound. Remarkable, that he hadn't had that awareness until now, that it had taken ancient Adigian and that old fortress to stir it.

Early evening on a rail trip, the train passing through the same town, himself on the way to Taiben, a guest of Tabini-aiji, all those years ago . . .

Making notes for the University back on Mospheira, attempting a sketch of the fortress, since a camera would never be accepted in those long ago, nervous days of human-atevi relations . . . back before the station had found new occupants, back before there was a space program, back before the paidhi had lived in the Bu-javid's noble apartments.

In those days the aiji inviting a human guest to Taiben was itself unprecedented. Revolutionary.

Teaching him the use of a firearm, and giving him a small, concealable pistol, had been a thunderbolt. Defend yourself, had been Tabini's implication, though at the time he had had no idea how imminent that necessity would be. It had not been a large gun: It was a small enough weapon to fit his hand, to fit very easily into his coat pocket—one of the concealed sorts that atevi maidservants might have tucked away when they only looked unarmed. Banichi had replaced it with another, slightly heavier, the night that he had arrived in Bren's service, never to leave him.

Tabini had seen conflict coming, hadn't he? The aiji had made his own decision to draw the paidhi into the thick of court activity, and gotten—oh, far more than Tabini had ever bargained for, that was probably the truth; but likewise Tabini had already known what he was going to ask for his people, hadn't he? More technology, more change—he had never offered more than Tabini was willing to take, and use, and go with, clear to the stars, and to societal change, and technological revolution that did, in the end, exactly what paidhiin had been appointed to prevent …

Paidhiin had operated on the theory that technological revolution would be devastating to atevi culture, atevi society. That it would mean another war, with the destruction of Mospheira or of atevi, or both. Paidhiin had resided quietly, down among the secretaries of the Bu-javid, and made their dictionary, and consulted on every word, every concept, building notebooks ever so tightly restricted to certain aspects of the University and the State Department, which supervised them.

He had broken those ties years ago. He had become part of the court. He had all but renounced connections with Mospheira in the end.

And that town had turned out to cheer them—to cheer Tabini-aiji, not the Kadagidi—hadn't they?

They were Ragi. It was natural they'd be on Tabini's side. But not, necessarily, on his. He had to remember that, and not expose himself to danger, not until he'd delivered the final load of information—things the Ragi atevi might not like to hear, but had to.

Turn in the road. He lifted his head, quite sure in his bones where they were, and dropped it back against his hands, then against the bus wall, Cajeiri sleeping soundly against his shoulder. He saw a map in his mind, a map that showed him the countryside between Adigian and Shejidan, a region crisscrossed with small roads between villages, population quite concentrated in this region, and with many towns of size.

It was a place where, above all else, they had no wish to engage their enemy. Nor would their enemy wish to engage them, here, in the heartland of Tabini's staunchest allies.

Had they seen the dowager? Was she all right? The boy was asleep again, against his shoulder. He had no wish to badger his staff with the unanswerable, when they were using their spare moments to think of details that might keep them alive.

Eyes shut. There was a period of dark, vaguely punctuated by potholes, turns, and once, the awareness of another episode of crowd noise, while the bus tires hummed over another stretch of concrete pavement.

Like going to the mountains over on Mospheira, that pavement sound.

Like holidays with his family, with Toby and his mother, he and his brother headed up the mountain to ski, their mother to soak up the fireside and a few drinks at the lodge . . .

Squeal of brakes. Loss of momentum.

He waked.

They had come to a fueling station: He saw the pump, and the dusty gray back side of a rural co-op building, with a red tractor with a harrow sitting idle, a wagon nearby piled high with sacks probably of grain, a railway car on a siding, typical of such places.

A truck was ahead of them at the pump. It moved on. They moved on, pulling briskly up to that point. He scanned all about them for a car, for any hint of one. At the same time he heard the bus door open, then heard bumping and thumping about the outside of the bus.

That surely meant they had found fuel, and were taking it on—insurance, he said to himself muzzily, and the boy, exhausted, never woke, though there was a quiet exchange of surmises between Jegari and Antaro behind him.

He doggedly shut his eyes, thinking their calculations about fuel holding out had been wrong. They had diverted over to this other source. They were still considerably out from the city.

The bus started up again, its doors shut.

"The paidhi is asleep," he heard Jago say, somewhere above him. "Let him rest a little."

He wanted to ask about the car, but they went away and he sank into spongy dark nowhere for an indeterminate time, before he realized the boy's weight had paralyzed his shoulder and he was in pain.

He moved. He lifted his head. He saw countryside rushing by, above a cloud of dust. He saw a bus overcrowded, with weary passengers sitting on the outer arms of seats, or outright sitting in the aisle, asleep, it might be, while a handful stood near the driver. It was the first time he had had a clear view out the opposite windows, and he saw a riverside, lined with small trees.

He shifted in his seat, chanced to wake the boy, who lifted his weight, blinked at the daylight, and asked where they were.

"Deep in Ragi countryside, young sir." Bren rubbed his stubbled chin and got his razor from his kit, down between his feet, with his computer. The razor still had enough charge to shave with, and he did that, while Cajeiri visited the accommodation to the rear.

He was still shaving when the boy came back and sat down, and watched in curiosity.

"Can it grow as long as your hair, nandi?" the boy asked.

"It might, young sir. But one has no wish to scandalize the court."

"Will you do it sometime?"

"What?"

"Grow it that long?"

"Much too uncomfortable, young sir. And not at all becoming. And it grows just as slowly as hair on your head."

"You would be as odd as the kyo."

"That I might, young sir. But by no means as round."

A laugh, a positive laugh on this chancy, desperate day. Cajeiri bounced onto his knees to see how his young bodyguard fared, the two of them having returned, one at a time, from their own visits to the accommodation. "Have we any breakfast?" he asked, and the two of them delved down into their gear and found grain and fruit bars.

"Would you like one, nandi?"

Now *there* was a good reason to have resourceful youngsters for company. He took the offering quite gratefully, tucked the razor back into his kit, and sat and ate slowly, finding it filled the empty spot in his belly.

All the while the land passed their windows, like a dream of places remembered. Not that far. Maybe half a day's travel by these weaving roads, until Shejidan . . .

Whatever that arrival brought them.

Algini came forward and spoke to the driver at one point, paused for a nod and a courtesy, and went back again, dislodging drowsing Dur fishermen the while. Then Banichi went back to Tano and Algini, while Jago talked to the driver, and then consulted the lord of Dur . . . all of which seemed unusual, and perhaps indicative of communications flowing from some part of their caravan. Bren wanted to snag Banichi on his way back, but could find no way to do so without provoking a host of questions from the youngsters: Banichi was looking straight forward at the road visible through the front windshield, and seemed intent on business.

A conference ensued, Banichi with Jago, and then

with the driver. Perhaps it was significant that they took a westerly tack at the next branching of the road—perhaps it was not. They bounced along, then hit gravel where another lane intersected.

"The other buses are not following, nandi," Jegari said in alarm.

Bren turned in his seat, and indeed, the reasonably unobstructed view out the back windows showed the other vehicles going off down the road they had been on.

That was it. "Pardon, young sir." Bren levered himself out of his window seat and, with stiffness in his legs, walked up to the front of the bus, where Banichi and Jago both stood on the internal steps, watching the road ahead.

They were on a downhill, and a train was stopped on the tracks in the middle of nowhere. A train with a handful of trucks and a couple of automobiles gathered beside it.

"What are we doing, nadiin-ji?" he asked, spotting those two cars with some hope. "We have left the column."

"They will meet us," Jago said. "We have other transport."

The train, clearly. A diversion off their route. Switch and confuse, he had no trouble figuring that. And the cars.

It occurred to him, then, that there was a train station beneath the Bu-javid itself.

And the dowager must have communicated with them, because there was no one else with the brazen nerve to divert them to that route.

He drew a deep breath, already laying out in his mind what he was sure was the dowager's plan of attack, telling himself the while that the dowager was stark raving mad. Having made herself a target all the way cross-country, now she was hijacking a passenger train—my God, he said to himself, relieved to think she was safe—and appalled to put the pieces together and guess what she was up to.

And all the while he had a longing vision of the hall outside his own apartment, his staff—his long-suffering staff, and Ilisidi's. Home.

But changed, there. Attack had come down on Tabini's people. Edi was no longer in charge there, that wonderful old man.

For that among other things, Murini deserved no mercy—if they were in the position of dispensing judgments.

The bus bounced and pitched its way along toward the train, and Tatiseigi's borrowed automobile was there among the trucks and several other cars: He could not see the dowager or Tatiseigi, but he at last caught sight of Cenedi standing on the bottom step of a passenger car, and at that welcome sight his heart skipped.

A body leaned against him, hard, and tried to worm past him, which in all this bus full of tall adults could only be Cajeiri, intent on a view out the window.

"Cenedi!" the boy cried, having gotten his face near the glass. "Great-grandmother must be in that train car!"

"That she will be, I am sure," Bren said, moving his

foot out of danger, the boy was so intent on leaning as much of him as possible against the passenger railing. The bus gave a final lurch, then an abrupt, brakehissing halt cast Antaro against him. The girl murmured, "One regrets it deeply, nand' paidhi."

"One hears," he answered absently, seeing the bus door opening, and himself caught in that press at the doorway with his computer and his baggage stranded back at his seat. There was no way to reach it. "Jagonadi! My baggage!"

"We have it, nandi," Tano said from the aisle, and that was that. The door was open, the way led out, and Bren managed to negotiate travel-numbed legs down the high steps. The last had to be a jump, down onto the graveled slope beside Jago, Banichi just ahead of them and Cajeiri and the Taibeni pair hard behind.

"Hurry out of the open," Banichi urged them and the youngsters alike, and Bren asked no questions. They had stopped by Tatiseigi's car, which was bulletpunctured all along its side, and they made all haste toward the nearest open door, that of the third car behind the engine.

Up the steps, then, and face to face with an old and ridiculous problem, that human legs just did not find train steps easy. He hauled himself up to the first step at Cajeiri's back, and, Cajeiri having struggled up on his own comparatively short legs, the boy turned and irreverently seized his arm, to haul him after.

And then straightway forgot about him, as they reached the aisle. The car, furnished in small chair-

and-table groupings, was crowded with atevi in formal dress and Guild black, along with a scattering of Taibeni in woodland brown, most of them armed.

"Mani-ma!" Cajeiri cried out, and zigzagged his way through his elders to reach his great-grandmother, who sat—God knew how—sipping a cup of tea beside Lord Tatiseigi, who had his right arm in a bloodstained sling and a teacup in the other hand.

The crowd cut off the view for a moment, until Bren had maneuvered his own way through. Just as he did come near, the train began to chug into motion.

"Sit!" Ilisidi said, teacup in one hand, cane in the other. She tapped the nearest vacant bench, and Bren cautiously came forward, bowed, and took the seat. Cajeiri sat down. So did the lord of Dur, and one of Ilisidi's young men brought the tea service.

Bren took a cup. It was hot, strong, and warmed all the way down to a meeting with his rattled nerves, no matter that his heavily armed staff was still standing watchfully by, like most others in the car, and that he still hadn't seen his computer. Tano turned up through the press, carrying it, made sure he saw it, and he nodded gratefully, yes, he had noted that. He could let go that concern.

Another sip. He felt moderately guilty, drinking tea when his staff had none, but there were moments when being a lord meant setting an example of calm and dignity, and he did his staff as proud as he could, reasonably well-put-together, shaven, thank God, and clean despite his sitting on the bus steps. Of the several of those of rank, Tatiseigi looked the worst.

"We are very well, mani-ma," Cajeiri piped up, in response to his great-grandmother's question. And: "Where is my mother, great-uncle?"

"With your father, nephew."

"In the plane?"

The plane seated three people, and she could be with Tabini—if Tabini was in the plane. Bren's ears pricked up, and Ilisidi stamped the ferrule of her cane on the deck. "Silliness," she said. "She will be perfectly well, great-grandson. Trust in that. One is," she added, looking directly at Bren, "grateful to the paidhi for taking care of this difficult boy."

"A pleasure and an honor, aiji-ma." It had been both, relatively speaking; but meanwhile he had an impression of many moving pieces in this operation, actions screening actions, and the casually revealed chance that Tabini, if Damiri was with him, was not in that airplane. "One is extremely glad to see you in good health, aiji-ma, and one is most concerned for nand' Tatiseigi's injury—"

"Gallantly gained," Ilisidi said, the shameless woman, reaching out to pat the old curmudgeon's good arm. "Protecting us, very bravely, too."

Tatiseigi cleared his throat. "A piece of folly," he pronounced, "an outrage, a thorough inconvenience, this upstart and all his relatives. And the car was not sprung as well as it might have been."

Likely he *had* been in great discomfort. Bren gave a little nod, a bow.

"One is ever so glad to find you safe, nandi."

"Glad!" A snort.

"For the sake of the stability of the center, nandi. You are the rock, the foundation on which all reason rests. One has always said so, in every plan."

Tatiseigi fixed him with a very suspicious glare under tufted brows, and had a sip of his tea. Another snort.

"The paidhi has said so, indeed," Ilisidi said, "and has understood your trepidation at receiving him under present circumstances. He expressed this sentiment to us, did you not, paidhi-aiji?"

"Very much so," he said. He was entirely unable to remember exactly when this was, but Ilisidi was on the attack, headed for a point, and one never argued.

"It was by no means trepidation," Tatiseigi said. "We are not trepidatious in the least. Cautious. Cautious, we say! Caution has kept this particular rock dry and steady all these years. Caution will carry us to the capital!"

"A wise and prudent lord," Bren said, steadying the cup in his hand, and noting that the lord of the Atageini had happily adopted his metaphor. Lord Adigan of Dur presented compliments, received the dowager's appreciation of his attendance. The wheels of the car had by now assumed a thump as regular as a heartbeat, a rocking sway that made the liquid tea shimmer under the light from the windows. The staff had filled a vase with hothouse flowers, red ones, to honor a Ragi lady, dared one say, and quietly set it on the table, inserting it into a little securing depression in the center.

It was all quite, quite mad.

But infinitely better than the bus. One hoped the walls of the car were better armored.

And that the effort to secure the switchpoints and stations ahead had succeeded.

"Another, nadi," Cajeiri suggested, hopefully offering his empty cup to the steward's view. "With sugar!"

And where *is* Tabini at the moment? Bren wondered, wondering, too, what the plane was up to. Nothing more than distracting the Kadagidi? Or just what had young Rejiri agreed to do with those bottles of petrol?

Where was Tabini, where were the Ajuri, the rest of the Atageini, whose lord, injured, would likely have wanted his personal physician? Had they gotten into the other cars? And what of the rest of the convoy, speeding across Ragi territory, presumably continuing on toward the city of Shejidan?

Faster and faster, surely to the train's limits of safety. The stewards found small paper cups from another car and managed to serve everyone a deluge of hot tea, gratefully received. Under a barrage of youthful questions, Ilisidi sat primly upright, her cane against her knee, her hooded eyes scanning the passing scenery as she answered what she chose to answer, frequently flattering Tatiseigi, who drank it down like medicine . . . the old man who had been late to every battle of a long life now rolled along, decorously wounded, in the vanguard of a desperately dangerous attack on the capital.

The train was going to get there ahead of the buses,

one had no question: the rails were the primary mode of transport in the land, vulnerable to stoppage and switching, but if security had put them on the train, that must have been solved. The question was what bloody business was going on out across the district. If part of the Guild, all the security staffs of all the houses backing the aiji's return, had drawn other sections of the Guild into it—bloody indeed. The Guild did not take half measures.

The steward offered a refill of tea. He took it. Ordinarily tea did not include sugar, but Cajeiri's request had brought a small dish of sugar rounds to the service, and he wanted the energy: He used the delicate little scoop to slip several little balls into the tea, and drank it down, wishing there were something more substantial in the way of food: The youngsters' sugary snack was wearing thin even for him.

Cenedi came into the car from the forward door, arrived in a deal of hurry, and went straight to Banichi and Jago, who in turn roused up Tano and Algini, while Cenedi went after Nawari and two others of his team . . . *something* was going on outside this tea party, Bren thought. It wasn't proper for a lord to get up and go inquire when such things happened, but he did cast a look at Banichi, which missed its mark, or the emergency was acute. Banichi headed for that forward door, and so did a number of others.

Trouble forward, Bren thought. "Aiji-ma," he said calmly, "one observes there may be trouble on the tracks. One might well brace for that eventuality."

"We have observed it," Ilisidi said calmly, passing

her teacup to a steward. And sharply: "Andi-ji!" This, to one of her youngest men, who had moved quietly into her vicinity. "What is Cenedi about?"

"Someone is reported to have pulled a bus across the tracks, aiji-ma." The young man came and dropped to one knee. "And to be defending its position with arms. But this is a distance away, and others in the district are working to clear it. One doubts there will be any great inconvenience to us."

One of the points against using the rails, Bren said to himself, resolving not to disgrace his staff by showing alarm. Lord Tatiseigi, meanwhile, had called his own chief bodyguard over for a running discussion, and Antaro hovered anxiously, while Jegari went to the left-side windows and attempted to get a look forward—useless, Bren said to himself. There was nothing to do but sit and wait and hope they did get the bus off the tracks.

Something thumped across the roof, going forward—instinctively the stewards' looks went aloft, to see nothing, to be sure, and none of the lords looked, but it was clear enough, all the same, that someone was moving along the roof of the cars, and moving fairly briskly.

Their own security, one hoped.

A sudden second noise, then, above the steady racket of the wheels on the track, that of a low-flying plane, passing overhead.

"Well," Tatiseigi said, addressing himself to the lord of Dur. "Well! Do we surmise the origin of that racket, Lord Adigan?"

"We would surmise," the lord of Dur began, but

just at that moment small arms fire popped from somewhere outside, and Antaro and Jegari flung themselves between Cajeiri and the nearest window, pulled him down as tea went flying. Security all around moved, and two young men seized Ilisidi to move her safely out of her chair. Bren slipped down to floor level with not a thought to dignity, except to avoid spilling his cup—one could grow quicker in that operation, over the years. The only one sitting upright at the moment was, God save them, Tatiseigi, who was waving instructions to security and demanding they take action.

"They are acting, great-uncle!" This from Cajeiri, from floor level above his crossed arms, as Jegari tried to get over to the side of the car. "You should get down!"

A window shattered. A red flower in the bouquet exploded in a sudden burst of petals. It was entirely astonishing . . . for the split second it took for fire to rattle out from along their roof. Hope to God, Bren said to himself, that it *was* their own security up there, that they still controlled the train, and that no one would manage a roadblock.

"A car!" Jegari, from his knees, risking a glance out the window.

"Get down!" Cajeiri shouted at him, a high, young, outraged voice, and Jegari immediately squatted down as fire laced across the windows.

Something exploded then. Jegari popped his head up and stared out the window.

"It blew up!" Jegari cried.

"Down!" Bren yelled at him, and Jegari ducked.

More fire from their roof, then. A dull, distant boom which there was no way to attribute.

Silence, for the space of a few moments after.

"We shall sit, now," Ilisidi declared, her aged bones surely protesting this undignified business, and her young men assisted her to sit up on the tiles. Tatiseigi sat in his chair, meanwhile, with his security bodily shielding him; the more agile lord of Dur had taken to the floor with the rest of them.

A thump forward, at the juncture of the car with the one forward, and Banichi came in, a little wind-blown, and carrying his rifle in his hand. Attention swung to him, and he gave a little bow.

"The attempt has fallen by the wayside, nandiin," he said. "There was a bus on the tracks, briefly, but the village of Cadidi has moved it, at some great risk to themselves and their property."

"To be noted, indeed," Ilisidi said, and, "get me up, get me up!"

Cajeiri scrambled to join the effort—the aiji-dowager was a wisp of a weight to her young men, and Cajeiri was only able to turn the chair to receive her, and to assist her to smooth a wisp of hair.

"Will someone shut that cursed window?" Ilisidi requested peevishly. Wind whipped through the gap, disturbing their hair.

"One fears it is broken, nand' dowager," the head steward said, the stewards moving to sweep up glass and recover the flowers. The steward gallantly proffered one surviving blossom, and Ilisidi took it, smelled it, and remarked, with a small smile, "They tried to shoot us, nand' paidhi."

"Indeed," Bren said, on his feet, and knowing he ought to stay out of the way, but Banichi was on his way back to the forward door, and curiosity burned in him. "Banichi-ji. Are we all right?"

"We have agents at the junctions and the way is clear," Banichi said, delaying. "But it must stay clear, Bren-ji. This far, we are all well. The opposition is not."

"Well done," he said fervently. "Well done, Banichi-ji."

"Our lord should *not* come up above to assist," Banichi said, not without humor, and not without truth. Banichi knew his ways, and was reading him the law of the universe.

"Go," he said in a low voice, "go, Banichi-ji. And be careful! Trust that I shall be."

Banichi ducked out in a momentary gale of wind and racket, and was gone, leaving him to walk back to his seat and pretend the world was in order.

"What did Banichi say, nand' Bren?"

"He reports they have cleared the tracks, young gentleman."

"That would have been that boom we heard," Cajeiri said.

"Do you think so, young sir?" Ilisidi said, grim and thin-lipped. "It may not be the last such we hear."

"We are still a target," Tatiseigi said, "a large target, and damnably predictable in our course."

"Very much so, nandi," Bren said, "as you made yourself on the way here, did you not?"

"And paid dearly!" Tatiseigi declared, his face drawn with pain as he moved the injured arm in its sling. "This was a Kadagidi assault! They knew that I personally would travel by automobile. First they destroy my own vehicle, and now they have shot my neighbor's full of holes!"

"Shocking," Ilisidi said dryly. "But more than the Kadagidi are involved."

"They knew, I say! They had every reason to know that their neighbor was in that vehicle, and ignoring all past neighborliness and good will, they opened fire!"

"Perhaps it was the Guild instead, nandi," Bren interposed, seeing his only window of opportunity, perhaps, to avoid a very messy feud between the Atageini and the Kadagidi—the burned stable, even the fatalities out on the grounds and the damage to the house might be accepted as the result of high politics, in which bloodshed was not unknown; but to think the Kadagidi, his neighbors, with whom he had such a checkered history of dangerous cooperation, had made a particular target of a vehicle they had every reason to think carried the lord of the Atageini—that, *that* had clearly offended the old man on a deeply personal level. "We might not have cleared all of them in the—incident."

Tatiseigi gave a noisy cough, a clearing of his throat, and one could see that new thought passing through his head: Tatiseigi was above all else a political creature. He had likely had a dose of painkiller, not to mention the discomfort, and he might not be at his sharpest at the moment. It looked very much as if he had given Tatiseigi a thought worth weighing: Not the Kadagidi, but an ambitious would-be Guildmaster who had made one overconfident move, brought Assassins into his lands, and failed. *There* was a situation of national scope, from which he could mine far more than from a local border feud.

"The paidhi is not a fool, is he?" Tatiseigi asked Ilisidi.

"Never to our observation," Ilisidi said. "Why else do we favor him?"

"We have the means to claim that it was Guild," Tatiseigi observed, "when we appear in the tashrid. That has value."

"Indeed," Ilisidi said, "granted we can proceed that far down this track."

Cenedi had arrived back in the car, looking satisfied, his graying hair blowing a little loose from its queue in the chill gust from the window.

"Report," the dowager said, and Cenedi, still looking uncommonly pleased, gave a little bow.

"The way is clear, aiji-ma. Towns have turned out patrols on their own, to guard the switch-points at Modigi and Cadai-Hadigin. The enemy has made another assault on the convoy, but to no great effect. Two vehicles have had their tires shot out, but those responsible did not linger in the area, and appear to have taken damage as they left."

"Hurrah!" That human word, from Cajeiri, drew the dowager's cold look.

"More," Cenedi said, with a glance at the lord of Dur, "the young gentleman from Dur has landed safely, refueled, and taken off, after dropping his petrol bombs in assistance of the village of Cadidi."

"Excellent news," the dowager said. The lord of

Dur simply inclined his head, relieved and proud, beyond a doubt.

"The best is last," Cenedi said. "Shejidan has turned out in the streets, and word suggests that Murini has gone to the airport to seize buses and fuel."

Dared one hope? Dared one possibly hope that Murini was going to leave the capital without a fight?

"Sit down," Ilisidi said. "Sit down, 'Nedi-ji, and have a cup of tea."

"Aiji-ma." In days previous, Cenedi might have demurred, disliking to inject himself into a privileged gathering of lords; but days previous had worn on him very hard. He sank into a chair and waited while the staff brewed up the requisite tea.

Bren got up for a quiet word of his own with the staff. "Our bodyguards have been working without cease for over twelve hours, nadiin. Might one request any foodstuffs you have directed to those assuring our safety?"

There were bows, assurances of earnest compliance that he did not doubt. He returned to his seat and sat, unease churning in his stomach, despite the good news from Shejidan. All they had been through was preface to trying to sneak an entire train into the city, up the line that led to the Bujavid . . . and all the population in Sheijidan turned out in their support could not deflect a well-aimed bullet.

If he were Murini, attempting to defend the city, he would bend every effort to stopping that train, knowing damned well where it was going.

If he were Murini, he would bring all force, all ingenuity to that effort. He would blow up track.

That said something of what the young man from Dur was doing up there in his airplane, flying ahead, tracing the track, making certain of their route and communicating with their security as best he could. There were no bridges between here and Shejidan: there was that to be thankful for—he by no means wanted to imagine explosives waiting for them.

Gone to the airport, however. Within reach of airplanes. And buses. Buses might have a dozen uses—perhaps to make a blockade. Perhaps to be sure the populace of Shejidan was limited in their resources.

Perhaps, please God, to board a plane and get out of town . . . Kadagidi territory had nothing but a dirt strip to receive him, and possibly—just possibly—the Kadagidi themselves had their doubts about Murini, whose rise within his own clan had been checkered with double-dealing and a far greater affinity for the politics of the south coast than those of the Padi Valley. The south coast was where Murini would have most of his support, and there were city aiports down there that would receive him, no matter if Sheijidan was in revolt.

Sandwiches were going around. Cajeiri took three, but his grandmother made him put two back. They were not that well-supplied.

Bren took a sandwich and a precious bottle of fruit drink, more welcome than tea. And iced. Folly to eat any sandwich without knowing the contents, but a cursory investigation between the layers turned up

none of those garnishes he should fear for toxins . . .
he took small bites, savoring them, enjoying the fruit
drink that had been so far from the menu during
their voyage—and, being modern, not on Tatiseigi's
very proper menu, either. Sugar insinuated itself into
his bloodstream, and unhappily produced nothing
but the jitters: He was that tired.

The plane roared over their heads and came back.
Cajeiri's young bodyguard, near the windows, got a
look and exclaimed: "There he is! The plane is rocking from side to side!"

A visual signal. Just what it signaled, one had no
idea.

Cenedi had excused himself and left the car by the
connecting door, in a gust of wind and rush of noise
from the rails. As the forward door shut, a sandwich
wrapper escaped Cajeiri's lap and swirled about
madly. It fell among the seats, disregarded, as Cajeiri
got up to go to the windows himself.

*Bang!* went the cane. Cajeiri stopped as if shot, and
came back to his seat, never a word said.

Meanwhile his two surrogates continued to peer
out the broken window, windblown and intent on
something in the sky.

"There is another plane!" Antaro cried. "They are
flying side by side."

"That," said the lord of Dur, "might be young Aig-
ino, from the coast. My son's fiancée."

Fiancée, was it? And a second plane, coming to
their support? That gave them much broader vision
over the countryside.

"They have flown off," Jegari said, kneeling on the

seat by the window, and putting his head out. He quickly drew it back. "Toward the south."

Toward the capital.

"Keep your head inside, nadi," Jago said to the young man, and to Bren himself: "Your staff would be easier in their minds, nandi, if you would also move slightly to the interior."

"Indeed." He gathered himself up and settled again in a more protected position, next to the dowager, with an apologetic and deferential bow. "Aiji-ma."

"Sit, sit. We should be extremely angry should some chance shot carry away the paidhi-aiji."

"One is greatly flattered, aiji-ma." The change of seats put him equivalent to, notably, Dur, who looked unaffected, and the Atageini, who looked at him with disapproval, but he bowed especially to Tatiseigi, who seemed a little mollified.

Another boom, somewhere near them, and in a little time Antaro called out that there was a plume of black smoke on the right of the tracks.

More, a report came from forward that persons had attempted to blow up the tracks between Esien and Naiein, and that this attempt had been thwarted, no agency specified—which argued that Guild was involved . . . on their side.

Sweets went around, little fruit pastries, and another round of tea, while the train ran full-out, blasting its whistle on two occasions, once when it passed through the outskirts of Esien. People there lined the trackside, waving handkerchiefs at them.

Then—then they puffed up a rise and began to

gather speed on the downhill. Bren could not resist getting up from his seat and taking a look out the window beside Jegari, as the track made a slight curve, one he so well remembered.

A city lay in the heart of that valley, a sprawling city of red tile roofs—Sheijidan. The red tile was all grays and blues at this distance, but his heart knew the color, and the wandering pattern of the streets, and the rise of the hill in the center of the city, on which sat the Bu-javid itself, the center of government.

Jago interposed her shoulder, getting him away from the windows, but others had stolen a look, too, and the word *Shejidan* was in the air.

"We may meet opposition here, Bren-ji," Jago said. "Or we may not. Word is that Murini has taken nine buses from the airport and headed south. But one is not certain Murini is with that group."

Buses, was it? Not toward Kadagidi territory, not toward his own clan, definitively, but toward the Taisigin, his allies on the coast?

"Presumably," Jago said to him, "we are to believe the Kadagidi have some internal dispute."

"Dares one hope it might be true?"

"One has no idea one way or another," Jago said. "But the action, the buses going toward the coast, is not what one would expect if the Kadagidi were firmly supporting him. He might have taken a plane. He may yet. We believe nothing until we have better confirmation."

He took his seat. He saw Tano and Algini with their heads together, and Algini talking on a pocket com to someone. Shortly after, Cenedi, who had been absent for perhaps a quarter of an hour, came back from forward, and consulted with them and with Banichi, while Jago talked with one of the Atageini bodyguards, with a grave and interested look.

Lords derived none of this information, to be sure. Bren sat and watched the passing of trees and hillsides, familiar places, a route he had used numerous times in his tenure in Shejidan. He held the memory of the city in his inner vision . . . his own apartment, and most of all its people, his staff, who might or might not still hold their posts—he could not imagine they were still there. He hoped they were all still alive.

"Nandi." Tano came close, and squatted down to eye level. "The rest of our number, in the buses, are somewhat behind us. The rail has taken us by a more direct route, and attempts to sabotage the rail have not succeeded—the Guild itself has acknowledged the restoration of authority."

"Extremely good news, Tano-ji." It was. He burned with curiosity to ask whether Algini's return from space might have precipitated something on the ground within the Guild and he longed to know precisely where Tabini was. But the one he would never know, and the other he would learn in due time; he would not corner Tano with demands for information on operations. "One is gratified."

"Indeed," Tano said. "Now the word is, from Cenedi, that the dowager's intent is to invade the Bujavid itself. Those who do not wish to take this risk may take the opportunity to leave the train. It will stop at Leposti to let any such persons off, if there is a request."

"Will she take the young gentleman into this venture?" He was appalled to think so, but he very much thought, by all he knew of custom and the demands of leadership, that for the boy to back away now might be something he would have to explain forever.

"It is a service the paidhi might do," Tano said, "to take charge of the young gentleman in whatever comes. My partner and I—we would ask leave to go with the dowager, if matters were in that state. Banichi and Jago would go with you; and Nawari would go with the young gentleman, to assist."

"You would assist the dowager."

"As much as we can, Bren-ji. We must."

Curious, curious choice at this crux of all events— Banichi and Jago, whose man'chi was with Tabini, departing with him; Tano and Algini, whose man'chi was much shadier, going on with the push inside. "I shall never hold any of my staff against their better judgment," he murmured. "But what shall we do, if that is a choice?"

"There will be a car," Tano said, "at Leposti."

Which could not be far, if his reckoning of position was at all accurate. Leposti was a suburb of Shejidan, almost absorbed in the growth of the capital, but outrageously independent; oh, he knew Leposti and its delegates, who had been violently insistent on a troublesome separate postal designation . . . a world and a way of life ago.

"We shall do what seems wisest, Tano-ji, with all hopes for the dowager's success."

"Baji-naji," Tano said. "I shall tell Banichi to prepare."

He was on the verge of losing Tano and Algini both to a danger where his staff, against all his wishes, couldn't stand together, couldn't work together. He felt desolate—didn't want to withdraw his small force, didn't want to leave the train.

But he didn't want an innocent boy in the direct line of fire, either; and he understood the thinking that had brought Cajeiri this far—the inexorable demands of the office he might hold, the appearance of having come as far into the fray, for his future, as a boy could; and having done so, to lay back just a little and stay alive, while others took the risks.

He understood that. He understood what his own job was, and what the dowager was asking of him— survive. Report. Support Tabini and Tabini's heir.

He sat there, the computer's carrying strap hitched high on his shoulder, and Banichi came to him, leaned over him, a shadow between him and any view of the countryside.

"Tano has spoken to you, has he?" Banichi asked.

"If my staff thinks this move wise," he said, "I understand the reasons."

"Excellent," Banichi said, and gave a little bow of his head. "We are approaching the meeting point. The train will stop briefly. Come with us."

"The boy—" he began, but Banichi was already walking away, leaving him to wonder whether to make a formal withdrawal, and say good-bye to the dowager, or just to get up and leave.

It was a Guild operation. He decided on the latter course, and got up and quietly followed Banichi to the front of the car.

Jago had drawn Cajeiri and his young staff with her; Nawari had joined them—no question now that the dowager was aware of the operation, and that her whole staff was.

"We do not wish to leave mani-ma," Cajeiri said, as firmly as any adult. "We refuse."

"The dowager's orders, young sir," Nawari said. By now the train was perceptibly slowing, the wheels squealing on the iron tracks.

"Move quickly, nandiin," Jago said, and hurried them out the door and into the wind, the ties moving below their feet, under the iron grid that was the platform between the cars. A ladder led off this open-air platform. The coupling that tied them to the car ahead flexed and banged under their feet as the train squealed to a halt.

"Now," Banichi said, seizing young Antaro by the arm, "change your coat, nadi, and your ribbon. Change with the young gentleman and be down those steps—stay low, be wise, and keep your gun out of sight. Trust to the staff with you. They are all Guild, and one is the dowager's."

"But," Cajeiri said, as Jago whisked the ribbon first off his pigtail and then off Antaro's, exchanging red for green.

"Stand still, young sir." As the wheels were still squealing, she tied the red ribbon onto Antaro's pigtail, straightened the too-tight coat, which would not button, and spun the girl about for a few quick words. "Straighten your shoulders, keep your head up. Be the young lord."

"Yes," came the teenager's staunch answer.

"By this you both protect him," Jago said, "as any Guildsman would do, and better than any of us. Go, nadiin!"

The train had scarcely stopped, but the two youngsters took off down the steps as quickly as possible, hit the gravel with Nawari behind them, rushing them along.

"I should be with them!" Cajeiri protested.

"Hush and take the ribbon," Banichi said. "You will need it. And put on Antaro's coat, young sir. This is the dowager's order. Move!"

"But," Cajeiri said, to no avail, struggling with the slightly oversized jacket.

"Come," Jago said, "and you will ride in the engine."

The engine, was it? Bren hitched up his computer strap, negotiated the passage between cars, and opened the door from the platform into the next car.

They entered with a gust of wind into a car the windows of which were defended by Guild of various houses, Atageini, mostly, Taibeni and Dur, not to mention Cenedi and the dowager's young men, plus a few more whose faces Bren did not see. Their passage through the car drew only cursory looks, a nod or two toward Cajeiri, but these people had their attention fixed on the passing landscape, the open fields and occasional hedgerows.

They were drawing close enough to the capital to

pass through more towns such as Leposti at any moment, where they might meet help—or opposition. Jago kept a fast pace through the car, Banichi bringing up the rear, but pausing a moment for a word with Cenedi, who nodded to something. Banichi cast a look back, as if in thought of the dowager.

So much Bren saw in his passing the door. In the next moment the wind hit him, the racket and rush of the unprotected platform, next to the thunder of the engine, an area where watching one's step was life-and-death. A ladder confronted them, a straight-up ladder, atevi-scale, and the whole platform vibrated with the joints in the tracks, with the deafening noise of the locomotive over all and under all.

"Nandi," Jago shouted into his ear. She took the computer strap from his shoulder, indicated he should climb first, and he did, hauling himself up the widely spaced rungs as fast as he could, aware by the vibration in the rungs that someone was on the ladder behind him, likeliest Cajeiri . . . he heard the boy shout something to someone, but he didn't stop or look down. He came up at nose-level with a catwalk, exposed to the raw wind, and hauled himself up onto that gridwork, kneeling on the metal surface and holding to the railing—thank God there was a railing. The train was passing through empty countryside at the moment, with a town in the distance.

And a swing of his head forward, into the wind, brought him the unexpected sight of a banner aloft, streaming flat out in the wind, atevi figures atop the train, sitting or lying, weapons braced. That banner was the red and black of the Ragi, of Tabini's house.

*That* was how the towns and villages turned out to mark their progress. *That* was the declaration they flew, unmistakable defiance of the authority claiming Shejidan.

Wind battered him as the train began a long curve. He felt Cajeiri's presence behind him. He summoned strength to wind-chilled muscles, hauled himself up off his knees, holding to the catwalk rail, and moved as briskly as he could along the outside of the generator and engine. The engine gave off the breath of hell itself, heat and fumes stinging and making his eyes run. Above all was the racket, and the rumble and the power of the machine, shaking his fingers to numbness on the railing.

The Ragi banner—outrageous and uncompromising: *Know us, know this is the moment, if Ragi will stand up and be counted. This is the moment, if man'chi will draw you.*

Why send off Antaro in the heir's coat? Why send Cajeiri up to the engine? Diversion, to be sure . . . but should anyone think the young lord would leave this train, this banner?

Except if security feared a traitor in their midst, in contact, somehow, with Murini's forces.

Such a traitor might be, one of Tatiseigi's men or one they had no way to know among their other allies.

But would the heir desert his father's cause, under such circumstances? Would he leave his great-grandmother?

Murini would, in a heartbeat. It was the recipient

of the information that counted: Murini might believe the boy would go. Murini always had, changing
sides with every breeze . . . a long, long history of fast
footwork.

Quivering iron railing slid constantly under his
hands. Wind battered him as the train's turn
smoothed out, gathered speed, and carried the ex-
haust away in favor of cold, rushing air. His catwalk
ended in another ladder. This one brought him down
to a small, sheltered platform with a door into the
cab, while another ladder offered steps downward.
The driving wheels thundered under the small gridwork platform where he stood, making it impossible
to hear.

Light footsteps shook the ladder above him. Cajeiri came down, and the gridwork platform was too
small to gather company, with Jago and Banichi coming after. He reached high for the latch of the metal
door and with his utmost one-handed effort,
wrenched it open and shoved it wide. Guild in black
leather met him as he shouldered his way past the
metal edge, men holding heavy weapons angled up in
the narrow corridor. Hands reached down, helped
him climb up the last high steps, pulled him safely up
into the short cab corridor.

Detail overwhelmed him, doors, guns, banks of
switches, levers, gauges whose purpose he understood but had no idea how to read. He had to trust
the armed men at his back. He was concerned with
the whereabouts of his staff, seeing Cajeiri had
climbed in after him.

Then Jago arrived up the short steps, exchanged a few words with the Guildsmen on duty, and indicated with a shove at Bren's shoulder that he should keep on moving down the short corridor into the cab itself.

He cast a second look back, unsatisfied until he saw that Banichi had gotten inside and the door was shut.

Switches, gauges, and levers. He made the passage along beside the power plant itself. Ahead of him, around a slight dogleg for the engine bank, a white light glared through the engine's broad windshield, offering a hazy view of the sky. It silhouetted a handful of armed personnel and others who must be the engineer and his crew. He walked forward, seeing too little detail in the unexpected light.

One man in that crew turned his head, and he recognized a familiar, light-edged face.

"Aiji-ma," he exclaimed, utterly confounded.

"Paidhi-ji." Tabini seized his arm and pulled him forward, into a nook between operators' seats, moving him into a safe, warm place. And made a second reach. "Son."

"Tai-ji," Cajeiri said, completely amazed at being likewise hauled into Bren's nook. The heir presented an unlikely figure, overwhelmed in a Taiben ranger's green jacket, small hands exiting the sleeves to grasp hold of the seat nearest. The driving mechanism under their feet thumped like an over-excited heart as Tabini reached and took his son by the shoulder.

And in that moment, in the forward windows at

Tabini's back, the city itself appeared, a sprawl of red-tiled roofs serpentining this way and that. High above it all rose the hill of the Bu-javid, where they were going, if any information still held true.

"How is your great-grandmother?" Tabini shouted at his son.

"She is very well, tai-ji, but Uncle Tatiseigi has a bullet in his arm and they sent my bodyguard away disguised as me, which I did not want! Where is ami?"

Mama, that was.

"She is with the buses, with her father and the Ajuri," Tabini said, and spared a hand for Bren's shoulder, on a level with his son's. "And you, paidhi-aiji. Are you well?"

"Perfectly," Bren answered, finding his breath short and his whole grasp of the situation tottering. "Perfectly well, aiji-ma."

A faint buzz penetrated the thunder of the locomotive and a shadow of wings spread over the windshield and diminished: A plane sped low overhead, streaking low along the track in front of them, then rose as it reached a hill, skimming like the wi'itikin in flight.

Scouting the track ahead, Rejiri was, and in utter hubris, letting them know he was up there—up there, all along their way, watching the track, advising them, making their hazardous course possible, an airborne presence elusive as quicksilver, there when they needed him. The boy that had set the nation's air traffic control in an uproar had redeemed himself today, no question, and they saw him rise, with a waggle of his wings, off on a course toward the distant heights of the city.

An explosion puffed smoke beside the plane. Another. Rejiri waggled his wings as if to chide the agent of this reckless attack, and flew on undaunted.

# 8

The little plane made a brazen, lazy circle all about the heights of the Bu-javid, reconnoitering—and clearly challenging the opposition to take a shot at it. Bren watched it from a relatively armored position in the engine cab, sure that this time, after days of being shunted aside, deprived of vital information, and relegated to a marginal existence by the Atageini, he could no longer complain he lacked a firsthand view of events. He had his computer slung on his shoulder, resolved to protect the machine from all accidents. He had Banichi and Jago standing near him, which he would have chosen above all things. He also had Cajeiri marginally in his charge—someone had to have the boy in hand, since Tabini, who was near him, was conferring not with Ismini, his own head of staff, who was nowhere to be seen, but with Cenedi and Banichi, the three of them laying plans the rest of them would follow.

This train was not only aimed at the center of the city, but about to force its way into the very heart of the hill on which the Bu-javid sat, that was increasingly clear: Tabini was determined to drive it as deeply as it could penetrate into the tunnels that led to the rail station inside the Bu-javid.

And, Bren thought, if he were in charge of Murini's defenses, and only pretending to have fled, the very first thing *he* would do was park a locomotive in those tunnels—the only obstacle available that could possibly stop this iron juggernaut. Stop it, and jam the tunnel with the resulting wreckage.

It was not a comforting thought. Presumably Tabini had thought of it. Presumably Guild in Tabini's man'chi were running ahead of them, making sure this did not happen. One had no way of knowing if Ismini and the team that had guarded Tabini during his exile were part of that effort, or were serving as decoy, or if there was some other reason for Tabini's reliance on older, better-known Guild help.

And where were the buses and the trucks at this point? Where was the majority of their strength? Gathering more supporters, they might be, but the buses were traveling a circuitous webwork of roads leading toward the city—still out in the country, news of their coming stirring others to join—or resist—the passage into the suburbs of Sheijidan, doubtless, but not making the kind of time they made.

Tabini's advance had met no great resistence, however—not yet. And Sheijidan itself was a strongly Ragi city, not strongly affiliated with their varied Padi Valley cousins, who were Ragi only in part, and in part not, and married into this and that other ethnicity—the hills, the coast, the south. The city itself would surely have borne Kadagidi rule very uneasily.

The boy standing beside him, their young vessel of all key lineages, brought in the Padi Valley's confused bloodties—and profited more from that heritage than Murini ever could or would, if the day went their way. It was demonstrable in that caravan of buses and trucks that the whole Padi Valley, Murini's birthplace, had fallen in with Tabini's advance on the capital. No question this boy's return from space would ring the death knell of Murini's hopes . . . unless this boy should die, or be proven to have fallen under unacceptable influences—

The paidhi's, notably, which state of affairs he himself had vehemently denied to all listeners, all the way from the coast.

So why in hell did Tabini insisting on bringing him with the boy, in the engine cab, in this most public of gestures?

Because Tabini, stubborn as they came, didn't intend to fail in this attempt, that was what, and he intended to make Murini a dead issue, incapable of protest or politics. The paidhi-aiji, one could only think, was still part and parcel of all Tabini's decisions, the adviser, the arbiter of his more outrageous opinions—and, though the paidhi himself had doubted it at times, it seemed demonstrable now that Tabini would not step back from that position. Some might see the paidhi as a liability. But others, diehard supporters of the aiji, might see the paidhi as the single binding-point of everything, every choice, every controversial step Tabini had made on the way to this upheaval: *Take me back, accept me intact, accept my decisions, and keep your objections behind your teeth,* his challenge seemed to be. *Admit I am right, and then have my son after me, this ultimate uniter of all clans, or bring me down, and lose my son, and lose his promise, and let a feeble union of the south coast and the small clans rule over nothing but chaos—choose that instead, and be damned to you all.*

Maybe it wasn't quite that harsh an ultimatim in Tabini's mind. Maybe he was sweeping the paidhi along out of some sense of policy he meant to maintain. But nothing in Tabini's past had ever suggested completely idealistic reasons, nothing except the aiji's absolute conviction that without him, and ultimately without his heir—there was no way to hold the *aishidi'tat* together, and without the *aishidi'tat,* there was no way for atevi to compete with humans and rule their own planet.

The scariest matter was—adding it all up—Tabini happened to be right.

Lurch. Jolt. The train passed by the airport, swung onto a familiar track, hitting a bump Bren remembered in his very bones, from his very first days on the mainland. Men in Guild black stood by the side of the track, lifted solemn hands as the train passed their position—hands empty of weapons, some, and others lifting rifles aloft in salute.

Guild had left their official neutrality. Guild had moved. The airport was at their left.

Was Murini still there, or might these Guildsmen have taken action to dislodge him? Had signals passed to Guild among them?

"Is there any word," he asked Jago, "nadi-ji, is there any word yet of conditions inside the hill itself?"

"There is dispute in the train station," Banichi said, clear understatement, "so the report is, nandi."

"And Murini? Has he been proven to have left the airport?"

"There is no word," Jago said. "Certain persons are looking for him."

*Looking* for him, was it? No one knew? Could the Guild itself have completely mislaid the self-proclaimed aiji of the *aishidi'tat?*

He didn't think so. The Guild knew where he was. There was a firefight or a standoff going on somewhere, that was his guess, and the side of the Guild they were communicating with had not been able to verify who was on the other side, so they had gotten no information they were willing to bet on.

"Can you talk to my grandmother?" Cajeiri asked, pressing up beside him in the apparent hope that communications were active.

"One is in communication with Cenedi, young sir," Jago said, "who is in communication with her."

"Tell her I am with my father," Cajeiri said plaintively. "Tell her and Uncle."

"She knows and approves this move, young sir," Jago said. "Indeed she does."

A deep breath from the boy, who leaned on the metal console and peered out the bright windows ahead of them. "Good," he said. They passed scattered buildings, the outliers of the airport. Streets were deserted, windows ominously shuttered along the way.

So had the airport train ordinarily been, when they had traveled in Tabini's personal car, that with the red velvet cushions, the thick, doubtless bulletproof blinds.

The door opened, a rush of wind and noise, and shut: Tano arrived, went straight to the aiji's conference, delivered a few words and left, acknowledging Bren's glance only with a slight bow of his head.

Another turn, and the train, at fair speed, rumbled through the commercial edge of the airport. Here, in this unlikely district, ordinary people had come alongside the track, near the road. People waved as they passed, and Cajeiri, leaning toward the side window of the cab, waved back.

"Dangerous, young sir," Jago said, setting herself between him and that window, and Bren put out his hand and moved her back as well, not disposed to let her make herself a living shield. She gave him one of those down-the-nose looks she could so easily achieve, touched his hand gently, then removed it.

"Bren-ji," she chided him. "You do not protect us. *You* do not protect *us*. Shall I say it, fortunate three?"

He was obliged to say, however reluctantly: "I shall rely on you, Jago-ji."

"I wish Antaro and Jegari were here, now," Cajeiri said. "I wish Antaro had not taken my coat." And then an apparent thought: "Can you contact them, too, nadiin-ji?"

A deep frown, on Jago's light-touched face. "We do not attempt it, young sir, for their safety, in order for the ruse to work. They may contact Cenedi, if they can."

"But there is no word from them?" Cajeiri was distressed. "There is no word at all, nadiin-ji?"

"Being wise, they will not chatter back and forth, young sir," Banichi said. "They will move quickly, and they will move unpredictably, as if you were in their care. We cannot answer your questions."

"They should not have gone at all," Cajeiri muttered, head ducked, his mouth set in a grim line. "They should not have done it."

Jago said sternly: "Jegari and Antaro are not your human associates, young sir. Never mistake it. They are not Gene and Artur."

A scowl. And a young man left to sit on a jump seat, head bowed, not so much sulking, one hoped, as thinking about what she meant, in all its ramifications.

A human was totally out of place in that transaction: Man'chi pulled and pushed, and it was an emotion as extravagant and sharp and painful as anything humans felt—no reason he could offer could make it better for the boy, to be told, indeed, they were not Gene and Artur. What they did was exactly comprehensible to the boy's instincts, if he would give way and listen to them. The paidhi had absolutely nothing to contribute in that understanding.

But in the next moment, while the engine gathered speed after the curve, Tabini crossed the claustrophobic aisle to lay a hand on his son's shoulder and point out the ways one should exit the engine if they should crash inside the tunnels . . . how ladders led to traps in the ceiling, and how he should, if worst came to worst in the tunnels or before that, find a small dark place inside the tunnels and wait until dark to get back down the hill.

"Yes," Cajeiri said, paying close attention, and Tabini found occasion to touch his son's cheek, approving—

Push and pull of emotions, curious combination of harsh and soft treatment to Bren's eyes, but the emotional tide in the boy at losing his companions had shifted back again, become a bright-eyed, active observation of his surroundings, his assets, the proper course to follow to gain his father's approval—one could all but see the wheels turning.

And one knew this boy. He aspired to be a hero. If he got the chance he would do extravagantly brave things, if security or the paidhi didn't quickly sit on him and keep him out of the line of fire . . . God, how did a human reason with the new spark in those gold eyes, that combination of empowering sacrifice for his own welfare and the heady draft of fatherly approval?

The train slowed for another curve in that moment, as the sun came between buildings. It cast their shadow against a grassy hummock beside the tracks, and showed the shadow of their train, the fluttering transparency of the banner spread above it, the low shapes of persons on the roofs of the cars. People all along could have no doubt who they were, and where they were going.

And still they turned out as the train passed the edge of residential districts with the tunnel looming ahead, men, women, children waving at them, one group with a stick with red and black streamers attached.

A short transit through a parkland. Then a tunnel

appeared in the windows, a tunnel, a dual fortification, a gateway that could be closed.

It was not.

Here we go, Bren said to himself, as if preparing for a dive down a snowy mountainside. Here we go. They were remote yet from the Bu-javid: It was the entry to the underground, the common train system that ran through the heart of the city. It would not be the greatest point of danger, unless their opposition cared nothing for casualties.

The tunnel widened to embrace them. They were swallowed up in darkness with only a row of lights in the ceiling to show their way, and those widely spaced. The lights of the engine itself illumined rock and masonry, and the double ribbon of steel that carried them. The noise changed to an echoing thunder that obscured chance remarks inside the cab.

One hoped the people on the roof were safe. It was certainly not where he would have chosen to ride out this journey.

But if there was to be an obstacle, they and he would be among the first to see it: The engineers would have at least as much warning as the headlamps and radio contact provided . . . not that there was damned much they could do about it. They were moving much too fast now for his liking, fast enough, he feared, to compact the cab into tinfoil if they met another train on their track.

Whisk—through an urban station, with lights on either side and other tracks, a strangely deserted station, where only a scattered few stood on the platforms watching the train pass. Two other city trains were parked there, and those were dark and eerily empty of passengers.

Whisk—into the dark again. The engineer, underlit by the control panel under his hands, was talking to someone on his headset. One hoped it was good information and good news.

Whisk—through another station, likewise deserted, only this one held a freight train, and a handful of shadows, one of whom waved a lantern, and the train slowed.

Back into the dark, then, more slowly still, swerving—if memory served—exactly where the airport train always swerved, where it switched to the Bujavid track. In a moment they hit the switch-point, a noisy crash.

Faster and faster, then. They were headed for the Bu-javid depot, now, right up into the restricted track.

Ought we not to proceed with more circumspection? He wanted to ask Jago that, but he had dissuaded Cajeiri from such questions, and found himself biting his lower lip as they began, yes, definitely to climb and then to turn.

"How is the track ahead, nadi?" He finally couldn't help himself.

"Clear, as far as our report runs, Bren-ji." Because she knew him, because she knew he was trying to think ahead, she added: "The floors above are at present another matter."

Murini hadn't pulled out all his supporters. Perhaps Murini had gone, and left them to take the heat—but it would not be easy. Granted one could believe the reports of where Murini was any more than one could rely on those about Tabini.

Whisk. Another lighted space, with no trains at all, only deserted platforms, amber-lit in the gloom, empty rails gleaming. He remembered it as the station that carried government employees to the foot of the hill.

And still the train climbed, its speed necessarily reduced by the bends in the track. It was inside the hill.

"The paidhi and the young gentleman should go to the aisle aft now," Banichi came to them to say. Bren perfectly understood: They were getting close to the main station, that station which served the higher levels of the Bu-javid. If anywhere, this was the place that would be defended. Nobody had thrown a train at them yet, but he would lay no bets now.

"Come, young sir," Bren said, collecting the boy with an arm about his back. "Let our security do its job."

"I have a gun," Cajeiri announced, this boy scantly eight.

"Keep it in your pocket," Bren said, "as I do mine. If you draw it, you will immediately strike an enemy eye as a threat, and you will attract bullets to both of us, vastly annoying our bodyguards."

"I want to fight!"

"Not even your father wants to fight, young sir, nor do I. Let us stand here at the start of the hallway, and not be in the way of those whose business it is to protect us. That is our best service."

"My father is up there!"

That he was, right up near the windows, which security would not like, but there was damned little arguing with Tabini at this moment. The headlights of the train picked out rough-hewn rock in their distant view of the windshield.

Then smooth concrete, and always that row of lights along the top of the tunnel—lights dimmed to insignificance in the blaze of fire that burst ahead of them. The whole train shook, and kept going through a sheet of fire, right on to the white flare of artificial light that dawned in the windshield.

Multiple tracks, the broad platforms for freight and passengers, cars on the siding and another train engine apparently moving, but on another track, headed out.

Home, the station from which he'd left on every journey . . . and seen now through the windshield of an engine cab bristling with firearms, a vantage on the place he'd never in his life imagined to have. The whole Bu-javid was above their heads now, the hill, the capital, the center of Sheijidan and the *aishidi'tat.*

The train slowed, hissed, squealed to a halt, and suddenly a fracture appeared in the windshield glass, silent, compared to the scream of the brakes. No one even ducked—only one of Tabini's guard stepped between him and the window, and at Bren's elbow, Cajeiri moved forward.

"Do not have the gun out, young sir," Bren said, grabbing a coat sleeve and wishing he could confiscate that deadly item from immature hands. "Keep your head down."

"But—" from Cajeiri, and at that moment Jago stepped near and seized Bren's arm. He seized Cajeiri's in turn, and took him where Jago led, which was back into the short corridor, and, bending low under the window, toward the door and the ladder down to the outside.

Out the door then, into the echoing cavern of the terminal and the reek of smoke and explosives in the station.

Jago stopped them half a breath—they were not the first out on that short steel platform: Banichi was. Banichi went down the ladder to the track itself.

"I shall follow you very closely, Jago-ji," Bren said at her back. "Use both hands for yourself, if you please."

"Yes," Jago said shortly, and dived down after Banichi.

It was relatively quiet, given the noise from the idling engine right at their backs, given, Bren thought, the pounding of his own heart, which he swore was keeping time with the train and just as loud. Two deep breaths on that little nook of a platform. Banichi's whistled signal pierced the ambient noise.

"We shall go down and to the right," Jago said, "along by the wheels, then up onto the platform. Follow."

She moved, instantly, and Banichi was out of sight. "Stay with me," he said to Cajeiri, and scrambled after Jago, down the atevi-scale ladder, down beside the massive driving wheels. Jago moved ahead of them, staying low, below the concrete lip of the platform, and Bren saw Banichi was up ahead, where a straight steel maintenance ladder led up to the main level. Banichi set a foot on it, reversed his rifle, and put the butt up above his head.

Fire spattered back, missing entirely.

"They are not Guild," was Jago's acid comment.

Not Guild. Banichi had ducked down and moved down the trackside, evidently on the hunt. Fire was echoing out from the top of the train.

"Stay here," Jago said, about to backtrack, and about that time fire broke out from behind them, from up on car level, about where Ilisidi's car was. Fire came from the windows as well as the top of the cars, directed at what, Bren had no idea. His mind supplied the broad panorama of the Bu-javid terminal, where a loading dock and broad passenger platform ran side by side in the large artificial cavern, with its pillars and buttresses. About fifty meters from the passenger terminal, a handful of freight and business offices, their very walls part of a massive pillar that went up several stories; and about twenty meters beyond that, a rock wall and the inset of a bank of lifts that went straight up into the offices and residences of the Bu-javid itself, doors tastefully enameled in muted tones, themselves an artwork—not to mention the several tapestries and the vases, designed to provide passengers tranquility and pleasant views, before the bustle and hurry of the trains.

Fire rattled out and richocheted off the train engine over their heads. More fire came from right above them, out the windows of the cab, and presumably their people on the roofs of the train had not stayed any longer to be targets—were likely either down within the train or had gotten off onto the platform immediately as they came in and moved out. The whole cavern resounded with gunfire, first in one direction and then another, and he had lost sight of Banichi in one direction and suddenly missed Jago in the other. They had left him—left him altogether, which they rarely did. She was off down the trackside.

His job was to stay low and stay out of trouble, and this he was resolved to do. "Come," he said to Cajeiri, spotting a nook beside the massive drive wheels, a nook that led right down under the engine itself, a place grimy and black with grease, but a veritable fortress against most anything that might come.

"What if the train should move, nandi?" Cajeiri asked.

"Then lie flat," he said. But the train had gotten itself into a position at the end of the line; only the roundtable could face it about, and that only after the cars were detached. Their train was not moving, and could not be moved, no matter a deafening explosion that filled the track area with stinging smoke.

Cajeiri moved to get out. Bren grabbed the coat and hauled him back.

"Great-grandmother," the boy said.

"The aiji-dowager can take care of herself, young sir. Stay with me. Guild is positioning itself out there, and that thick smoke is part of it. This is not the time for us to be wandering loose."

He could not read the boy's face in a dark now compounded by thick smoke. Next, Bren thought, the lights might go. But he heard distant shouts, people calling out for someone to move south.

They were certainly not Guild, he said to himself. He maintained one arm about the boy, the other snugging his computer close. The only flaw in his plan that he could see was that his own staff might not realize he had gone to cover, but he had no means to tell them except to use a pocket com, and that might not be prudent—even if they had time to answer a phone call. He heard little short whistles, low and varied in tone—difficult to get a fix where they were, but those *were* Guild, likely their own Assassins moving and advising one another of their movements in a code that seemed to shift by agreement . . . much as he had heard it, he recognized only those signals his staff made with the intent he understand.

Boom. And rattle. The ground itself shook. The lights dimmed significantly, not that there was a thing to see from their vantage between the wheels, and meanwhile the smoke had sunk even to low places, stinging the eyes and making his nose run. He blotted at it, and found his calves cramping as he squatted there, not a good thing if they had to run for it.

Someone moved near them. He saw legs, out between the wheels, but the smoke and the shadow obscured identity.

"Bren-ji."

Jago's voice.

"Here," he said, and let go of Cajeiri's coat. The boy crawled out ahead of him, and he exited on eye level with Jago, who leaned on a rifle, kneeling on the end of a wooden tie beside the rail.

"We are making progress," Jago said. "We have secured the platform. Forces are moving up inside the

Bu-javid itself, level by level. The Guild has concentrated its efforts."

"On which side?" he was constrained to ask.

"Tabini-aiji has taken possession of the Bu-javid," was Jago's answer, wrapped in the obscurity the Guild favored. "And Murini is confirmed to have left the airport, by air."

No damned specific information about the Guild, not even from Jago, not so the human mind could gather it.

"We are winning," he paraphrased her.

"Baji-naji," she answered him, that atevi shrug, and said then, "we have to move."

Something else blew up, shaking the concrete walls of the trackside. Jago pushed him into motion, and Bren grabbed Cajeiri's sleeve and shoved him ahead in the stinging smoke.

Where are we going? it occurred to him to ask. But they reached the short upward ladder, and Jago shoved them aside to go first, taking it in three moves, a rifle swinging from her shoulder.

Bren shoved Cajeiri up next, and followed right up against him, pushing the boy over the rim as Jago seized first Cajeiri and then him, dragging them into motion. Smoke was thicker above, stinging their eyes. Shapes—support columns, pieces of equipment, baggage trucks, moving figures—appeared like shadows and vanished again in haze. They crossed the broad platform, running toward the central lifts, from which the whole space of the station fanned out. There were shouts, whistles, and they dodged around a column.

Are we going upstairs? Going up into the heart of

the Bu-javid seemed to Bren a dangerous proposi-
tion, to put themselves into the fragile mechanism of
the lift system, the towering shafts an easy target for
sabotage. He was not anxious to do that, but he was
not about to protest anything Jago thought necessary.

The wall and the bank of lifts came up at them, a
darker gray in the smoke, and several shadows by
it—these were surely allies: Jago had her rifle in
hand, and did not raise it. Whistles sounded. Jago answered in kind, short and sharp, and they reached the
carpeted vicinity of the lifts themselves.

"Nandi." Tano was there. So, for that matter, was
Tabini-aiji, with his guard. Tabini snatched his son
into his care, welcome event. Bren bent over, catching his breath, wiping his eyes. Lights were at half.
Such lights as there were lit blazed in the high overhead like multiple suns in fog, contributing a milky
glow aloft, but no distinction to the shadowy figures
out across the terminal platform.

"We are going up," he heard. It was Tabini's voice,
leaving no doubt that was exactly what they would be
doing.

No one protested, not even the aiji's security. A
door opened in the wall, a clearer light shining
within, where there was no smoke—and it was not
the lifts Tabini proposed to take, but the emergency
stairs, Bren saw . . . emergency stairs, atevi-scale, and
the highest climb in all of Shejidan.

Guildsmen pressed their way into the stairwell
slightly ahead of Tabini, and the rest of them were
clearly going with Tabini, affording no time for questions, no time, either, to ask where Banichi was, or

Tano or Algini, none of whom were immediately in sight. Jago pushed Bren and the boy up metal stairs that resounded with the thunder of climbers above them.

Up and up the steps, three landings that had no exit, a space occupied only by the height of the station roof, a fourth landing, where several Assassins stood waiting to wave them on up and up. Bren found his legs burning, his heart pounding—Jago had the weight of the rifle, a sidearm, and ammunition, and he could only manage the computer and his pistol, himself, with the atevi-scale steps and a body that had spent the last couple of years sitting far, far too much. The rest of their force climbed behind them—he dared not slow them down, so he sweated and climbed, while his vision went hazy and his breath tore through his throat.

He bumped Jago hard when, at a landing, they reached an abrupt stop. He couldn't see, couldn't catch his breath, everything gone to tunnel vision. He heard Cajeiri ask him was he all right, and he couldn't get breath enough to answer, only bent, leaning on a safety rail, the computer a leaden weight on his shoulder, but he had it, he had the heavy pistol in his pocket—that had not fallen out; and Cajeiri patted his back, exhorting him to breathe.

Then Jago's free arm came around him, warm leather, great strength, absolute concern. He managed to straighten his back, then to get the edges of a real breath and center his haze of vision on an open door.

Tabini and his guard occupied that doorway. There

were figured carpets in clear light. Paneled walls. He didn't know precisely what floor it was, but maybe the first of the residential levels, above that of the courts and the legislature. He heard shots, somewhere down that hall, thought incongruously, hazily, of that fragile paneling.

"We are in, Bren-ji," Jago said, heaving at him. "One is sure the aiji's forces are ahead of us."

Beat and beat and beat. The heart had survived it. Cajeiri was safe. Bren flung his other arm around Cajeiri's shoulders, and Cajeiri's came about his heaving ribcage, and there was nothing for it but to walk, Jago with her rifle at the ready.

They passed the door. And there, blessed sight, Banichi stood, rifle in hand, and Algini next to him, giving directions, waving them down what was, yes, the first level corridor, a place of priceless handwoven runners, carved plinths supporting ancient porcelains.

"We are clearing the upper floors, nandi," Banichi said. "The adherents of the Kadagidi have not generally stayed to meet us."

Bren wanted to sit down on the spot. His legs all but tried to do so on their own, but he locked his knees and kept his feet under him. "Very good," he managed to say, the first thing he had gotten out of his throat. He had no sight of Tabini or his guard at the moment. Jago drew him on down the hall, with Cajeiri, until they reached a small conversational area, with an incongruous bouquet of flowers in a low vase on a table, everything *kabiu*, everything in

meticulous order, as a rattle of shots went off somewhere down the hall.

He didn't sit down. He thought if he should sit
down, he wouldn't get up. He stood leaning against
the paneled wall, his eyes darting in the direction of
the gunfire, which had ceased.

Jago watched that direction, too, and all others,
until a Guild Assassin trotted down the corridor toward them, with no hostile intent evident.

"We have the lifts," that woman said, and Jago
made a move with her rifle, signaling they should go
now.

They jogged back the way the woman had come,
down past the door they had used, and on around the
corner. The majority of their party was there, Tabini
in the lead.

And shots exploded off the wall in a shower of
plaster and stone fragments. Bren began to reach for
his gun, but a body hit him and Cajeiri at once, a
black leather jacket up against his face, his back
against the wall, Cajeiri next to him: Jago had covered them both, and he felt her body jolt hard, heard
an intake of breath.

"Jago-ji!"

She spun about against them and let off a burst of
fire, her muscles jumping to the recoil of the gun she
held one-handed. Then the pressure of her weight let
up. She stood rock-solid, facing back down the corridor, and now, Bren was able to see, other Guildsmen
had taken off back the way they had come, to secure
it against any advance.

"Jago, you were hit."

"Bruised, nandi." She swung about and herded them both into a position sheltered from the corners. Tabini had moved to cover them. The armor inside the jackets, Bren thought. Thank God.

Then Tano showed up in the hall from which they had come, waving an all-clear, and stances relaxed all around. Tabini came back to see to his son, to offer Jago a nod of appreciation which she received tight-lipped, with a bow.

"The Kadagidi staff has asked to remain in their premises, aiji-ma," one of the Guild reported. "They will admit our personnel as far as the foyer, and plead they have had no contact with their authority and cannot withdraw."

An unenviable position. Bren feared for his own people.

But there were conventions exempting domestic staff—if there was any staff in that establishment that wasn't Guild.

"Granted," Tabini said. "Set a guard on their door and outside their windows."

And monitor all communications. That went without saying. Even a human from the Island knew that would happen. He drew two relieved, shaky breaths in succession, knowing where Jago and Tano were, wishing he had a notion where Banichi and Algini had gotten to, or what was going on downstairs.

Then a report came in—he heard half of it—that the buses had reached the heart of the city, and that they were coming toward the hill.

"Mother is coming," Cajeiri said confidently, in his higher voice.

Mother, and perhaps, if the business downstairs had gone well, great-grandmother and great-uncle would come upstairs and help Tabini restore order. The Guild around them was taking a more relaxed stance, as if what was flowing in electronic communications was reassuring. Bren took the leisure to cast a worried look at Jago, to be sure she had told him the truth: Her face showed a little pain, but she occupied herself entirely with reloading, her dark face utterly concentrating on that, and perhaps on what reached her by the communications unit she had in her ear.

The lift worked. The racket in the shafts near them reported the cars in motion, and Bren had thought they had shut that down. Bren cast a worried glance in that direction, and at Tabini, who had spared no glance at all for the noise and the sporadic gunfire somewhere downstairs, as if he knew very well what was going on. The lift passed them, stopped somewhere on the floors above.

"Secure the audience hall," Tabini said, and that hall was on this floor, the main floor, which communicated with the outside via broad, public stairs, down to the U-shaped road—the road by which the arriving buses might most logically attempt to come in and discharge their passengers.

A pair of Guildsmen moved off in that direction, and vanished around the corner.

Silence then. For several whole breaths there was no racket, no sound of combat. Bren counted off his heartbeats, about the time it would take the Guildsmen—a man and a woman—to reach the public areas.

A door boomed open in a great vacancy, in the empty audience hall, a place ordinarily crowded with petitioners and favor-seekers, and noisy as a train station. It sounded lonely and hopeful now, the beginning of a new authority, the civil government opening its doors again for business . . .

And doubtless, in the prudent atevi way, any domestic staff or clericals still in the building had taken cover in their own areas, shut doors, locked them, and sat waiting for the Guild to sort out the business of state . . . sat waiting to be summoned by whoever won the contest and opened such doors.

Tabini gave a wave of his hand. Forward, that gesture said; and it was no time to lag behind. They moved on quickly around the next corner, into the broad public corridor.

The outer doors of the Bu-javid were still shut— the doors that at all hours and in every weather stood open for any citizen to visit the lower halls, to deliver petitions to the offices, to visit bureaus and secretaries, and most of all to deal face to face with their aiji in the public sessions.

"Open the doors," Tabini said, first of all orders after the opening of the audience hall, and security moved at a run to go unlock those huge doors and shove them open wide—not without a certain readiness of weapons and a cautious look outside.

What came in was the dark of night, and a breeze came with it, a breeze that would clear away the stench of gunfire and smoke, a breeze that stirred the priceless hangings and ran away into the farthest reaches of the floor.

The audience hall stood open and safe. Tabini sent Guildsmen in to join the others, and then walked in himself, the rest of them trailing after. The place was in decent order, give or take a stack of petition documents, heavy with seals and ribbons, that had scattered across the steps of the dais.

"Those will be collected," Tabini declared, treading a path among them, up the few steps to his proper seat. He would by no means ask Guild staff to do that secretarial business. Petitions were the province of the clerks, who had not yet appeared.

Tabini took his accustomed place. Beckoned, then.

"Go, young sir," Bren said, urging Cajeiri with a little push, and Cajeiri drew up his shoulders, straightened his rumpled, borrowed coat, and walked the same path as his father, to stand by his chair.

A second time Tabini beckoned, and Bren had the overwhelming urge to look behind him, to see if Tabini meant some other person of note—Tabini would not be so foolish or so downright defiant of criticism as to want him to mount those stairs. He should not. He had to find a way to advise Tabini against it, but could think of none.

Tabini said, definitively, "Nand' paidhi. Join us."

There was nothing for it. Bren walked forward, as far as the steps, and there sat down, as he had, oh, so many years ago, when he was only Bren-paidhi, and had represented Mospheira, not the aiji, in Sheijidan. A divorce case, Tabini had been hearing then; and he had been a different man, in that quiet perspective—

A man who had had to defend his bedroom against assassins. Or rather, Banichi had had to, that night.

Banichi was not with him now. Jago hung back near the door. He had never felt so publicly exposed and entirely vulnerable.

And he hoped to have done the right thing—not to stand by Tabini on the dais, but to resume his former post. He hoped people reported that. He hoped Tabini would understand what he advised, a restoration of the paidhi's former status—most of all that he would take that advice, and not shipwreck himself on old policy.

There was a little murmur in the hall. It fell away into a hush. He could not see Tabini's face, not at all; but he could see the faces of the crowd. He could see Jago and Tano, and saw that Algini had slipped in by the door to join Tano. He began to worry about Banichi—began to be desperately worried about him. Banichi had never left him so long, in such a moment of danger. He tried to catch a hint from Jago's face, whether she knew where Banichi was, or whether she was in contact, and he couldn't read a thing. Her impassivity far from settled his sense of dread.

"Let them come," Tabini said. Someone had just said that the bus caravan had passed onto the grand processional way, and that crowds were in the streets, welcoming them and joining them on their route. "The hall will be open, no exceptions."

It was an incredibly dangerous gesture. It exposed the aiji and his son to potential attack, not necessarily from Guild Assassins, but from some mentally un-

balanced person, some furiously angry person who
had lost fortune or family. The Presidenta of Mospheira would never dare do such a thing, despite all
the Mospheiran tradition of democracy and access to
institutions. But that the aiji of Shejidan made that
gesture—

He was not on the ship, or the station. One thing
overrode all questions of security, among atevi, and
that was the sense of choice in man'chi. It was the absolute necessity for stable power, that rule not be im-
posed. There had to be that moment of equilibrium,
that choice, baji-naji, life or death; and in that real-
ization of how things must be, Bren felt a certain
chill.

People began to trickle into the hall, lords of the
*aishidi'tat,* heads of clan, officials, clericals who had
kept the state running while Murini claimed to rule.
In each case, they came and bowed and proclaimed
their man'chi, and in each case Tabini nodded, asking
a secretary, who had quietly appeared among the
others, and another diffidently come forward to
gather the scattered documents from the steps, to
write down the names.

A paper of formal size and thickness was found, a
desk was drawn up to its position near the dais, and
the second young man, a junior clerical, placed there
the petitions that he had gathered from the steps, a
formidable stack of parchment, heavy with the ribbons and metal seals that proclaimed the house or
district of origin. There were too many for the single
desk. A second table was found, sufficient to hold the
rest of them; and in all of this, the first secretary, writ-

ing furiously to catch up, made records of the names and house of everyone who had come to the audience, the hour, the date, the vital numbers.

An old man presented himself, a senior servant of the Bu-javid itself, who offered his devotion to the aiji and wished to restore a sense of *kabiu* to the place, and wished to move the skewed carpet in the middle of the hall, of all things, its pattern again to run toward the steps, as it had tended.

"No, nadi, with all appreciation," Tabini said from above. It was as if the old servant had wanted to build a wall at the base of the steps. "But place it about. Full about, if you will."

Not keeping the presence that had come in from departing, nor yet lying as a barrier, but reversing the flow of the room, allowing what came in from the door to flow up to the dais, the reverse of what had always existed there. Even the paidhi had no trouble understanding that gesture. The crowd moved back and even lordly hands applied themselves to straightening that ancient, priceless runner, aiming its knotted-silk patterns from the door toward the dais.

In a moment more, a handful of other servants had brought in bare branches of the season, and vases of seasonal pattern, and tables stolen from the halls. Two more servants, from some deep and untouched storeroom, had found Ragi banners, red and black, and brought them to stand in their places, while others took down the Kadagidi colors.

"Unstaff and fold them," was the aiji's declaration. "They are the Kadagidi's banners, not Murini's. Send them to the Kadagidi. They may bring them back to this hall again."

A little stunned silence followed that quiet statement, like the shock after an explosion, and Bren did not so much as blink, though his mind raced, and he wondered if the Kadagidi would accept that gift—their banners returned to them without remark and undamaged. That "not Murini's" declared, seemingly, that if the Kadagidi could free themselves of Murini's leadership, they would find their way back to the grace of the Ragi aiji.

No reprisals. No general purge of clan leadership.

Nothing, either, so gracious or politically convenient for the Kadagidi as the aiji himself executing the culprit and taking on the onus of a feud. The Kadagidi clan itself had a choice: To take measures, or find itself at extreme disadvantage in the restored aijinate—even at war with the aiji's growing authority, which looked to be more solid than before the trouble.

No, it was not as gentle as it sounded at first blush. It forced a very, very uncomfortable decision on the Kadagidi.

Would they kill their own kinsman? Exile him? Break man'chi? The little silence that had followed that remark had perhaps understood that situation at gut level, a good deal faster than a human brain could reason its way through the matter, but likely enough, Bren thought, even atevi had had to think about it a heartbeat or two.

And the reaction among the Kadagidi would be split—split right down the dividing line of factions that surrounded any provincial power, those favoring this and that policy, this and that way of managing clan affairs. There was always another side to any clan-aiji's rule, and this little statement reached right in with a scalpel and cut certain taut threads within the Kadagidi clan itself.

Not gentle, no. Likely to have bloodshed, not all over the country, but specifically right within the very halls to which Murini's flight might now be taking him. Let *that* statement go out over the airwaves, as it surely had gone through Guildsmen present, to the Guild authority, whatever it was at the moment—Tabini-aiji, reputed for sharp decisions, was back in business.

And something had clearly happened inside the Guild, among all those delicate threads of man'chi held in precise tension, among Guild of various houses and districts. Guild black was prominent here, weapons in hands, weapons supporting Tabini-aiji.

From general paralysis of the Guild, change had happened catastrophically, from the moment Guild authority had moved in on Tatiseigi's estate—drawing a lethal reaction from high-up Assassins in Tabini's company, possibly in Ilisidi's guard, and—a fact which still stunned him, but which was very logical—possibly a very high one inserted into the paidhi's household. Assassins continually in the field, his, and Tabini's, and Ilisidi's—met a company of Guild officers who must have thought themselves the best, the most elite, likely equipped with the latest in surveillance and weaponry on the planet, arrived to carry out a very surgical strike—and they just hadn't moved as outrageously, as fast, as the field agents. Arrogance had expected Tatiseigi was underequipped, and hadn't reckoned on the heavy weapons and explosives Tatiseigi's house had accumulated over the years, in its proximity to Kadagidi provocations. Tatiseigi's antique equipage and old-fashioned notions had doubtless occasioned scorn and derision in the Guild, and despair in his own staff. But a shed full of explosives, as one could easily imagine existed in a rural, forest-edge estate, where the occasional stump had to be removed. (Had the aiji not wanted such caches registered, in those early, innocent years, when they were blasting roadway for the rail? And had not the lords turned very secretive about what they had, what they insisted they needed for themselves?) Lord Tatiseigi's store, had been, perhaps, just a little excessive for stumps ...

One could certainly imagine that train of events, at least, creating a very shockingly effective resource to deploy in general defense—God knew, Tatiseigi could understand blunt-force explosives. And his own staff had brought in items the planet-bound Guild had never seen. Arrogance met spaceborn technology, was what.

And met Guild members who hadn't been present for whatever underhanded maneuver had set Gegini in a position of authority.

A woman in Guild black came from the door, bowed. "The buses are coming up the drive now, aijima. A crowd is following afoot and in vehicles."

"Let them in," Tabini said, and Cajeiri, who stood at his father's arm, said, in a slightly elevated voice: "That will be mama."

"That it will," Tabini said, and in a few more minutes there was a general gasping and squeal of brakes outside, audible even in this thick-walled hall.

And if only, Bren thought, finding his hard-used legs were going quite numb and tending to shiver on the cold stone, if only this arrival didn't rattle a sniper or two out of the woodwork, they were home. *Home,* and Tabini was solidly back in power.

His own apartment was upstairs, in whatever condition. As Tabini's was. The halls of the legislative branch were just down the corridor. His imagination painted them dark, the lamps of democracy and debate momentarily gone out.

He imagined a plane in flight, Murini's people trying to decide where to go, if they had not picked out a landing site already. There was an airport at Mei, in the Kadagidi holdings, and that was the most logical, a pleasant enough town at the edge of the foothills ... if he dared bring his growing trouble home.

A hubbub came up the outer steps, came into the outer hall, stressed voices, voices calling out directions, but none raised in alarm. A clot of people pressed as far as the doors, demanding to be let in, and yet hanging back in fear or diffidence.

Then, "We shall all see the aiji," a feminine voice said in no uncertain tones, and guards at the door gave way to Damiri herself, entraining her young cousin, her sister, and her uncle and aunt and the lord of the Ajuri, all of whom swept into the hall in a wave of heraldic color and dynastic determination. Damiri walked ahead of them, left her uncle and grandfather to reach the steps, and to climb right past Bren to stand by her husband and her son.

That reunion Bren turned his head to see from the corner of his eye, a restrained exchange of slight, sedate bows, a little touch of the hand, wife to husband, son to mother. There was no wild outward demonstration, nothing of the sort; but he knew beyond a doubt one young heart was fluttering hard, and youthful nerves were at their limits. Ilisidi would be ever so proud of her handiwork, Bren thought. Everyone in the hall had a view of the lad's comportment, and it was formal and atevi to the last degree, even while other contingents from the buses were crowding and jostling their way into the hall.

"Tabini-aiji!" someone called out, and other voices joined in, "Tabini-aiji!" It became a chant, an echo in the high hall, and it went on, and went on until Tabini shouted out, "We are here, nadiin-ji!"

Which raised more cheers, rousing complete, aggressive chaos in the hall. Baji-naji, Bren thought, looking out over the tight-pressed crowd, in which black Guild uniforms mingled indiscriminately with the travel-worn colors of civilians from the central provinces.

A happy event. A Ragi event dominated by Padi Valley ambitions, the return not only of the Ragi aiji, but the heir of their own blood, in a tumult that went on and on and on, became a contest, a rivalry precarious and dangerous.

Bren felt the strength drain from his bones—was

anxious for his own people, and most of all anxious
for the impression he created for Tabini, this close
to power. He was not popular in the Padi Valley,
there was no question. He sat still, tried to look
decorous, wishing he could just creep down the
steps and see if he could gather his staff and get
away to his estate. He presented a disheveled appearance, not to mention a sweaty and grease-
stained one, black streaking his hands, smudging his
coat, probably his face, God only knew. Pale colors
meant he collected dirt.

And if he lived to get out of this hall, if some Assassin didn't take him out before the night was over,
upstairs was his dearest ambition. He wondered if his
own apartment still existed, if there could possibly be
a bath, and his own favorite chair, and above all his
staff, safe and intact.

He didn't let himself settle too deeply into that
hope. Most of all he was worried for his bodyguard's
safety—knew that they were committed to the aiji's
survival at the moment, in which his own safety came
second if not third, and he desperately wanted to get
Jago within range to ask her about Banichi, whether
he was safe. He saw her. But she stayed out of his
reach, and spent her attention on the crowd, scanning
faces, it might be.

Then he spotted a conspicuous coat near the doorway, an ornate, too-small coat, and a second teenager
with a handful of green-and-brown-clad Taibeni.

So did Cajeiri. "Taro! Gari!" the heir cried out,
startling the assemblage to silence, and a boy who
had learned some of his manners in the back corri-

dors of the *Phoenix* starship went plunging down the steps to reach his young staff . . .

Who had the planet-bred good manners to bow very deeply and bring the rush of enthusiasm to a quick halt. They bowed, Cajeiri bowed. The room— and startled security—let out a quiet exhalation and settled.

Bren did not look back to see Tabini's reaction, or Lady Damiri's. The moment passed. The young rascal wanted to bring his staff right up onto the dais with him, as security staff had assumed positions near his parents, but the young people had more sense. Antaro shed the too-small coat, exchanged it on the spot for her own, outsized on Cajeiri, and if there was a witness present who didn't realize what that exchange was about, his instincts needed sharpening.

"Son," Tabini said gravely, and with a single backward look, Cajeiri climbed back up the steps to stand with his parents.

The youngsters were safe, Bren said to himself, feeling his legs gone numb. That business had gone right. The youngsters had gotten through, the decoy, if it had worked, hadn't been fatal, and everyone had come through on that side. Was that Ismini, back there near the door? Was it Ismini and his team Tabini had sent with the decoy?

For his own safety, however . . . there was no such easy answer.

Then he saw one large and very welcome presence loom in the doorway—a little frayed, it might be, his uniform jacket cut and showing its protective lining, and even his hair stringing a bit about his ears, but

Banichi had come in, and with him, Nali, one of Ili-sidi's young men, in no better form. They spoke a word or two to Jago, gave a little nod.

A little shiver started, absolute chill setting into Bren's bones, as if the final reaction had waited all this time to get a hold on him. He tried to keep his muscles warm. He heard Tabini's voice above him, thanking his suporters, declaring Intent on anyone who aided Murini henceforth—documents would be filed; the Guild would function as it legally was supposed to function, a force for order, atevi order and law.

"At a certain time, and before the hasdrawad and the tashrid, we shall have an accounting," Tabini said. "The Bu-javid is in our hands again. Where is the master of the premises?"

There was a little confusion. But a tall old woman, her hair completely white with age, came forward to the foot of the steps and bowed deeply.

"I am here, aiji-ma, in my father's place."

"Madam," Tabini said, "take account of the staff, those in our man'chi and those unreliable."

"I have such an accounting," the head of staff said, "and have kept it daily, in my head; and chiefly unreliable, aiji-ma, the head of house security and his immediate staff, who are no longer on the premises."

"We know where he has gone," Tabini said. "There will be amnesty for minor faults. Do not mistake, madam, the names or the man'chi of those remaining."

A deep, deep bow. "To the best of my knowledge, aiji-ma, I have my list, and will give it."

"Do so," Tabini said, with that curtness only allowable in lords. "Assume your father's post, madam. Arrange the house, with immediate attention to our residency. My security will move in, immediately, expecting good order."

"Aiji-ma." A third, and deepest bow, and the old woman turned and walked away—one sure power within the house. Bren knew her, long her father's right hand, doing all those administrative tasks that kept the halls clean and the priceless heirlooms of the people's hall safe and maintained, down to the polish on the doors and the cleanliness of the carpets underfoot—not to mention the credentials of the lowliest sweeper and the most elegant arbiter of *kabiu.* Those eyes, however old, were very keen for minutiae, and that mind was sharp.

And upstairs, doubtless at this very moment, whatever Murini might have left in the aiji's apartment was being searched out, dismantled, rearranged. Very soon she would have domestic staff going through it.

"Those of you who have residence within the halls," Tabini said, "see to it. Those who have residency in the city, see to your own man'chi. Those of you who will house in hostels, we shall stand all charges: Apply to the master of accounts, with appropriate records, within prudent bounds. The *aishidi'tat* is intact and safe tonight. Go to your residences!"

A cheer broke out, happier than the last, minatory expression—a cheer for being home, for being back in command of things—for the world being set right, dared one hope?

Bren ventured to get to his feet, to find his legs

again, sore and weary as they were, and after a few tries, made it up. Tabini had gathered his staff about him, Ismini and his men with them. The lord of the Ajuri pressed forward, asserting his presence and his influence; the Taibeni, Keimi himself, with Deiso, moved in, asserting the rights and presence of their clan. Several others that had been marginally involved pressed close, including the head of (Bren recognized the woman, but the name escaped him) a major shipping company, in one of Shejidan's notable houses, vying for her share of attention. No few of Shejidan's powers had come in, and pushed their way into the approaches to power.

Reshuffling of the deck. People who had supported Tabini and those who had hedged their bets on both sides, all pressed hard to make sure they had the aiji's ear at the earliest, and offered their support, now that the balance had tilted so strongly toward a resumption of Ragi clan rule.

Bren took a careful step down, onto the floor, child-sized and not seeing over the crowd. But Tano was there, quickly, and immediately after came Algini, who gave a little bow, his face as grave and sober as ever.

"One apologizes, nandi, for actions taken without consultation."

Algini, who so rarely spoke, who never had admitted that he might have a man'chi higher than the paidhi, higher, even, than that to Tabini-aiji. And if he did hold such a man'chi, then, presumably, his partner Tano might hold the same. But there was no graceful way to ask. Dignity consisted in accepting what Algini offered, and doing it with good will.

"One has never doubted your duty, Gini-ji, or your goodness."

That last addition seemed to startle Algini, whose eyebrows lifted just a little, whose mouth took on a rueful—was it humor? Or something else, from this man of many man'chiin?

"One has never doubted the paidhi's qualities," Algini said, and bowed deeply. "In any event. Excuse us, nandi. One fears Lord Tatiseigi has taken residence. There are arrangements made."

Taken residence. Taken *his* residence, that was.

Well, damn! The old lord had survived, for which the paidhi could be very grateful; but he had also, always the double-edged good news, taken his apartment back, reclaimed the premises that Lady Damiri had graciously alloted to the paidhi-aiji, along with its staff, and *he* had nowhere to go, tonight.

"The dowager is well?" he asked Algini.

"Well, indeed, and she asks the paidhi and his staff take residency in her quarters."

*That* was a shock. He was ever so relieved to know Ilisidi had made it through—but the invitation was another double-edged item. "One would be very grateful," he murmured.

"We should go there, nandi," Algini said, and he obediently went with Algini, as far as Banichi and Jago, who stood near the door. The lot of them were relieved of all responsibility, one supposed, for the heir and his staff.

So they were home, and relatively safe. Concern for his secretarial staff occurred to him, but his security staff already had its hands full, just seeing to him, and the domestic staff that would have seen to domestic details and relayed messages for him had just been reappropriated by Lord Tatiseigi. He might call in staff from his coastal estate—assuming it was still standing—but he had no residence to call them to; he needed urgently to inquire after the safety of those people as well. Ten thousand domestic things needed attention, and the staff he did have was exhausted, likely as distressed as he was to learn that they were to be dispossessed of their place in the Bu-javid, that familiar beds and baths were not going to be available.

"It seems we are to lodge with the dowager, nadiin-ji," he said to Banichi and Jago, finding his voice unexpectedly hoarse. "One hopes we can have a few hours' rest tonight."

"Those premises will be secure, at least," Jago said—that was a plus, no question, the premises in question being those of a district no other lord would want to offend. The place was a veritable museum of fine carpets and heirlooms of Eastern origin, and those had surely stayed intact, whatever the troubles.

In the meanwhile, one could guess where Lord Tatiseigi would choose to lodge for a number of months, certain damages having occurred to his estate.

God, he had so wanted his own bed tonight, his own bath—his own staff. But they had never been truly his. And unwelcome as the news was, it had come in advance of any awkwardness, since the principals never had to negotiate the situation. No need, therefore, to be told at his own door that he could not come in, no need to sit miserably in a hallway until someone noticed his plight. Algini had arranged things. Ilisidi had.

"So, well," he said, hoping that external demands on his staff now were satisfied, and that he might get a message or two through to various people, not to forget a phone call to the Island, if he could manage it. "Nadiin-ji, one hopes that we all may go upstairs."

# 9

A bath, at last—a deep, soaking bath. And if nothing else, Madam Saidin, chief of staff in what had been his apartment, had sent his personal belongings to Ilisidi's premises—coats now surely out of style, clean shirts, clean linens—trousers that were not the snug fit they had been. He had dropped weight, not an unwelcome notion. The shirts and coats might fit, but strained the shoulders a little.

And there were Ilisidi's servants to help, servants expert at putting a wardrobe in order, in dealing with ragged, grimy nails and bodily cuts and bruises—not to mention providing an array of unguents and salves, providing a good shave, and, thanks to Jago, a deep massage on the broad dressing bench. He might outright have gone to sleep in the course of that process, but he fought the urge, and gathered himself up dutifully to be dressed and combed and fussed over, all in deference to the dowager, who, it turned out when he presented himself in the library about two hours before midnight, had made the other decision, and taken a lengthy nap.

For once staff information had failed him. It certainly would not be proper for a guest to be found asleep in the dowager's library, and he had no wish to crush his clothes, this first time a borrowed staff had dressed him. He thought of going to sleep, then decided someone in the household should stay awake a little longer to see if any emergency turned up.

So he called for tea and sat and shut his eyes between sips, in the selfsame library, swilling cup after cup of fairly strong tea, while he hoped his own security had found the chance for a little sleep, leaving matters to people Cenedi could call on.

Not so. Banichi turned up, washed, newly uniformed, but looking unaccustomedly tired. "Nandi," he said, in that formal way which indicated business.

"Sit down, Banichi-ji," he said, indicating a substantial chair, wishing not to have to strain his neck to see Banichi's face, and Banichi, unaccustomedly, sat down to give a report.

"Your staff and the dowager's have been gathering information," Banichi began, "and we have a list of unreliable persons, none of whom reside here, but Madam Saidin has undertaken to remove two maids to the country."

"Indeed." Removal, with the redoubtable Madam Saidin, could be more extreme than that, if she were entirely convinced of treasonous acts.

"More," Banichi said, "we have a reasonably accurate tally of Bu-javid general staff, and are acquiring others."

"One regrets the necessity of such measures," Bren murmured.

"Regrets, but your staff does not hesitate, Bren-ji.

Nor shall we permit any of these persons to come into your vicinity or the aiji's, or the dowager's." A breath. "One regrets to say, too, that certain lords have retreated to their estates, there to reconsider their man'chi and perhaps work their way back into favor."

"Word of Murini, Nichi-ji?"

"His plane has indeed landed in the south, in the Taisigin Marid, but he has disappeared from view— only to be expected, nandi. He may already be dead. It would be prudent of that clan. But he may also have decided to go into hiding until the wind settles."

"That man," Bren said, considering every syllable, "has deserved no pity."

"He has not," Banichi agreed. "Nor is he likely to obtain it from Tabini-aiji. There is too much bloodshed. The Filing has been made. Any Guild member can carry it out."

"Our staff on the coast," he began, in the curt manner of ship-speak, and decided, weary as he was, he had to amend that two-year-old habit.

"We have attempted to contact the coast," Banichi said before he could draw his next breath, "and have spoken to Saidaro-nadi, who says that they have suffered some attacks, but no losses. A number of persons attempted to steal your boat, but were frustrated to find a chain across the inlet. They abandoned it against the shore and fled, after doing internal damage and attempting to set it afire."

One could only imagine the scene. And damn it, he loved that boat. "Brave Saidaro."

"The boat is completely repaired," Banichi reported. "The house dared not venture as far as market, and has sustained itself by fishing and by digging shellfish, and by frequent gifts from Lord Geigi's staff, which fared very well in the crisis. Your staff would take the boat up the coast at night and load on supplies from Lord Geigi's estate—Lord Geigi's estate remained unassailable, since it is an Edi estate on an Edi shore, in an Edi district. One understands there was some shooting between the Edi and their neighbors to the southwest, and there were some Guild movements, all privately directed, nothing of Guild orders for the duration."

"Indeed." An appalling notion, the whole coast at odds, and with Lord Geigi up on the station, Murini's folk had still had to handle the Edi district very carefully. Though Maschi clan, he was a very popular lord over the Edi. "One wonders that Murini could restrain the Taisigin from running afoul of the west coast." The Taisigin occupied the southern coast, long at odds with the Edi; but one could see, too, that the Edi had long had a network of connections of marriage and history that ran all along the coast northward, into districts on which the center of the *aishidi'tat* relied for food—notably fish, a staple of the diet, in quantities the south alone could not supply. "But one believes Murini may have run up against certain economic facts of his existence."

That drew a little smile. "Certain economic facts of the world as it has become, not the world as the Kadagidi would like to pretend it might again become. Shejidan has come to appreciate its frozen fish, indeed, nandi."

"Bren-ji." It nettled him when his staff withdrew into formality with him in private, where *Bren-ji* would do ever so well. "One is very tired, Banichi-ji. One is ever so tired, and Bren-ji is an ever so much warmer blanket."

"Is it?" Banichi was amused. An eyebrow moved.

"Than nandi, yes, it is." He managed a smile. "One appreciates a warm blanket, now and again, Nichi-ji."

"That one may," Banichi said, and added: "Salads," which made him laugh despite sore ribs.

"Are we safe here?" he asked.

"One believes, yes, we are safe."

"It would be a good thing if one could make a phone call to Mosphiera."

"No, it would not be good," Banichi said, "for the paidhi to do that so soon."

"Indiscreet," he said.

"Exactly."

"Then the paidhi will be entirely circumspect, as long as need be."

"Certainly until the paidhi has reported, officially, to the legislature."

He understood that was coming, and only in the weakness of exhaustion had he voiced the thought of contacting Mosphiera, which would get their reports the way they had gotten other information, via the coastal settlements, and by rumor and radio. He, on the other hand, had to be concerned how such contact would look. Not so much substance, as perception of substance, people watching the wind to see which way it would blow in what was, potentially, a new regime. "Will the legislature come?" he asked. "Is it convening?"

"It has been called," Banichi said. "One has no knowledge as yet, but yes, certain ones are on their way."

"My office staff." The thought had gnawed at him ever since he had heard the situation on the ground. "One hopes they reached safety. That they may be induced to come back."

"Shall we make inquiries in that matter?"

"Among other things that must be urgent for my staff, nadi-ji. Perhaps if we only issued a public appeal."

"Such things are always accomplished down appropriate and secretive waterways, one believes your expression is."

Through appropriate channels. He had to smile. "Indeed. Indeed, Banichi. But let the word loose, down those ways, however it has to be done. I shall need them before long—if I stay in office." And a darker thought. "And if they have lost by being loyal to me, Banichi-ji, would I insult them by offering compensation?"

"It would by no means insult them, nandi," Banichi said.

"Bren-ji."

"Warm blankets," Banichi said, leaning forward, arms on knees. "One understands, Bren-ji. Warm blankets and a safe bed tonight."

"You should see to your own, Banichi-ji, you and all the staff. We are under the dowager's roof. One trusts that Cenedi is well. And Nawari. And the rest."

"A few nicks and bruises. But Cenedi—" Banichi made a little hesitation. "Cenedi-nadi is quite done in, and will not sit down, not for a moment, except the dowager has given him a firm order, which he is contriving not to obey."

"He is a brave man," Bren said, and added, relentlessly and with deliberation: "So are you, Banichi-ji."

Banichi glanced at the floor. It might be the only time he had ever taken Banichi so far aback.

"Very brave," Bren said doggedly. "And one will never forget it."

Atevi could blush. One had to be looking closely.

"One had better see to duty," Banichi said, making a move toward the chair arm.

"One should accept praise, Banichi-ji, where it is due," Bren said.

"We are a quiet Guild," Banichi said.

"All the same," Bren said. And added: "Very well done. One will not inquire regarding the Guild. One is very grateful to all the staff."

That seemed to be a poser. In another moment, Banichi lifted a shoulder. "Algini and Tano have a strong man'chi within this house. Your bringing them back to the continent was a great favor to them. They express deep gratitude."

*Murdi.* That *gratitude* word, different than man'chi.

"And man'chi?" Another small silence. In earlier years, he might have hesitated to inquire into that silence. Now he was relatively sure of the facts. And of Tano and Algini. "Will they be ours in future?" he did ask.

"They have never ceased to be of this household,"

Banichi said, and folded his hands across his middle. "The Guild never discusses its internal matters. But Murini's ally is dead, the old master has reasserted his authority. Algini is bound not to discuss it, but, Bren-ji, he and Tano are now free to continue assignment here. They wish to do so. They are not able to answer questions." A shrug. "But one doubts that the paidhi has many questions to ask."

It was a shock, even so, to hear it stated. Bren cleared his throat of obstruction. "No," he said. "No questions. They are welcome, very welcome."

Banichi listened to that, seemed to turn it over in his mind, perhaps trying to parse what he knew of humans and one particular human, and the faintest look of satisfaction touched his face. "Algini is required to be here. Technically, he cannot have man'chi within our household, but he holds it to Tano. And we may discuss this in *this* house because Cenedi is very well aware of the situation. That the paidhi guessed—one is not utterly surprised. It will not likely surprise Algini."

"You will tell him I know—at least I suspect—he has other ties."

"One is constrained to tell him," Banichi said. Guild law, one could guess, constraints of what he, too, was.

"One has no great concern for honesty. Tell him I have the greatest confidence in him."

"Indeed," Banichi said.

"But—" he began, had second thoughts, then decided to plunge ahead into what was not legitimately his business. "Tano. Man'chi to Tano, you say."

That required some consideration on Banichi's part, deep consideration. Finally: "Tano has become his partner."

"Become."

"They are old acquaintances, different in man'chi. They have acquired one, through Tano, to this house. They have become what they are, quite firmly so. One *may* have more than one man'chi, Bren-ji."

Banichi had never spoken so directly about Guild business, about the household, about the extent to which the Guild held man'chi within the great houses. He wondered why this confidence now, except that perhaps it was only what another ateva would have known, or guessed, more easily. He had a slight reluctance to ask any more questions on the topic, fearing, for reasons he could not define, that he might learn more than he wanted.

"These are dangerous times," Banichi said then, as if he had read his mind. "If Jago and I were ever lost, the paidhi should know these things. Consultation with the aiji's staff or the dowager's would produce good recommendations, but what surrounds you now has been very carefully chosen, and can be relied upon."

The aiji's selection, and the Guild's, and, up on the station, he had Lord Tatiseigi's man, Bindanda. Not to mention others presently out of reach. He had, Mospheiran that he was, failed deeply to analyze the politics of early recommendations to his staff, at first. He had realized certain things on his own about later ones, sometimes having to be told—bluntly so, as Banichi had chosen to inform him now.

"One should rely on them, then."

"Jago and I would recommend it."

"Baji-naji."

"Baji-naji."

But it was not a pleasant thought, not at all. "You are not to take reckless chances, Banichi-ji. One earnestly asks you not take reckless chances."

"This is our duty, paidhi-ji."

"I am most profoundly disturbed even to contemplate it."

"Nevertheless," Banichi said calmly. "One must."

It was like feeling his way through the dark. "Do you recommend taking on additional staff? Ought I to do that, to provide you assistance?"

"There is none I would rely on, except Taibeni, who would be willing, but quite lost and unhappy in the city. Best keep the staff small as it is. One is much more content inside the dowager's establishment. Lord Tatiseigi's is much more vulnerable to outside man'chi, even Kadagidi man'chi."

"Not Madam Saidin." Madam Saidin had been their own chief of domestic staff, when they lived in that apartment. Now she would surely manage for Lord Tatiseigi.

"Not that one. And one may trust she has looked very carefully into the associations of all persons on staff, and she will attempt to learn everything. But they are still a midlands staff. The dowager's is all eastern, most from her own estate at Malguri, or thereabouts. They would not be influenced by Kadagidi interests, or by southern, not in the least, no more than Jago or myself. If you ever must make a choice, listen to the dowager."

It struck him he had no idea where Banichi's home district was, or what his familial connections might be, and he had never asked. He was not about to begin now to inquire into what Banichi had never deemed his business. Banichi he took on trust, absolutely, in a human way—having no other way to be, not really, not even after all these years. It remained a humanly emotional decision, not based on reasons Banichi himself could exactly feel.

It worked, however, Banichi being what he was. And he felt secure in that human judgment, for the satisfaction it gave his human instincts. Trust. Man'chi. Not the same, but close enough, however complex.

"One understands." He picked up his teacup, discovered the tea gone ice cold and his hand incapable of holding the cup steady—fatigue compounded with far too many emotional confidences. He drank it to the lees and set it down before he spilled anything.

"The paidhi should take the chance to rest," Banichi observed.

"The paidhi is dressed. The paidhi will by no means put the dowager's staff to another change of clothes."

"The dowager's staff is accustomed to meticulous duty. Your own security staff believes you should rest, Bren-ji. Your staff insists, for all our welfare. Come. Into your suite."

He had already begun to listen: It was curious how the very effort of getting out of the chair suddenly seemed all but insurmountable, and the legs he had taxed running the stairs had gone very sore. But he stood up. He went with Banichi back into his borrowed quarters, and there Banichi himself took his coat and summoned staff.

He let himself be undressed—made no protest, as he would have done with his own staff, that a once-worn coat need not be pressed. The standards here were the dowager's, and he offered no opinions, only sought the smooth, soft depths of a feather bed, soft pillows—utter trust that Banichi and Jago and his own people were somewhere near.

He missed Jago. He wished she would rest, but he was already so far gone toward sleep that he had no idea where the others were.

The rest was dark, and a handful of dreams, one that lingered near to waking, that someone was rattling dishes, stirring a vat of priceless porcelain cups with a stick, and saying that they had to make tea because the ship was running out of that commodity, and that they had to grow flowers, because flowers were getting scarce, not to mention carpets being turned the wrong way.

It was not the sanest of dreams. He thought that he was on a boat, on Toby's boat, since the surface under him seemed to be heaving like that. He thought that Jago had come to bed, since he felt a warmth near him.

Or perhaps he remembered it, because when he waked he was alone in the large bed, in a very soft place, and he had no great desire to move for, oh, another century.

But duties came slithering back into his forebrain, not that he knew what, precisely, he had to do, but he was sure he ought to be ready to do it, whatever came. He lay there a luxurious ten minutes more, then dragged himself toward the edge, stuck a foot out into cool air, drew it back, nerving himself and re-warming the foot—then flung the covers off and braved the chill of an ordinary autumn day.

In Shejidan. That was the miracle.

They were in Shejidan. In the Bu-javid.

Home alive.

In the dowager's suite.

He found a robe on the clothes-tree and flung it on, on his way to the accommodation that pertained to the guest room.

A servant intercepted him. "Will m'lord wish a bath?"

He was chilled to the bone. "Yes," he said. He wanted it, very much.

It did take the chill from his bones. It afforded him another chance to nap, his head against the rim of a huge, steaming tub, until he had quite warmed himself from outside to in. A small cup of hot tea, offered while he sat steaming in the tub, brought his body temperature up inside, making it necessary to get out and cool off—in fact, his very skin steamed as he toweled himself dry. Breakfast—breakfast might become luncheon, perhaps one of the dowager's luncheons, but at least in a dining room, not out on the freezing balcony, with the current chance of snipers . . .

He came out of the bath to dress, at no point seeing one of his own security staff, and hoping that they had taken to bed themselves. Security present at the door was a pair of Ilisidi's young men, in whom he had the greatest confidence, and the domestic staff absolutely insisted he have more tea and a couple of delicate fruit-flavored cakes, the paidhi having missed breakfast.

A third?

"The paidhi is quite full," he assured the young lady who offered the dish. "These are quite large cakes, on the paidhi's scale of things."

"Indeed, forgive the forwardness, nandi."

"Indeed, nadi, there is no point on which to fault anything. The hospitality is flawless."

"Nandi." A deep bow, and every sign of astonishment and pleasure: One had to wonder how often the staff heard the word *flawless* from the aiji-dowager; and one, again, had to remember whose household this was.

But he sat dressed, finally, rested, if sore, warm and full of sweets, and simply enjoying the play of live fire in the grate, that very earthly pleasure, when a servant brought in a silver bowl with a message cylinder.

*The Lord of the Heavens' chief clerk,* it said, *begs to offer respects and esteem on the occasion of the lord's safe return to Shejidan, and hopes that his services will again be required. The staff has preserved papers, correspondence, and records in various places of safety and is prepared to return to duty immediately at the lord's request, beginning with the acquisition of our old offices and equipment within the Bu-javid, if this can be accomplished, with the lord's authority. One will assure the lord of the unfaltering man'chi of the entire staff, without exception.*

God. The records, the correspondence, the mountains of paper, the translations of manuals and technical specifications, all kept safe?

And the staff, all loyal, with all that had gone on? Amazement was the first reaction—never doubt of the majority of the staff, but *all* of them?

And ready to return to work before the smoke had even cleared?

He was deeply, deeply touched.

"Did this come by messenger, nadi?" he asked the servant, who stood waiting for an answer.

"One believes this to be the case, nandi."

"Paper and a cylinder, if possible, nadi, for a reply. My own kit is on the station."

The requested items arrived. He sat down. He wrote: *The paidhi-aiji is profoundly grateful for the devotion of the staff and of the chief clerk in particular. One can offer no assurances of proper quarters at this hour, but if you will provide a means and address for reliable contact, the paidhi will place this matter among his highest priorities. One leaves all other details of timely summoning and fit lodging of staff to your capable management—*

Dared one assume the paidhi would even survive in office the next few days?

Or survive at all, for that matter?

*—and urges you closely observe current events for the safety of yourself and the staff, with profound appreciation for your honesty and service.*

He dispatched the letter, trusting staff would be able to find the gentleman who had delivered the note. He wished he could rush out to the halls, embrace the old man, assure him of his job, all those humanly satisfying things—but in the very moment of thinking of it, he heard the distant pop of gunfire, and paused a moment, asking himself how safe the Bujavid was, or who might just have been shot.

Guild business? Mop-up?

He was far from confident, and had no wish to make the elderly gentleman more of a target than he had been, by bringing civilian staff prematurely into the building.

Besides, the answering of general correspondence, which that staff handled, had to take a back seat to more urgent business, such as finding a place to live that did not impose his presence on the dowager's generosity, such as getting some indirect word to Mospheira, to let Toby know he was alive and to let Shawn know Tabini was back in power. Banichi was quite right: Pursuing contact across the straits was a potential for trouble, something he dared not have misinterpreted or noised about as evidence of his reattachment to human interests.

The presentation to the hasdrawad and the tashrid came before everything . . . granted that Tabini really meant to let him speak freely.

Most of all—he had simply to stay alive for the nonce, and keep his head down, and not take walks in the hall, even escorted, until the dust settled.

He settled down to a little rest after the late breakfast, a little quiet time with his notes, a little time for his long-suffering staff to go on sleeping, if only they would do that. What had been a very small staff in the dowager's employ would, he hoped, begin to accrete old members of their own, filling out the numbers, but by the time they increased to any degree at all, he had to settle the apartment problem. He did think perhaps he should send a personal note to Madam Saidin, who had served him very kindly, and who now was back in the service of the Atageini. He might send flowers to her and the staff there, perhaps, if he had any funds at his disposal, though accessing such funds was usually a staff job ... and staff was what he lacked ... and then there was the matter of *kabiu,* in choosing what to send ...

Everything ran in a circle, and right back to the necessity of finding quarters somewhere in the Bu-javid, this ancient building wherein apartments were inherited over centuries, and where the contents of said apartments tended to resemble cultural museums, priceless art and antiques, each carefully arranged according to the numerical rules of *kabiu,* adjusted to the presence of a particular family. The Atageini had afforded him the old apartment, since Tatiseigi had been in the country and Lady Damiri, who had been using it, had moved in with Tabini. One might say the Kadagidi residence within the Bu-javid might be up for a new occupant, and very likely Murini had governed from those premises rather than set up in Tabini's apartment—but it would hardly be appropriate for a court official to set up there against the will of the Kadagidi. Murini might be a fugitive and his demise foreordained, but the Kadagidi themselves were an ancient clan, and to insult them would only slow the process of peacemaking and create a problem. No, the Kadagidi would be back, once man'chi had been settled. They would claim their valuables and their treasures, and their premises and precedences within the network of residencies, and to imply anything else would create a problem of lasting resentments, a cause that simply would not be allowed to rest.

So, well, he might find himself lodging down in the garden apartments again . . . opposite the aiji's cook, without a staff, as he had started. In a certain measure he wished he could take that option, go back to his pleasant little ground-floor rooms, in which he had availed himself of general services, rather than having a personal staff: But *that* was not the case, now—he had managed to lodge Banichi and Jago in those early days, but his life was far more complex, and his duties had gotten to be such that he hardly knew how to proceed about anything without extended staff, with specialists among them. He had staff up on the station who might well come down from his apartment there once the shuttles were flying again—granted that Tatiseigi would surely reclaim Bindanda's services. He would very much regret that, not alone because the man was an excellent cook, a good tailor, and a very clever observer; but there was Narani, that worthy old gentleman, and the others—and if they did get the shuttle fleet flying, that was certainly a staff long due a chance for blue sky and a little rest.

Well, well, he said to himself, it was a case of having far more problems than power to solve them, where it regarded housing and offices: He did not dispose of Bu-javid residences, and there was no sense battering himself against the situation. And until he *did* have staff he could not set up to provide for staff: circular problem. What had taken him years to build and Murini days to demolish had to be restored, but there was not a single move he could make until his problems reached Tabini's desk—and there was likely a pile of those waiting, all with far higher priority.

Jago turned up, looking wearier than she had seemed last night, all the energy of combat and hazard ebbed out of her. She accepted a cup of tea and some small cakes, which she had no trouble disposing of. She sat in the other chair, informally so, ankles crossed, and reported Banichi, Tano, and Algini all still asleep.

"As they should be," Bren said. "Rest as much as you can, Jago-ji."

"We shall certainly do so," she said. "We have a notion of bringing staff in from the coastal estate, but as yet we have nowhere to lodge them."

"True. Not to mention one has great concern for their safety, to make such a trip."

"Regarding such affairs," Jago said with a deep sigh, "the dowager's staff has arranged a formal dinner this evening. A message will arrive."

God. Already. He had no energy left for verbal fencing. But Ilisidi wished to have her fingers deep into whatever was going on, one could imagine. She had been unable to be everywhere at once in the fighting and now wanted all the details, while the irons were still hot. "Will the aiji attend?"

"One understands so," Jago said. "So will the Astronomer, the Ajuri, the Taibeni, and the Atageini lords. Not to mention the young gentleman."

Familiar company—give or take the Ajuri. "Everyone, then."

"Everyone," Jago said, and added, before he could even think of it: "The staff has sent for certain items of current fashion, and the paidhi will not be inglorious in his appearance."

He wanted to go fling himself face down into the very soft bed and stay there for days.

Instead he took notes until he could no longer postpone preparation—making sure he remembered all the details of recent days. He took a very long soaking bath, until his fingers wrinkled, had a leisurely second shave, a long encounter with thick towels, and finally gathered the fortitude to face formal dress.

Jago's "current fashion" turned out to be velvet lapels, easily applied by a clever staff. Fashion seemed to have recovered sensible moderation in the lace—in fact returning to an earlier style, which made the shirts from his oldest wardrobe, so the servant said, quite adequate, and very fine quality. The latest cross-belted shoes he absolutely could not come by, to the staff's distress, but footgear was always a problem on the mainland. He went with a comfortable pair of old ones, ineffable luxury of comfort, and kept the traditional queue for his hair and the paidhi's white ribbon, though the staff suggested that the Lord of the Heavens might possibly go with blue . . . so little this staff understood of what lay beyond the visible sky.

He stayed doggedly by the white, relying on the one modest title that he knew how to defend, and the modest position of a court officer with real and historic basis—although the dowager's major domo, who looked in on the proceedings, was certain that they should send for the dowager's tailor and go down into the city to exert some special effort in the matter of the boots, at least for the following day.

The paidhi was only glad to see his staff had had the same luck with wardrobe, recovering comfortable uniforms from the apartment that was now the Atageini premises. They turned up only slightly scraped and burned, as far as showed below cuffs and above collars—Banichi had a bit of a cut on his chin and several on his hands, but looked otherwise unruffled. Clearly Banichi had survived and there was no statement on the health of the persons who had caused the damage.

And meanwhile the sun had declined and one could actually muster an appetite.

He'd ever so quietly hoped, at least in the depths of his heart, that it would be a relatively homey, simple meal, nothing fussy and many-coursed.

It was evident from the formal reception, Ilisidi seated in the eastern manner, and the bustle of the servants over seven different offerings of drink—fortunate seven—plus the arrival of two southern members of the tashrid, anxious for their safety and redemption, and six from the north, perfectly triumphant in the action the north had taken—that it was no simple family affair.

It was the grand dining hall in Ilisidi's suite, a room, oh, about the size of a train station, and Tabini was unfashionably late, arriving barely ahead of the stated serving time, with a great cloud of attending secretaries, and with Damiri, with Lord Tatiseigi. Almost invisible in the flood of adults, was a very starched and proper Cajeiri, his two young bodyguards looking exceedingly uncomfortable in court dress—they being no Assassins, they looked more like young city gentlemen than Taibeni foresters.

"Nand' Bren," Cajeiri exclaimed, much too loudly, darted through a screen of adult bodies, and chattered on about how he had moved into his parents' residence, but how he was very soon to have his own rooms, and his own staff (how they were to manage this in a general shortage of apartments, one had no idea) and how he was already writing a letter to Gene and Artur and all the rest of his young human associates.

"Young sir," Bren said, "one is ever so glad to hear such news. But recall that the names of your associates aboard the ship are foreign to present company. These elderly gentlemen are often extremely alarmed by foreign names, particularly when it suggests your father's son has been influenced by humans."

A small sulk. The eight-year-old was back. "Then one will not be pleased with them. One will never be pleased with them."

"They have excellent qualities, the paidhi-aiji assures the young gentleman, and they have served the young gentleman's interests ever so well, at great personal risk and loss of property. Be patient and persuade them cleverly and slowly."

The scowl persisted through *patient,* but at *cleverly and slowly* gave way to a deep frown, a thinking kind of frown, then a dark glance aside at adult company and back again. "Are these people your enemies, nand' Bren?"

"Some of them certainly believe the paidhi has not served their interests. They have lost property and suffered greatly from the upheaval. One is certain, young sir, that the dowager can much better explain—"

"She calls them fools. She calls them very short-sighted. She says they have no good grasp of the numbers." This last in a whisper not quite adequate, but at least the boy tried to keep his voice down. Bren looked for escape, managed only:

"It is a very delicate situation, young sir. One begs you watch and listen—and by no means use any word of Mosphei' in these people's hearing."

"Not even 'damn fools'?"

Wicked boy. It was not the best acquisition he had ever made, and not the paidhi's best moment that had let him pick that up, in the depths of space.

"Especially not that," Bren said fervently, and the young rascal swaggered off, smug and victorious, to talk to his great-grandmother, who was engaged with the volatile lord of the Ajuri.

Bren kept quiet and drew over to the side, pre-tended to sip the offered wine, wanting to keep all his wits about him and earnestly hoping the youngster was not going to follow days of extraordinarily good behavior with a catastrophic letdown.

The Astronomer had arrived with Tabini, and while he had been talking to Cajeiri, the court mathematician had shown up, the two old gentlemen now involved in an ongoing debate and very little noticed the summons to table. They were still in the anteroom, passionately flinging numbers about, when the rest went in to dinner.

"Well, well," Ilisidi said, immediately seated—the privilege of age and rank—in her position at the head of the immensely expanded table. Tabini and Damiri occupied the places beside her, with Cajeiri—not to mention Tatiseigi and the Ajuri at either hand of that family group. Bren wanted a seat much removed from the high table, but servants directed him to a seat uncomfortably high and on Tatiseigi's left hand, in fact, but there was no objecting. One sat where one's host's staff indicated and made the best of it. The Astronomer was seated just next, and that chair was vacant, the old man still engaged outside the hall.

"Here we are," Ilisidi said as the buzz of movement diminished, "family and guests. One is ever so gratified. Do sit."

One sat, even the aiji and his family.

Appropriate expressions of appreciation followed, a general murmur, and then the host's recommendation of the first course, in all of which there was, thank God, a moratorium on politics. The Astronomer and the mathematician strayed in and found their places, fortunately not near one another, and the Astronomer began asking Bren questions which, again fortunately, pertained to the abstract character of space and travel through it, not the details of their trip itself, and distracted him from any conversation with Tatiseigi, who, having Damiri next to him, was interested in talk up the table, not down.

It was an extravagant and otherwise very *kabiu* dinner, security standing formally behind each participant, everything in season, wonderfully prepared—with due indication from the dowager's attentive staff and a graceful and quick substitution for every dish that might have proved inconvenient for a human guest. Bren sampled the dinner ever so slightly, finding his stomach, having had chancy fare for days, was not amenable to a surfeit of rich food. There were seven courses to get through, again, fortunate seven, forecast by the number of the varieties of drink offered at the outset, and the portions were atevi-scale.

A massive effort. There were seasonal flowers on the tables all about. A whole beast appeared, offered as the main course—it was the season for game, and there it sat in the middle of the table, horns, hooves and all, done up in glaze that, fortunately, in Bren's opinion, contained a fair amount of alkaloid. The paidhi took fish as an always correct alternative, quite happily so, while the beast was diminished to bone—the cook must have started that dish the moment Ilisidi arrived at the apartment, or optimistically before that.

There were fruits of the season, there were grain cakes, which were, if not the ones with black seeds, perfectly safe, and very good with spiced oil; there were eggs with sauce, one of Ilisidi's favorites. There was a secondary offering of fish, and shellfish, with black bread—never eat that one, Bren knew. And last of all came a sweet course, a dessert, a huge confection, more architecture than food, the presentation of which drew great appreciation—Bren nibbled at a very small slice of cake with sweet sauce, sure it at least was safe, but it was absolutely beyond his power to swallow more than two bites. Endless rounds of tea, and the absolutely mandatory compliments to the chief cook and his staff . . .

Then Ilisidi, host and mistress of the table, invited her grandson the aiji to speak. A silence ensued, a deepening silence, as Tabini stared fixedly at his wine glass, and turned it a full revolution on the table.

"Nandiin," Tabini said then, in that deep voice, and Bren expected a lengthy speech, full of plans. "Nandiin, there was bloodshed in the Kadagidi house, when the traitor's plane announced its intention to land. One believes that preceded his decision to turn south. There, he was allowed to land."

Chilling, both in implications of an in-family bloodletting, a purge within the house—and in implications the southerners had been very unwise to allow that plane to land. One remembered that Tabini had twice offered amnesty to that clan. One suspected it would not happen the third time. An infelicity of two leaped into Bren's mind, in Banichi's voice.

Another silence. Another revolution of the wine glass.

"We are informed the tashrid will have a quorum by dawn, the hasdrawad by midafternoon," Tabini said further, while the wine glass turned in his fingers.

Then those unsettlingly pale eyes flashed up, squarely at Bren. "The paidhi will deliver a report to the joint body before sunset."

Bren's heart sped. Thank God he had put in the time to have it ready, edited down from two years of notes to Tabini. Thank God, thank God. A final polish. That was what it needed.

"Aiji-ma," he said with a little nod of his head.

"We have received reports," Tabini said, still in that deathly, biding silence, "from the coast, from the north, from the east—" With a nod toward his grandmother. "We have asked that the people keep shops and shutters closed until the legislature has ruled. This is for public safety, and for public attention to the radio, so that they will know what is done. This is our decision. Those of the two houses who have come foremost, those on their way at our first summons, their names we know."

Another revolution, in silence.

"We have been immoderately generous throughout our administration," Tabini said, "in our treatment of those who have offended us. Those who have offended twice, and those who have offended the people, however, will find no such generosity. We do not admit that Murini has ever been aiji. None of his decrees has legal force. Such administrative matters as he signed must be presented again, or allowed to fall, from the greatest to the smallest act. We look for a list of these matters to appear on my desk, sorted into public and private categories, within two days. Any matter, however small, which does not appear on that list will not be considered for confirmation. Any omitted matter must be submitted as a new action."

It could be done. Clerks would have the lights on all night, but surely it could be done, given the court penchant for record-keeping and lists. It would be every grant of title, every court judgment, even divorce decrees which had found their way through the lower court system to the aiji's audience hall, every Filing of Deed or Intent, every adjudication, every assassination or fine: In short, every act public and private that Murini might have signed during his tenure. Most, purely administrative, would get a glance and a stamp; some would receive much more attention. It was, in effect, an audit of legal grants and confiscations, of awards and contracts, of alliances between houses, everything that might affect man'chi or empower one clan over another.

A mammoth job. One wondered whether, as with his old staff, the aiji's surviving staff had begun to come out of concealment, and whether, as with the university students making off with the vital books and papers from their library, the aiji's old staff had been able to preserve certain record books. It would be ever so helpful if they had.

The faces of those legislators present were very solemn.

"Yes," they said, almost in unison. "Yes, aiji-ma."

"Be it absolutely clear," Tabini said, in that same

low tone. And then: "This is my grandmother's table. I will have no more to say."

"Indeed," Ilisidi said, and gave a slight move of her hand. "We are weary. We are quite weary, nandiin. We shall present the traditional brandy in the parlor, but one is quite certain there will be no notice taken should certain of our guests depart to urgent duties."

Dared one assume it was time to go? It was a delicate decision—a political decision, whether to take his human presence into the parlor and mix his controversial self into very fragile atevi business, or to consider himself dismissed to quarters, bring up his computer, and hope to God he could find a viable printer in the household.

He decided on the latter course. The company rose, some to the parlor with their security, some to the foyer for a good-bye to their host, and he managed to slip aside and to get a glance at Banichi, whose sense of these things was usually much more reliable.

"One thinks we should go to our rooms," he said under his breath. "We have papers to prepare."

"Yes," Banichi said simply, confirming it was a proper thing to do—whether the other would have been proper, Bren had no idea.

But he was glad to get back to his own small refuge in Ilisidi's suite, and to shed the formal clothes, and to put on a dressing gown for a late session over the computer, a hunt, a final hunt for exactly the right words.

He was aware of movement about the apartment, was aware of some sort of consultation between

Banichi and Jago, and some sort of communication flowing to the outside. A crisis didn't take the night off. People were moving, he was quite sure—planes were flying, trains were rolling, legislators were spending a night on the move, huddled in small groups, discussing in advance of more specific information. And worrying how the measures they had taken to survive Murini's seizure of power might look now—there were bound to be very worried men and women on their way to the capital at this hour, and a certain number trying to figure out whether they should run to the farthest ends of the continent or still back Murini, or whether it was indeed, all up for the revolution.

Blood had already flowed within the Kadagidi house. There were bound to be other realignments in progress.

He worked until the letters blurred. He refined. He memorized. And a request to Ilisidi's staff brought a small plug-in printer, a machine capable of taking a format his computer could deliver, and a great stack of packaged paper. He loaded it, he set it to work, he informed the knowledgeable servant of his requirements and, with paranoid misgivings, left it to print and several servants to collate and convey it to a copy machine which would, they assured him, run much more rapidly than the printer.

He was, at that point, exhausted, and realized he had only taken the first sip of the brandy staff had poured hours ago. His hands and feet were like ice. His eyes blurred on ordinary objects. He sat in his bedroom, warming the brandy and his hands together against his middle, and studying his feet, seeing whether concentration could send blood down to warm them, or whether that would have to await his going to bed.

And he was very, very far from sleep at the moment. Far from sleep and needing every minute of it he could manage. Perhaps a second brandy. He didn't want to take one of his few pills—they lingered, and he couldn't afford to be fuzzy-brained facing—

He didn't want to imagine it.

Jago dropped in, not on her way to bed, clearly: She was in uniform and armed—she was only looking after him. "Will you not sleep, Bren-ji? Staff is asking."

Staff had been too wary of his glum mood to enter the door, he read that.

"Sleep does not come, Jago-ji. The mind will not sleep." At the moment the mind was half elsewhere, mistaking the shadow of a dim bedroom for the deep dark of space, nights that went on forever and ever, measured only in the deep folds of a ship's progress. He was there. He was here. He wandered between, trying to assemble his arguments for a planet that viewed him as a traitor—on both sides of the strait: Humans because he served the atevi aiji, atevi because he had set burdens on them and left them. A thick mist seemed to settle about him, and then to give way to an atevi room with Jago in it. "How is the staff faring?"

Jago hesitated a moment. Then: "I am the staff, at moment. Tano and Algini are in a special meeting at the Guild. They have asked for Banichi to attend. We would not both leave you."

"If *he* needs you—"

"One believes they are arguing for cancellation of certain Filings once accepted."

"Against me?"

"Against you, among others, nandi."

"Not *nandi*." He felt uncharacteristically fragile at the moment. "If they come to any harm, Jago-ji, if they come to any harm over there—" What did he say, what threat was enough, against the Guild itself? "I will go after them."

The slightest of smiles. "We believe Tano and Algini will return after the meeting. This is a duty they owe. But it is very likely they are in the act of reporting facts they have observed, and resigning any man'chi but that to this house."

That, he thought, might not be the wisest thing. "Perhaps they should wait until tomorrow for that," he said.

"Then it would hardly matter, would it?" She settled on the substantial footboard of the bed. "I have remained to protect you from any untoward business in the dowager's house, which we know will not happen, and Cenedi is annoyed with us, but he understands the form, and I understand it. Banichi would not leave you to anyone else, not even Cenedi. And I trust that if the Guild fails to be reasonable, Banichi will be back, all the same, and we shall simply await the damages to be filed."

It was humor, as Jago saw it. He managed a faint smile for her effort. And felt better for it.

"So," he said, "we are in no acute danger. Nor is the house."

"If there is danger, at this point, it would come from the Guild, or from individual members acting within their man'chiin."

"So, but Murini is in the south. Perhaps on a fishing boat headed for the remote islands. Anyone acting for him must surely consider that acting for the Kadagidi would be better, and they would not let him land."

"True."

"So have a brandy. Come to bed. Banichi will surely not disapprove."

A quirk of a smile, a downcast look, and she shrugged out of her jacket and its armor.

It was not exactly lovemaking, but she was warm, warm enough to take the chill out. He drifted off to sleep, waking only when Jago, who had never taken the earpiece off, slipped out of bed and left the room.

He got up, put on his dressing gown, shivering with chill, and got as far as the door before she came back again and put a warm arm about him.

"Banichi is back," she said, a shadow above his head, "and says Tano and Algini will be here before morning. They have a matter to attend."

"What?" He was half asleep and too chilled and worried for indirection. His mind pictured Guild business, a shadowy and bloody business, but Jago's powerful arm folded him close and held fast, while her breath stirred his hair.

"Back to bed, Bren-ji." The old way of speaking, that *Bren-ji:* our so-easily-shocked paidhi, that tone said. Don't ask, don't wonder, don't be concerned. This is not your business.

"Tell me when they get back," he insisted. "Wake me and tell me, if you have to."

Sometime before dawn she did.

Then he burrowed his face into the pillow, murmured an appreciation, and truly went to sleep.

# 10

Tano and Algini were there by morning, Tano with a slash across the hand, and with just a little stiffness about his movements. And not a word said, nor ever would be said, if it had been a matter within the Guild itself. One dared not ask. Bren only caught Tano's eye, nodded, Tano nodded, looked satisified, and Jago, while the house staff served a light breakfast, said that there was nothing that should immediately concern the paidhi.

Had they set aside the Filing on the paidhi's life? One had no idea. And there was that troublesome *immediately concern.*

Hell, Bren thought, and had an egg with sauce, and a half a piece of toast, thinking about his notes, the points he had to make, and wondering whether the printing would be done, on a primitively slow printer and copy machine.

Banichi came into the little sitting room/office at that point. "The legislature, Bren-nandi, has a potential quorum. They will assemble at midmorning."

That, on the traditional atevi clock, was fairly precise, about ten in the morning, which was about two hours, and the egg and toast suddenly weighed like lead. "Excellent," Bren said, numb. "How is the printing?"

"It will be done," Banichi said.

"Is there any possibility, nadi-ji, that we can employ a screen?"

Banichi's face, rarely expressive on a problem, showed sudden doubt.

"We would not wish to be controversial on that matter. Have we bound the copies?"

"Not yet."

"Printed images, then. Can we insert them?"

God knew no innovations, particularly not in the tashrid, even if the likely venue was the hasdrawad.

"We can manage," Banichi said, and added: "Unfortunately the images will be in monochrome, Bren-ji."

Banichi and the rest of them had gotten spoiled by the conveniences of the ship. They would have to make do on a very critical point, in images which would not look as real, or perhaps as reasonable, to the suspicious eye.

"I had better dress," Bren said.

"Staff will assist," Banichi told him, and he got up from the small portable table, walked back to his bedroom. He had not even time to look into his closet before the dowager's staff arrived to take over the selection and preparation of garments, the meticulous details of a court appearance . . . which freed a lord's mind to do more useful things.

Like worry.

His security staff was nowhere within reach at

the moment: That argued they were backstairs in consultation, or seeing to something useful to the occasion. They had left him to the dowager's staff, rare as it was for at least one of them not to be with him. He had put his computer away for safety. He trusted it was still in the desk, and that he was with allied staff, but all the same he worried, and felt exposed, and very, very lonely for the duration of the process. He wondered *was* the computer safe, and whether some new threat had taken his staff off to deal with it . . .

No information was hell. And he tried to remain pleasant with the dowager's servants, and to express gratitude, and to approve the extraordinary efforts that had transformed a several-years-old coat into something he trusted would be suitable. He was numb to aesthetics, felt the silken slide of fine cloth on his skin, felt the expert fingers arranging his hair, the snug comfort of a meticulously tailored coat, all these things, while his mind was racing in panic between the safety of his own staff and the order in which he had his data.

The dowager's major domo came in to survey the work, looked him over, bowed, and reported the printing was done, the last-moment insertion complete, the binding in progress.

"Excellent, nadi," he murmured, and tried to haul up enough adrenaline to get his mind working on last-moment details. He did not ask the embarrassing question, Where is my staff? He simply trusted they were there, spread too thin, doing all they could with limited resources, and the one thing they could not manufacture was time to do all they had to. Tabini-aiji was calling the shots, Tabini-aiji was setting the time of their appearance, be it straight up ten o'clock by Mospheiran time or farther along. "One expresses utmost gratitude."

Likely the domestic staff was attempting to handle his needs *and* the dowager's all at the same time, not to mention the printing and paper procurement— enough to fill a small truck, when all was done—not to mention very critical things Cenedi might lay on them. It was a heroic effort of the staff, from kitchen to doorkeeper, he was very sure, not only for duties ordinarily in their line, but for a clerical effort that ought to have engaged a full-fledged office.

Other staff had come in, not in the dowager's colors, domestics in modest, house-neutral beige, and for a moment they were no different to his eyes than any of the domestic staff, perfect strangers.

And then not.

"Moni? Taigi?" They were a little thinner than he remembered . . . from downstairs staff, and then moved to his service, to his estate on the coast, and then to retirement, by all he remembered.

Deep bows, and scarcely repressed delight. "We are back, nandi," Taigi said—Taigi ever the talkative one. "We are ever so glad to see you safe, may we say?"

"A welcome sight, a very welcome sight." He was thrown back years, completely derailed from his current concentration, and utterly puzzled. "Have you come from the coast?"

"Your staff sends their utmost regard," Taigi said.

"And wishes to send representatives to the capital to assist, nandi," Moni said, "in whatever way possible."

They were Guild, he ever so strongly suspected it. And given the recent—hell, current!—upheaval in that body, he was just ever so slightly nervous about their appearance here—scared, was more the point, but he put on his best manners, and collected himself. When had he ever been afraid of Moni and Taigi? How could he be?

"One has very many needs," he said, "and first of all with the printing. Please, nadiin-ji—in ever so great a stricture of time—consult the dowager's major domo and inquire if the printing will be finished within the hour? And ask how are we transporting it all to the legislature?"

"Indeed, nandi," Taigi said, and the pair turned and left, leaving him—

Shaking, dammit. Two old acquaintances, two former staffers turned up, and he could manage no decent gratitude, only a moment of panic, a feeling of utter nakedness. He had been safe within the cocoon of the dowager's residence, safe, for the only moment in years that Banichi and Jago had actually left him— and then two people from his past showed up, and he outright panicked and invented a job for them to do, a job that wasn't particularly polite to the dowager's staff, and entirely unnecessary: The printing would be done—it *would* be done, and if it looked otherwise, the dowager would press other facilities into service to see that it was done. He feared the pair had come expecting to resume their old intimate relation with him in this crisis, perhaps simply to help him dress for court, with the earnest good will of all his staff on the coast.

He was already dressed, thank God, and had no need to let them touch him. He felt guilty for his suspicions, and his panic, and the state of mind he'd gotten into, but he couldn't find any confidence in the situation. He stood alone in the room for one cold moment, every organized thought flown out of his head, all his preparation for the legislature completely lost from memory—he didn't know which loose end to grab first, or at what point to recover himself.

Concentrate on the speech, he told himself, but staying alive was his foremost responsibility—his utmost responsibility to everyone involved.

He took three strides to the door, found one of the dowager's staff out in the hall, her arms full of printed, bound books, doubtless his.

"Forgive me, nadi," he said in a low, urgent tone. "Set those aside and take me to Banichi or Jago or Cenedi. Immediately."

"Nandi," she said, bowing, and searching desperately in the baroque hallway for somewhere safe to set her burden. "Please follow." Her conclusion was simply to clutch the heavy stack to her bosom and go, and he followed after her, back the way she had come, back to a door only staff would use, and a corridor as plain and severe as the ordinary corridors were ornate. Thick carpet-deadened steps here, minimal lighting cast the place in shadow as well as silence, and she led him quickly along one corridor and another until they reached a small, close room, a place of thickly-baffled walls and a little brighter lighting.

Banichi was there, with Cenedi, with Jago as well, and Tano. All eyes looked in his direction, fixed in absolute startlement.

"Nandi." From Banichi, quietly and respectfully.

And he suddenly felt the fool. Felt like bowing, being out of his proper territory and with no good reason behind his flight from his own premises.

"Moni and Taigi just came in, nadiin-ji. One could not entirely account for their provenance. They claimed relation to the estate. I set them to query the major domo, regarding the printing." He found himself a little out of breath, and Jago had already moved, past him, back down the corridor, on an investigative track. He added, inanely attempting to keep the conversational tone: "I came here."

"Curious," Banichi said. "They would know better. And staff let them in."

"We were watching," his young guide said.

"Unacceptable," Cenedi said, and left on Jago's track, with his own man on his heels and the young woman with the bound texts hard pressed to keep up.

"One hardly knew," Bren began awkwardly, left alone with Banichi. "I held them in good regard."

"Their reputation and their clearance was once impeccable for their assignment," Banichi said. "Their current behavior is not. They have used accesses they no longer own to get in here. Bren-ji, go down that corridor to your right and exit the door."

He didn't question, except to say: "I left my computer on my desk."

"Yes," Banichi said, and Bren delayed no second longer, only went quickly where Banichi told him to go, to an unfamiliar plain door at the end of a service corridor.

That door opened into an ornate room behind a partial curtain—and led to the dowager herself, who, seated by a high window, looked up as he walked out from behind that curtain and into her presence.

"Aiji-ma," he said with a deep bow.

"There is an alert," Ilisidi said straight off, her mouth set in a hard network of disapproving lines.

"These were staffers of the lower court residency, aiji-ma," Bren said, "and once part of the staff on my estate on the coast, but retired from service. Now they claim to represent the estate staff. Many people have fled to safe venues. It is possible they are telling the truth, aiji-ma, and protective of me."

"My doorkeeper is grievously at fault," Ilisidi said, "for attempting to finesse this situation uninstructed, if nothing more."

Attempting to observe and protect, without interfering between him and former servants. The young woman with the printing had been right by the door, give the staff that. There might have been others hovering near and ready.

But if the two had been Guild, they very likely would have been too late.

"They may indeed be innocent staffers of mine, aiji-ma. And there was one of your staff by the door."

"As certainly should have been!" Ilisidi said, and the cane hit the floor. "My major domo is himself questionable, at this point. These two persons should never have been allowed inside the residency, and the paidhi's life is not a disposable resource!"

"Cenedi is investigating, aiji-ma. One has every confidence—"

"One has no idea how this staff of ours has ever survived our absence," Ilisidi snapped, the head of the cane tucked against her chest. "Damned fools! Two years of managing for themselves and they develop their own channels, excluding all higher authority! Delusions. Delusions of competency. This will *not* be acceptable."

"One has no wish to blame—"

"The person at the door was overawed by credentials," Ilisidi said grimly. "By paper, and seals, not by weapons. A junior staffer was set at the door. *Here* was the error, and my staff will answer for it. An investigation will be undertaken, now."

They had overtaxed the meager staff since their arrival. Most of Ilisidi's staff had gone east to Malguri, at the other end of the continent, during their absence. The remaining few had stayed up all night trying to cope with the speed of events, and knowledgeable people had to sleep sometime.

But some head would roll, figuratively at least; and Banichi was right. Moni and Taigi, old employees of the Bu-javid, should damned sure know the hazard of subterfuge with any high lord's staff . . . let alone the aiji-dowager's. Whatever became of them, they surely, surely knew the dowager's staff was not to trifle with.

"One cannot defend these two," he said regretfully. "Except that the habits of the lower courtyard and my estate have neither one been stringent. One asks an investigation, before any extreme measures."

"Ha!" Ilisidi snorted. "Sit down, paidhi-aiji, and let staff mend these bad habits."

"One has no plausible excuse for these persons," he said despairingly, and subsided into a gilt chair, by a window that looked past a balcony rail onto the crazy-quilt tiled rooftops of the city under a blue, crisp sky.

"Appalling," Ilisidi said sharply. "Are we prepared for this address?"

"As prepared as one may be, aiji-ma," he said, trying to recapture the loose ends of his reasoning, the pieces of attempted logic that rocketed through his mind. A loud thump resounded through the walls, another distraction shocking his nerves. He tried to ignore the situation.

"We shall be at hand to corroborate the paidhi's account," the dowager said without missing a beat. "But we look to the paidhi to exhibit his ordinary eloquence."

"One only hopes to oblige, aiji-ma," he said, and at that moment Nawari, who had his arm in a sling this morning, quietly opened the door and said,

"The intruders are both contained, nandi."

"Well." Ilisidi said, as if this disposed merely of the lunch menu, not his former staff, for whom he had a deep and wounded sympathy. "We are ready. We are quite ready, nand' paidhi."

"Whenever the aiji-dowager chooses," he murmured, hoping that thump had not involved his computer.

But Ilisidi tapped her cane, told Nawari, "We shall go downstairs," gathered herself to her feet, and that was that. Scarcely seated, he got up, straightened his coat, earnestly hoping for his own staff to turn up.

Jago did, with the computer slung over her shoulder. She entered by the same door, gave a little bow, stood waiting.

There was no way to ask, with the dowager in charge, exactly what had happened. He was no longer master of the situation, not while the dowager directed her staff, not while Cenedi had taken charge, and had links, surely, to Tabini-aiji's staff—whom they failed to trust, quite. It was all disquieting. But whatever the state of confidence in the other staff, one had a notion that persons were moving throughout the lower floors of the building, that the legislature, both houses of it, were moving into session.

Where is Banichi? he wanted to ask Jago. What happened? What about Tano and Algini? Are we taking our direction from the aiji's staff? But the only source of information was Jago's strictly formal deportment, her quiet competency. Everything was as right as it could be: His staff was doing all that could be done, and his questions were no help at all. He was going downstairs in close company with the aiji-dowager, in more security than Tabini himself could muster, and that was that.

A little tug at his coat cuffs, lace straightened. He hoped his face didn't show the sense of panic he felt.

And he was very glad to pick up Tano and Algini in the hallway, the two not conspicuously armed, but very likely quite well-equipped beneath their leather jackets. Cajeiri turned up with his two young body-guards in court dress, not, as would perhaps have roused regional hackles, in Taibeni green and brown. Tasteful, quiet, a little lace at collar and cuffs, hair done back in green ribbon. Cajeiri's queue, more dis-ciplined than ever in his young life, was tied up in complex red and black, the Ragi colors, and his coat was deep Ragi red, with black vines stitched subtly across the fabric—quite, quite splendid, with black lace. The dowager was in ordinary splendor, black and gold with just a hint of red. The paidhi felt quite overwhelmed in comparison, a lack of conspicuous-ness he judged his best and safest statement. Lord of the Heavens, Tabini had named him; but it was the paidhi-aiji, the aiji's interpreter, who had to render his account.

The doors of the dowager's residence opened, with an immediate unfolding of security outward, and about them, and behind. Bren fell in behind the dowager and the heir, with Jago beside him, and Tano and Algini behind. He was content to be deeply buried in the entourage of a legitimate lord of the As-sociation. Underfoot were the priceless hand-knotted silk runners, the ornate inlay work of the floors—overhead, the lamps that time had changed from live fire to electric, but the panels that softened the electric glare were carved onyx that had originally shielded live fire from drafts. On either hand, rare hardwood panels and tapestries and niches and ornately carved tables holding ancient porcelains, vases, and statues worked in rare blues and reds and greens, centuries old and untouched by the violence that had run these halls.

Of Murini, they had no further word, but the danger was not past—would not be past, if this meeting failed to achieve reunification, or if Tabini failed to pull a coalition together. The whole thing could break down again with a new claimant, or three or four, fracturing the Association into districts, with no single voice clear enough to prevail. If that happened . . .

He tried not to let his thoughts scatter. They had just passed the lift, the dowager choosing to take the stairs down, stairs which had their own security provisions, and which provided solid footing all the way down. They were in no great hurry. The dowager proceeded at her own pace, the ferule of her cane tapping the steps at measured intervals, and only once Cajeiri lifted his voice to ask if the lift was broken.

"No," was the dowager's clear response, and no further information. But it was utterly in character for the holder of Malguri to disdain the lift, to choose her own way down—

And to have her security fling the doors open onto the main floor hallway, secure themselves a standing place in a place thronged with legislators, mostly gathered down by the lifts—gentlemen and ladies with their own entourages, who, by this maneuver, were set at a distance from the dowager's arrival, and set off-balance.

*Bang!* went the dowager's cane when a hubbub rose and a few started to surge forward to take possession of the dowager. "We need no assistance!" she declared, her voice echoing hard on the impact. "We are here for the joint assembly. Where is my grandson?"

"Not here yet, nandi." It was Tatiseigi who turned up among the legislators, with the Ajuri close at hand, and the lord of Dur with his son. The Atageini lord gave a stiff and slight bow, but when Ilisidi extended her hand, the old man's expression changed, and the second bow was deep and gracious, before he took that offered hand—took it and joined their processional, the Ajuri and Dur sweeping in with them, the point of an advance that split the crowd of senators and representatives—

The more so, since certain lords of the tashrid, not to be outdone, swept in beside the Atageini and Ajuri and Dur, in the vanguard as they headed down the hall to the legislative chambers. Advance, hell, Bren thought. It was a processional, a rivalry to be as close to the dowager as possible, a sweeping of the hall of every damned member of the house of lords, who were not going to linger to politic around Tabini. The dowager, notorious for her conservation of the east, not even a member of the Western Association, which was the clear majority here, had swept up the west in a rush to claim precedence, and likely—Bren did not gawk about to see—no few of the hasdrawad might press after.

The door wardens opened the double doors of the hasdrawad assembly, and the dowager and her security and her allies marched in, and down the sloping aisle toward the dais, climbing the steps. A number of seats had been brought in, old and ornate chairs set on either side of the dais, in the well, in rows of fortunate seven, and the lords nearest Ilisidi claimed the foremost, the hindmost having the back seats, and, indeed, Bren saw, a sizable number of the hasdrawad had flooded in after them, with more arriving by the moment. There was a growing buzz in the chamber as the dowager mounted the steps and took a seat arranged for her, with cushions of Malguri's colors, and Bren hesitated, wanting to take his seat on the steps, if he had had his way, but on the dowager's left was a seat with white cushions, a white that glared unmistakably in the muted light of a hundred ancient lamps. The paidhi's colors. The aiji's orders—no damned way those colors had been set there in any misunderstanding; and he had no choice but climb the steps and take his place.

"We have the computer," Jago said at the last instant. "We will be at the right."

"Yes," he said, finding oxygen in short supply, and climbed up and sat down, for the first time having a view of the entire assembly—the tashrid with very few vacant seats, the hasdrawad's own desks rapidly acquiring occupants, though clots of consultation lingered in the aisles. The chairs reserved for the aiji and his consort were dead center, still vacant; but a small commotion had arisen in the hall outside, and he was by no means surprised when a second wave swept in, this incursion headed by Guild security, a great deal of security. Members of the hasdrawad cleared the aisles. Members seated rose, and the seated members of the tashrid rose, and suddenly Tabini and Damiri were present, walking down the right-hand aisle toward the dais.

# 11

**B**ren rose and stood. Cajeiri did. The dowager gathered herself up last with a slow and apparently effortless move not using the cane, painful as it might have been, and they all stood as Tabini and Damiri moved down the aisle, and up the steps, and took their places in the speaker's circle, all this in an undertone of comment, voices blurred and mixed in the vast echoes of the chamber. For the first time since their encounter in Tirnamardi, Tabini stood arrayed in court splendor, a black coat glistening with black woven patterns, not quite animal nor quite pure design, with black lace at his cuffs, and a spray of rubies glittering on his lapel— a shadowy eminence with those pale, pale gold eyes raking the assembly.

Bren felt lightheaded, grateful when first Tabini-aiji and then Damiri and Cajeiri and the dowager sat down. He took his seat simultaneously with the rest on the dais, and saw at that moment a commotion near the doors, as, yes, amid the milling about of members seeking their seats, the dowager's household staff arrived, carrying stacks of papers.

The report. His report.

He let out a breath, seeing at least a part of his duty discharged. The treaty with the kyo was in those pages, no matter what happened hereafter. Photographs were there to convince the skeptical, everything to make the report credible, if even the dowager's word failed to persuade the diehards to reason ...

But these in attendance were not the rebels, he told himself. These were the legislators who had stood up to Murini and the Kadagidi claim. These were, among others, canny men and women who would already have conceived their own plans, protecting their own interests, ready to assert their power the moment the fragile convocation so much as shivered, let alone fell into discord. One could still hope these powerful lords conceived the *aishidi'tat* itself of vital interest to their constituents.

The documents spread across the chamber with ordinary dispatch. The legislators were accustomed to receiving printed materials at ordinary sessions, and few broke the seals or delved deeply into them. Most present found greater interest in small, hurried conversations with neighbors and allies, interspersed with speculative dais-watching, darting looks toward the aiji and his household—how the boy has grown, they might observe; or the dowager looks in fair health; or note that the consort is beside the aiji, and the Atageini lord has come in person, in the first row of the tashrid. And is that the lord of the Taibeni in the hall? Does anyone know him by sight?

Slow breathing, Bren chided himself, and slow the

heart rate. This would take time. There had to be a certain amount of maneuvering and posturing, and he was a veteran of the legislature, if not of joint sessions. He did some surveying of his own from his position on the dais, picking out this and that lord, even spotting a few who had been on the Transportation Committee, scene of his last battles before his personal world had undergone upheaval—before a shadow on his bedroom curtains had announced his life was going to become something completely different.

Years ago. They all had changed. The world had changed.

And changed again. At the moment he had nowhere to live, and his staff was farther from him than they liked to be, in very chancy circumstances.

Deep breath. He heard the bone-deep sound of the *eis,* that man-high tubular bell that called the hasdrawad to take their seats. At that sound, the movement in the chamber became a definitive slow drift toward places, the buzz of conversation fading. Lords found their temporary seats down in the well. Representatives of the populace, many of them mayors or sub-mayors, eased into their desks . . . among them, perhaps a few who had supported Murini before or after his attack on Tabini, and now, seeing the tide going the other way, they took the risk of showing up here—maybe to have their contrary opinions heard, maybe to pretend they had never faltered in their man'chi to the Ragi lord, or maybe just to find out what decisions might be taken here, and decide where they wanted to jump next.

A second deep hum of the bell stilled the air. Closer and closer to the moment. Bren moved his fingers and feet slightly, to prove to himself that they *would* move, that, when he had to stand up, he could. Otherwise he felt numb, dislocated in time and space, and tried not to entertain either foolishly generous or uncharitable thoughts toward certain faces he spotted in the general assembly.

Third stroke of the bell. The senior of the hasdrawad ought to get up and bring the assembly to order, on any ordinary day, but it was Tabini who stood up instead, that sleek, dark presence, tall even among his kind. He appeared grim but not accusatory. He was precise and confident. And in that distinctive deep voice:

"Nandiin, nadiin, all points of the north and west and center are secured. We have firm assurances of the east. The Kadagidi have not permitted the traitor to reenter their house. It remains to see whether any houses of the south will prove hospitable to him and his adherents."

"Nand' aiji!" someone shouted out, from the middle of the tiers of desks, and others took up the shout: "Aiji! Aiji!" Legislators rose more or less in a body, all shouting and shouting, and Tabini stood still, letting it go on for what approached five minutes, before he lifted his hand and returned the salutation.

"Representatives of the people . . . lords of the ancient houses." The hand dropped, and there was fervent silence. "We accept your declarations. We will resume the ordinary business of the *aishidi'tat,* foremost of which—"

The representatives were sinking into their seats. But one figure was starkly different, hand lifting, and of a sudden footsteps thundered on the hollow dais, security moving like lightning as that hand moved upward.

Bren leaped to his feet, seeing only one thing—the man on whom the whole world depended, his dignity making it impossible for him to dive for cover. Bren hit Tabini waist-high with all the force he owned, chairs going over with their fall, security swarming over both of them, just a half-heartbeat later.

He and Tabini and a third and fourth body had hit the platform together, very solid ancient timbers, and as soon as he knew the other bodies were the dowager's security, Bren clambered off Tabini's person and scrambled aside, lying on the floor as shots deafened his ears. They were exposed to everything: The dowager and the boy were up here in danger—but Jago had reached him, and Jago's body cut off his view as she crouched by him, gun in hand.

Tabini got to one knee, and stood up forthwith, to a thunderous cheer from the chamber. A second cheer: Tabini had pulled his son protectively to his side, and Damiri had stood up with them.

The dowager, Bren thought in alarm, and on hands and knees edged a little past Jago to get a view of the dowager sitting quite untroubled in her seat, her cane planted before her, and Cenedi standing between her and the general chamber.

He found himself winded, bruised, and shaken beyond good sense. He tried to imitate the aiji and get up, but Jago laid a heavy hand on his shoulder. In the next instant another shot went off, and he jumped, pure reaction.

"Banichi," he said.

"Banichi is attending the problem, nandi," Jago said quietly, rising and facing the hall. "We did not have confidence in the aiji's security."

"But if *they* would have assassinated him—" he asked from below.

"Not him," Jago said, beneath the rising buzz in the chamber, the racket of chairs being moved or set back up. "*You,* nandi. The Guild has no inclination to strike at the aiji: they knew Murini would go down soon. But we have not let the aiji's security near you. Or the young gentleman, for that matter. One requests you stay down a moment more."

To make a move that fatal, that absolutely fatal to the shooter, just to get him . . . He was not surprised that someone wanted to kill him; but the aiji's own guard, and to do so in such a wild, fanatic way, so at odds with the ordinary way the Guild worked—

What Jago said made no damned sense. The shooter had risen from among the legislators, from the hasdrawad, had he not? He had had a seat there? Did a person of such stature pay that high a price, all to shoot down a court functionary?

One did, if such a move struck caution into the aiji, if it robbed the aiji of the aiji's fiercely held human contact. One did it, if it took power out of Tabini's hands and put it in others'; and if the aiji's own guard *knew* what was going to happen—and let it—

His brain raced wildly. He recognized a high-speed fugue for what it was, and tried to gather his wits into the useful present. He felt bruises atop other bruises—hitting Tabini was like hitting a brick wall and it dawned on him that he'd brought the aiji down publicly, a human embarrassment at the most critical of junctures. Tabini was back in command of the situation, though tumult was still racketing and echoing in the chamber. Tabini ordered something or someone removed and of all things—

Of all things, another voice ordered men detained who happened to be the aiji's own guard—shocking enough; but the voice echoing so loudly through the chamber was Banichi's.

That did it. He had to see what was going on. He started to his feet. Jago quickly thrust him back down.

"What are they doing?" he asked.

"The Guild is attending its business," Jago answered him in a low voice, while he kept his head down. "Banichi has taken down the target. Now they take the collaborators."

Cenedi and his men meanwhile had formed a living wall of body armor before the aiji-dowager and Cajeiri, standing there, hands on weapons. Cajeiri's young guards were right with them, armorless and unarmed, but putting their bodies between the young gentleman and harm.

Tabini, meanwhile, had set himself in front of Damiri, who was also on her feet, and several voices from the chamber had lifted in indignation, Tatiseigi's among them, decrying the action of fools and traitors to their own houses, and cursing damage to historic premises.

The *eis* thrummed, three insistent strokes. The vibrations overran their own echoes, and hurt human ears.

It hurt atevi hearing, too, perhaps far worse than that. He saw Jago's grimace, and when the sound cleared, the chamber seemed hushed and stunned.

"Nadiin, nandiin," Tabini resumed, as if nothing at all had happened, and there was a last moment movement of chairs and bodies, a diminishing buzz of conversation as the legislature tried to get itself back to order and decide whether it was safe to sit down.

Time, clearly, for the paidhi-aiji to get up off the floor before he became an object of complete embarrassment. Bren gathered himself up with Jago assisting, her body still between him and the chamber, which more or less shielded him from view as he regained his chair.

"That was *grand,* nandi!" Cajeiri leaned forward, whispering much too loudly, and the dowager's cane thwacked the boy's shin.

Grand. Hell, Bren said to himself. He had affronted Tabini's dignity in front of the whole legislature. He'd maybe saved the aiji's life in the process, but he doubted it: it turned out the shooter had likely missed because the attack was aimed at removing him and not Tabini, and he had plunged straight in front of Tabini. Security in the chamber had immediately pounced on the shooter, and the aiji of the *aishidi'tat* had been flattened by the very human who was the target—it was a damned comedy, not a rescue.

A second disturbance, this one to the rear of the

dais. Heads turned, bodies poised for another dive to the floor. But whoever had just hit the ground stayed there, and Tabini-aiji elected not to give it more than a passing glance.

"We accept the support of the quorum," Tabini said calmly. "All officials in office at the time of this interlude resume their offices as if there were never disruption; those who have accepted office from the false regime have never had authority, and their acts—excepting the ordinary civic business of marriage and divorce, are subject to careful review, with prejudice. If there are office vacancies thereby created, let a local vote fill those positions within five days, in public meeting, and report the outcome to us. All rights abrogated by the false regime are restored, all possession given by the false regime is reverted subject to review, and all other acts under that regime's seal are subject to review. The man'chi of some may have wavered in the face of outright false-hoods and deceptions, but we accept its return, as we accept that certain houses may have acted under constraint and entirely without choice: Their actions will be given benefit of the doubt."

The exhalation in the room was almost audible, along with a little settling of very anxious people.

"The Guild leadership will support the *aishidi'tat*, and untoward action will be dealt with summarily."

There was still blood on the floor, the paidhi had no doubt whatsoever, and the smell of gunpowder permeated the chamber.

"The actions of the false regime constituted a self-serving seizure of power, allied to a sentiment of dissatisfaction among certain individuals of certain houses, not even of general benefit to clan or province. Let the hasdrawad and the tashrid judge the validity of whatever complaints have been lodged, and if inequities have hitherto existed, let them come to light, and let the whole *aishidi'tat* examine them and correct them. If they have existed, we maintain they are the gift of nature, baji-naji, which bestowed mineral riches here and fishing there: Such gifts as one province may bring to the *aishidi'tat* are to its profit, but *not to extortionate profit*. We have attempted to distribute public works equitably among the provinces, based on three criteria: the least damage to the environment; the greatest economic need of the citizens; and the most efficient transport of resources. Wherein we have erred, we will hear such matters: Be it known that the location of such facilities was *our* choice, *not* the paidhi-aiji's, who neither administrated nor settled the choices. Hear me clearly: Those who have laid all discontent at the feet of the paidhi-aiji and the humans have taken a simple and incorrect answer to flaws that the *aishidi'tat* must address. The faults are in ourselves, nadiin, nandiin, and human presence has only shone a light on the matters we need to mend within our own institutions. Were we wrong to build a presence on the station? Were we wrong to hasten every effort to secure atevi participation in the human mission to this far station? Were we wrong to elevate the paidhi-aiji to lordly rank, to enable him to represent us with authority in these far regions? And were we fools to send our heir out to this far place, to see with his own eyes what truth there is out there? We think not. Now we have reports that the mission succeeded. We have waited to hear the results, in confidence that they could be presented in this chamber, under these circumstances, and that the legislature would sit in judgment of the facts. Here we have come, at personal risk to many of you. And here is my heir, here is the aiji-dowager, and here is Lord Bren, with a report the gist of which is in your hands. We have not seen it. We have not influenced it. We have not forbidden or suggested any part of it. Judge!"

Tabini swept an unexpected hand sidelong, toward Bren.

And stepped aside.

It was his moment, his turn to speak. He hadn't his notes. Jago quietly walked into range and gave him the computer case, and said, quietly, "We have taken the images, nandi, from the printing and Tano is prepared to show them at your request."

Thank God. Thank Jago and Tano. He walked to the centerpoint of the dais, the speaker's point, and had the presence of mind to bow to the aiji, to the dowager, the heir, and independently to the has-drawad at their desks and the tashrid sitting down in the well, all the while his mind was juggling the pros and cons of trying to open up his computer and bring up the records, or just get to it before the audience grew restless.

He set the computer case on the ground against his leg. Bowed again, to gain time to collect his thoughts, and to try to focus his wits on the numerical intricacies and pitfalls of courtly expression. Setting up—was impossible. He would lose them.

"Nadiin, nandiin," he began, trying to overcome a little buzz of comment from the chamber. "The case for or against the paidhi-aiji rests on whether or not I have properly served the aiji, the *aishidi'tat,* and the people of this continent, and the report is in your hands; one need not repeat it verbatim. We never misled you: We reported to the aiji our apprehensions that without atevi presence in the heavens, decisions would be taken by humans aloft and on the planet, decisions that would profoundly affect your welfare." The buzz simply would not die. He had grave doubts that people at the back of the chamber were hearing him, and it set him off his rhythm. He wished he had delayed to turn the computer on. He wished he had some control over the visual presentation that he could evoke.

"Nadiin, nandiin," he said again, and restored a little quiet. "The paidhi-aiji urged extreme and upsetting haste; he by no means denies that. And in fact an action was about to be undertaken, since the ship-aiji Ramirez had preserved a secret that came out only at his death: That humans in the far depths of the ether had contacted foreigners, and that they had abandoned a populated station out in the depths that would be in dire danger of foreigner hostility . . . that there was great danger of foreigners taking that station and deciphering records which would lead them to attack this world."

The buzz rose up again, and someone shouted out,

as the hasdrawad would, with speakers of lesser rank, "This we know! Go well beyond this, paidhi!"

"Nadiin." He bowed, to cover his confusion.

"And *why* risk the heir on this adventure?" someone shouted.

Another murmur, loud and long.

A movement brushed against him, unheard in the racket. The young gentleman himself had gotten to his side, and what the dowager or Tabini or Damiri was doing in the background, Bren had no idea. Cajeiri could move like lightning when he was motivated.

But it was no time for a gesture of the heir's solidarity with his influence—it was the worst thing.

"Because if we had stayed here in our apartment we might be dead," Cajeiri shouted. "Because Murini would have killed all of us if he could reach us. My father wanted me to go out and learn everything I could about the humans, to see and to make sure they were telling the truth! And it was indeed the truth! We saw what happened—we saw nand' Bren deal with the station, we saw him rescue the people, we saw it all, we talked to the foreign humans, so did my great-grandmother, and we know nand' Bren is not a liar. He did everything my father asked and saved all sorts of people!"

It was a shocking declaration, particularly from an eight-year-old. It was, one suspected—except the lapses in grammar, the mingled negatives and the confused symmetry of numbers—the dowager's own words. That young voice shocked the chamber at least enough to diminish the buzz of exchanges, probably while adults added the items and took into account whether the three-part *we* was the singular, the regal *we*, or the number of persons acting.

The lord of Dur stood up, in the tashrid seats. "Did the paidhi not just go to the aiji's defense?" Dur shouted out, and Bren's heart went thump and the warmth drained from his face.

Go to the aiji's defense. Never mind the assassin had been aiming at *him*.

Go to the aiji's defense—like the mecheiti after the herd leader, fences and barriers be damned. Go to the leader—like everything native to the world. He'd outright flattened the aiji of the *aishidi'tat*—he'd afflicted Tabini's dignity and simultaneously made Tabini a target in the process. But Dur's statement produced a racket of debate in the chamber that did not die away.

And what did he then say if the assembly took that move of his for proof of that deep atevi emotion? Use as fact the misapprehension paidhiin had spent generations denying, that there was, after all, an atevi sense of man'chi operating in a human? Claim that the two species felt things exactly the same, when what he'd felt most was a desperate sense of priorities, a visceral outrage that one shot could take out the one man who could knit everything together?

The War of the Landing had started on such a convenient misconception, allowed to bubble along in the subtext.

"Nand' Bren came to rescue me!" Cajeiri shouted out at the assembly. "And nand' Bren saved everybody in the foreign station! And *we* met new foreigners who were angry at us, and we ended up talking to them on their own ship, because nand' Bren rescued one of them, too! His name is Prakuyo an Tep and he is very respectful of my great-grandmother!"

There was the matter, inside out and hind end foremost, but the new item in the mix created two breaths of bewildered silence, in which first Tabini-aiji and then Damiri moved near their son. Then, with a crack and a measured tap of her cane, Ilisidi rose and came forward to stand by Cajeiri, a solid front, the entire leading family of the Ragi clan.

He bowed, clearly become an extraneous particle in this line, willing quietly to cede the floor to authority and postpone any explanation while atevi sorted out their own business.

*Bang!* went Ilisidi's cane, silencing every murmur, and every head in the chamber turned toward the dais, in a moment of breathless silence. Bren respectfully froze in place.

"A fool would urge us to stay out of matters in the heavens and let humans dictate such things as they understand," Ilisidi said. "A fool would argue we could build the necessary machines with no fleeting disturbance to our social schedules, not a ripple in our occupations and our attention to the numbers of this world. But we are not fools, and we know the one is not wise and the other is not possible. No, this generation is not a generation of fools! It has sacrificed! This generation has secured its command over this world, an authority which the ship-aijiin and even the Presidenta of Mospheira acknowledge. The ship-aijiin appointed a ship-paidhi to consult with Tabini-aiji on all matters, acknowledging that nothing of value comes from this world but that the aiji in Shejidan sends it. Were you aware of that? But the rebel attacked and tried to kill her, as he attacked the aiji himself. Are you aware that the foreigners we have met in the farthest distance of the ether have acknowledged the authority of my grandson as governing, binding, and safeguarding our world? If Murini failed to tell you such things, why, it was surely not because he would wish to conceal the aiji's success from you. It was because *he,* being only a shortsighted upstart and ignorant of every needful activity of educated governance, had appointed no observers aloft. He had constituted no authority in the heavens, he wielded no authority in affairs of dire import to the world, and he not only proved utterly ignorant of the numbers of the wider world, he even failed to govern the continent or satisfy the reasonable requests of its regions and associations, sowing only discord and jealousy, and attending to not even the proper benefits of his own region! Bad numbers, false numbers, nandiin, nadiin, inevitably lead to wider error. Baji-naji, the universe does not tamely bear a fool on its back! We, on the other hand, know the numbers that do exist, numbers as wide as the distance we have traveled. More, we have numbers reported by foreigners who have voyaged still farther, into territory as yet unexamined and unaccounted—numbers contained within the records of our voyage. We have reported all these numbers to the Astronomer, whose records his devoted students rescued from fools bent on destroying them . . ." A mild buzz, quickly suppressed by a crack of the cane. "Ask the paidhi-aiji why they would so urgently wish to destroy these numbers."

God. Bren's mind went blank, utterly blank, in that second.

Then snapped back into focus. He took a step forward, found breath enough to make himself heard over the murmur.

"Truth," he said, "is in those numbers, nadiin, nandiin, and those numbers clearly favor the government which has led atevi through these delicate points of balance. Peace is possible, through the outcome of a mission planned by Tabini-aiji and supported by this body. Knowledge brings to this world the true numbers of the universe, and baji-naji, the universe still orders itself, caring nothing for fools. You have the greatest opportunity and the greatest danger. The ship-humans, through a series of mistakes, had made these foreigners their enemies. The dowager and the heir themselves gained the respect of these foreigners, who are encouraged to know that their kinsman is in charge of an association of such wide-reaching power, and they have ignored the offense of the ship-humans, concluding the error is now corrected. They may well visit this world to pay respect to such an authority. One has every confidence they will be met by a strong and impressive association which will assure the integrity of its own territory. Nadiin, nandiin, you have the report of the voyage. Images are provided within the document."

Now let the murmur loose. Now let legislators look

at one another and flip through the pages of the document, but before they could get to the back, where those pictures were ...

Seize the moment, Bren said to himself, and aloud: "Tano."

A breath later the chandeliers dimmed and two of Ilisidi's men, as smoothly as one could wish, brought a screen up on the dais, set it beside the aiji and his household, and unfolded it.

Light flared, then, and an image flashed up which drew a collective gasp: Prakuyo an Tep, gray and huge—and emaciated, as one would not realize, who did not know the kyo. Difficult to apply scale to the first images, until the picture of an improbable afternoon tea, and that huge, gray face bent close to Cajeiri's, in every intimation of benevolent exchange.

Murmuring in the chamber became a racket. Someone stood up, shouting: "What is this creature?" And someone else shouted: "Quiet!"

"That is nand' Prakuyo," Cajeiri's high voice declared, its pitch rising over the thunderous murmur. "And he is now an associate of ours!"

One was ever so glad photos of Gene and Irene and Artur were not in the file, too, Bren thought distractedly, feeling the whole business suddenly spinning out of control. A human voice could not carry over that racket. His carefully prepared presentation went to the four winds. But Cajeiri's light voice rose above the racket.

"Prakuyo was a prisoner of the wicked station-aiji, but nand' Bren went in and got him out. Nand' Bren figured out how to talk to him, and so did I! Nand'

Prakuyo is very respectful of my great-grandmother. All the kyo are!"

*Bang!* went the cane. "There is a tradition among the kyo," Ilisidi interjected, a calm dose of orderly information, at which Bren's racing heart somewhat caught its beat, "of entirely decent respect for elders. More to the point, nandiin, nadiin, the kyo confess to us they are not the only foreigners in the region. This is the primary reason they were so very ill at ease when humans came trespassing in their territory. They are themselves not adept in dealing with foreigners. They do not know how to conduct reasonable relations in such situations. Neither, in fact, do the ship-humans, who have never dealt with any authority but their own. Our expertise, and that of the Mospheirans, in the manner in which we share territory, was very useful in sorting out these previously mismanaged relations, and our skills may prove even more valuable in the future." Another murmur from the assembly, and Ilisidi's cane banged the hollow floor like thunder. "Like it or not, nadiin, the universe contains other people of independent will and means. We have met two others. If we had not put our noses out there, the kyo still would have found us, sooner or later, and what then would they have found? Persons adept and capable in the wider universe, or not? Would they, in their inept management of foreign matters, have fallen on us with weapons instead of the humans' petal sails? We have suffered one ill-planned incursion and dealt with it in long experience. We have become much wiser, since. Let us deal with the next encounter at the safe distance of our station, where we and our human residents can establish our authority, take sensible charge of negotiations, and keep human fools and atevi fools—and we each have them in numbers!—from dealing with these new foreigners, who doubtless have fools of their own. They will not land, as humans did. We have that assurance. The kyo will not seek residence even on our station. They may indeed visit us to express their sentiments of respect, and it is imperative that they and territories beyond them be met with the unshakeable and reasonable authority they expect, or they will call us liars. Their arrival may come within the year, or not for several years. But come it will!"

"Indeed," Tabini said, himself somewhat taken aback by the vehement direction of Ilisidi's address, a tone that had utterly shocked the chamber to silence. On the screen, where images had stopped cycling, was the image of Prakuyo and two of his kind, two very well-fed kyo in their robes, entities who could not possibly be mistaken for atevi or human.

"We have said," Ilisidi declared. "So has our greatgrandson." Thus stifling any more commentary from Cajeiri, who, with Ilisidi's hand on his shoulder, was obliged to keep silent.

"Aiji-ma," Bren said after a breath, completely off his balance, "I have by no means finished the detail of my report, but the dowager seems to have covered the essence of it very well."

"The paidhi may usefully confirm it," Tabini said. "Take the floor, nand' paidhi."

Bren bowed—shaken, and with a flood of other, more dangerous knowledge racing through his brain, knowledge that Ilisidi had only brushed by, in that remark about fools in abundance. He had no wish to complicate Ilisidi's good effect by telling the assembly that there was trouble out in deep space, but he had no wish to compromise the future by letting the assembly assume a peace that was not true, either.

"Nadiin, nandiin," he said, standing on the speaker's spot, and bowing. "It is a wide and complex universe, the numbers of which we have begun to know with far greater accuracy. It was a wise decision that sent the aiji's son out to see and understand these things—it was a very wise decision, because the aiji's heir now is favorably regarded by these individuals. We have made a fair beginning of dealing. There is word of other foreigners, unknown to us—" A small murmur that quickly faded as he continued, "—but there will always be foreigners. The universe is very large. The more we know, as a world, the more authority we have."

Ruling the solar system posed a decided problem to a governing body at this very hour struggling to rule its south coast, a governing body with only earth-to-orbit transport at its disposal, and with part of its citizenry still debating the wisdom of being in space at all. He knew what he was dealing with. He saw the shocked looks, heard the stubborn murmur of discontent that wished to take all the unhappy surprises the universe had handed them and lay them at the paidhi's door.

"The only conveniently habitable world in the solar system is yours," he said. "Human authority in the neighborhood will leap up to speak for itself if you do not claim your own sovereignty over any further visitation, and one humbly urges the *aishidi'tat* to assert overriding authority in the very near future and see the shuttles flying again. One has no doubt that Mospheirans and ship-humans alike will respect an atevi assertation of rule, since each has found atevi authority reasonable and sure in their representations. When other foreigners pass through the heavens, as they will, as the aiji-dowager has so clearly put it, meet a sensible, strong authority on the atevi station; they will deal with the *aishidi'tat* up above, and not intrude onto this world." For one dizzy moment a weary brain simply whited out, all order gone from his thoughts as he lost his place. The dowager had taken over his speech and done it very well, covering the point that should come next. He could only complicate matters by going on. He needed simply to end it and sit down before he undid everything. "Wherein the paidhi's haste to bring atevi into space has caused distress to districts and individuals, the paidhi accepts all blame. The aiji will be your source of justice. As for my report, you have it in your hands."

It seemed enough to say, if lame. He bowed, backed off the speaker's circle, and for a moment was so disoriented in the dark and glare of the projector and the screen he had doubts where his chair was. He blinked, found a hazy navigation point, and backed a few steps toward it, casting a human shadow on the image of the heir and Prakuyo an Tep at tea.

Tabini took the speaker's circle.

"This assembly will stand adjourned until the

morning," Tabini said. "We will *all* read the paidhi's report."

Thus preserving the aiji's impartiality and a deniable distance: so Jago had said. Bren located his chair, but only in time to stand in front of it as others rose. The assembly in the shadows rose, bowed, and the murmur this time was subdued and dim in his ears.

He had not done at all what he hoped. From the attempted assassination to the dowager's taking over the core of the information, things had not followed the script, and he had lost all his threads, absolutely lost them. But maybe it had gone well enough, except his ill-conceived dive at Tabini.

The dowager went for a few words with her grandson. Cajeiri went to talk with his mother. The chamber lights went up. Bren hesitated, then decided to collect his security about him and get back to the dowager's apartment as quietly and quickly as he could.

"Paidhi." Tabini spotted him, and crossed the small distance in a couple of strides, to which he could only bow and try to explain his actions.

"Aiji-ma."

Tabini seized his arm in an atevi-strength grip. "We will remember," Tabini said, which was what one said in accepting a personal debt; and then it dawned on him Tabini meant his presumptuous dive for the floor, that atevi instinct could only construe as great devotion, the most charitable construction Tabini could put on matters—knowing the paidhi had been the target. But it was still a human reason: Tabini of all people should know that; and he couldn't have

Tabini starting to think otherwise, not even in the most secret and illogical depth of his heart.

"Aiji-ma," was all he dared say, and bowed desperately, and found himself let go and excused. He wanted only to get back to the dowager's apartment where he could sit and reassemble the pieces of the last hour. He was losing the coherent memory of what he had said to the assembly. He hadn't yet examined his sense of atevi logic to figure how the blowup within Tabini's guard could be construed by the aiji's enemies. He only knew it was going to create controversy, particularly as the paidhi's guard had taken over, along with the dowager's.

Who were eastern.

Wait until that hit the news.

He bowed his way to the edge of the group, found Jago and Tano with him, and said, "We should go back to the apartment, nadiin-ji. Quickly."

"Nandi," Jago said, never questioning the decision, not explaining where Banichi and Algini were at the moment. Bren had the notion of business in progress, business likely regarding the would-be assassin, and deep inquiries among security that had led far outside the chamber and possibly all the way to the Assassins' Guild—where Algini had a word or two to say.

But best, he thought, that he should clear the scene and render matters less complicated for his staff. There was a problem, a serious problem working somewhere in the vicinity, no question of that, and Jago and Tano needed to get him to safety and get back here to support Banichi and Algini in whatever was going on.

He headed for the side door, kept quiet the entire way out of the assembly and into the small service hall, where a few bodyguards waited, notably Ilisidi's young men.

Safe, then, he said to himself, drawing an easier breath. Trust Ilisidi's men, yes, absolutely. Just let them live through the next dozen hours. Let Algini's allies win inside the Guild.

And let *him* get a phone link to the Island, and a relay to Jase up on the station, to explain the good and the bad of the current situation. Rumors had to be flying from the capital to the coast by now. He wasn't sure how long he might stay in office—or stay alive; he wasn't sure what might develop if he never got to explain to Mospheira or to Lord Geigi exactly what had gone on, before it grew more tangled than it was, and before they had to send another paidhi over here to try to deal with a general discontent with humans.

They exited quickly into the main hall, headed for the lift. The carpeted, beautiful hall outside had a gathering crowd of legislators and their staffers, particularly those of the tashrid, seeking their own apartments upstairs as the legislature left the chambers. Such a traffic was nothing unusual after a session. It was not what he wanted to encounter. He'd hoped to have beaten it in his retreat.

"The paidhi," someone exclaimed, and heads turned. "Nand' paidhi," someone addressed him, and that address he was obliged to acknowledge: The speaker, the man coming toward him, was the lord of Dur, to whom he owed ever so much.

"Nandi." He bowed, and by then others were pressing on him with enthusiastic protestations, Jago and Tano establishing a line of retreat to the lift car by the reach of arms toward that wall.

"It was extraordinary, extraordinary," Dur said to him, as he heard the lift door open. Other legislators pressed close about him, even touched him, all positive, thus far. The lift made its departure, most of the crowd blocked from reaching it.

"Baji-naji," he murmured to Dur's enthusiasm, that eternal expression of events in imbalance. "One expects security to be quick in investigation of the matter—one fears now it was aimed at my person, and one was entirely wrong to have moved near the aiji—" Not to mention flattening him to the floor.

"But well done," the graying lord of Maidin said— a woman who had supported the aiji in critical votes, and the expression found several voices in approbation, and more hands actually touched him, a strange and uneasy sensation among atevi, who did not touch, except among intimates. It was eerily like an atevi family occasion, as if, among these diverse lords some sort of current was running that he could not tap or quite understand—an intoxication that led ordinarily dignified atevi he did not even know to brush hands against his back, his shoulders, and, stranger still, led his bodyguard to allow it. Anyone could approach him, anyone could touch him, and the lord of Hajidin actually gripped his arm with bruising force, and let it go again.

"Nandiin," he said, shaken by the pain. It dawned on him that, the aim of the threat aside, he alone *had* been in position to do what many in the hall would have instinctively done. He had carried out *their* instinct to protect their aiji, no matter his own, human-driven reasons for doing it, and the motion was what counted with them. *That* was both the trap and the fact of the case. He had acted *for* them. It was that tricky word *murdi,* that almost meant gratitude, and somewhat meant surrogate, God help him—Jago and Tano didn't extract him not only because this crowd posed no threat, it had a political dimension. It wasn't forgiveness they offered the paidhi; atevi were never keen on forgiveness, in their own pragmatic way, having no trust in its future, given their own passions. It was acknowledgment of a feeling they felt that *did* have a future, a sentiment of belonging and identity, and he was utterly awash in it, carried along by it—literally, as the crowd's pressure moved him away from the lift and into a corner.

Lord Tatiseigi appeared in the mix, arm in a sling, the lord of the Atageini capturing his person from his other possessive protector. There was a fierce strength in the old man's good hand, at least enough for a human, and *it* closed on his arm.

"Lord Bren," the old man announced, "the guest of the Atageini, the protector of the heir—" Lord Tatiseigi let no one forget *that* heredity. "And clearly of the household of the aiji-dowager, our ally and associate, *and* of the Ragi of the center. The Padi Valley Association stands firm in its solidity. The upstart who has troubled his own house and usurped rightful authority within the Padi region has been refused admittance. Let fools receive him, and let the Associations of the center—"

"And west!" someone shouted, while the blood left Bren's hand and his bodyguard found no way to rescue him. Now the younger lord of the Ajuri had shown up and pushed in.

"—and the west!" the old man said, not missing a beat, nor surrendering him to Damiri's father, "and the east and the north and the south, besides! Let us gather up the power and deal with traitors as they deserve! Approbation, we say, approbation for the safe return of the aiji-dowager and the heir, our great-grandnephew, and our support of the Ragi aiji and his allies forever!"

The old bastard, Bren thought, wondering if his arm was going to break; but the Atageini lord had cannily swept up the broken bits of the alliance and gotten them all concentrated on the dowager, the heir, and Tatiseigi's relationship to the aiji—never mind one inconvenient human, who found no breath to speak and wished he could only get his arm free.

"And the paidhi-aiji!" Dur shouted out, reinserting the human into the argument.

"The paidhi-aiji!" several cheered, and at that point, thank God, the old man finally let go his arm. Bren resisted the urge to grab the injury and massage it. He bowed, instead, bowed several times while backing up, in the manner of a mere court official, not the vastly overtitled Lord of the Heavens.

"And never forgetting the bravery of the lord of the Atageini and his people," Bren threw in, in a breath within the racket. "And the Taibeni, and the lord of Dur, who have come so many times to our rescue—" A fast breath, and a chance of rapid escape. "Nandiin, your leave. The paidhi will leave matters in very capable hands."

There were cheers, a few pats on the back and on the aching arm. But he escaped the corner by retreating along the wall to the lifts, and Jago, again thank God, had likely used a security key to get control of the nearest one and hold it open for him.

He made it inside. He leaned against the wall, looking at Tano and Jago.

"Well done," Jago said.

"Was it?"

"Well done in all things, Bren-ji."

The *Bren-ji* was the part that warmed his soul. Not nand' paidhi, not Lord of the Heavens. Just Bren-ji, whose staff no one could equal.

# CJ Cherryh
## *Classic Series in New Omnibus Editions*